❧ THE ❧
KALEVIDE

LOU GOBLE

BANTAM BOOKS
TORONTO · NEW YORK · LONDON · SYDNEY

THE KALEVIDE
A Bantam Book / November 1982

Maps by David Perry

All rights reserved.
Copyright © 1982 by Lou Goble.
Cover art copyright © 1982 by Jim Burns.
This book may not be reproduced in whole or in part, by
mimeograph or any other means, without permission.
For information address: Bantam Books, Inc.

ISBN 0-553-22531-6

Published simultaneously in the United States and Canada

PRINTED IN THE UNITED STATES OF AMERICA

O   0 9 8 7 6 5 4 3 2 1

THE KALEVIDE

The Kalevide, the national epic of Estonia, like the Finnish epic *Kalevala* from which it is descended, is one of the great legends of Europe. Son of the godling Kalev, who came to Viru on the back of an eagle, and Linda, mistress of the birds of the air, the Kalevide is at once a mortal hero with human failings and weaknesses, and a mighty champion with a god-given mission to preserve a nation.

Here, for the first time, this ancient saga of sorcerers and demons, lovely maidens and enchanted swords, gallant battles and stalwart companions is retold in modern English. Its bold storytelling, its sweep of action and adventure, its great themes of life and death, make *The Kalevide* an epic that rivals the greatest fantasies of all time.

Bantam Science Fiction and Fantasy Books
Ask your bookseller for the books you have missed

THE
KALEVIDE

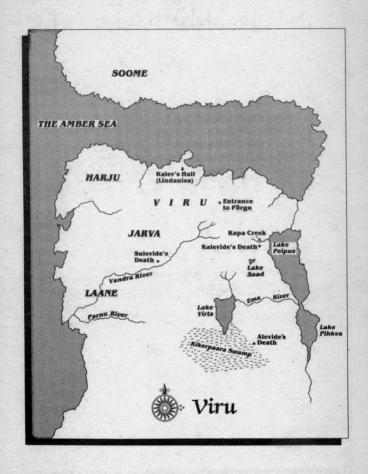

SOOME

THE AMBER SEA

HARJU

Kalev's Hall
(Lindanisa)

V I R U • Entrance
to Põrgu

JARVA

Kapa Creek

Sulevide's
Death •

Kalevide's Death •

Lake
Peipus

Lake
Saad

Vandra River

Ema River

LAANE

Lake
Virts

Parnu River

Lake
Pihkva

Alevide's
Death •

Kikerpaara Swamp

Viru

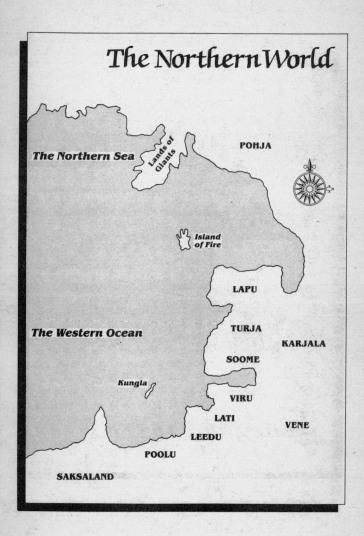

The Northern World

The Northern Sea

Lands of Giants

POHJA

Island of Fire

LAPU

TURJA

KARJALA

The Western Ocean

SOOME

Kungla

VIRU

VENE

LATI

LEEDU

POOLU

SAKSALAND

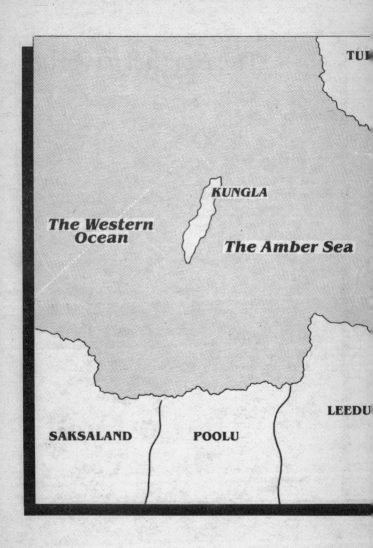

TUI

KUNGLA

The Western
Ocean

The Amber Sea

LEEDU

SAKSALAND   POOLU

JA

KARJALA

SOOME

VIRU

INGRIJA

VENE

LATI

PIHKVA

VITEBSK

The Lands of the West

AUTHOR'S NOTE

The Kalevide is an archetypal hero, like Gilgamesh and Herakles, Siegfried, Beowulf, Cuchulainn, even King Arthur. Here are the motifs of European myth, the posthumous birth, the mighty sword, a magic ship, a mysterious quest. The Kalevide meets monstrous beasts and defeats vile demons; he wages the war for his people's future. Yet despite his prodigious strength, he is all too human, clumsy, confused, torn by doubt and loss, slow to learn. He has fits of irrational rage, falls asleep, forgets his mission, and if he is not quite sane, that merely ensures his membership in the company of heroes. The Kalevide is the hero of Esthonia; his epic is the *Kalevipoeg.*

The *Kalevipoeg* was composed by Frederick Kreutzwald in 1857–59 from the oral literature of the Esthonian people, much as the great national epic of Finland, the *Kalevala,* was collected earlier by Dr. Elias Lönnrot from Finnish lore. (The two epics are related, even as the Finns and Esthonians are.) The *Kalevipoeg* was translated into English by W. F. Kirby in *The Hero of Esthonia and Other Stories* (2 vols., London, 1895), which I have followed in writing *The Kalevide,* leaving out a few minor episodes and adding more drawn from other Esthonian folk tales and my own fancy. With a few exceptions the songs and magical charms included here are authentic, if somewhat abridged, taken either from the *Kalevipoeg* itself or from *The Pre- and Proto-historic Finns, both Eastern and Western, with the Magic Songs of the West Finns* by John Abercromby (2 vols., London, 1898). In all cases the versification, such as it is, is my own. I have not tried to follow the original meters.

Viru, the land of the Kalevide, is, or was, Esthonia. It is not, however, the Esthonia a traveler would see from a train between Tallinn and Tartu. To see Viru he must return along the track in time and understanding, disembark, and board another carrier to a world not quite his own. Accordingly, descriptions of the land or people here will not correspond to those of the Esthonia that is, except by coincidence.

[xi]

To the extent that the events of the *Kalevipoeg* have historical foundation, and they do, they belong to the thirteenth century. I have deliberately chosen, however, to set *The Kalevide* in a more far away and abstract time. A true hero has no place in the real world, not even the real world of fantasy. This is his eternal tragedy; the hero is doomed to stand on the cusp between mythic time and history, and there embody the promise of return to another age of dream.

Lou Goble
Eugene, Oregon

PROLOGUE

A man with no legs rides a white mare. Neither one moves. Both are fastened forever in front of the mouth of a cave leading into darkness. The man is balanced precariously on his horse's back. His left hand clutches her mane for support; his right, clenched in a fist, is caught in a hole in the cliff. It feels to him as though someone inside the mountain is holding on to him, but it is only the stone. Anguished moans well from deep within the throat of the cave. The man with no legs prays for them to end.

The white mare is starving. Long ago she grazed the last grass growing around her feet; now only the dust of the earth will feed her. Once her coat was bright and silver-white; her mane flowed like rippling water when she ran. Now her hide is hairless and yellowing with the long drought of years. Only a few tufts of her once beautiful mane are left; the man on her back has torn out the rest. Ribs show through her dry skin like the bars of a cage imprisoning her life. Her legs have become sticks, so brittle they can barely support the weight of her rider. Once strong, the white mare is now so fragile that if anything touched her, she would crumble like the dust that feeds her.

Once the man with no legs was young, but that, too, was long, long ago. Now he lives without age, without life. Although he can no longer speak, at times his mouth moves in mute recollection of words too long forgotten in his mind, for he knows there are things he has done which he should recall, acts he should remember, deeds to lament, people he has loved whom he would like to mourn. All are forgotten, all lost to time. He has forgotten who he is and where he is. He no longer knows why he is there, so long at his post, caught with his hand wedged so firmly in the rock. All that is left to him is to wonder whether he will ever be released. He wonders, too, who is inside the cave, and why he is moaning so.

PART I

1   Kalev died before his son was born, his seventh son, the son who was to be his heir and bear his name before the world, the single one who was to keep his dreams alive. He died before the child could see his country, before he had a chance to learn to be a king.

One moment only lies between the life of deeds a man has done and what he hopes to do, and in that frozen moment, when everything is new, Kalev was struck down. Whether it was by some sudden air-borne sickness, or by a sorcerer's secret shot, or simply age, no one ever knew. Kalev fell, and cold earth caught him. Although his legs twitched and trembled enough to show that life still lingered, it was a mockery of the strength that might have been. Above his body the weathered remains of a horse's skull, nailed to the crossbeam of the gate as the emblem of his reign, leered at him with a broken smile. Overhead a single sea gull wheeled on the wind and screamed.

One moment. It caught him standing by the entrance to his courtyard, gazing at the open grasslands in front of his homestead, but in that moment he was not seeing the grasses dancing or hearing the whispers of the breeze. He saw instead only the inward visions of his dreams. Four horses grazed on the pasture; he beheld instead herds of thousands, thundering on the plain. Beyond the field stood the dark line of the forest, but in that moment he never saw the trees. He gazed instead upon the gray walls of a city rising. Instead of his own wooden hall and outbuildings, instead of his workmen's huts of bark, he imagined rows and rows of high buildings built of stone, along stone streets like canyons leading toward his palace, the high hall of Kalev-Viru, king. In his vision he saw the city and the black smoke pouring out of chimneys from the forges of his smith-houses and armories, the cellars of his country's strength. In that moment he watched troops ride forth from his city, men clad in iron armor and mounted on horses wrought of steel, armies meant to march on far highways, warriors bound to subdue the world.

Kalev called his country a kingdom. Others might have seen only a farm hacked out of the forest, supported by the folk of a small hamlet nearby. Nevertheless, Viru was a kingdom, for the people hailed Kalev as a king. He had taught them that much, and more. Alone he had come upon the country—come from the north, come from the sky, come on the wings of an eagle—to claim it for his own. Alone he had cut the forest and cleared the land. He had felled the oak and birch and pine and all the lesser trees, and while he was attacking the primeval wood with his iron blade, the people had appeared before him from their homes among the trees. They came to mourn each giant that fell, gathering around each mighty trunk to sing songs over it as over the body of an ancient friend, but though they grieved, they never fought to save the trees, for they had no weapons other than their sadness and their love for living things, and that was not enough to withstand the invader's assault. Kalev, new to the land, scorned their simplicity, but when the people were homeless he built them homes. He offered them protection; he provided for their wants. He taught them new skills, for he knew he would need them to build his kingdom. He used them, and he changed them.

Before his coming, the people had been content to haunt the forests, to prowl like beasts, to forage for herbs and fruit. They sucked the honeycomb as if it were meat. Kalev gave them knives of steel to replace their blades of copper, silver, and gold. He taught them how to till the earth, to sweep the sea; to keep goats and sheep. With access to easy stores of food they ceased to wander the far, hidden paths of the deep wood. They settled in hamlets and villages. For their keeping Kalev gave them work to do. They began to herd cattle, the folk who once had talked with deer.

Kalev's only enemy was the forest. The people believed the trees were kin. Once he had seen an old man, an elder of the land, full-bearded and clad in peasant rags, standing in a grove, speaking to a gnarled and ancient oak, not worshiping, merely gossiping as if with a brother. This he could not understand. For him the woods were too dark, too filled with powers even he could not control. Trees, he believed, were to be cut down for timber, timber for buildings. The forest must make way for cities.

In his dreams he saw deer paths and sledge trails becoming straight roads, paved with stone, linking Viru with the lands of the west, Poolu and Saksaland, with the castle lands, the remnants of the Old Empire, in the south, with the principalities of

Vene in the east and beyond, to Permu, to the far nations of the Golden Khan. He would build a port with stone piers from which armed ships would sail to Kungla, the fabled island land of weath. Viru would become a center of trade and commerce; it would swell with riches and power. All the world would bow before its might.

Kalev had already extended hegemony over Harju and Laane, the western regions near the sea, and over Jarva, the central lake district. Though few people lived in these parts, and those who did scarcely understood the importance of a king's power, it was a beginning nonetheless. His borders extended to the swamps of the Lettish lands of Lati and Pihkva and to Ingrija where only sorcerers and witches dwelled. Soon he would stretch his arms to embrace those neighboring nations. He would build first a kingdom, then an empire. So he saw it, so he dreamed. This was his destiny: to rule.

Then, in a moment, a sea gull screamed. A broken skull grinned. Kalev's visions dissolved. His city crumbled, thick walls collapsed, the citadel tumbled to the ground. The armies he had marshaled vanished in a blinding mist. The dynasty died. If it had not been for the son unborn, Kalev's dreams of power would have been dispelled forever with the wind.

Without thinking, Linda flew across the courtyard to catch her husband as he fell. The possibility of evil lurking in the air never crossed her mind. She flew to him like a bird whose nest has been attacked, without regard for risk to herself or to the child within her womb.

Linda had been sitting on the long porch of Kalev's high, timbered hall, sitting as she always sat, on a low, three-legged stool, clad as she was always clad, in a coarse brown woolen dress, spinning, as she always spun, a gray-tan linen thread on a spindle, while her two small sons, Paari and Jaani, played at hounds and bears around her skirts.

Three small birds, a bluebird, a swallow, and a fat-bellied house finch, were perched on the porch's spindled railing, chirping and chattering with light-hearted voices, as if they had no care for what might come. These were Linda's companions, given to her by her mother, the Woman in Blue Stockings, as a token of the days before Kalev came and claimed her and her land. Linda was of the elder race of Laane. Like all her people, she had been changed by Kalev; he taught her new ways and new ideas. He guided, and she let him lead. In all things but her birds. He had always mocked them, and her when she whistled and hummed along with them, but no matter how he scoffed and rebuked her for foolishness, she would not give them up. They were her only friends.

Kalev was unconscious when Linda reached him. His face was set and his eyes blind. She touched his legs and tried to straighten his body. The two young children on the porch screamed until the old woman who swept the hall whisked them inside to keep them safe from harm. Linda cradled Kalev in her arms and crooned sadly over him, but in the open yard there was nothing she could do for him.

In desperation she half-dragged, half-carried him to the bath-house behind the great hall, where it was warm and clean, and health was served. She laid his body on the long wooden bench, then shut the door on the world outside so that none, save the child she carried, could witness the service that she did.

A large copper cauldron sat on the ever-ready coals. Linda fed the fire and fanned the flames to bring the water to a boil. Leafy willow whisks, simmering in the copper, added their fragrance of the scent of smoldering cedar wood, cedar for curing, and steam. She splashed sweet water on the heated stones of the hearth. Clouds boiled. The enclosed air of the bathhouse became stifling. Clumsily, she removed Kalev's clothes and kneaded his twisted muscles. His body lay inert and still at last, free of its spastic trembling. As she scrubbed him with hot bathwhisks, her thick hair fell from its coils, hanging heavy and damp around her face and shoulders. Linda pulled off her dress and shift, so that, naked, she could share whatever powers she possessed with the steam. She began to sing.

She sang the songs that must be sung to bring fresh steam into a bathhouse, the songs which foster health and open the ways to greater powers. Linda was no wizard; she was not schooled in the deep crafts of incantation which true healing requires. The only charms she knew were the lowly songs women sometimes sing in times of trouble. Nevertheless, she took great care to shape her words precisely. The names she chanted must be correct, the flattery true, the rhythms exact, if the magic were to work.

Linda called on the forces, high and low, that she knew. She appealed to Kivutar, mistress of pains, and her sluttish maid, Kipula, to bind the ills that had attacked her husband and to carry them away, to hide them, to cast them into the sea, to bury them beneath the blue-spotted stone. She summoned Vanamuine, lord of song, and Ukko himself, high lord of clouds, to help her, to come into the steam and aid its healing, to breathe golden

[6]

warmth over Kalev, to bathe him with honey. Thus Linda of the Birds sang. This was the magic she knew, bits and snatches of songs, old songs she had heard her mother sing, a scattering of verses borrowed from the true songs of power, scraps of the deep lore which might have been overheard from wizards, the true masters of the art, and passed from mother to daughter, all blended together and confused in the lifetimes of those who did not know, or understand, the hidden powers bound within the words, and it was not enough.

Kalev did not recover. Although his body relaxed, because of the steam, he improved no further. He could not move. His eyes, though open, showed no life. If they could see at all, it was only Mana, the dark one of shadows, who lingers always by the shoulder of every man.

When, after hours of struggle, Linda realized she could accomplish no more, she opened the bathhouse door and stepped out into the open air. Her hair was matted and soaked with steam, her body was soiled with her own sweat and Kalev's waste, and she was exhausted. Although it was midsummer, the fresh air felt like a winter's wind. She shivered from the chill and her own fatigue. Her three birds fluttered to her, greeting her with laughing voices, rejoicing as she emerged from the house of the dead. Singing and whistling, they tried to cheer her with foolish words, but for once she hardly heard them and had no heart to answer.

Only a wizard, Linda knew, could save Kalev now. Only such a one could read the illness, discern its origins and so discover its cure. Few wizards remained in Viru. Most had retired to the distant north in the years before the changes came, before Kalev himself swept down upon the land, but one might be summoned nonetheless. Even a wizard far away could be called and with his art could come, regardless of the distance.

Yet Linda hesitated to cast the spell. Like all her people, she felt awe for the race of wizards, awe mixed with reverence and tinged with fear, but although it meant opening the way to forces more powerful than she knew or understood, she knew she must try, or Kalev would die. Kalev would have scoffed at her notions, as he had scoffed at all her people's arts. He would have laughed, except that in his life he rarely laughed, and now in the coming of his death his face was frozen and he could not even smile.

Linda tied her silver brooch to a length of thread unraveled from her dress and, standing in the center of the courtyard, spun it seven times around her head to call the alder-beetle out of the forest. When it came, she cupped it carefully in her hand.

[7]

"Go, little sister," she whispered to the small red and black bug. "Go to the northland with my words. Fly to Soome, to Turja, to Pohja if you must. Find me a wizard, little one, one renowned for his healing gifts. Fly swiftly, sweet one, and beg him to come to Kalev's bedside. Bid him bring his drum and alder chips to learn the cause of Kalev's illness. Hurry, dear one, hurry from my heart. The wizard will know the songs to draw the dark torments from Kalev's body and restore his strength. Speed now, sweet beetle. Fly."

With the word she cast her messenger to the sky. It circled, seeking the direction it should travel.

"To the north, beetle," Linda prayed anxiously. "To the north."

The north, however, was the direction of ill omen, and the alder-beetle was afraid and confused by the weight of her mission. She turned westward, instead, and shot away as fast as she could fly.

Linda spun her brooch desperately to call her back, but it was too late. The beetle was bound on her own adventure and would return when she would. Sadly, Linda went back to the bathhouse to resume her vigil over Kalev. He did not change. Days passed into days, and there was nothing she could do but wait.

Once a day for seven days she spun her brooch to give the alder-beetle strength for her long journey. In her mind she imagined the vast distances she must wander to the west. If the beetle crossed the world she knew—a world she had never seen but had learned from the songs of strangers and from Kalev's tales—then she would fly across the water, across three kingdoms and a fourth, to the end of the earth, to the edge of the western sea, and then beyond. Across the ocean she would find a mist-shrouded islet where a mountain rose. Behind the mountain she would see, as Linda saw in her distracted dream, the silver moon balanced on the water.

Perhaps the beetle would deliver her message to the moon, but in vain. The moon would not answer. Silently, it would close its eyes and sink softly into the sea. Linda needed a wizard, not the moon. A wizard is the one with wisdom; the moon is merely a poor, sad-eyed youth, a lover ever looking for his love. It has no lore, only longing; poetry, not power.

When that alder-beetle did not return, Linda finally called another, although she was reluctant to trust too many messengers with her words. The second beetle also shunned the north, to her dismay. This one flew east, across the wide, unbounded wood where strange spirits live which are best left undisturbed. Beyond the forest she would cross sweeping grasslands, steppes like oceans, flowing green and gray beneath the summer sky. Across two rivers and a third, over a rough mountain chain and another, this was the eastern world, until finally, in the farthest distance, if she fared so far, she would meet the rising sun. Red-faced and jovial in the morning, by midday it would burn angry and fierce. The beetle would flee the sun's consuming heat, only to be lost in the emptiness of the desert.

Linda's third messenger wandered south, across the width of Viru, over the low hills and across the lakelands, skirted the wide marshes where no one went willingly, then flew through the deep forests beyond. Here and there, outside the borders of Viru, there were small clearings where bands of Letts and Vends and wild men dwelled. These the beetle passed without notice, not that she was wise enough to know a wizard from an outlaw, but she had set her heart on the evening star. The south was said to be the way of luck, the star its symbol. Gleaming in the twilight, it had none of the sadness of the moon and none of the rage of the sun. Nevertheless, the eye of the evening star was fixed. It would not look at the alder-beetle; it would speak no word, neither of comfort nor care.

For three weeks Kalev lingered in the borderlands between life and death. If he did not return to health, at least he moved no farther into that grim realm from which no mortal man might walk again. Linda tended him as best she could. She kept his body clean, she fed him food he never tasted. She lived entirely in the bathhouse now, while the elders of the village watched over the farms and cared for her two sons.

Eventually Linda summoned a fourth beetle, knowing it was futile, needing to try nonetheless. There was no one else she could send. No person could cross such distances, and her birds were not given to carry such tidings. Nor would she part with them ever, not even for Kalev.

"Go north," she pleaded, offering the last beetle to the air. "Go north, little sister, find a wizard there, for me, for your friend." She was too weary, however, even to notice the direction this one took.

Faithfully, she leaned over Kalev's body and stroked his brow. She washed some of the filth from his loins, then just sat looking at him tenderly. Once he had been so strong and hard, and now he lay so helpless, muscles soft, flesh limp. She sang softly. She might have been a bird sitting on her nest, or crouched over her fallen mate until he was dead, and like a bird, she would wait an extra day before she flew away.

[9]

As Linda sang tunelessly, thoughtlessly, new words formed in her mouth, words she had never sung before. They came to her from nowhere, or from the air. Perhaps it was a song she had heard once long ago in the house of the Woman in Blue Stockings and then forgotten. Excited now she listened closely to the words she was singing. It was a northern chant. Perhaps her beetle had found a wizard and this was his message to her. She sang louder. The song seemed summoned out of her by a force beyond her knowing. Strength swept through her body. This was the time of turning. She had prayed for so many days and now the gods were answering. She touched her husband; strength and the new words flowed out of her and into him.

> Old man, old one, Vanamuine,
> old as time, needed now come
> hither, come here, summoned
> here, where a sick man lies
> dying, here, struck by evil
> unknown in name, an illness
> of unreckoned origin. Old one,
> old one, hither, hither come,
> here, the floor is rotting
> under foot, the roof decaying
> overhead above this man.
> Vanamuine, sweep away the plague
> with your bathwhisk; a honey wing
> will quench the sparks, a golden wing
> will raise the evil sickness
> to the sky, Vanamuine.
> Vanamuine, give a portion
> to the storms, to rocks; winds
> carry it away from here.
> To the north, far, away, to sea,
> beneath black mud bury it;
> in the blue stone beyond earth
> hide the ill where none will know.

Thrice over, Linda sang these words, each time with a stronger voice, and then she was finished. She fell back exhausted, her body shaking from the force it had received and released. Gently she wiped Kalev's face, wet with her tears. As her fingers touched his eyes, his eyelids flickered.

She sensed the spirit inside him straining to emerge, to speak through frozen lips, and her own will cried out to his. Together

[10]

they pushed back the cloak of darkness that had engulfed him. At first Kalev uttered only croaks, harsh inhuman noises brought back from behind death's domain. Soon, however, the sounds fell into patterns she knew to be words. Trembling, Linda bent over him, anxious to hear what he would say and equally afraid.

"The kingdom—" he muttered; his tongue could hardly hold the word. "The kingdom—" as though it was the only idea left in his burned out mind. Of all that Kalev had ever known or felt, this was the one portion he must leave behind. "Kingdom— Viru—youngest son—mine—my heir—"

The words collapsed into a meaningless jumble, then ceased altogether as Kalev lapsed again into that state lying between unconsciousness and death. The effort spent in speaking had taken the last of his strength and he could bring himself forward no more. Although his eyes remained open, they lost the last of their luster. Linda stayed by him. She leaned back against the dripping wall and watched and waited for whatever would come. What else could she do? She had sung her last song; she had nothing more to give. She was too spent even to think about his words. All she knew was he had not spoken her name.

Linda's last hope, the tiny alder-beetle carrying her message to the north, traveled very far for so small a being. She braved the gray waters of the sea's long arm between Viru and Soome. She fought the wind. She flew through fogs raised by sorcerers to shield their land from the eyes of strangers. Searching for the one who could serve Linda's need, the beetle crossed and recrossed fearful fenlands from Turja to Karjala. She followed long chains of lakes leading far away into the hidden northland.

A solitary man stood on a high outcropping of rock scanning the horizon, a knotted blanket looped around his neck, a small bagpipe tucked under his arm. The alder-beetle passed him by. A wind-enchanter is not a wizard. The winds are his domain, not words. He knows no healer's songs.

Beyond Soome, beyond Turja, she entered the forbidden realms of Pohja where true wizards were said to dwell. Bleak and gray, barren, to eyes blind to the wonders there, this was a country so remote it remained untouched by the concerns of mortal men. Here, in retirement, the race of wizards lived, each one alone, each one at home in the misty reaches of the vast, unbounded space that is the north. One by one they had left the lands of earthly care, hurry, and change, to seek peace where none but wild geese bred. There, in quiet solitude, each one practiced his private arts and followed the life of learning he chose to live while in their former haunts men of a new kind came upon the land, men like Kalev, whose songs carried a more strident note, the ring of iron.

Hidden in a circle of hollow hills surrounding a silver lake was a small hut woven of willow boughs and thatched with golden moss. It was so concealed from the world that none could have found it ever unless its contriver allowed it to be seen. The wizard sat beside the shining pool smoking a long stemmed pipe in peaceful reverie. A fishing line trailed from his hand into the water. A pike played with the end of the floating thread.

The alder-beetle dived out of the sky to light on the wizard's waiting hand. Twitching her wings and waving her antennae, she told him of her journey and its origin. Gently, he touched her with his fingertip to still her fears and ease her fragile mind. A venture through the northland would tax greater persons than this.

While the beetle rested, the wizard contemplated her message and Linda's need. He smiled wryly. Even if he had cared for Kalev, he could not save him. All arts have limits, his no less than others. What the moon has blanched, what the sun has seared, what the evening star has withered with its frozen eye, can never bloom again.

Long before Linda could call the alder-beetle home again, Kalev died.

2   Linda bathed Kalev's body in four pure waters, salt water from the sea, sweet water from the spring, soft rain, her woman's tears. She clad him in a silk shirt and wrapped him in a satin shroud fastened with a belt of silver. She smoothed his hair with a golden brush and silver comb and last of all a light caress with her fingertips.

No one came to help her when she laid him on a sledge and dragged it from the courtyard, through the gate, under the leering, broken skull, across the wide meadow. She was Kalev's wife, his widow; this was her burden alone. Only her birds even watched.

Kalev's horses were gone. In the weeks of his illness they had run to freedom beyond the pasturelands. Perhaps they would be captured by other folk and kept; perhaps they would be slain and eaten by the outlaws or demons who lurked in the darkness of the wood. Whatever their fate, no friendly horses were ever seen again in Viru.

Linda brought her husband to the crown of a knoll overlooking the sea. Here he had often come when he wished to be alone and when he wanted to survey his country. On one side, the great primeval forest spread far across the south and west, broken only where he had cleared land and laid bare the coastal plain. On the other lay the open sea, which he had seen as a road to the world beyond Viru. Here he could keep guard forever.

Scraping the turf with her hands, Linda prepared Kalev's last bed. Her birds perched on her shoulders and fluttered about while she worked, whistling, chirping bright sounds of foolishness just to share the joy they knew. Oblivious to grief, they chuckled about the summer and the sweetness of ripe fruit. Linda put up with their nonsense patiently, but could not join it. She was too listless for laughter. At last she sent them off to scurry for their suppers, so she could sing farewell to her husband without their childish chattering.

Facing north, toward the land of Kalev's origin, she spread her arms to the open sky and chanted the songs of mourning sung by people of her kind. Not knowing what hymns his fathers might have sung, she could only bury him with the reverence that was within her. While she covered Kalev's body with a warm cloak of earth, she sang again, a short song of parting to him and another song to the earth to receive him with kindness. Begging the earth's forgiveness for any hurt she had done with her digging, she planted blue harebells and golden starflowers around the tomb to mark the wound. In time their roots would reach downward, deeper than usual, and tendrils would twine about Kalev's bones. Flowers would spring from his naked cheeks and flourish from the hollow sockets of his eyes.

In the months that followed, Linda lived alone in the great hall which Kalev had built, passing her days without plans, without purpose, with no other company than her birds. Her two sons remained in the care of the elders of the village at the forest's edge. Kalev had fostered all her other children into foreign lands; Paari and Jaani would remain close. She might have kept them with her, but Linda no longer had the strength to bear their prattling noise and play. Only the child within her womb shared her life now, and he seemed to absorb all that was left of her spirit. He was growing rapidly now; daily her body became more unwieldy. Often in that time she would take out her spinning, intending to work a thread, only to find herself, some time later, sitting motionless, devoid of thought, distaff and spindle lying forgotten in her hands.

Once Kalev had filled this room. Now there were few reminders of him left, some tools, a knife, a copper cup. Kalev had not been one to clutter shelves and cupboards with trophies and trinkets. The very starkness of his side of the hall was the mark of the life he had lived. The only important mementos of his years in Viru were the empty iron hooks on the wall and the Book.

The hooks were to have held his great sword. It was to have been wrought for him by a northern smith with a blade that would never break, never even lose its edge, a point that would never blunt. Forged of iron and fire inseparably joined, shaped with deep magic imbued within its steel, and instructed with such spells of swordcraft as only the master smiths of Soome could know or understand or control, it was to have the power to cut and kill and never know defeat on this earth. For years Kalev had dreamed of this sword, and for years it had been in its shaping, but he had never seen it, and now he never would. Eventually Linda would hang herbs and skeins of yarn on the unused hooks, and she would forget the purpose for which they were driven into the wall over the hearth, as she would forget that somewhere in Soome there was a sword waiting for its master.

The Book was more mysterious. It was a wizard's book, a book of power, inscribed in the age before this age, in the time when the great masters dwelt within the forests of Viru. Bound between heavy iron plates, unadorned except for some graven signs which none could understand, and fastened with leather straps and iron chains, it contained all the spells and prophecies, the lore and powers, that meant life and freedom to the people of Viru. So it was said, and most believed, though none knew for certain. The Book was never opened, and no one really knew what secrets were inscribed on its pages. No one was left who could read its script; no one remained to write in it again.

When the wizards quit the country to seek a surer peace in the north, they had carried their Books with them to keep them from the hands of unworthy men. Somehow, however, Kalev had learned of this treasure, located, and recovered it. Somehow he had wrested it from the one who was its keeper and so returned it to its home.

The Book belonged to Viru. That was his sole reason for wanting it. He had no interest in reading it; he did not even try, disdaining all the wizards' arts. Nevertheless, once it felt iself in its homeland, the Book began to release its powers by itself; it continued to work for the people. The mere fact that it was there ensured success and fortune for Viru. So long as it remained, the country could not be conquered nor the people vanquished in battle.

Linda, however, feared the Book. She alone of Viru's people could sense the unseen tentacles of power that seemed to writhe from between its covers. Some of them reached far across the fields and forests; some remained in the hall. Some touched her; some worked their way into her womb to touch the child growing there. Others merely twined around themselves and wound mysterious patterns in the air. Because she could not understand the forces radiating from the Book, or know them for good or evil, she shunned the niche on the west side of the hall where it was chained. It too was ignored and then forgotten, until an hour when it was too late for remembering.

Often, in her loneliness, Linda would go to the knoll where Kalev was buried. She might have returned to Laane, to her early home, where life was simpler, but Kalev's last words had barred that haven to her. He expected his youngest son, the one unborn, to be his heir, so she must stay in Viru to raise him to be a king, and she did not know how.

The earth over the grave was dry. Although the herbs and flowers she had set were growing, the ground was bare in many places. The signs of the tomb were too stark and easily seen. Linda moved a stone to cover a grassless patch. That stone led to another, and another. Over the days and weeks moving stones became a ritual, a mindless repetition without apparent reason. Without thinking, she piled them one atop another until the entire grave was buried. Even then she continued.

The blocks were heavy; laying stones was far harder labor than planting flowers, and it was made more difficult by the child swelling between her sides. In the last months he had grown so large she could scarcely stoop to lift a stone. Nevertheless, she persisted, for no other reason than to be doing it. She dragged the granite blocks by hand up the steep slope of the seaward side of the hill and shoved them awkwardly onto the pile. It became a high mound. Once, the image of a cairn over a tomb formed briefly in her mind. This, she remembered, was one of the burial rites Kalev had said was practiced by his people. That impression drove her to work harder. She would build a monument on his grave; it would be something concrete for Kalev's child to see. It would remind him of the father he had never known, and perhaps there the future king would find the guidance, and solace, she could not give.

The heavy skies of autumn pressed ominously on the land. Clouds foretold a storm; the sea reflected their warning. Waves ran rapidly over the ledges along the shore and crashed on the rocks at the foot of the knoll. Linda worked frantically to finish her day's labor before the sky itself should fall. That she might leave, go home, return another day, never occurred to her. All she knew was that what she had begun must be done. Yet the harder she worked, the worse it was. Once she slipped and fell between two stones, too weak to rise. Lamenting her fate, desperately lonely, she wept. Her tears formed a pool between the boulders.

Winds came out of the north and east, cold, biting winds. A new pain ripped through Linda's sides, and she knew it for her child. She groaned. It was not yet his time, and yet it was. The son within her would not wait for the day decreed for him. "Ukko," she whispered pitifully to the clouds. Why must he be so impatient? Why couldn't he wait for a brighter day, when she was ready to receive him leisurely? Another pain seized her womb, and she knew that whatever she might wish, the time had come for Kalev's heir to take his place in the world.

Whimpering softly, Linda crawled from her resting place and scrambled clumsily over the crown of the hill, leaving behind, unfinished, the mound raised to her husband's memory to deliver the only monument he ever wanted. The wind pressing at her back drove her across the meadow. The clouds sank lower, to crowd the earth with their fullness. She cried aloud pleas to the sky for comfort in her haste.

Alerted by Linda's birds, two ancient women from the village greeted her at the bathhouse door. They had already built up the fire to heat the room and boil water, filling the chamber with healthful steam. They had kindled it in secret so no stranger, no passing sorcerer or bearded witch, should know their business or cast a spell of evil over the new-born child or his mother in this time of innocence and openness. For luck, the wood they burned was from the back beam of the barn.

By the time Linda arrived, the bathhouse was ready to receive her. Behind its sealed door, hidden from all eyes, the two old women helped her remove her clothes. They crooned old songs and caressed her to calm her and help her relax. Linda let them minister to her as they would; she was concentrating anxiously on the pangs that were regularly upon her now.

[16]

She knelt on the straw and cushions on the floor. As she opened herself to the time that was soon to come, the sorrow she had felt on the knoll disappeared. With a new sense of peace and worth, she joined her voice with the others', singing a protective song to ease and speed the birth and to ward away all blights and ill enchantment. Billows of steam rolled around her; even the clouds were singing. Leaning forward, she braced her head against the wooden bench. In the mist all shapes were blurred; the patterns and forms of things seemed to be spinning. Only the pains in her belly were constant and firm. The two women, no longer visible, moved through the vapors like spirits. Beneath the eaves, unseen by anyone except Linda in her confusion, were two shadowy strangers who had come with the steam to watch over the birth and attend the mother in travail while Viru's king was born. One of them, clad in rough peasant garb and bearded, was the old one, Taara, himself. The other, round-faced and jovial, was Rougutaja, master of birth and midwifery. They had come to bless the child and the mother. Linda closed her eyes and lurched from a rending pain.

Gentle hands stroked her sides; perhaps it was one of the women, perhaps a god. With soft tallow and honey the moving fingers rubbed her naked loins, her thighs and hinder parts, and between her legs. All the while the voices sang. Their songs were directed to the child, to the small one, to the traveler, as he was called, to come into the world, to join the race of men, to breathe the open airs, to play with other infants. They called on all the mysterious powers to speed the child's delivery, to spring the fleshly gates, to unbar the doors of bone, to cut through all bonds and obstacles, to open the fertile oven, to let the small one, the traveler, come bouncing forth.

With the passing words of the songs, the pains came more quickly and insistently. Linda groaned, and then cried out. The hands held her as she writhed from the movement within her. These pangs were far stronger than any she had felt with her other sons; none had ever torn her so. She opened her mouth to cry again but could not; she could not speak or sing. Then, suddenly, like a flood bursting through a dam, her own prayer for childbirth poured from her mouth to fill the tiny room:

> Ukko, high one, lord
> of earth and cloud, raise
> the golden axe, strike now
> with silver hatchet, hew
> the fleshly threshold, break
> the locks of bone apart.

Open window holes, cut
open vents that the traveler
might pass through, the small one,
one of little strength, a tunnel
that hither he may come.
From the oven, Ukko, drop
the flat stone, from the well
a pebble, from the woman's lap
a boy-child from her hips.
Or death will enter; life
flee this womb in pain,
the belly's fearful throes.

Ukko, high one, lord
of cloud, come hither, free
the small one for his journey.

As though a key were turned in a lock, or a pin pulled from a
hinge, Linda felt the hidden passage within her middle open. The
gate swung freely; the door-posts parted. Something inside her
seemed to separate; her very bones spread apart. In that moment
she opened her legs and strained every muscle in her body to
focus all their strength upon her womb. She smiled and groaned
at once, and in that look and sound there surged all the urge that
is life. Suddenly his head appeared and in a rush Kalev's heir
was born.

Leaning against the steamy timbers of the bathhouse wall,
Linda lay back on the floor, exhausted. One of the women had
taken the infant and quickly washed it with a fragrant water in
the manner of her people; the other had gone to proclaim the son
to the open air. The chamber itself rang with the baby's first loud
cries. When the old woman returned the child to her, Linda
cradled him against her breast and gently rocked him while he
cried. Her soft skin was slippery with a mixture of sweat and
steam, but to the small one she was simply the center of great
warmth.

After a while she held him up to look at him, and then she
laughed, with relief, with joy, with complete and satisfied fatigue.
His tiny legs waved foolishly in the air as she shook him, and
she laughed at his absurdity. He was so helpless and small, such
a contrast to his sire.

Even so, when Linda considered him carefully, as a mother
will, she saw that, indeed, her son was large for one new-born,
larger than her other sons had been. She imagined how he would

grow; soon enough those tiny legs would be long and thin, like his father's. He would have Kalev's golden hair, but her own dark eyes. His skin would be lighter than hers, darker than Kalev's. She looked into his unformed face to read his future but could see little there. If he grew to be the son his father wanted, he would be a hero and do great deeds, winning honor and glory for himself and for Viru, but Linda lacked the seer's art and could not know his end.

Wisely, the two women slipped out of the bathhouse to leave her alone with her lusty, screaming child. The hot clouds of steam, their work completed, were released through the air vent. Yet, before the vapors were entirely clear, the two hidden figures stepped out from the corner to make their departures. With a smile, Rougutuja touched the infant's lips. The old one, Taara, spoke aloud.

"He will not die by the hand of man," he decreed, then disappeared with the other through the mist.

Linda named her child Sohni, but he was always called the Kalevide, Kalev's son.

3   Winter came over Viru like a war. Winds marched across the frozen fields to assault the lonely hall where Linda and her infant son lived alone. Cold gusts sought the cracks between the timbers. They hissed and whistled, then howled through the nights like outland raiders or demons. Inside, only one small fire held off the cold. Kept constantly burning, it gave just enough warmth for the two to live. The only light in the wide room came from the hearth and from the flame of a single pine splint flickering in its copper holder above the baby's cradle. Beyond that close circle of firelight darkness loomed huge and empty; shadows lurked like spirits in the corners.

The Kalevide was fretful. Wearily rocking the cradle, Linda wondered what was troubling him, an icy finger of the wind or the dark demon-dancing of the shadows across the room. Suddenly he screamed. His mouth stretched full width, red cheeks swelled, and an explosion of sound, such as had never before been heard in Viru, burst from his infant lips. Perhaps somewhere in the darkness dwelt a spirit which only a babe could see; perhaps it was only a simple stomach pain. Whatever it was, when Linda bent over him to pick him up, he kicked and struggled and would not let her touch him. Nothing she could do would comfort him. Rocking the cradle did not soothe; her lullabies went unheard beneath his shrieks. The Kalevide merely thrashed wildly on his bed and screamed.

Every night for a month he raised the same shattering cry, only to be calm again when morning came. The night returned and brought fresh screams of torment. Linda sang to him until she lost her voice. She offered lilting cradle songs, she chanted simple charms, anything to give him sleep, but nothing did. As the nights passed without change, she began to pray for sleep for herself as well. All her songs closed with the burden,

> ". . . and the mother,
> let her sleep; the infant's slave
> has need of rest as well."

It was without success. Linda soon began to fear that, indeed, some demon had attacked her son or a sorcerer had cast an unkind spell on him. Why, she did not know, but she believed it could be so. The malevolent ones were known to strike the innocent.

On the month's last night, the Kalevide, still screaming at the top of his lungs, rose out of his cradle. He stood, clutched its sides for support, then shook its thin wooden slats in rage. A new fury seized him. His face became distorted in a mask of agony. His eyes seemed to turn in his head; his baby's hair stood straight out from his scalp. With her fingers Linda made a swift sign to ward off evil as he tore his swaddling clothes apart. Then, naked, he smashed the cradle to pieces with his hands. Like a chick newly hatched from its shell, he started to crawl about on the floor, awkwardly at first, but soon learning to move at will. In his infant nakedness he had won his first true moments of freedom.

That night and thereafter the Kalevide slept comfortably, occupying Linda's bed while she slept in a pile of straw on the floor. In his first act of his own, the Kalevide had climbed upon the cot, where he sat regally until she acknowledged it as his. Linda was content to let him keep the high place; she preferred her nest of straw. It reminded her of her youth, when she had always slept in such a bed. Yet there were times, many times, when the Kalevide was wrapped in sleep, when she would slip into bed beside him to hug and hold him close through the long, dark night.

Linda nursed her son until he was three years old and would have nursed him longer if he had not weaned himself. His appetite was too great; not even Linda's ample breasts could meet his hunger. He might have sucked her very life from her. At three he was as large as a six-year-old child should be.

While Linda worked at her woman's chores about the house, cooking or cleaning or spinning, always spinning, he played on the floor beside her, or, when the weather was warm, in the yard outside. Often, to amuse him, she shaped tiny toy deer or oxen by bending soft pine chips to form legs and horns. Though they pleased him well enough, as all toys pleased him, his chief delight was the wooden horse that Kalev had hewn from a tree trunk once many years before. The young Kalevide would climb upon its back, flourish a small wooden sword, and proclaim himself the emperor of the world.

When he was older, he would sometimes pull rushes and twist them into chains to pass the time. Linda showed him how to plait them properly, so they would not unwind at once, and how to bind them into bracelets and necklaces. She also taught him to weave simple baskets out of willow twigs, for he seemed eager to fashion objects with his hands. At times he would try to carve small animals out of wood or to fashion rude figures or utensils from clay, but he was clumsy and awkward and most of the shapes were unrecognizable, even when he identified them as bears or dogs or deer. Nevertheless, although any cup or bowl was likely to be unusable, Linda would take each one and admire it proudly. She kept them all. Every lump-like animal, every misshapen dish was praised and placed on a shelf or in a cupboard. Soon they occupied all the vacant places in the house, and more filled chests in the storehouses. Linda's pride was genuine; she saw in each wretched shape the craft of her child's hands. If he had formed it, that was enough to please his mother.

Although Linda may have admired these products of his groping, the Kalevide did not. He knew they were ugly and ill-formed and useless, and he wished she would throw them away. Something inside him, like a voice from far away, told him they were no good and he must not be satisfied with any of them. It insisted that he could do better, that he should do better, that he must do better. In frustration, he would throw down his tools and scatter his materials with an angry sweep of his arm. His hands were too large, he would cry in rage, then storm out of the house to play at something else.

In the courtyard his wooden blocks lay where he left them. Squatting on the ground, he would arrange them carefully into a miniature city. Although he had never seen a city, he had found inside himself the pattern of what he wanted to build. He spent hours aligning these blocks to represent houses and harbors, placing a high wall around them, which he pretended was stone. So he played. Too often, however, before he ever completed his city he would knock it down. The buildings became ruins, the harbors wrecked, the walls destroyed, forgotten as he turned instead to playing at Kurni, the game of his people, sometimes called tipcat. Picking up a stick, he would flip the wooden blocks into the air and bat them far across the yard. In no time at all he could scatter them everywhere over the meadow. He loved to see them flying, like birds, framed against the sky and laughed aloud each time he sent one spinning away toward the woods.

Sometimes he ran, as fast as his legs would take him, away from the house and down to the shore where he would play by the sea. For long hours he was content to stand at the edge of the cove, in the shadow of the knoll where Kalev was buried, skimming stones across the water. Ducks and drakes became his favorite sport; it was the one feat at which he could excel. As he grew older he learned to skim the stones in long multiple leaps, until they fairly slid on the silver surface of the sea.

He used to run home proudly to tell his mother. "I threw one across the cove," he would declare. "I threw one for a league, for two leagues, for three."

"Did you?" she would say.

"Uh-huh—and I stood on my head to watch it go."

Then Linda would laugh and hug him and call him her sweet berry.

"Am I your berry?"

"Of course you are."

"What kind of berry?"

"A bearberry."

"Is that good?"

"Umnh-hmn."

"I'm glad."

And the Kalevide would squirm into her lap, upsetting all her spinning gear.

"Tell me a story," he would plead.

"If you like. What shall I tell, the one about Two True

Friends, or the one about Three Brothers Who Went Forth To
Find Their Fortune, or Silly Smudgeface Who Became A Prince?"

"Tell me about the Woman In Blue Stockings, because she
was your mother."

"Silly boy, you always ask for that one."

"I know it. Tell me again."

Linda sighed. "All right, silly, but you must promise to listen
very carefully and not interrupt."

"I won't."

Then she leaned back and closed her eyes for a moment.
Although she had told this story many times, it was worth telling
over if he would remember it in time. It was a story of the elder
age, before the old ways changed and the new possessed the
world.

"Once there was a woman who lived alone in Laane," she
would begin.

"You always start that way."

"That is how the story begins: Once there was a woman who
lived alone in Laane, which is west of here. She was the Woman
in Blue Stockings, and she lived in a tiny, little home hidden in
the trees of Taara's ancient forest. Each morning in the springtime, the Woman in Blue Stockings would leave her little cottage
to walk along lost woodland paths and through green meadows
which were just awakening with dawn. On her arm she carried a
large wicker basket filled with wildflowers, and as she walked,
she scattered these flowers all over the earth. In the woods she
spread her sweet blue violets and jewel-like white anemones. In
the open glades she strewed buttercups and cowslips in carpets of
gold. And everywhere the flowers touched the ground, they
grew. Soon the earth was covered with their colors. All day
long, while the Woman in Blue Stockings walked, little winds of
springtime tugged playfully at her ribbons; misty morning dew-
drops sparkled on her slippers. The Woman in Blue Stockings
wore a silver veil through which everything she saw was real.

"Through the day she sang, and, as she sang, the words that
flew from her mouth were birds. The birds she sang in the forest
fluttered away to live in the trees and thickets, the secret sparrows
and wrens and thrushes and noisy woodpeckers. In the meadows
and clearings her birds hid amongst the tall grasses, tiny golden
finches and bluebirds and larks and nightjars. At river sides and
lake shores the Woman in Blue Stockings sang ducks and geese,
and in the marshes cranes. All the birds she sang sang with her;
they joined their songs to hers and soon the world was filled with
birds."

"Is that where your birds came from?"

"Yes, but this is not their story." Perched beside her, Linda's three companions, bluebird, swallow, and house finch, were asleep. They already knew the tale she told.

"Some of the birds the Woman in Blue Stockings sang," continued Linda, "soared high, high into the blueness of the sky."

"Hawks!" he cried.

"Yes. But some soared higher yet, high beyond the limits of the clouds. They flew so far they left the world behind; these became the stars that sing always in the heavens.

"One day, in the spring, when the Woman in Blue Stockings had spilled the last of the flowers from her basket and sung the last of her songs for that day, when she was returning to her tiny house by way of the winding track a lost cow had made, she found a fat, brown hen in the middle of the path. She picked it up and put it in her basket to take home with her. A little later she came upon a grouse's egg nestled in the moon-shaped footprint of the cow. This she tucked between her breasts to hold it warm and safe. Finally, not far from her cottage, she found a young crow with a broken wing. She took this too, slung over her back like a bundle of bath whisks.

"That night, in her storehouse where she kept her most precious things, the Woman in Blue Stockings made a nest for the hen and the egg by lining her basket with soft lamb's wool. The crow she threw behind some boxes in the corner. Soon the hen began to grow. She grew and grew until her head bumped the lid of the basket where she had been sitting on the egg. She grew for three months, and a fourth, until one day the Woman in Blue Stockings went back to her storehouse to look at her darlings. And what do you think she saw?"

"A chicken!"

"No, silly, the hen had grown into a beautiful young woman with long, shining hair like honey. This was Salme. The egg, meanwhile, had hatched into another maiden; she had dark brown hair, and this was Linda."

"It was you!"

"It was me, and Salme was my sister. But the crow was an orphan girl with black hair. Salme and I didn't like her much, so we made her be our servant. She cut and carried wood for us, cooked our food, prepared our baths. She was a maiden of all work. The black girl was very sullen and not at all nice to look at. She had a crooked arm and could not speak. But she was the one who would remain with the Woman in Blue Stockings in after days."

This was the story that Linda told of her beginnings, and it pleased her to think that it was true. In later years, however, the Kalevide rarely asked to hear it. He was no longer content with such simple fables; he wanted bolder tales.

"Tell me of my father," he would clamor. "Tell me of his origins."

Because this, more than anything else, was important to him, Linda tried to please him.

"I cannot tell you where Kalev came from," she would begin. "That is something no one truly knows. But it is said that he was born somewhere beyond the world's end. Beyond Soome, beyond Turja, beyond far Pohja. Beyond the lands where cold winds dwell. Beyond the water and the sky. This much I can tell you, my son, for this I know is true: Kalev came from the north.

"On the back of the black north wind three brothers flew. On the backs of great eagles wrought of dark iron, they soared, their golden hair streaming in the icy air as they sped through the sky over many lands in their long journey to the south and to the east.

"The eldest of the three ventured far, far across the eastern forests and the boundless plains. He crossed the rivers and the hills that divide the East from the West until at last, in the country of the Golden Mountains, he became a merchant and a trader. His merchandise was arms. He sold weapons in the endless wars between the peoples of the Uraltai and the Riders of the Khan, so it is said, and he sold his deadly wares to warriors of both nations and so thrived well from their strife. Nor has he ever returned from there; he may live in that country still."

"But he wasn't Kalev."

"No, that was his elder brother."

"I'm glad."

"The second of the three brothers flew eastward over the northern fens and fells of Turja and Karjala until he was lost to the ken of man. Some say he became a warrior wandering among the peoples of the waste, selling the services of his sword and crossbow. He may have settled with some tribe or he may have died on the ice. No one knows. Some say he was captured by a wind-enchanter, and some believe he became a sorcerer. Some have said, in darkness and in secret, that he took service with the Sarvik himself."

"Who is the Sarvik?"

"Hush, my sweet one, that is no name that we should speak."

"But who is he?"

"Sh-h-h, sometime I will tell you. You will learn when you are grown, but boys should not think of him, for he is not nice. Instead I will tell you now of Kalev, who was the third of the brothers and the fairest of them all. He steered his iron bird south across the Amber Sea; east he flew, across the land of Laane, and on across the land of Harju. He skimmed above the treetops until Taara in his wisdom brought him to earth to land on the shores of Viru. Here he cleared the forest and here he settled. Here he vowed to found his kingdom. It was his home; someday it will be yours."

Then the Kalevide would reflect on the long future lying ahead.

"I miss him, sometimes," he said.

"Of course you do."

"He could show me things, and teach me how to do them right."

"I can show you things."

"I know. But it isn't the same. He would make me do them better."

Linda bent to kiss him, but he pulled away.

Only many years later would the Kalevide, his mind still dwelling on his father, ask how Kalev had come to take Linda for his wife and how she had left the Woman in Blue Stockings to go away with him. Thus he learned, without being aware of it, of the time the ages changed, the moment when the music sung in Laane faded and the louder note of Viru rose. This was the tale Linda told:

"I have told you of Salme, and I have said she was beautiful. Because she was so beautiful, suitors from all over the world came to court her. Rich sons of merchants and the sons of princes sought Salme's hand, but although all brought her splendid gifts, she refused every one. And when she refused them, they courted me, for that is the way of eager men. They seek brides to comfort them and do not much care which women become their wives. Even the prince of Kungla asked for my hand, offering me golden chains if I would wed. But I too refused them all, even the prince of Kungla. I had no mind to marry.

"Nor was it merely mortal men who courted us. The moon and the sun had heard of Salme's beauty, and both sought her hand. One night the moon drove into our courtyard in a sledge drawn by fifty horses all shining black. Salme would not have him, however, nor would I, for he was a pale, sad young man, who had to work by night and sometimes by day, traveling, always changing. Soon he went away to seek another love in an endless quest. It is said he glimpsed her once in a river beneath a bridge, but that is another story long to tell.

"The sun arrived next day with an escort grander than the moon's; he came clad in a bright golden coat and bold yellow boots. Nevertheless, Salme sent him away as well, for he was far too spiteful and angry; even his eyes burned. Although he could be kind and gentle, too often he was cruel and hard, causing great harm upon the land through heat and drought. In a rage the sun left us behind.

"It was when the son of the north star arrived that Salme found her love. He brought with him the calm of the deep night and the peace of great distance. Ever steadfast and constant, he served to guide the ways of men and never seared the earth. Salme took him gladly for her husband.

"I will not tell you of the wedding now; in time you will celebrate a wedding yourself and will see then the customs of our people when a man and a woman wed. It is a grand festival, filling many days and nights. People came from all around the land to rejoice with Salme and the north star's son. The cottage was filled, and so was the courtyard and beyond. While Salme dressed herself in the bathhouse, with my help, all the people danced and sang outside. They danced all the dances of Laane and Harju, of all the westland and all the ancient wood. Even trees came to celebrate the wedding, and they danced with their roots and branches."

"Trees? No."

"But it is so, for I saw them myself. They danced to the singing of the old ones, the wise ones, who know the songs that stir the hearts of men, who weave true magic in their words and music. When these sing, the rest are still; all draw close to hear the words. Everywhere the world draws close; beasts of the wood and birds pause to listen. And the trees are moved.

"Then, while the eldest of the old ones sang, a new voice was heard. Over the heads of the people, a harsh, strident sound rose in a foreign song, painful to hear. This was not the music of the forest and green meadows; it was a chant of men marching to bold adventures, defying every force in the quest for glory and fame. Oh, it was strong. Too strong. It silenced forever the elder's song.

"The stranger who sang did not take the painted singer's bench, as our bards do, nor did he play the five-stringed kantele.

[27]

No, he stood in the center of the room and strutted as he sang. The folk fell back to give him space. He was new to the country; no one had seen him before. Tall and handsome with his long golden hair, dressed in belted tunic and leather breeches, leather boots adorned with bright silver chains. And he wore a sword. He was the only one there with a weapon.

"While he sang, I say, the stranger danced. He drew his sword and turned in a proud, driving dance. He strutted like a cock. He bobbed, he weaved, he brandished that sword in the rhythm of his chant. And he was dancing for me. His motion wove a spell of power around me until my heart could not move except to the beating of his heels on the floor.

"Once he had captured me, the golden stranger announced himself to the people."

"Kalev!" cried the boy.

"Yes, Kalev. Your father. He, too, had come to Laane, to the home of the Woman in Blue Stockings, to court a bride. He, too, had heard of Salme's beauty from afar and desired her. And he, too, unable to have his chosen one, chose me. For he would have a wife. I had refused the other suitors; I had refused the sun and the moon. I had refused the Lord of Waters and the Lord of Winds, but I could not refuse Kalev. I had been trapped by the spell of his dance."

"I'm glad."

"You are? Why?"

"Because then he could be my father."

"And so he came to be. But most who were there weren't glad; they opposed the marriage because Kalev was a stranger. The Woman in Blue Stockings did not like him because he had interrupted the elder's singing. But there were a few, mostly younger people, who did approve. They cheered his bold manner and brave appearance. I think many of the young men envied his sword. Everyone said he was more handsome than the prince of Kungla. To me it did not matter if any approved or not. In my heart I was bound to him already.

"Kalev wanted to leave at once. It was far, he said, to his home. Yet ill fortune follows when a wedding feast is cut short, and I did not care to leave so soon. I needed some time to gather my belongings and to dress myself as a bride. So I was in the bathhouse when Salme and her husband departed. Never more would she return to Laane. Her only home now lay beyond the clouds in the north star's hall. When I heard the sledge drive away, I ran to the door, but all I could see was a swirl of snow and a mist of starlight. I cried to her; I called, 'Where are you going?' but all I heard was the sigh of the wind through the pines. I have never seen my sister since.

"That was my first moment of sadness. I would have wept if I had not been heartened to think that I had Kalev to wed. He would protect me from all future loneliness and sorrow. So I trusted.

"Soon after Salme's departure we left, too. I hugged the Woman in Blue Stockings once, quickly, then snuggled under the rugs beside my husband in his sledge. He raised his whip, and we were off. The Woman in Blue Stockings called something after me, but I never heard her words. We were gliding too swiftly on the snow. Flying through the deep forest night, I leaned on Kalev for warmth.

"All through the night and the next day and another night and day, we drove without rest. All the wood was wrapped in snow along the trail from Laane to Viru. All the forest was still. The trees were watching us; all the world was waiting. Something had happened. It was a moment of turning. Kalev had taken me for his wife.

"In Viru I became the mother of his children, the mother of his daughters, who are gone, and the mother of his sons, of which, my little bear, you are the last. And that is the story of how I wed your father. Yet there is more:

"When the sledge carried me away, the Woman in Blue Stockings sang three birds, my bluebird, my swallow, my fat house finch, and sent them after me. They were her gift, and they were her messengers. They bade me not to forget my old father, the moon, who stood before the door, nor the sun, my ancient uncle, by the storehouse, nor to forget my brother, the birch tree, by the window, or my sister, the willow, by the bathhouse, nor all my kin and cousins of the woods and meadowlands, not to forget the birds.

"For a moment I had forgotten, in the moment Kalev carried me away, and so in after days these things could never be recalled as I had known them once. Yet with the birds to remind me, I shall remember them always. And I shall not forget the Woman in Blue Stockings and the life she taught me.

"When I had gone, the Woman in Blue Stockings was left alone. Her daughters had gone to other worlds; only the poor orphan girl remained. And when the Woman in Blue Stockings turned to her to lament our leaving, the black-haired slave was mute. She opened her mouth to speak, but she could only caw like a crow.

"These things the birds have told me. They are my companions, they are my friends. They do not grow old, for they have been touched by the lips of the Woman in Blue Stockings. And so I love them dearly; they remind me of her and of my life with her in Laane. And you should learn to love them too, my pet, for they are more than the silly bundles of feathers they seem to be. Listen to the birds; they will always sing you the truth, if you will only believe them.''

The Kalevide was not listening, however. He was dreaming of his father dancing with the sword and of his sledge rushing through the snow. For a long while Linda sat beside him silently, trying to remember once again the day she had married Kalev and left her haven in Laane. She could recall the day, the wedding feast, its songs and dances, all its outward trappings, but none of the inner reasons why she had followed Kalev as she had. The feeling of that moment was forever lost; all that remained was the bare knowledge that she had had a great need. Now so much time had passed that it was difficult even to relive in memory those days long past, and impossible to retrieve that time to live it over again. She must be content with the way things were, for she had no others. This, too, she had learned in the house of the Woman in Blue Stockings.

4   Often, in the ensuing years, Linda took the Kalevide into the forest so he could meet the trees and woods and learn to enjoy them as his friends.

"The pine woods," she said, "are called the Lord's Forest, as the oak groves are Taara's Wood."

"Why?" he asked half-heartedly. Just then he was more interested in discovering what hid under the stone he was turning over: grubs and beetles and slugs.

"No one knows," she answered. "These are just the names we use. The oak has always been sacred among our people, and it has always served us well. That is reason enough. Do you see that coppice of birch trees? Birches are the Maidens' Wood. They are very modest. See how they lean away from us and tremble? Alders are known as the Wood of Poor Orphans; the alder tree is dear to mourners."

It was part of the education she wished him to have. As the Kalevide grew older, she tried to teach him all the crafts and lore she knew, in the forest pointing out useful herbs and roots and showing him which were the fruits and nuts to keep and which to throw away, which berries were sweet to eat and which were ill, which would open his bowels or, even worse, would kill. She taught him how to find a honey hive and how to take some of its comb without offending the noble bees.

Now that his legs were grown long enough to keep pace with hers, they coursed the wide corridors of the forests far from their home. At times they played at being animals, slipping through thickets on the twisting paths of deer and smaller creatures. Linda was nimble in the wood. Bent double, she could slide through the underbrush with scarcely a sound, no more than the rustle of the birds whose paths she followed. The Kalevide was clumsier. Without caring what disturbance he caused, he walked upright, crashing carelessly through dry brushwood, scaring off any small animals he might have seen. Sharp thorns and briars caught on his clothing; vines and branches lashed his face. He learned to ignore the pain. Often he tripped over fallen logs or stepped unwittingly into sinkholes of mud; yet every time he picked himself up and went on unperturbed. These were joyful times for him: to be within the forest, to be with Linda among the trees.

Sometimes they sang, old songs with their tales of elder days, and chants of ancient learning. Although he was an indifferent pupil, Linda wanted her son to absorb some of her people's words of power. He should know the secrets of healing and of shaping, all the names and origins of things, so he could survive in the world without violating the rhythms and harmonies of the earth. It was important that he master the spells that turn the forces which make the world alive, for although a man may live, and even thrive, without these charms and lore, the one who sings will walk with peace throughout his days and will not offend the balance of the earth.

Once, in early summer, while gathering willow boughs for bath whisks, they came to a tiny pool of pure water, where a spring bubbled out of the ground and filled the hollow space between the roots of a giant beech tree before slipping away in a thin silver stream. Sunlight, pouring through the branches of the tree, splashed in patches on the water. While the Kalevide waded in the icy pool and laughed at crayfish scuttling away from his naked toes, Linda sat on the mossy bank, nibbling a bit of golden honeycomb purchased from the bees for a song. They had traveled far that day, farther than the Kalevide had ever gone before.

"Isn't it wonderful to be alone?" he cried. "Just you and me all alone where no one else has ever been."

"Mnh-hmn."

"I think we should stay here always and always. Just the two of us and the forest forever."

Linda spread her legs lazily. Looking at him now, she thought how much he had grown lately. His body was like a young oak tree, though he still had much of the softness of childhood on him.

"But others will be depending on you some day," she said. "Has my little bear forgotten he must be king of Viru and live with the people and rule them? That was Kalev's plan for you. Those were his last words, that you were to be his heir."

"I know it, only sometimes I forget."

"You must not ever forget."

"I won't."

"We could stay this one night alone in the forest, though, if you like. We could sleep here in a nest of trees."

"Oh, yes, let's!" Thoughts of the kingdom were chased very far away.

As evening deepened, Linda told him stories of wizards and wind-enchanters and evil-hearted sorcerers and demons and dwarves, the silly ox-knee people, who were wicked but easily outwitted. Although the stories were frightening, and meant to be, spun of the stuff of darkness as stories of the night should be, the Kalevide was not frightened. He was with his mother, and she would protect him always; after all, she knew all the songs to drive sorcerers and demons away. He laid his head on her shoulder and put his arm around her waist.

Later, as he was dozing, so that his rest would not be disturbed by darkness's spells, she told tales told by people everywhere, of daring princes and strange beasts, of maidens lost and treasures found, of ploughboys who were brave and grand rulers who were wise, of heroes who ventured on long voyages and simple folk who outwitted the shrewdest villains. When he slept, the Kalevide dreamt of fighting sorcerers and wrestling demons, killing ferocious beasts with his hands, and even rescuing beautiful princesses.

Linda did not sleep for a long time, however. The sadness of what she must do in the morning kept her awake. In the silence of the night she could no longer deny to herself the secret reason she had brought her son to this far, beautiful, lonely, hidden place or the sacrifice she must make so soon. Only with the first faint glow of dawn did she begin to drowse, and then, it seemed, it was only to be awakened immediately by a rough hand shaking her shoulder.

"Wake up! Wake up!" The Kalevide was shouting. Linda opened her eyes at once expecting, after her fitful night, to see a ring of outlaws, or demons, or worse, surrounding them. "Wake up!" he cried joyfully. "It's morning!" The sun had just come to touch the treetops.

"Oh, my honey." She wept and embraced him and held him very tightly. The Kalevide was confused, and vaguely disturbed.

An hour later, after they had bathed in the pool and eaten lightly, Linda told him what she had feared to say the day before.

"Do you see that path between those two oak trees?" she asked. Every word was difficult. "Today you must take that path by yourself. Listen, my pet, listen, my little honey bear, listen carefully, that path will lead you through the forest a little way, then you will come to a marshy ground, follow the trail around to the left, always to the left, and soon you will come to a small lake. Across the lake is a smith's workshop. You must go to the smith and tell him Kalev sent you. Tell him Kalev, not Linda. Can you remember all that? Remember, Kalev."

"I don't understand. Why? Where will you be?"

"The smith will teach you the ways of working metals and making tools, which you will need to know to keep the farms of Viru when you are king. There are many such skills you must learn. I have taught you the things I know. I have shown you the forests and green meadows; I have introduced you to the birds and small animals and plants. I have taught you a few songs. But there are many songs I do not know. I cannot teach you the mysteries of men."

"But why won't you come with me? Please, you have to. I've never been alone in the woods before."

"I cannot. Oh, my sweet one, I would if it were allowed, but the pathway to the smith's is closed to all women. If Kalev were alive, he would have taken you. But then I would not be here with you now and we would not have had our night in the forest together. Now Kalev is dead, and you must go on alone."

The Kalevide stared at her in desperate anguish. He had never been separated from her before, and now she was sending him away. Her pain made it no easier to bear.

"Go," she said miserably. "Between those trees. Hurry. Follow the path, to the left. Go, sweet son, come back to me."

* * *

Long after he was out of sight and the last sounds of his crashing through the trees had faded, Linda returned to Viru, to the companionship of her birds, who alone stayed close to her. With her last words buried in his heart, the Kalevide plunged through the wood. Although the trail was plain enough, he often strayed off it, blundering through the underbrush until chance brought him back to the path again. Tears in his eyes made it very hard to see.

As the hours drew on, he dawdled more and more along the way. At midday he slept in a hollow tree; by midafternoon he had only passed the marsh and come to the shore of a small lake ringed by low, mound-like hills. Here he lingered, loath to go on. For a long while he played idly by the water, skimming stones and making up stories. Across the lake, barely visible, a plume of gray smoke rose from a cleft in one of the hills of stone.

A small, round hut was backed against the mound. All around it were piles of rock and slag and cinder, pits where charcoal was made, trenches where ores were smelted. Farther back were strips where the earth's hide had been scraped for iron. Even the marsh and lakeside had been dug and dredged of their metals. Everywhere the ground was torn and scarred, desolate and dead. No signs of life appeared anywhere around the hut, no birds sang, no grass grew, no people stirred. Only a faint ringing sound, coming, apparently, from the earth itself, interrupted the deathly silence. If it had not been for Kalev's command, and Linda's plea, the Kalevide would have gone no farther.

Hesitantly, he pushed on the small copper door of the cottage. It swung silently open into a dark and empty room. Built in the manner of the old ones, except for the metallic door, the hut was no more than a simple dome of bark over a sunken floor. It had no windows. In the center of the single chamber a chimneyless hearth was built beneath an open vent in the roof. The hearth was cold.

At the rear of the cottage the wall was welded to the rock of the hollow hill. Through a cleft in the stone came the faint sounds of voices mingled with the clang of metal work. The voices disturbed the Kalevide. He had expected the smith to be alone. Perhaps it was customers, he thought hopefully, and then he thought perhaps it was demons.

"You, boy, you come in here," bellowed a voice through the thick wall.

The Kalevide crawled fearfully through the cave's dark grinning mouth. The sharp scent of hot metal stung his nose; he

[34]

choked on smoke. Blinking tears out of his eyes, he peered around to see how many people were there, but it was too dark to distinguish shapes. A dim red glow revealed a forge; thick smoke billowed off its coals to seek the crack in the earth overhead.

"Come in, boy, come in," the voice roared again. "Will you look at the size of him! How would you like to feel those hands stroke you, my sweets, my tender ones?" The last words were not addressed to the Kalevide who was stumbling forward toward the living light.

Out of the darkness hobbled the smith. He was shorter than the Kalevide, but greater in girth. His arms were like barrels. The hair on his head was short, black and frizzled, as though it had been singed rather than cut. Throwing his hammer and tongs down with a loud crash, he seized the boy's hand in a crushing grip.

"Come in, boy, be welcome. Let me have a look at you; let me see the size of you."

"Please, sir, I'm to say that my father—that Kalev sent me."

"I know that, boy. I've been expecting you. Look, my sweets, look at his size. If he has the strength to match his growth and a will to match his strength, he should make a proper smith. By the ores, another Ilmarine or I'm a woman. Come in here, boy. How old are you? Are you a virgin?"

"Please, sir. . . ."

"I say, are you a virgin, boy? Not that it matters much, but the metals prefer the touch of a new boy who is still innocent. Don't ask me why; no one knows. But it is so. Who can know all the ways of metals, eh, boy? Who can know all their wanton secrets? Perhaps they want to corrupt you themselves; no smith stays chaste for long. Say, boy, let me see your legs." Without giving the Kalevide a chance to move, the smith seized the cuffs of his trousers and jerked them up over his knees. "Long and straight, look at them, my pretty ones, long and straight. But for how long, I ask you that. Here boy, look at this, now." The smith pulled up his own cuff to show the knot of muscles that had warped his left leg and left it a little shorter than his right. "Now that's a smith's leg for you, boy. Yours might grow like that if you become a smith. Think of it, boy, standing by your anvil, wielding your hammer, heavy enough, raising it high over your head, rising, so, on your toes to put more power in your swing, so, pounding down with all the weight of your body behind the blow, so, all that power driven into the opposite foot, so. Hammered down, boy, hammered down. Did you ever wonder why a smith always limps? Hammered, even as the metals. There you have it, boy, the mark of a true smith, the sign of his ancient clan. Why, it is said that Ilmarine himself was so crippled he couldn't walk at all, just wheeled himself about on a silver cart. Now there you have a smith!"

The Kalevide shuddered. "Please, sir?" he began.

"Speak up, boy, no room for silence here."

"Please, sir, who were you talking to just now when I came in? I can't see anyone. Is it spirits or demons?"

"Spirits, boy? No spirits, except the spirits in the ores. I was talking to the iron. Always talk with your metals, boy, when you work with them. Remember that, talk, and listen too. It pleases them and makes them willing to be handled. I will teach you. That's why you're here, isn't it, to master the ancient craft? To meet the metals' spirits? I will introduce you to them all in time: sweet silver, supple gold, placid copper, cruel iron, lumpish lead. You will learn them, boy, and love them well if you become a smith."

Even while he was speaking, the smith was rummaging in bins, boxes, barrels, heaps on the floor, pulling out samples of his ores, nuggets, lumps of earth, bars, ingots, delicate leaves. "Here's foolish gold, boy. Warm-white tin," he would announce, holding each piece aloft, then throwing it back in the pile with a crash. "Cool copper, boy. Here is iron. Beware of iron, boy; iron will bite unless you know the true songs of origin. I will teach you."

Without waiting to see if the Kalevide was heeding at all, he stepped across the cave to the forge and began pumping heavily on the bellows. The coals blazed from sleeping red to bright orange into white and blue. A blast of light burst across the blackened room. The Kalevide covered his eyes and cringed. The smith thrust an iron bar into the fire, pumped some more until it glowed with an angry white-red heat, then, jerking it out with a heavy pair of tongs, he waved it once under the Kalevide's face and slung it down across the anvil. The Kalevide flinched back. A wisp of acrid smoke off the seething iron burned his nose. He was afraid to cry.

Heedless of the child's horror, the smith started hammering at the hot iron, all the while speaking coarse words and chanting a discordant song. The clamor of the metal beat pain into the Kalevide's heart; the dissonance pulled like a hook in his bowels. He longed to clamp his hands over his ears and run and hide, but he was fixed, as though it were he in the grip of the smith's tongs being hammered, and all he could do was stand in anguish, staring, while his master displayed his skills. His lessons had begun.

After an unmeasured time, the smith held up an ox-shoe, still shimmering with heat. He stoked it once more in the fire, its colors slid once more slowly from gray to blue to red to orange. When it was white, he threw it suddenly into a bath of old urine. The Kalevide recoiled from the stench. The smith fished the shoe out and tossed it to him to show off his work. Taken by surprise, the Kalevide dropped it clumsily. It fell loudly at his feet. Even that sound was hard to bear. The smith paid no mind. The shoe became another piece of dirty rubble littering his foundry floor.

"Hey, boy, are you hungry?" he shouted. "Have you eaten? A smith must build his strength as well as his tools."

The Kalevide nodded numbly. He had forgotten about food; he had lost track of time altogether. In the depths of the cave it was impossible to tell day from night. Too much was happening too fast, and it was all overwhelming. If he was hungry now, it was only because he was always hungry. He was more relieved to have a respite from the rasp and hammer of metal against metal. The smith limped over to a small stove built behind the forge and returned with an iron kettle filled with a dark, gray stew. He banged down two freshly wrought copper bowls, ladled them full until gravy slopped onto the floor, tipped up a half-empty keg of nails, sat on it, motioned for the Kalevide to do the same, handed him a wide silver spoon, and set to shoveling meat into his mouth. Although the stew was greasy and peppered with the grit of cinders and metal filings, the Kalevide ate hungrily. He was too stunned by the smith and his surroundings to do anything else.

While they ate, the smith spoke of the metal craft. He told the Kalevide of Ilmarine, the father of his race, for unless a man knew the origins of the craft, he said, he could never hope to master its secrets. Ilmarine was the great primeval craftsman, the world's first smith and master of all metals, who first shaped solid, earthen things, Vanamuine's brother. As Vanamuine first worked with words and music, Ilmarine first wrought with hard wood, clay, stone, and metal. Each shaped the world in his own way.

"They say Ilmarine could work life into a thing of metal, boy," the smith said. "Once he even shaped a bride for himself of gold and silver, though the marriage failed. She turned out to be a cold wench in bed. But there you have an artisan, boy. Think of Ilmarine if you dream to be a smith."

The Kalevide had no such dreams, but refreshed by his meal

and emboldened by his rest, he determined to accept the fate allotted him. This, after all, was Kalev's choice for him.

"I will try," he said bravely. "If you will teach me. Will you show me how to make swords and things?"

"I will teach you, boy, all that you can learn. But swords, boy, swords? Is that your dream? It will be long before you put your hands to a sword. Your time here will be taken up with ploughshares more than swords. And scythes, boy. That is our craft here. Knives for cutting meat, perhaps, not men. Arrowheads for hunters. We teethe rakes, boy, and fashion kettles for the womenfolk. We forge hinges for doors, shoes and fittings for oxen, boy. That is our work. And nails."

"Didn't you ever make a sword?" The Kalevide was disappointed. He saw glory disappearing into drudgery.

"No weapons are shaped in this foundry, boy. The men who trade with me have no desire for swords. Your father, Kalev, I am told, went across the water for his. In the north, in Soome, there is a smith more famed for the craft of blades than any man alive; Kalev dealt with him. Now, do not misunderstand me, boy, I do not say that swords are wrong. A swordwright is a proper smith and there is an art in a well shaped blade, as there is in anything well formed. But in this land we do not deal in swords or sabers. In Viru there is no need.

"Another thing you should understand, boy, if you think to learn the trade. A smith does not make anything. Not swords, not nails. No man, not even the master, Ilmarine, makes the smallest tool. He shapes, that is all."

The smith's voice dropped from its deep rumble and roar, like the blast of his furnace, to become gentler, more thoughtful, as he tried to explain what was ill-suited to words. It was one of the deep mysteries of his craft. He tried to tell how the smith merely takes materials he is given by the earth, mixes and molds them, heats, beats, bends, draws, tempers, edges, shapes in any way he will, but nowhere in the process was there any making. The origins of his works were in the earth itself, and it was origin that gave things their powers.

He spoke of other mysteries as well. All the smith's works, born of the earth, would in time return to the earth. Iron would rust, copper decay. The earth would strip away any pattern and form the smith instilled in his work to reveal it for what it truly was, merely metal.

"You asked if I ever made a sword. The sword is only iron, boy; ask who made the iron."

The Kalevide was not listening, however. He was asleep. The

smith's words droning in the hollow cavern, so different from the raucous clangor earlier, had lulled his anguished senses. In that single day his world had changed from the sunlit forest morning to the smoke-filled foundry dark, from childhood's bright carelessness to an adult's steady purpose. He had taken his first steps to join the company of men, steps intended to lead him to the rule and mastery of Viru, and they had exhausted him.

5   The Kalevide had no idea how long his apprenticeship with the smith lasted. It might have been days or weeks or months. In the darkness of the foundry the passage of time meant nothing. Moments were years, years moments. No sunlight ever entered that hidden world. The forge alone gave heat and light; the hearth was the center of life. Day and night were one. The smith worked when he pleased and slept when he chose; the Kalevide toiled when he was told and longed to sleep more.

Nor did he ever handle metals, although that was the sole reason for his being there. Before he could work with copper or iron, his master said, he must first learn their songs of origin. Unless he knew how to speak to them, in words they would understand, he would never win the metals' confidence. If he even tried to touch them before he had mastered the rudiments of power, their spirits would either turn against him or else flee forever from his control.

Yet the Kalevide had no sense for these songs of smithcraft. They were so different from the verses Linda had sung to him, songs of birds and wildlife and friendly growing spirits, or the words he had heard that helped bread rise or ale ferment or to bring seeds forth from the ground. Nor were they like the ballad songs with their tales of adventure and the feats of heroes; those he could have joined in gladly. These songs were dark; they possessed strange words and stranger rhythms. They seemed to have been born deep beneath the mountains in the underworld far below the earth's outer skin. Their sounds were screechings in his ears, tortured, demented cries too painful to sing.

"The song of copper, boy," the smith declared. "Learn it first as copper is the first metal for a smith to work." He sang:

Hiisi's girl,
Hilahatar,
Hiisi's mistress,
Hiisi's mare,
Hilahatar,
on a rock
urinated;
on a rock
mare's urine
dried; urine
dried red
copper; urine
grew: copper
ore, poured
like urine,
copper smelting.

The Kalevide groaned. He covered his ears and cowered behind the anvil, but he could not shut out the pounding, hammering rhythm that surged through the song and seemed to resound off the cavern walls. The song of iron, he knew, was far worse. It told a long and terrible tale reaching into the very roots and origins of the world.

Since the Kalevide could not learn the smith's songs, and the smith would not let him touch even the rudest ores without the songs, he put the boy to work pumping the bellows while he himself sweated at forge and anvil. He hoped the Kalevide might thus absorb some of his lore and then accept the rest.

In between his chants and his coarse, crooning words to the metals, the smith lectured on the secrets of his craft. He described the different natures of the different ores: copper is calm, iron angry, burned in the fire but cold at heart. He spoke of the fire: the smith's first tool, without which his hammers, tongs, files, and saws were nothing. It took the fire to melt and mix the ores, fire to soften plate for shaping. The fire's heat flowed in the metal's veins and fibers, loosened its will, made its spirit malleable and amenable to the smith's control. He told how a smith persuades his metal but never compels. If he should try to bend it against its will, it would break, he said, or it would flake instead of bind, hence the smith must always talk with his metals, sing to them. Know their origins, he would reiterate, know how to charm them and how to please them. A smith must understand their secrets and learn their subtle, intimate ways, known only to their lovers. He must listen when they spoke in return, he said, and hear the sounds they made beneath his hands, feel the way they moved to his touch. Caress them with words, he said, caress them always, with songs, with hammers, with files, touch their innermost spirits, satsify their most wanton desires. He might flatter, cajole, even lie and deceive, but he must love them truly.

To the Kalevide it was torture. The forge-room was hot and stifling. Everything tasted of soot and burnt iron; everything reeked of smoke and foul urine. His head was filled with the constant banging of metal, a ceaseless echo of hammering and cutting, the rasp of files. The smith may have called it caressing his metals; the Kalevide thought it was horrible. Even in his random periods of rest his ears rang with the remembered shriek of beaten and twisted metal.

His work at the bellows was bearable only because it spared him having to touch the metals themselves. He was too frightened even to approach them. When molten streams of smelted ore were poured from crucible to mold, he had to turn away. When a bar of iron was thrown across the anvil, he cringed at the sound. When the smith described the spirits locked within the metals, when he sang his dreadful songs, the Kalevide was too revolted to listen.

In time he might even have adjusted to his agony if it had not been for the unending darkness adding to his despair. In his long hours hidden behind the forge, the Kalevide found himself longing for the quiet and calm of the forest and green meadowlands. He missed the silly singing of the birds and the sweet smells of wildflowers in his hands. It was hard to be locked away from the world, even if that was the way of men. The foundry seemed too much like a tomb underground. Nothing changed. He lost the count of seasons that was the rhythm of the living world. He no longer knew the year.

Occasionally the smith would leave his forge to dig fresh ores from the countryside or to burn charcoal in the wood or to trade with the men who came through the forest to seek his skills. He never took the Kalevide with him, however, or let him see the daylight. When he left it was always with the instruction to stay by the bellows to keep the fire constant, lest he spoil whatever work was in progress, but the Kalevide seized these moments to rest. As soon as the smith went out, he would leave his chores and curl up behind the furnace to sleep, only to be roughly awakened, too soon, by the smith's hard poker prodding him in the back, driving him back to work.

Even when he slept the Kalevide knew no peace. The pounding and ringing and roar of the forge filled his dreams as they filled his waking hours. He had visions of being burned by sparks flying from heated metal, of sweltering and choking on poisoned fumes, of being attacked by smiths wielding swords. When he woke, the Kalevide was consumed by the torment of his master's hammering at the anvil and wrenching metal in a vise. His days became the nightmare that his sleep had forged. Until once, when the smith left him alone longer than usual, the Kalevide woke from the terror of his dreams and fled.

The blast of sunlight outside the cave blinded him, but still he ran, around the lake, through the marsh, without heeding where he ran, only rushing to escape the region of his captivity. He felt as though he had just emerged from some hideous underworld and wanted only to immerse himself in any living realm. Marsh or meadow, field or forest, it did not matter so long as it was out of the depths of the earth. At night he slept in the arms of trees; in the day he wandered aimlessly through the woods. Three days passed before the Kalevide finally found the path that led him home to Viru.

Linda knew of the Kalevide's coming long before he came. Almost as soon as he left the smith's, her birds brought her the news, overheard and passed in song from wind to water to wood. Through the eyes of the children of the air she watched her son's progress and was on the porch to greet him when he came through the gate. Dragging his feet, he crossed the courtyard to her. Without speaking, she embraced him fondly so he would know he was welcome home again.

The Kalevide tried to explain why he ran away from the smith's. He wanted to tell her the horrors of his months there, but before he could speak she put her finger to his lips to silence them.

"It does not matter," she said. She thought it was enough.

"It does matter! Don't you see? I failed, I ran away. My father wouldn't have run. He would have stayed, no matter how hard it was. He would have listened to the smith and learned from him."

"That may be, but Kalev could work with metals. He enjoyed the feel of iron in his hands. You are not your father, that is all. The work did not suit you."

"I'm his son, though! I should have stayed whether it suited me or not. I should have seen it through, as he wanted me to, but I couldn't and I ran away."

There was nothing Linda could say, except that Kalev was dead and could not guide him now.

Later they spoke of what the Kalevide wished to do. There were still many useful crafts he could learn, skills vital to the kingdom's rule. Linda suggested he become a mason, to build with brick and stone if he did not care for metal, or a carpenter, to work with living wood. The Kalevide merely shook his head. Nor was he interested in being a shoemaker or a potter or a trapper or a trader. Remembering he had always liked to fashion small figures with his hands, Linda thought he might shape jewelry, beautiful brooches and rings of gold and silver.

"It is not much like the smith's brutal work," she said.

"I'm too clumsy," he said dismally.

"Then what would you like to do, my pet? I will not send you off to learn the arts of war."

Without either of them realizing it, she had just closed the door to the one course which he would have taken, which would have returned his self-respect, and which would in time have led to the fulfillment of his father's goals.

"I don't know," he replied. "Couldn't I just stay here with you?"

"Of course you may."

"But I will still learn," he said brightening. "I'll learn all there is to know about the farm."

"Of course you will."

Thus, in the mornings that followed, for weeks and months, the Kalevide walked to the fields with the ploughmen or the reapers who worked his father's land. When seeds were sowed, he raced about chasing blackbirds. At harvest time he flourished scythe and flail with the rest. Yet often, too, in the heat of the day, he would be found asleep among the stooks of corn or ricks of hay.

Although he toiled beside them, the villagers never tried to teach the Kalevide. They were not master craftsmen; he was not their apprentice. They did not think to tell him the mysteries of growing grain or the meaning of the seasons or the songs required for planting and reaping. Everyone assumed, since he was Kalev's son, he knew these things already. Kalev had brought husbandry to Viru. Surely, thought the elders, he had implanted that knowledge in his own seed.

For the Kalevide this became a carefree time. No one demanded anything of him; no one criticized. He believed he was learning useful skills, and he never had to prove how much he knew.

As he grew older, the Kalevide's brothers, Paari and Jaani, would sometimes take him along when they fared into the forest.

They were both young men now, and although they still lived with their foster parents in the hamlet at the edge of the wood, they watched the affairs of Viru with interest and helped their younger brother when they could. They showed him how to hunt small game for the table and how to set simple snares for squirrels and hares. They even tried to teach him to kill larger game with crossbow and spear, but he had little skill with those weapons. A quick, hard-thrown stone was more to his taste.

Often, too, the Kalevide would wander far away from the others to walk alone in the forests that surrounded all tended lands. There was a great peace for him beneath the vast canopy of branches in the ancient groves of Taara which had never known a woodsman's axe. Here more than anywhere else he felt at home. Strolling slowly among the trees, he would talk with them as he could talk with no one else, not his brothers, not even Linda. Sometimes he would merely sit, cradled in the forked roots of an oak or nestled on its wide, arm-like boughs, and sing songs to it as he might sing to a loving father.

Nevertheless, the oak was not his father, and he could not escape the feeling that he had thus far failed Kalev miserably. His own inner need to accomplish something grand for Viru demanded more of him. Thus one day in autumn he decided suddenly to plough the wide, untilled field in front of his father's gate. There, when springtime came, he would sow the land with barley, enough to feed all his people and more to sell and bring the country wealth. Where Kalev had once imagined herds of horses galloping on the ground, his son foresaw golden fields of growing grain. The visions were different, their goals the same.

Filled with youthful exuberance, the Kalevide set out early in the morning, when no others were around to watch or worry. He hitched the great iron plough of Viru behind his mother's broad-backed ox and, kicked the blade into the field's hard earth, as he had seen the ploughmen do. The ox lumbered forward. As if by wizardry, a deep furrow opened behind the knife cutting the earth's dark skin.

As daylight brightened and the sun pursued its unending journey, the Kalevide strutted proudly behind the plough. The single furrow lengthened. It lay like one long extended snake across the naked plain. Others might have ploughed back and forth across smaller sections, but since he had decided to till the entire field, the Kalevide vowed not to turn until he reached the edge of the forest. It was well past midday when he got that far.

Thinking it might be wise to rest a while before proceeding back again, the Kalevide turned the ox loose to graze on the wild grass growing by the wood while he himself lunched on a loaf of bread. The sun overhead was warm, the air filled with a smell of fresh-turned soil mingled with the scent of fallen leaves. The Kalevide was pleased. At last he had done something on his own which everyone could see and admire. With a sigh of satisfaction, he lay back on the grass to sleep a while.

Asleep, he dreamed of his days in the smith's dark workshop. The glare of the sun on his face became the blaze of the furnace; the distant drumming of a woodpecker was the pounding of a hammer. The awful throbbing in his head shook him as though he were the metal being beaten. Waking with a start, the Kalevide was at first uncertain where he was, aware only of the silence around him. He was alone, no longer in the smith's dread prison underearth. The plough was where he had left it. Only the ox was gone.

Frightened to think it was lost, he shouted its name, but there was no answer except the whispers of branch and grass in the quickening wind. The sky was clouding over; the sun had nearly set behind the trees. Looking anxiously across the wide plain and seeing no sign of the wandering ox, the Kalevide concluded it had strayed into the forest, which was even more frightening. In the wood it could be captured by the dwarves or demons or other uncouth folk who made their livings apart from men.

Frantic now, the Kalevide plunged into the forest to look among the trees he knew. He crossed and recrossed familiar paths without finding a clue, until, as night fell over him, he sought shelter in the bole of a tree. He was afraid to go home. Through the slow hours until dawn, he tried vainly to remember songs to keep the valuable ox safe from sorcerers and other evil wights, but all he could recall was a charm against a bear, which he sang, hoping it would suffice. When at last he slept, it was to suffer fitful dreams of a tribe of dwarves feasting on the ox's uncooked carcass, devouring it all, entrails, hide, and horns, so nothing would remain to remind the world that there had been a living being.

In the first light of morning, the Kalevide resumed his search northward through the forest. Though he called for the ox repeatedly, no answer ever came. There were no tracks or traces. The beast seemed to have been carried off the earth by magic. Hurrying along the woodland trails, he became more and more frenzied in his search, until he forgot he was looking for something real and ran instead from a desperate need merely to run. Heedless of briars tearing his clothing and branches whipping his face, he raced wildly through the trees. The trunks of oaks and alders became a blur to his eyes. The forest birds fell silent, frightened by his anguished cries. Only sea gulls screamed overhead.

Then, suddenly, he stood on the shore. One moment he was beneath the thick cover of the wood, the next he stood under the open ocean sky. Stunned by the sudden change, he stopped abruptly. In the colorless sky, the scavenger gulls wheeled in an endless parade. In front of him spread the sea; beside him rose the knoll where Kalev was buried.

The same savage hurry that had sent him rushing through the forest now drove the Kalevide up the hill to his father's grave. Scrambling over the rocks that cluttered the seaward slope, he scraped his hands and shins, but he was too frantic to heed them. In his childhood he had often sought refuge on this hill. He had come in happy times and sad, but most often in the times when loneliness overwhelmed him and he needed the sound of his father's voice. Here, by the cairn his mother had raised, he had knelt and cried to hear one word, but no sound had ever come from the grave.

Grasses grew between the stones of the monument. A few of the yellow faces of golden starflowers and the blue eyes of harebells could be seen, but most were hidden by the thick tangles of branches and beds of bracken which had claimed the mound for their own. Over the years, leaves had blown between the granite blocks to remain and form soil, but instead of pretty flowers, thistles grew. The Kalevide was enraged. All at once he tried to tear the briars out, but the thorns hurt too much.

"Father," he cried. "Father . . ."

The need inside him could only cry in pain; it could not speak in words. Desperately he ached to hear the voice he had never heard. A small rodent ducked into a hole between the rocks. A lizard slipped over the stones. No other living creature dwelt nearby. No sounds were to be heard but the constant calling of the gulls. The Kalevide gazed mournfully at the mute burial mound. Then, in despair, he dashed headlong down the path to Kalev's hall.

"The ox came home yesterday afternoon," Linda said, not to chide but to relieve him. The Kalevide never heard.

"I was at my father's grave," he shouted angrily. "It was all overgrown with weeds and thorns."

"I know."

"You know? Then why don't you take care of it? He was your

husband, wasn't he? Didn't you love him? You almost sound pleased.''

"The earth cares for Kalev's tomb," she said tenderly. "What more could I do?" She tried to touch him, to fondle his golden hair as she had done when he was small. He pulled away.

"I don't know. Keep it clean or something. It's so overgrown you can't even see the stones anymore.''

"It is the earth reclaiming its own. The earth is insatiable, so hungry it wants not only Kalev's body but the very blocks that cover him. In time the earth will grow over everything there is, so how can I keep his gravesite clear? The earth is not so sentimental; the earth is inexorable.''

The Kalevide threw himself into a chair across the room from her, a chair on the men's side of the hall, his father's chair. Silently he glared at her.

"The earth will always cover the scars we make," she continued. "It may take time, a long time by our count, but the earth will form new soil, seeds will sprout. Heather flesh and grassy hair will grow over the wounds we cut. When I piled the mound over your father's grave, I thought it would help you remember where he was. You know that now; you no longer need the stones. So long as you remember, Kalev's tomb cannot be lost. In after ages, no one will know. No one will need to know; no one will even think to care. The seeds of trees will come; the forest itself may climb the hill to claim Kalev's body. Through the long years all signs of the grave will be overgrown, and it will be forgotten. This is inevitable, and,'' she added, ''I would not have it otherwise.''

"Then why do we even try?" he cried in despair. "This farm, this land, they will be overgrown and taken by your earth, too, won't they? The ground Kalev cleared and tilled will be buried just like him, lost without a trace to show anybody what he's done.''

"In time. The earth is insatiable, it claims everything. One might hold it off for a while, a very little while by the world's reckoning, but the forest will come, or the marsh, or the sea. If the farm is well tended, if the fields are kept tilled, if the vines and creepers and saplings and all the other encroachments of the wood are cut back, then the earth might be forestalled. If the wetlands are drained to keep the swamps out of the meadows; if dikes are built to hold the sea out of the fields and levees to contain the rivers; if houses and barns and sheds and stalls and storehouses are built and rebuilt; if rotted wood is carefully replaced, if mosses are removed from roofs and timbers, if storm damage is quickly repaired, if . . ."

"Stop it!"

She looked at him.

"Must I do all this?"

"This and more, if you think to hold back the wild."

"It's horrible. How can a man do so much? And how can he do less and lose everything?"

"Kalev would have done it if he had lived."

"But how can I?" he said sadly. "I'm not my father. How can I hope to keep the land he claimed? I can't even plough a field. Look what I did yesterday. One dumb furrow, and that wasn't even straight. Then I fell asleep and lost the ox. I don't know how to do anything for the farm. I can't make tools to clear the land. I ran away from the smith."

"It does not matter. If you do none of these things, you still live. Let the forest come, let the marshes rise. They are good."

"No! It does matter. It mattered to Kalev, and it matters to me! If he hadn't died, Viru would be a kingdom now, a real kingdom. It's up to me to build it for him."

"Perhaps you ask too much, my little pet. You are not Kalev, after all. But do not worry about the farm. There is time yet, and there will be people to help you. The villagers will work for you. Let them hoe your fields and feed your herds; let other men mend your tools and build your barns. All you need to do is ask them."

"How can I?" he fussed. "I don't know anything. I don't know enough to ask them anything."

"Your brothers will help you. I will help you."

"What if they go away? What if something happens to you? What would I do then?"

"Nothing will happen to me."

"But what if?"

Linda looked at him sadly, sorry to see him so fretful, unable to help him.

"I will tell you a thing I heard once long ago in a dream," she said cautiously. "If anything does ever happen to me, perhaps this will help you. This is what I heard: Once you truly believe I am lost forever, then you will find me again."

"What is that supposed to mean?"

"I do not know," she laughed lightly to break the spell of tension. "That is the way of dreams. But be assured, my honey bear, the words are true. That, too, is the way of dreams. Now, come sit by me and I will tell you some other things I heard long ago, not in dreams but from your father, so you will take them to be true. He looked on the future of his land, and he foresaw only wealth and glory for Viru. He foretold riches and fame and power before all the world. And he predicted vast renown for you, his son. You would rule Viru and it would grow great and strong. You would be its king.''

It was an old story, one she had told him often before. She told it now because she knew it pleased him and would dispel the doubts and despair which for a moment had threatened to smother his precious life. To keep his dreams alive, Linda told him once again the tales of Kalev's dreams, of cities, of horses, of victories, of kings.

When the Kalevide left her side, he strolled away with a renewed sense of his own worth. Although he did not yet see how such greatness could be won, and Linda could not tell him, it was reassuring to know that it would come. It must come, for his father had said it would.

Slowly the Kalevide retraced his steps to Kalev's knoll. There, beside the cairn, he tried to speak words of thanks to the father he had never seen, thanks for this gift that he was given, the glory that was to come. As he stood gazing across the sea, his youthful fancy soared. He dreamed himself a white horse to ride, he clad himself in golden armor, and in his hand, which had never held more than a hay rake, he gripped a mighty sword. It was the eve of his fifteenth birthday.

6   The Kalevide sauntered blithely down the path to the hamlet at the edge of the wood, completely unaware of the sorcerer lurking in the pasture behind the hall. No one saw the evil one except meadow spirits, who turned their faces and fled in fear. Warped by the arts he practiced, his body was twisted and ugly. His arms were shriveled, his face disfigured, eyes oblique slits, nose a vulture's beak. Thin wisps of hair, less than a beard, dribbled down his chin. Tusks protruded through fleshy lips. He was clad in the fashion of his race, in a long robe of yellow skin which covered his pointed shoes. Once the hem had been trimmed with fur, but that had long since rotted away. On his head he wore a high, pointed cap, the sign of his power.

As soon as the Kalevide was out of sight, the sorcerer slipped stealthily into Kalev's keep. Before Linda's birds could cry alarm, he touched his filthy fingertip to their bills to put them into a deep, poisoned sleep. Unwarned, unprepared, Linda first saw him framed in the doorway, a frightful black silhouette ringed by the glare of the morning's sun on the sky, unmistakeable in its evil. With a shriek she shaped her face into a grotesque mask to ward off his power, puffing out her cheeks, rolling her eyes, pulling down one corner of her mouth with a finger. The sorcerer laughed hideously. He was supposed to vanish instantly at the sight; instead he stalked into the room, unafraid. Linda backed away, moving her left hand in a sign against all spells.

"Who are you?" she cried through her terror when this, too, failed. She knew too well what he was.

"You do not know me, Linda? I know you, Linda; Linda, I have watched you secretly for years. I have waited for you, Linda, waited long." He laughed again; it was a hiss, a whine. "I am your kin, sweet Linda. Kalev's kin, hence yours. I claim you for my own. Now, Linda. I have come to take you for my wife. To keep you, Linda; Linda, I shall keep you in my brother Kalev's place. That is the custom of our kind. When one man dies, his brother takes his wife; if not his brother, then his closest kin. I claim you, Linda; Linda, I will take you. Linda."

"Go away, foul thing. You were never Kalev's kin, no more than the weasel is kin to the golden marten."

"That may be as that may be, Linda mine; yet Kalev and I were kin. Be not deceived by the shape I wear. I can shape my body in any shape I choose. Would another seem more fair?"

For the briefest moment Linda thought she saw the image of her husband flicker over the sorcerer's misshapen form. In that moment she felt the deepest fear.

"I have come to take you, Linda; Linda, come with me now. Now. Come, Linda, come. To warm my misty home."

"You'll get none of me, black slime," she cried, despite the nausea rising in her. "Other men have sought me over the years, and none has won me yet. I'll wed no man and I'll not wed you."

"Rue, woman, rue your words, before I transform you into a frog, before I change you to a toad, before I charm you as an adder, before I shape you like an eel."

Suddenly Linda laughed. It was a thin, panicked laugh, but at least she could laugh that much.

"Oh, you're like all the other men, boasting of your powers, boasting, boasting. If you could do the things you claim, you'd have done and been done. Go away, you poor, poor thing."

A spot of yellow foam flecked the corner of his mouth. He snatched the linen tablecloth out of her hands and flung it aside. Where he had touched it it was smeared with dark, greasy stains. Everything the sorcerer touched was soiled.

"Woman, listen well. I am more skilled than you can know. I wield more powers than you can understand. I can bind the winds and raise great storms. I can cast all ills and torments from one man to another at my will. I can call up pestilence and plague. I can blight and I can burn. Demons come at my command; black demons do my bidding. The power of the Sarvik stands behind me." He rattled a sling of short arrows at his belt. "These are pains and sorrows, slut. Beware them. Beware me, before I drive them one by one into your ghastly woman's flesh!"

"Boasting, boasting. It will not win me, you. I'll not have you, not for all your pains and sorrows. Go away, go away from me, go away from Viru, before I send my eagles to tear you to pieces with their talons. I have one sharp-clawed eagle in my house and two more nearby who will protect me. Leave my house, you, before they come and claw your evil eyes!"

Like a cloud of oily smoke, the sorcerer departed, although his odor lingered. Nevertheless, although he withdrew for the moment, he meant to court her one more time before he destroyed her utterly.

When the Kalevide returned later that afternoon, accompanied by his brothers and their dogs, Linda was alone, singing softly to her birds, who were at last safe in a healthful sleep. Paari and Jaani rested casually on the long bench beside the hearth, the three dogs sprawled at their feet. The Kalevide sat in his father's high backed chair in the center of the hall.

"We're going hunting," he said to Linda. "It's Musti's first trial." The black puppy, Mustukene, looked up at the sound of his name and wagged his tail. He was Paari's and Jaani's present to the Kalevide for his eighteenth birthday.

Linda looked at her sons but could not reply. Words choked in her throat. For all his life she had tried to spare the Kalevide pain; she could not tell him of the sorcerer.

One of the dogs scratched at a flea, his leg thumping noisily on the wooden floor. The rest of the hall was silent. The Kalevide sensed a little of his mother's distress. "Are you all right?" he asked.

She nodded and waved him away, as if to say they should go if they were going. Tears were close to her eyes.

"We will have him home tomorrow night," said Paari preparing to go. "We will spend tonight with our fosterers in the hamlet, then set out early in the morning."

"And we'll bring you back a good catch," said the Kalevide.

Linda smiled, to encourage him, to send him on his way.

"Come, Irmi, Armi, Mustukene," Paari called from the door. The dogs bounded outside. Jaani glided after them, tipping his cap to his mother as he left.

"Are you sure you're all right?" the Kalevide asked. "I'll stay home if you want me to."

She shook her head.

"See you tomorrow, then," he said. "Don't worry, I'll be all right. Come, Musti," he called to the puppy waiting faithfully for him.

In the deep night the sorcerer went secretly into a swamp. On a hummock surrounded by fetid, half-frozen, stagnant water, he stripped off his ancient robe of filthy hide and began to dance, naked but for his sorcerer's hat, his belt of magic, and his shoes. Turning to the four quarters of power, calling their forces to come to him, he cast a chant into the gray-black, clouded sky. Beating his sacred drum in the rhythm of his song, he drove his spells across the world.

The air of the marsh had been cold and heavy and hanging in a mist close to the ground. At his command it rose, and with it rose a venomed fog which seethed forth from the swamp and spread over the surrounding forests. With a loud cry he summoned winds which tore the cloud and carried it into far-flung lands. In the vapor were locked his words of hate and spite. He sang into the frigid wind and let his wicked spells be scattered over distant realms. His voice whined; it wheedled. His words were mumbled, shaped of sounds which were no part of human speech, but their message was borne to the minds of men in every land, heard, and understood.

So Linda had other suitors, did she? So others courted her flesh? He would see that no man would ever seek her again. No man would ever think of her except with horror. Out of the fog he formed a vile image of Linda to fill men's minds. Her beauty was ruined, her teeth were iron. She spoke words like white-hot tongs. Her breasts were like rotted fir wood, her nipples soft and moldy. Her legs were tree stumps, and her loins smelled like a sewer. So he sang and sang again, and drove the message across the world with the beating of his drum.

If men must seek for wives, he chanted, let them venture to

the north to take their brides from among the Fen-men. In Soome were endless rows of nubile maidens, all rich in gold, breasts hung with pearls, their bodies draped with gems, virgins all, but all lustful, waiting on the rocky shores. So he sang. Who knew what simple fools might believe and be lured to their ruin on the mist-hidden shoals of Soome, easy prey for his brother sorcerers?

In a circle the evil one danced, pounding his hollow drum, mumbling his words, pausing in his incantation only long enough to fire his short black arrows of enchantment into the air. The barbed darts of sorrow sped in four directions, his invocations rode them to every corner of the world. In distant realms they fell to earth in rain. In Viru and the nearby lands they imbued the mists themselves and entered the minds of men with every breath they breathed. Only Linda's sons were unaffected.

The Kalevide, Paari, and Jaani set out early in the morning. The elder two were armed with spear and crossbow; the Kalevide trusted more to the strength of his own hands. The three dogs raced ahead, their noses close to the ground, snuffling eagerly for the fresh smells rising from wet earth.

Mustukene flushed a rabbit first, chased it, helter-skelter, through the stubble of the unploughed field, around and down and back, following the hare's every turn, until a grouse burst raucously from cover and the pup leaped for it instead. The Kalevide laughed as both bird and beast went free.

"Look how quick he is," he boasted. "We'll catch hares by the dozens, and wolves, and foxes too."

"You can't eat wolves," Jaani said quietly.

"No, I suppose not. Well, we'll just keep the hares then, five score, or more." Both brothers smiled at him.

At the edge of the forest fresh osiers blushed crimson; yellow willows revealed the first young leaves of spring. The wood glowed like a golden cloud lit by the early sun. Patches of snow, just beginning to melt in the morning, dotted the meadows. The trees of the forest dripped silver water as their white covers warmed.

The dogs charged down the paths, keen for the scents of beasts that would be slow and stupid, drugged by the remnants of their winter's stupor. The three brothers followed cautiously behind them. Even the Kalevide tried to move quietly.

"They have something," Paari said quickly, as a new note came into the dogs' barking. Then they ran, heedless of noise.

They burst into a clearing. A bear rose up on its hind legs to greet them. Barking madly, the dogs danced in a half-circle just out of its reach. The bear spread its short forelegs as though to invite the men into its embrace, or to bare its breast for sacrifice. Paari stepped forward cautiously. The dogs fell silent.

"Ho, Otso, oh, sweet broadnose," Paari crooned as the forest hushed. "Ho, brother, my lazy honey-paws, oh, sweet golden Otso, darling small eyes—do not be angry."

He raised his spear, kissed its copper head, then thrust it quickly through the bear's thick coat, between its ribs, into its heart.

While his brothers dressed the carcass, Paari took the bear's claws and tail and fastened them to his belt for talismans. He strung its teeth on a sinew for a necklace, then, leaning back against a pine tree, he sang a song of tribute to the one he had slain. He sang to praise the bear's valor, to please its vanity, to appease the spirit whose life he had stolen. His song told of the origin of the bear and the manner of its death. It spoke small words of flattery and more of fame. This was Paari's offering to the forest whose child the bear had been, and to the others who dwelt deep within the wood.

As the timbre of his voice rose above the treetops, leaves opened and shone brighter than before. The alder and the willow unfolded yellow buds which blossomed to a brilliant green with the fullness of his song. Needles on fir trees turned to silken tassels; cones shone purple in the sun. On the tips of oak twigs acorns swelled; catkins spilled from birch branches. Tiny flowers sprang forth on maples and spread themselves like wings. The wild cherry tree awoke from slumber and revealed its pure, snow-white, sweet fragrant covering of flowers, which gleamed in the sunlight and would glimmer at night with the moon. The forest echoed with the music and returned the song to Paari so that his heart might be glad. His words were heard across the heaths and meadowlands where even nymphs wept tears of rapture.

Linda was standing at the hearth preparing soup when the sorcerer returned. He spoke no word but seized her by the belt with a clawlike hand. The strap broke as she heaved herself away. Standing perfectly still, still without speaking, the sorcerer bared his tusk-like teeth. The odor of offal rose from his body. Linda cowered against the wall on the woman's side of the room. She set her face and hands in all the signs against evil she knew. Her fingers danced in the air, drawing patterns to ward off dark powers. She sang. She called to herself such forces as she knew to combat sorcery. She chanted his wicked origins:

Orpoja's birth
I know; sorcerer,
evil one, I know
his origins: Orpoja,
evil, bred outside
the world; spawned
in ice fells; on fir boughs,
stones, Orpoja's birth
was laid aside to die.''

The sorcerer let her sing. She began a boasting song meant to drive fear into his heart while depriving him of his own power to cause fear. He muttered a few rapid, obscene words she could not understand. The song died in her mouth. All her strength and power was stripped from her. Unable to move or speak, she could only watch him with horror, watch and wonder why her charms had failed. Even the best of wizards have times when their spells go astray.

With studied indifference, the sorcerer selected a long, thick stick of birchwood from the woodpile. Linda could not even turn her head. Loathing surged inside her, sickened her, but she was powerless to release it. With one cruel stroke he clubbed her across the side of the face. She crumpled. Not quite unconscious, Linda knew what was happening to her but could not resist. The spell-cast stupor held her in bondage.

When he was finished he forced her into a deeper sleep. Gathering her up under his arm like a stolen hen, he carried her to the shore by Kalev's knoll, where his boat was hidden.

An elk stood absolutely still beside a pool beneath a slender waterfall. Water painted the gray stones silver. Where the shade of the forest touched the stream, thin sheets of ice glazed the rocks, yet the pool itself in the sunlight was perfect and clear. The elk held its uncrowned head erect and alert. Poised for flight, it gazed between the birches, black and white, at a man kneeling in the snow. Unseen farther off in the wood, two others held their dogs to keep them quiet.

The hunter raised his crossbow, aimed, and fired in the breath of a moment. His arrow pierced the deer's velvet heart. As it folded its knees and died, Jaani ran forward, knife in hand, to skin his prize. With its hide fitted over him like a robe and its tail tied to his belt, he became, if only briefly, the one he had killed.

Beneath the weeping branches beside the pool, Jaani sang his song of sad victory to release the elk's spirit to the forest. While he sang, buds unfolded on the bushes, and flowers bloomed, wild roses and red currant blossoms. Golden ears of grain swelling on the grasses ripened with the sun. Apples reddened. Kernels formed on nut trees and cherries filled with sweet juices. Red cranberries covered the hillsides; blueberries thrived by the marshes, blackberries beside swamps, yellow berries on mossy hummocks. Heavy clusters of purple fruit bent the branches of elder trees as everywhere the woods rang with the voice of his singing. In the silver pool and in the stream and in the more distant lakes water spirits wept white tears of joy.

Linda recovered consciousness in the bottom of the sorcerer's dugout boat. Though still in pain, she could move again. The sorcerer was shoving the boat into the water. She pleaded with him to release her, but in vain. In her heart she prayed to the sun and moon and to the spirits of the air to help her; they, too, were silent. The angry sun, sinking low, glowed with the color of blood above the ocean. The sad half-moon overhead turned away and closed its eyes. A wind blew up and swept, cold, across the sea; it held no hope for the woman.

Weeping, Linda longed for the comfort of her birds, but they were far away and drugged by evil spells, and they were too small to fight a sorcerer.

She prayed desperately to the forest and its daughters, the birch and willow with whom she had played as a child, to the fir and juniper, the rowan and the cherry which had always been her friends. None would answer. She called on the meadowlands and heathfields. Whispers were everywhere, in the trees, in the grasses. Nymphs and sprites danced wantonly. None heeded the pleas of a mortal any more.

Gathering her courage, Linda flung herself out of the boat and scrambled up the shingle to the rocky knoll. The sorcerer grabbed at her with a curse, but he had spent his powers and spells and must move slowly. He could not even conjure her return. Linda clambered over the sharp-edged stones that covered the hillside as the sorcerer started the steep climb behind her. He did not have to hurry, he thought, she could not escape.

She cried aloud to the great powers for protection. She begged the earth and sea, the air and sky.

"Help me,
Ukko,
Old one,
of clouds!"

With a crash of thunder, Pikne, lord of lightning, swooped out of the high white clouds, driving his bronze-wheeled chariot down the iron bridge of sky to spread flame and fire over the western world. The lightning blast exploded at the sorcerer's heels, shattering rock and knocking him senseless behind a boulder, where he was shielded from further wrath.

Linda kept climbing. "Help me, Ukko. Spare me!"

The forces of the world smiled after their way. She had known sorrow and pain; she need never fear outrage again. A sea gull screamed. Another blast of lightning ripped the sky. In its might Linda was transformed into a block of granite near the crown of Kalev's knoll.

The Kalevide stood head to head with a wild moor ox. Here was an animal more magnificent than any he had ever seen on earth. In the slanting light of late afternoon the aurochs's tawny hide looked golden. Its horns were longer than any man could reach; its flanks rippled with primeval strength as it pawed the ground. Gazing into its huge, well-like eyes, the Kalevide saw reflected the image of himself. How could he resist testing himself against such a beast?

The aurochs charged. The Kalevide lunged under its horn and grabbed it around the neck. Thus they remained, locked together, neither able to move, neither able to throw the other, neither one willing to sacrifice a step for fear it would be his last.

To the Kalevide the minutes seemed like hours, or days. Time became impossible. He could have passed a lifetime in that frozen pose. Every muscle strained. His back and arms and legs cried in pain but he would not let go. The aurochs planted its feet in the soft ground. Its breath was a heated wind. Very slowly the Kalevide pulled its head around. He pressed down heavily on one horn while heaving up on the other, twisting its neck until the beast was forced to kneel.

He knew then he had won. Quickly straddling its neck, the Kalevide continued to wrench the aurochs's head around. In one brief moment the golden ox yielded. It relaxed its muscles. Its broad head snapped around; its neck broke with a loud report. It died.

The Kalevide lurched to his feet, laughing. His body was covered with dust and sweat and was shaking from the strain, nevertheless he felt an exhilaration in him he had never known before. He had never realized he had such massive strength; he had never felt so invincible. A spirit swelled in him as though in its death he had absorbed the aurochs's power. He had found the secret of his life. Staggering drunkenly around the field, he wanted to swing the carcass over his head to present it, his victory, himself, to all the world.

He settled, however, for breaking off its horns, which he gave to his brothers, and taking an ear for himself for an amulet. At last, under the largest oak in the forest, he relaxed. Raising his voice as loud as he could, he sang his triumph. Wild beasts crept through the wood to hear his words and marvel. Fox and wolf, lynx and fawn came together, hidden in the trees and high grasses, to listen. In the trees, cuckoos, doves, magpies, larks, nightingales and jays joined their voices to his to spread the mystery of music throughout the forest. Swans and ducks and geese paddling on a silver river and a blue-green lake paused to hear the singing. Far away, the ocean's waves lapped against rocks in the cadence of the song. The crowns of great trees swayed like dancers. Clouds opened to let the sky hear the words the Kalevide sang. Tellervo, the daughter of the forest, and her sisters of the wood shed soft tears of rapture and sighed with longing for the golden singer.

"Come, we should go home," said Paari. "It grows late. Our mother will be waiting for us."

In the twilight, all the world was still. Peace lay everywhere, except in the hearts of three small birds flying mournful circles around a slab of stone. Many times they passed it; many times they paused to brush it with their wingtips. Then they parted, each to its own destination.

The first to leave was the swallow, with its red-brown breast, its coat of blue, its forked tail and laughing flight. It turned to the sea and flew a straight-line course away from its home, a course no longer marked by merry circles of joy. Into the mouth of the wind it flew, then, far from shore, it dived, to die, into the hungry waves.

The bluebird rose skyward. Above the sacred stone it flew higher, far higher, than it had ever flown, and, as it soared, it spread its blue wings wider and wider in a limitless embrace of the sky.

The fat bellied house finch, Linda's pet, flew the longest way. She traveled across the forests to return to Laane in the west where, she knew, the Woman in Blue Stockings was, and always would be.

7   "Did you ever see such a beast?"
the Kalevide chattered. "I know I never did. Did you see him?
Huge, I say. But I killed him. Grappled him down. Did you see?
Brought it to its knees. I broke its neck."

His brothers walked beside him silently, rather wishing he
would be silent, too. They were walking home in the long,
sloping hours of twilight, when the shadow of a man stretches
longer than his life. The wind whispered and the grass replied.
Soft sighs said the earth was settling into rest. Far away, birds
cried as they hastened homeward. Dusk: the hour before dark
when another world wakes, when light changes and there is
peace before the night creatures come. Soon eyes would peer
between the trees; soft feet would pad the meadow paths; silent
wings would sweep the air. In the east, darkness had already
gathered over the forest. Sleek, gray-black, it lay above the
treetops like an animal resting, like a panther protecting the
brood that nursed upon its body.

Paari and Jaani glided through the grasses like their lengthen-
ing shadows. Although anxious to reach home, they did not rush
lest they disturb the stillness lingering on the field. The Kalevide
never noticed the calm. He was too excited by his exploits.

"Did you ever see such hunting?" he crowed. "What a lot of
game! A bear, an elk, and my ox, my moor ox! I call that a good
catch. I do. Won't mother be pleased?"

To show off his new found strength he had insisted on carrying all their catch. His brothers were glad to let him, if only he
could be quieter about it! The three dogs trotted amiably ahead,
but only Mustukene had enough energy left to run, and even he
let rats and rabbits escape unmolested.

"There's the house," said Jaani. "I see the roof."

"Your eyes are sharp," said Paari. "I do not even see the
smoke."

"There isn't any. The house is dark."

"Then where is our mother? She should have a fire; there
should be light in the windows."

"Mother!" the Kalevide shouted, not to the others but to the
empty house. Throwing his bloody cargo to the ground, he ran
the rest of the way to the hall. A dread silence hovered over all
the buildings; they were empty, cast open to the wind. "Moth-

er!'' he cried again, but only an echo answered. The door swung open, untended, unguarded.

Inside, the fire was out. Dead ashes lay on the hearth. A kettle that might have contained soup was cold and covered with scum. A table and two chairs was overturned; logs were scattered from the woodpile. They found the belt to Linda's dress under a log and in a corner the silver brooch she always wore at her breast.

"Well, she struggled," Paari said at last.

"What do you mean?" the Kalevide asked.

"Someone carried her off. Against her will."

"It has happened before," said Jaani. "Men steal wives when they cannot woo them. That's how Kalev won Linda away from the suitors in Laane."

"No! Stop it," the Kalevide cried. "That isn't true! It isn't true now! It can't happen. Help me find her."

He rushed outside to look for signs of her. Better she be dead than captured, he thought, but she couldn't be dead. She couldn't, he wouldn't allow it.

"It is too dark," said Paari standing by his shoulder.

"There must be something to say where she is. You go west, Paari, and look along the forest trail. Jaani, you look east, and I'll search the shore."

"Better to wait for morning when it's brighter," said Jaani.

"But she might need us, need us now!" Without waiting for their answer, he ran down the path to the cove.

There was nothing there to see.

The sorcerer had taken his boat and left the land. When he recovered from the lightning blast and Linda was nowhere to be seen, he assumed she had escaped to her home and left it at that. He could return another time to claim her. She could not escape forever. If she hid, he would divine her hiding place; if she ran, he would pursue. He would make her suffer for spurning him.

"Her blood shall flow upon this earth," he vowed. When he spat, the gravel at his feet sizzled from the venom that burned his curse into the bones of Viru.

Hastily gathering up what he could of his scattered gear and tossing it into the bottom of his dugout, he shoved the boat into the water, anxious to depart before the powers which had blasted him could return.

The Kalevide walked sadly along the water's edge listening to the gossip of the waves and stones. It told him nothing of his mother. Restless gulls called across the night. His foot stepped on something caught between two stones. Gray, shapeless, obscene, it filled him with loathing when he picked it up, but it was only a limp, long, pointed felt hat. Not Linda's, he knew, but then whose?

"It is a sorcerer's hat," Paari said later when they had all returned to the gloomy hall. The cap lay on the table beside Linda's brooch and belt.

"A sorcerer has my mother?" the Kalevide exclaimed. He had been worried and afraid before; now he was outraged. His brother shrugged.

"We do not know. The hat tells us a sorcerer once touched our shores, that is all. It does not say when or why. It does not say he took Linda."

"It doesn't say he didn't either!"

"No, it does not say he did not. Nor does it tell us if he came to Viru from abroad or if he embarked from here to attack some other land. We do not know if he came and stayed, or came and left again."

"Well, I'm going after him," the Kalevide declared, snatching up the pointed cap. "If he took my mother, if he even touched her, he'll be sorry." He flung the hat angrily onto the glowing embers.

"Don't!" Jaani shouted, too late.

The hat flared once in a blood-hued blaze of light, then dissolved and disappeared. Only a thick black smoke hovered where it had been, and even that slowly uncoiled and sought the night.

"Now that was stupid," said Jaani. "That hat held the sorcerer's spells. We could have used it to ransom Linda. We might have turned the spells to work for us. Who knows what we could have done with it? Maybe it would have shown us where she is."

"I don't need it," the Kalevide replied. "I'll rescue her myself without any sorcerer's tricks. I'm strong enough. You know that, you saw me wrestle the ox. Mother told me once sorcery was evil and I should never deal with it. I'm not going to start now. Are you coming with me?"

"Let us wait for daylight," said Paari. "We need rest after our hunting, and we need to eat something before we can set out on such a search. Who knows where it will lead, or how long it will take? Linda could be anywhere by now."

"Perhaps Taara will send us a vision," said Jaani. "In the night a dream may come to tell us where she is."

"We must go now!" cried the Kalevide. "Don't you see? Think of the torture she may be suffering."

"We gain nothing by hurrying," said Paari.

"We gain time!"

"Time lost may be regained with thought."

"I don't understand you!" the Kalevide cried as he stormed out of the hall, slamming the door behind him.

"Go, then, little brother," Jaani said sadly after him. "Go, if you must. It's what you have to do, I suppose, and I pray you find what you are really looking for, whatever that is."

He and Paari settled down to eat and make their own plans for finding Linda. They would do what they could, but they would begin in the morning, when they were rested and the world was brighter.

Outside, the Kalevide was less sure of himself. The world was very wide: where would he begin his search? The night was very dark: how would he find his way? He felt completely alone, with no one and nothing to guide him. Unaware of where he was walking, he wandered randomly across the meadow until he came to the knoll where Kalev was buried. This, he thought, must be a sign. The tomb would tell him what no mortal person could.

"Father, speak to me," he begged, kneeling before the cairn of stones. At first his words sounded silently in his mind, but as he gathered courage he spoke aloud. "Speak now. You have never said one word to me, but now I need your help. Speak to me, Father, help me, please."

Within the earth, sand trickled into the eyeholes of a skull. Small stones rattled between ribs.

"It's me, Father, me, the Kalevide, Kalev's son, your son. Speak to me now, please. I don't want to disturb your rest, but I have to. I need you."

Grass grew around white bones; rocks pressed down on a fleshless breast. Wildflowers grew from the bowl of a broken skull. Lilies of the valley replaced its eyelids; harebells were its eyes. Crimson clover had become its blushing cheeks.

Tears filled the Kalevide's eyes. He did not want to cry, but all the emotion of his childhood rose in his chest and poured out in a stream from an inner well. For once, he opened his heart to his father as he told him who he was. He bared all his youthful longings, his sorrows, his troubles, his pains, all the burdens of boyhood which had gathered and grown in him so long. He admitted his doubts and fears and renewed his promises to do better than he had done. To his father now he said much that he had never said before, much that he had never told his mother. It had never been necessary to tell Linda all that was in his heart, nor could she have understood his longings if he had, for they were the longings to be a man. Now she was gone, and he must become a man to save her.

"Help me, Father," he pleaded. "Help me find her. Rise out of your grave and walk with me. Guide me. Show me what to do and where to go."

There could be no answer, only the sighing of the wind.

"Help me, come with me. She was your wife, my mother. If you loved her, help me save her. I do; I love her. I will rescue her. Won't you come with me? We can search the world for her together, you and I, father and son, together."

The weight of the tomb is mighty; the dead do not ever rise.

"Won't you give me a sign? One sign, a word, a sound. Something to tell me you hear and you care."

The wind blew cold from the sea. The stars overhead were bright and clear and numberless. Here and there, however, black patches appeared and grew and hid the stars one by one, shadows that meant there were clouds in the sky, and they too were silent and without a word. The wind whispers; the waves lap lightly on the shore. Stars and clouds, wind and sea, none bear tidings of Linda.

A flock of terns flashed over the waves, their white wings winking like starlight. They swept up the hillside and over the stones, and led the Kalevide to the edge of the knoll, where the largest boulders were, then skimmed away into the night crying "to sea," "to sea," "to sea." Misunderstanding their message, he followed them down the hill to the shore. Linda had always told him to listen to the birds in time of trouble; now he tried. Without hesitating for a moment, he waded into the water and began to swim northward toward the mist-hidden land of Soome. A sorcerer had stolen his mother, he thought, Soome was the land of sorcerers, the sea would take him there.

The Kalevide swam with his arms and steered with his feet, pulling himself through the peaceful water with strong, lunging strokes. Here the tides were gentle, and there were no currents. His body surged with power. The strength released in him when he wrestled the aurochs would carry him, he hoped, to his mother's rescue, however far that might be. Like a golden sail in the wind, his hair billowed on the water as he swam ever northward guiding himself by the tail of the Bear, which rose out of the wall of mist that shrouds the world's end.

Overhead and all around uncounted gems of sparkling light filled the wide night sky. One was Salme, the North Star's bride, his mother's sister. At her behest, myriad stars swam with the Kalevide. Reflected in the sea, they seemed to join sky and water together, to unite the vastness of heaven and the unbounded ocean. The world revealed its awesome emptiness. Never in Viru, where every plain and meadow is ringed by a wall of woodlands and all level ground is broken by hills, had he sensed such space or felt such silence. Not even the sound of his own splashing could disturb that power. Mortal sounds were swallowed in the depthless still of the night.

For a moment the Kalevide was touched by that void on the open sea, but it was too much for him. He kicked and plowed through the water, driven by the need for haste, afraid of being engulfed by the loneliness he had sensed. Some may find beauty in the untouched night; he preferred walls of solid earth around him. He wanted a world where place was sure and known, not the undefined openness of endless space.

Slowly the stars wheeled in their circles. Some sank; some rose. They were his only measure of time in the darkness. But for them, the Kalevide might have dreamed he swam for days or months. Time became distorted in the night that bore the stars, far away from sight of land. His arms grew tired and he longed for someplace firm where he could lie down and sleep, but not even a rock rose above the sea. His feet and legs felt like iron weights he was forced to tow behind him. When he paused in his swimming, they sank, pulling him under the water. Once he let them drag him down, to test the depth of the sea. He sank into certain darkness and devouring cold. With horror, the Kalevide realized there was no bottom.

A small rocky islet, alone in the middle of the ocean, jutted steeply upward from far below the waves where the water was deep, cold and black, with the solidity that comes from unfathomed depths. Stars, reflected on the swells, looked like bright stones or gold gleaming on the imaginary floor of the sea.

The Kalevide paddled slowly around the island, searching for a place to land before he was completely overwhelmed by weariness. Coming eventually to a small cleft in the sheer rock walls, he dragged himself across a narrow, coarse-sanded beach to a hollow sheltered by the towering cliff, where he collapsed on a bed of dried seaweed cast ashore by storms. Gentle breezes blowing through the crevice brought him the sweet scents of wet moss and grasses growing overhead. How he longed to sleep forever, the search for Linda forgotten in the flood of raw fatigue.

Far short of forever, however, he woke at dawn, drawn from his rest by the soft sounds of singing. In the midlands between sleep and waking, there seemed to be a deep-throated bird hovering above his head calling to him. For a moment the Kalevide thought of how his mother had sung over him when he was small. This voice, however, was far more beautiful than Linda's had ever been.

The singer, whoever it was, was somewhere on the cliffs above him, and it was a woman. That was all he could tell clearly. The song itself was muffled by the mists that had come upon the night. There were no words, or if there were, they were not important. All he heard was the note of rapture flowing with the wind. Gently the music bathed him; it washed the weariness from his body and drew him from the shadows of sleep. He rose, alert and young, strong, eager to stand. The song was summoning him. He stretched his arms; his muscles rippled, lithe and supple from the long night's swim. He would seek the singer: he would share her joy. His legs felt sure, his body taut, his loins hard.

A narrow path at the rear of the crevice led him to the top of the bluff. Here, in the slowly swelling light before day, he could see for the first time how very small the island was. It held only a single farmstead. Goats were tethered by a small cottage; their bells rang dully across the meadow. The grass was soft, like a bed, wet with dew and the breath of mist, but alluring nonetheless beneath his naked feet. A maiden was standing alone on the edge of the cliff.

8   Kaare sang to greet the coming day. Gazing across the gray expanse of mist and sea and the silver band in the east dividing dark water and dark sky, she spread her arms to the sun.

> Whither comes the dawn
> from darkness; whither comes
> the day from night? With life
> the sun approaches floating

> on the darkness; with light
> the morning brightens, gold
> and copper swimming. Hither
> comes with love the dawn.

Behind her, the Kalevide stood in rapture. Was this a nymph, he wondered, a water spirit, a daughter of the air? He was awed by her beauty no less than by her song. She seemed more lovely than he had thought a woman ever could be. Tall, taller than the other maidens he had seen, as tall as he was, golden-haired, hair like his own. Turned as she was, he could not see her face, but he imagined it was fair, far fairer than any goatkeeper's daughter should be. Her dress flowed over her body lightly to her feet. It seemed fashioned of a fabric finer than any mortal weave, russet-brown, embroidered with threads of gold and silver. A copper belt was fastened around her slender, supple waist. The maiden looked a little older than he was, yet with her poise and bearing she could have been without earthly age, one of the children of the meadow queen.

> Across one sea, across
> a second, the sun ascends
> in streaks of copper, gold
> upon the edge of ocean.

Her voice was rich and mellow, low, liquid. The melody sank to low notes; it rarely rose to higher tones. The result was a music shaped in a narrow scale, too haunting to bear. The rhythms which before had called him from sleep now awakened new sensations in his body. The Kalevide reached gently to touch her, to join the mystery within her which she poured into her song, but if she was aware of him at all, she gave no sign.

> A copper man, his body
> copper, crimson rises
> from the ocean, closer
> coming with the dawn.

The Kalevide longed to speak, to say something, anything, but his tongue was frozen, bound by the new desires surging in him, and she was lost somewhere in the depths of her trance.

> Copper body, copper
> head, his hair all golden,
> radiant, rising, lights
> the sky above the water.

He caught her urgently around the waist and crushed her against him. All he wanted was to break the spell that was wound around her, keeping her from him. She was too aloof, too remote, removed from the island, from the world, from himself. Kaare wrenched her head around to look past his shoulder. Unable to free her body from his grasp, still she gazed into the surge of the swelling sea.

> Copper face and crimson
> cheeks blushing copper
> betray kisses stolen
> on the couch of night.

She did not move or struggle when he broke her belt and unfastened her clothing. With arms limp and eyes unseeing, she stood while he ripped open her robe and pulled it off her. She still sang, even as he drew her linen smock over her head and stripped her shift off her back to bare her silver breasts.

> Above the sky the crimson
> man of copper towers,
> tearing clouds; bursting
> across the blushing sky
> crimson scatters, copper
> melting in the golden
> morning. Quickly comes
> with love the golden sun.

In desperation the Kalevide forced her to the ground. Awkwardly, heavily, he caressed her breasts and arms and thighs. She was so slender beneath him, his body covered hers completely. Oddly, he thought of the ox he had slain.

Even as he forced himself into her, she sang the ending of her song.

> Hither comes the dawn
> from darkness; hither comes
> the man of copper; crimson
> sunlight rises; morning
> breaks, the golden dawn.

[67]

As if summoned in that moment the sun broke suddenly over the horizon. Balanced on the edge of the world, it shot a streak of golden light burning through the mist, sweeping across the silver water to bathe the island in morning's glare. Finished, the Kalevide moved aside in the sunlight to gaze at the maiden beside him. Her skin was so fair, as if golden, her body smooth, glistening now with dew. More than anything else he wanted to talk with her. If she would only speak, he cried inwardly, if she would only give some sign that she had felt something of the power he had experienced. But she remained silent. She did not move, not to hide from his gaze, not to recover her clothing, despite the chill in the air.

"I never before . . ." he began haltingly. "It was the first time I ever . . ." What could he say? There were no words for the profundity he felt. How could he tell her his joy, his pride, his love? How could he make her feel it, too? When she sat up, she still did not look at him, but only stared into the eye of the sun across the sea. Nothing about her suggested she even heard him.

"Speak to me," he cried. "Say something. Please. Talk to me." He did not mean to be demanding; he only wanted to be gentle. "Please. I didn't hurt you, did I? I didn't want to. You didn't struggle. Didn't it mean anything to you? Won't you say something? Please. Are you angry?"

She did not answer; her song was finished.

In the silence between his words the Kalevide heard the sighing of the deep water sleeping below the cliff. Daylight filled the cloud-free sky. The mists had vanished. To the south the Kalevide could not see even the shadow of the land he had left in darkness the night before. Waiting for Kaare to speak, he glanced around the island. A hut stood at the edge of a tiny forest; two goats grazed by its door. The lawn was grass and golden moss, dotted with white-eyed daisies still closed in sleep. A few feet ahead of him was the cliff. Beyond that there was only empty space and the sea. He felt very alone.

"Won't you tell me who you are?" he pleaded, anxious to reach this beautiful maiden who had closed herself to him. He wanted her to turn those white shoulders just once; he wanted her to look at him. "You needn't be afraid," he said. "I won't hurt you. Won't you tell me your name? Please. I am called the Kalevide, Kalev's son. Have you ever heard of him?"

Having spoken his name and named his father, he waited, hoping for a response, even a flicker of recognition, but she remained perfectly still. He wanted to shake her. Then, suddenly, she screamed. She moved so abruptly that he froze, as though transfixed by a bolt of ice. In the moment of his surprise she leaped away in terror. On the edge of the cliff her foot slipped, and she threw herself over the brink. Her scream followed her into the darkness of the water.

Before her cry could die, the sound of it spread across the island and filled the hut where the elders slept. The old man rose in alarm and donned his clothes at once. The old woman, his wife, rolled over in the bed of blankets heaped on the floor.

"It is only a dream," she muttered. "Go back to sleep."

"It was Kaare," he replied. "I must go to her."

Armed with a stout club, the tiny man, shrunken with age and toil, scuttled across the meadow toward the bluff. His long, thin arms seemed as long as his legs as he ran sideways, like a crab, with his old knees bent. In the golden light of dawn, the shape of the Kalevide loomed overlarge at the edge of the cliff. The old man thought he was seeing a god. Frightened, he dropped his club and quickened his crablike pace.

The Kalevide looked down at the water. The turmoil in his mind seemed mirrored in the creamy eddies swirling over the stones below him. There had been no splash when the maiden fell. The ocean had opened its wide, smiling mouth to swallow her without a sound. She was lost without a trace in the deep depths. For a moment the Kalevide considered diving down to rescue her. Swim to the bottom, he thought, if there was a bottom, and find whatever dwelt within that darkness, but since he could see nothing down there that offered hope, nothing might be all he would find. His search would likely be futile.

Cautiously, the old man peered over the treacherous edge. In his arms he held the dress and smock and shift he had found lying on the grass. They proved his daughter had been there, but where was she now?

"She jumped," the Kalevide remarked.

"Aihhhh!"

It was a wail of dreadful loss, of lament and weary age. The cry that poured from the old man's mouth flowed into the very rock and soil of the island where it mixed with the sighings of winds in lonesome caverns. This wretched, pitiful wail roused his wife, as their daughter's cry had not, from the delusion of dreams and brought her swiftly to the shore.

"Are you her father?" the Kalevide asked, but the old man could not answer. He could only gaze at the hungry waves.

"What has happened here?" the old woman said to her husband as soon as she arrived. He could not speak to her, either; his sorrow was too great. Breaking away, he ran back and forth along the cliff-top looking for some way to rescue the child he loved.

The woman turned to the Kalevide. "What has happened here?"

"She jumped," he repeated. "She just jumped. I don't know why."

"Aihh." For a moment she staggered, struck in her heart by a blow more mortal than any club could deliver, but then she caught herself, and stood firmly.

"Who are you? What have you done here?"

"I am the Kalevide, Kalev's son."

"You! What are you doing here?"

"I'm on my way north, to Soome," he replied innocently, "and I just stopped here to rest. I'm trying to find my mother. She was carried off by a sorcerer, a sorcerer with no hat. Have you seen them?"

The old woman could not believe what she heard or that the Kalevide could care so little about what had happened to her daughter. She was about to reply angrily when the old man came running past them, his arms filled with rakes, hooks, nets, and coils of rope spilling behind him. Racing frantically along the bank, he began fishing for his child in the waves.

"We cannot talk here," said the woman. "Come with me. We will speak of your mother. And your father."

The Kalevide was confused. What did his father have to do with this? Nevertheless, he followed her. If she had news of Linda, he must hear it, and perhaps she would offer him some food. He was very hungry.

"Have you seen the sorcerer, the one without a hat?" he asked again when they reached the hut.

"The only sorcerer I have seen was many days ago. He paddled a small boat across the water from north to south. He had nothing to do with this. And," she added sharply, "he wore a hat." She ducked through the flap of hide that was the door.

"It could be the same one," he said, following her in. "Maybe you saw him when he was heading for Viru, and now he's on his return after working his evil."

The hut was low and round, a dome of bark and withes built over a shallow pit. It had no windows; the only door was a hole in the wall. Inside, the floor was matted with hides still covered with hair. A small fire smoldered on a tiny hearth in the center of the single room; its smoke trailed out through a vent cut in the ceiling. The Kalevide and the old woman squatted on the floor beside the hearth. She offered him a bowl of goat's milk, which he gulped down greedily.

"Tell me your name once more," she said.

"I am the Kalevide, Kalev's son," he answered with pride. "Have you heard of my father? He was a famous warrior before he died. He was king of Viru."

Her gaze probed him deeper than he liked, Her eyes were small and dark, blacker than jet, but quick and alive in spite of their age. He could not match their look and soon glanced away. The woman's hair was long and gray, in disarray from her hasty rising. Although bits of bone struck here and there were supposed to hold it in place, the hair spilled in wild tangles around her shoulders and down over her belt. She was dressed in a soiled dark dress that might once have been black or brown, but which now was merely drab with age. The woman looked the way Linda would have looked in twenty years.

Under her steady, intense glare, the Kalevide's boldness slipped. "Why did she do it?" he asked meekly. "Your daughter. Why did she jump? I don't even know her name."

"Her name was Kaare."

"Why did she have to kill herself? Was it a sacrifice? Something terrible seemed to frighten her, and she leaped. Or else she only wanted to get away from me. Was it to escape me?"

"What were you doing on the cliff?"

Was it an accusation? He could not tell.

"I—we—we were just . . . we were just talking and . . ." What could he say? A new sense of embarrassment flashed over him and left him looking stupidly at his feet. The woman noticed it and knew what it meant. She also noticed how quickly it passed from him. He felt no true regret.

"I didn't hurt her," he insisted. "I know I didn't hurt her. I told her my name and then she jumped."

"What do you know of your father?" she asked abruptly.

"My father? He was a famous warrior. He came out of the north to be king of Viru. He . . ." Again something in her look made him fall silent. "I know little," he admitted finally. "He died before I was born; I never saw him. My mother told me a little about him, about his deeds and valor. But I never knew him."

"She told you children's tales, little of which is true. Did Linda tell you what kind of a man he was? Did she tell you of the life they lived together? Did she tell you of the offspring she bore him? How many children do you think he made her bear?

Two? Three? How many sons did she have? Seven? How many daughters? Yes, there were daughters too, but they are not often remembered. There were five. Did she tell you of his women, the other women he had when he was away from her or when she was too heavy with child, his child, to please him? Did Linda tell you he used to come to this island, that he raped me on the cliff where you raped Kaare? Did she tell you he returned, again and again, until I was too old to serve him as he wished?''

The Kalevide stared at her in horror. He clapped his hands over his ears and shouted to shut out her words. ''Silence! Woman!'' It was a scream. She sat on her heels and looked at him with the same unwavering, malevolent stare.

When he calmed down, he tried to think, to understand. He had hoped to learn something of Kalev, but this was not what he had expected, or wanted. Yet now more questions must be asked, whether or not he wanted to know their answers. They must be asked to silence the questions that had no answers.

''Are you trying to tell me that Kaare was Kalev's daughter?''

''She was.''

''My half-sister? From when he . . . ?''

''Your sister. Kaare was Linda's daughter even as you were her son. She bore Kalev many, many children. All but the youngest were sent to foster homes to be raised in different lands by different folk. The sons were placed in the high halls of noblemen and princes. The daughters were sent to more humble homes to be reared until it was time for them to wed. Kalev brought Kaare here. He raped me—yes, use the word—he raped me on the cliffside and he used me often after that. He said his daughter would serve for his payment. She was a lovely child.''

''Did she know? Did she know who her parents were? I told her I was Kalev's son. Did she know I was her brother?''

''Of course. She knew everything.''

''Then I understand now.''

''You do not understand.''

''She jumped because she was my sister. . . .''

''Yes?''

''The horror she must have felt.''

''Was it greater than what you feel now? What horror do you feel?''

There was none. It did not matter to him that she had been his sister; she had been beautiful.

''But if it wasn't because I was her brother . . . then why?''

''This was her fear: not that you were her brother, but that you were her father's son.''

The Kalevide brooded for a while.

"I don't understand."

"What don't you understand? Kaare killed herself because she saw the father's son repeat the father's crime on her mother's child. She did not want the life that would follow, the life I have led."

"What? Oh—no, that isn't what I meant. I don't understand why the old man out there mourns so much. He must have known the girl wasn't his daughter. So why does he grieve for her now?"

"The girl was Kaare, and she was his daughter. She was his only child. Listen to me, to be a person's parent, his father or his mother, is not the matter of a moment, but a lifetime. Fatherhood comes from love, not lust. My husband, not Kalev, was Kaare's father because he loved her. That is why he mourns. Because his daughter is dead. Can you understand that?"

"You're not grieving."

"I grieve more deeply than you can dream. Was she not my daughter as well? I will bare my grief when you are gone and I am alone."

The Kalevide just looked at her. He was confused. He could not understand what she was trying to tell him and it made him uncomfortable in her presence.

"I'd better go," he said after a long silence. He remembered now he had other, more important things to do. Already he had lingered on the island too long, and his own mother needed him. As he started to rise, however, the woman caught his arm and held him with an iron-like grip.

"Stay," she said fiercely. "Do you feel no remorse of your own? I do not expect you to know shame, for you are your father's son, but will you not feel sorrow for your sister? Are you too young? Will you not reflect for one moment to understand what you have done?"

"I have to go."

"Wait!"

Before he could escape, Kaare's father appeared in the small, round doorway. In his arms he carried a long bundle wrapped in canvas which he laid tenderly by the fire before unrolling what he had rescued from the sea. It was not his daughter.

One by one the old man revealed the treasures he had caught: an oak tree, a fir, an eagle's egg, an iron helmet, a fish, a silver dish. Reverently he placed them on the floor in a ring around the hearth, each one set in place with studied precision, like a talisman on display, a totem to be worshiped. He could not explain. Tears poured down his cheeks; his grief twisted his mouth and face into a mask that was only barely human. Sorrow had claimed his tongue. For a long while he was busy adjusting and readjusting these objects, setting them exactly in their places, moving them about, shifting them by inches, until certain they were exactly where they belonged. With slow deliberation he arranged the limbs of the trees and laid the fish beside the silver vessel. There was no apparent reason in the pattern he made, the egg was not set close to the fire for warmth, rather it was left in the cold, damp helm, but to the old man it seemed vitally important that the pieces be put in their true places. The Kalevide wished he had left sooner.

"I could not find her," the old man moaned at last. "I could not find her. I cast my nets; I cast again. I plied my rake. You know my rake." He spoke only to his wife; in his grief he never saw the Kalevide. "I drew my nets and worked the hook but I could not catch her. I caught the oak tree first. Or else the fish. Perhaps it was the fish. I cast again; I raked some more. I hooked the fir tree with my hook; I caught the dish. The dish? Perhaps the helmet next. In my nets I found the eagle's egg, such a pretty egg. You see the things I found, but I could not find our Kaare."

He knelt forward and rocked until his head touched the floor. His wife consoled him; she wrapped his tiny body in her stronger arms.

"Listen, my husband," she whispered. "Tomorrow in the morning we will plant the oak tree and the fir. We will set them in the earth for our daughter and see if they will grow. We will see what becomes of each of these wondrous things."

The Kalevide left. There was nothing he could do or say to either of them. The old woman was stroking the short, wiry white hair behind her husband's ears, while he rested his head against her breast. Neither noticed the Kalevide's departure. They had closed him completely out of their close circle, for he did not share their grief. What he had done, he thought, had been done and could not be changed. It was more important for him to continue his search for his mother; no one would console him for her loss.

Plunging into the sea, he swam north once more. All around him the water burned with bright patches of golden sunlight scattered from the sky. The island shimmered ethereally. Once, and once only, the Kalevide looked back, as though to bid farewell to the place where he had lost his innocence. The rock cliffs glinted with light, like glass. Against the brilliance of the bright blue sky and shining sea the island looked as though it did not belong to this earth. If he had come to it by daylight, he would not have stopped.

Far below him, slow waves washed the feet of the cliffs, and in their swell were born the last words of singing from the unfathomed depths:

> Do not weep, my dearest
> father, do not weep,
> my mother, deep I dwell
> beneath the sea, my bed
> is laid within a chamber
> far below the waves; I sleep
> surrounded by the stillness,
> sheltered from storms, I rest
> within the sea's deep calm.

9   The Kalevide lay curled in a nest of sand and gravel, cold, wet, lonely, miserable, unwilling to move, his mind and body drugged by half a day's and a night's long sleeping. It had been a troubled sleep, disturbed by strange dreams he did not understand.

The old man and woman on the island had gone to the meadow where their daughter Kaare used to dance in the evening. There in her memory they planted the oak and fir her father had fished from the sea so that the earth might nourish them in her name. Since the iron helm was too damp a nest, the woman placed the egg in her bosom to keep it warm, and that night, when they slept in each other's arms, it lay nestled tenderly between them. In the morning they released the fish to carry greetings to their child in the deep.

By morning the oak had grown a hundred fathoms and the fir tree ten. By midday they reached the clouds of Ukko. An eagle hatched out of the egg the woman mothered. By twilight it escaped and flew away.

The oak scattered the clouds and threatened to tear the sky itself. Fearing the damage it would do, the old man set out to seek someone who could cut the tall tree down. His wife, meanwhile, went into the meadow with a golden rake, copper-handled, silver-tined. She raked three swathes of hay. In the third she found the body of her eagle, beneath its wing was a little man, less than two spans high. In his hands he held a tiny copper ax.

While the old man searched far and wide for a wizard or anyone to fell the trees, the great oak spread. Its branches blackened the island, hiding the sun and moon and casting all the land in dismal shadow. The day grew darker than the night. When the islander returned, disappointed, from his search, the woman led him to the storehouse, where she kept her private treasures, to show him the eagle and the dwarf she had found under its wing.

"Will you fell the oak?" the old man asked.

"I will," the dwarf replied, "in exchange for my freedom."

"You shall have it, and a dish of gold."

The dwarf went to the meadow and chopped at the oak tree for a while, then he too began to grow. First by ells, and then by fathoms and by leagues, he grew until he towered with the tree. For three days he hewed at its trunk, and on the third day it fell, covering half the island and half the sea with its branches.

From the trunk he fashioned two great bridges, one stretching south to the shores of Viru, the other arching northward to the fells of Soome. From the spreading branches he built ships, merchant ships from the stout central boughs, traders and fishing craft from the crown. Rowing boats were carved from sticks and children's boats were whittled out of the chips. From the tangled roots he built a town; the scraps made houses for the poor folk, widows, weak old men, and orphans. Last of all he fashioned a little room from the tiniest twigs. A minstrel sat there and sang his songs of oak trees.

The Kalevide groaned awfully and sat up. Fog enveloped the beach. Behind him, barely visible through the mist, lay the hulk of a boat, half-hidden in the sedge by a trickling stream. Hollowed from the trunk of a tree, it might once have been polished and smooth, a pleasant vessel to skim the waves like a bird, but now it was gray and weather-worn, a sad ghost of a ship, its rough wood crumbling at a touch. It was a sorcerer's, the Kalevide thought. Only sorcery could have kept it afloat.

The thought roused him enough that he started inland, trudging along the stream, trusting it to lead him to the sorcerer's lair. It was his only guide through the maze-like forest of Soome. The fog followed him, disguising everything. Shapes formed and vanished in the haze. Soon the very contours of the earth seemed to change wihout regard for sense or reason. That was the nature of that evil land. The world itself was warped to keep outsiders from the inner domains.

The creek flowed through a narrow gorge, a crease scratched across the land by a claw. The path grew steeper. He was climbing a mountainside. Bramble and briar forced him to wade; the water was icy cold. He stepped into pools like pitfalls; he tripped over hidden logs and jagged snags. He scrambled up smooth and slippery rocks washed by ages' water, often sliding to the bottom, forced to climb again. No other man would have gone so far, but the Kalevide did not know how to turn back, not if he meant to find his mother. Where he walked, he told himself so often it became a chant, the sorcerer had walked, and what the sorcerer could endure, he could endure as well.

The canyon continued to narrow until he began to imagine the hills of each side were closing together to clasp him in their stone embrace. In a panic, he thought he saw sharp trees coming at him through the fog. They were armed with bristling spears aimed at his heart. He longed to be an eagle.

On a barren ridge of slag-like stone he stood at last above the fog. Beyond, the land was clear, though dark, caught in shadows cast by high clouds. The trees of the forest offered no bright colors. In the nearer valleys there were only black spruce. Farther away were alders, which had not yet begun to show new leaves. They did not even have that blush of yellow which signifies spring's first kiss.

"Alder trees," the Kalevide said, "the mourner's wood."

Far away a thin river wound through the forest, shining in the distance like a silver ribbon dropped by a woman long ago. Near the water, a wisp of smoke rising from a small clearing indicated human habitation. As soon as he saw it, the Kalevide was convinced he had found the sorcerer's settlement. Who else would live in such a far, forsaken land? All that remained, he was sure, was for him to carry Linda from this hold and his quest would be done. With a joyful shout, he plunged down the mountainside, scrambling through scree, racing for that distant clearing.

Beyond the first barrier the land set no obstacles against him. The Kalevide crossed the second valley, and the third, before climbing another hill to view the farm he had spotted. Like most settlements, it had a central hall surrounded by a circle of smaller sheds, barns, and other outbuildings, but here the hall was little more than a hut, and the other buildings were scattered about without order or arrangement. They were all decrepit, hovels stricken with the blight and poverty which clasped the northern lands.

"Just what I would expect of a sorcerer's haunt," thought the Kalevide smugly.

Around the buildings was a low wooden fence with so many of its logs fallen that it seemed no fence at all. It would keep neither attackers out nor cattle in. Behind the barns a few small fields had been cleared beside the stream, but they were bare, the soil pale and neglected. Beyond the fields spread the dark reach of the endless forest. In a marshy ground between the hut and the wood, three bent women in yellow robes were harvesting what they could from the earth.

Nettles. No one in Viru still lived on such fare, but in the north, where life was hard for everyone, they were still cultivated. In the early springtime the tender shoots served well in soups and salads, in porridges and puddings. Later in the year the older stems were used to flavor ale. They also provided a fiber as durable as flax; their leaves and stalks gave fodder for geese and goats. At year's end the roots were dug to draw their dye.

From his vantage point on the hill, the Kalevide anxiously studied the women laboring in the field. He thought they were slaves and feared one would be Linda, but she was not among them. At first he was relieved to think she had been spared such demeaning toil. Then he realized that that must mean his mother was imprisoned within the sorcerer's house, there to suffer horrors unknown.

He rushed toward the farm. The women, fearing he was one of the giants such as are spawned in the far north, fled in terror. No one else noticed his approach. The rest of the farm looked deserted. The Kalevide peered boldly over the broken gate leading to the courtyard. Inside the enclosure, asleep on a sack of feathers, lay a single man.

Uncontrollable wrath rose in the Kalevide's breast. He went back into the wood surrounding the lonely fields and wrestled with a sapling oak until its roots broke out of the ground. With his hands he ripped off its branches to shape the trunk into a club. When he whirled it around him, the air roared. Small creatures in the forest trembled and cowered, afraid of the thunder.

Heedless of stealth, the Kalevide strode back across the clearing and pushed his way into the courtyard. The farmer started from his sleep to see the stranger advancing toward him with a heavy club swinging brutally in his hands. It was too late to escape or hide. In desperation the small man tore at the sack of feathers and flung them all in the Kalevide's face.

The feathers engulfed him as a cloud, a black haze, an evil shadow distorting vision. The Kalevide stepped back, but they surrounded him. In his eyes they became a host of fierce warriors, demons summoned from the underworld by the sorcerer's dread call. Floating in the air like a mist, they appeared vague and indistinct at first, then seemed to rise, to stretch, to reach beyond themselves and pull themselves into human, or nearly human, form. They were larger than dwarves, but smaller than men, black, evil shapes, thousands of them. All bore weapons, blades, axes; all wore hooded caps of black leather; all were clad in armored robes of black feathers. Their faces were black; their claws were yellow. In human voices they cried in the Kalevide's ears.

He swung his club and struck one after another. He knocked them out of the air, but as soon as one fell, another rose. They swarmed around him like crows around an eagle. Again and again he struck. Only when he broke one's back did it become a feather again lying still on the ground. Bracing his feet, the Kalevide wielded his club as though he were threshing grain. The host scattered, broken bodies covered the courtyard, and still he swung until he had swept them all away to the farthest corners of the yard. In defeat the demons crawled back into themselves, and only feathers remained strewn over the earth.

The Kalevide turned. Deaf and blind to any further spells that might be cast on him, he towered over the poor, frightened man.

"Ha, sorcerer," he shouted. "Your sorceries have no power on me. No demons can defeat me; I defeat all demons. I destroy all sorcerers. You will tell me where my mother is."

The man fell to his knees and hid his face. He trembled too much to speak.

"Tell me, you. What have you done with my mother? Where is she? Speak before I kill you."

"Please, have mercy," whined the man miserably. "Don't hurt me, please."

"Hurt you? I will kill you. Tell me where she is."

"Are you crazy? What have I done to you? I have done you no harm."

"Where is my mother!"

"What are you talking about? Your mother? Please, what do you want?"

"My mother!"

"You are crazy. Go away. No one is here. What, am I your father that you look for your mother here?"

"Lies! Wicked lies! Tell me now where she is. Linda, Kalev's wife, my mother. Tell me what you did to her. If you have hurt her, I will kill you. I will break your head like a jackdaw's egg. I am her avenger.''

"Please. Have pity. I have done nothing. I know nothing. Don't hurt me. I am only a poor man. What do I know? No one is here. I do not know your mother."

"You lie. You came to Viru; you took her away. What did you do with her? Don't tell me you did nothing. Don't try to tell me you did not find her alone when I was away and she was helpless. Ha, sorcerer, you ask where I was and why I was away. Need you ask? You lured me away, you sent me away, you cast a spell on me so I would go hunting with my brothers. You knew I would never leave her. You knew I would have stayed where I should have stayed. You ask where I was? In the forest hunting, because you, sorcerer, you blinded me to her need. You lulled me with sorceries or I would have watched over her. Do not blame me for leaving her alone; it was your doing, fiend. You came while I was away and you seduced her, my mother. You carried her away. Now, I want to know where she is!''

"Perhaps she went off with another man?"

"You lie!"

"I do not know your mother. I never saw her."

"Do not say that! I will not hear you. You stole her away."

"Maybe she is dead?"

"She is not dead. You lie; I will not listen. Say no more."

Angry beyond his knowing, the Kalevide raised his club in both hands. The man, unable to move, cowered in front of him.

"Look for her," he whispered. "Look all you want. Look everywhere. She is not here."

The Kalevide would not hear him. He swung the club down against the side of the man's head and sent him sprawling halfway across the courtyard. Then began the long search for Linda.

He was alone. Except for the small man, lying unconscious, the farm was deserted. The women he had seen were gone. The Kalevide found their belongings in a storehouse, but nothing that was his mother's. Calling for her, he ran through the small central house but it was empty. He broke down every door and smashed every lock looking for secret rooms, but there were none. The house yielded no trace of Linda. Outside, he searched every stall and shed and ransacked all their many chests and cupboards seeking some sign that she had at least been there once. With his stick, he poked through piles of rubbish and debris; he even dug about in the midden without finding so much as a brooch or a pin he could call hers. There were bones, but he trusted none of them were his mother's. The thought made him sick.

Some of the smaller buildings he pulled to the ground, just to hear them crash. The noise, resounding around the countryside, satisfied his rage. The Kalevide vowed to destroy the sorcerer's estate to avenge his evil deeds.

At last, weary of his wreckage, he returned to the courtyard. The man was gone, he had crawled away to find shelter of the woods. The Kalevide did not care. Let him go, he thought; revenge would wait for another time. Re-entering the empty house, he wandered forlorn through the vacant rooms, speaking his mother's name. His wrath was spent, replaced by simple loneliness. Tears of longing rose in his eyes as he stared stupidly at the ruin of the rooms. Only Linda could comfort him, and she could not. Finally, at a loss what to do, he threw himself down on a mattress torn from the farmer's bed and wept himself to sleep.

Fearful dreams visited him in the night, however, tormenting him with visions that would have terrified him if he had remembered them when he woke. They showed him scenes of battles and murders, rapes and pillagings. Black armies out of unkind lands marched across the earth and trampled living seeds beneath the hooves of iron horses. In the wave of naked warriors, carnage strewed a blackened world; black smoke coiled off the charred bodies of men. The Kalevide watched while the spears of faceless knights pierced friends he loved. Most horrible of all, he saw a sword, wielded by no hand, dismember the body of a living man.

By morning, though, the dreams softened so he could wake without madness, and he beheld his mother as a maiden, playing with her sister, Salme, in the meadows. Both girls swung gaily arm in arm together, their skirts swirling about their waists. Both were decked with garlands of wildflowers, and behind them their sad-faced servant watched with furtive, melancholy glances. When he woke, the Kalevide remembered little of his visions, half seen, half sensed. Only their feelings lingered, and he ached with deep longing for his mother.

Although the farmer had not dared to return, the Kalevide knew he could not stay there long. He was convinced now that Linda was far away. She had never come into this wretched north, and his entire search for her had been vain. He wished he had never left his home in Viru.

Walking away from the farm, he took a path different from the one by which he had come, for he no longer remembered the direction that would lead him back to the shore. Indeed, it seemed to him that the very forest had changed in the night. Trees appeared where he expected none; streams flowed through meadows where he looked for deep woods. This was sorcery, the Kalevide told himself, the power that changes familiar forms in the dark.

It mattered very little to him now where he walked. Any path would do, for although he wanted to return to Viru, he no longer knew where that was. The trail he took led him first eastward through the forest, and then turned north. It wound in and out of the woods, wandered around low hills, went straight across meadows and past numerous small, half-frozen lakes. The way was not easy, but neither was it hard. He could walk where it went, but it went nowhere.

Darkness falls early in the forest, early and swiftly and completely. The Kalevide was trapped by night while still in the middle of unknown land and forced to sleep on the wet ground beneath a fir tree. When dawn broke, his clothing was crusted with rime. The earth around his face was feathered with the fragile filaments of frost. Lying immobile on his hard bed, his body seemed frozen in a knot, his hands clenched between his knees. He prayed he would not shatter from the cold.

He could not move. Lying very still, he summoned strength to combat the ice that claimed his veins. Was this, too, sorcery? One eye cracked open. Overhead, the sky was low and gray. Soon snow would fall, and the forest was not thick enough to shelter him. He felt utterly alone, lost in the middle of a world that hated him.

He opened the other eye. On the tip of a willow branch sat an early thrush, singing a song to presage spring. As soon as it had caught his attention, the brown bird changed its song. "Come with me, come with me," it seemed to sing. Painfully, the Kalevide rose; he stamped his feet on the frozen ground and blew steam out of his mouth. The thrush flew away. "Come with me, come with me."

He followed. Leaving the easy trail behind, the bird lured him through dense thickets. The Kalevide struggled to keep up, crashing over small saplings as he tried to keep it in sight. Still the brown one called to him. Soon the forest thinned; the thrush flew on without stopping. It led him far across an open down and then, where four roads met, it left him.

In dismay the Kalevide watched it flying away, higher and faster than he could ever follow. He knew then that he had been abandoned. The bird had toyed with him as everything in his life had toyed with him, deliberately leading him astray, and then deserting him at the very point where paths diverged and nothing told which one to take. He had been better off in the forest, or so it seemed to him. There he had not needed to choose.

Despondent, he sat down in the middle of the deserted crossroads and buried his head in his arms, bitterly cursing his fate. The moors on every side seemed the same frost-hued gray. The sky was gray. He could not look at either. A few fat flakes of snow fell around his head without cheer. They kissed his brow but did nothing to brighten the dreariness he felt. Sadly, he reflected how everything he had ever known had led him, as the thrush had led him, only to leave him alone in the middle of his need. His father, his mother, his brothers. He felt abandoned by them all. Even the sorcerer had forsaken him without giving as much help as he could, and should, have, he thought, oblivious of the irony, and wished he had gotten more information out of him before letting him get away, or else that he had killed him outright.

"If I had had a proper weapon," he said to himself, "he would have told me everything. Where Linda was, how I should return to Viru, everything. He would have begged to tell me, if I'd had a sword."

Then he remembered. Soome, the land of sorcerers, was also famed for its smiths. That was the one thing he had learned in all his time as an apprentice. Kalev himself had bought his weapons here. His former master had told him that, and the old woman on the island had said as much. How could he have forgotten? If only he could find that swordsmith, he thought, he could buy his proper arms. If he were weaponed well, with an honest sword, he would be better equipped to save his mother, once he found her.

Four roads divided; all seemed the same, and no marker said where any of them went or in what direction the smith would be found. While the Kalevide sat on the frozen ground and considered which way to go, a small, dark figure appeared in the distance. Down the northern road it came, walking with a strange, hobbling, hopping gait. When the person was quite close, the Kalevide could see it was a woman, an aged hag, wrapped in a black shawl reaching to her feet. He could only glimpse the blue-gray stockings on her thin legs and her face hidden by the hood. Her skin looked gray in shadow, but her eyes were bright and black and quick. Her nose was like a beak. The Kalevide wanted to laugh; she looked too much like a bird. Then his smile died. She spoke, and her voice was a raven's croak.

10   "My son, my son," the raven woman rasped, "so far from home, my son. Have you lost your way, small one, to come so far from home?"

"I am not your son," the Kalevide said sullenly.

"You are who you are, and you are where you are. Are you wise enough to know either, or why?"

"Don't ask me riddles. All I want to know is how to find the smith. And I need a place to sleep tonight. Is there a hamlet up ahead where you come from?"

"I have come down the northern road, my son, farther than you know. Do you not know the north? Have you not heard of Turja? Have you not heard of Lapu? Have you not heard of Pohja? Have you not heard of Pōrgu beyond the world? Do you not know the omens of the north? Seek along the northern road and you will lose your way indeed."

"Old woman, all I need is a bed and some warm food, and you tell me about far places. What do I care about Turja, or Pohja, or Pōrgu? I'm looking for a swordsmith."

Squatting on the ground beside him, the black-cowled crone drew a dark, whorled spindle from the folds of her cloak. She began to spin a lock of dusty gray wool into a dingy thread.

"If you seek the smith, seek not the north. Venture not along the northern roads whence I have come, or you shall find no more than sorrow. Such is the omen of the north."

"Listen to me, you old witch, do you know this country, or don't you? Stop prattling about other roads and tell me where to go!"

"Go west," she croaked. "Go where you will. Go west. Follow the road to your left, always travel to the left, to the west. Your journey is not long, but neither is it short. It is not hard, nor is it easy. Walk along the western road, walk for one day and for a second. Always to the left, always to the west. Your path will cross the downlands and enter a forest. Follow the road. It will come to a wooded mountain, and there it will divide. Take the leftmost turning; always travel to the left. One path leads around the mountain's left side; the other around its right. They join again beyond the mountain. Take the road that leads you to your left."

"Why left, if both go around the mountain? Is it shorter that way?"

"Do you listen as I tell you? It is not shorter, but neither is it longer. Take the leftward turning, lest you be lost. Travel westward. You will reach a river. There turn left and walk along its bank, now southward. Pass one waterfall, and a second, and a third. You will reach a headland rising above the lake. Across the lake there is a house where fishers have lived, but none live there now. Beyond the house there is a mountain. There, in the mountain, you will find your smith."

Her message completed, the old woman replaced her spindle with its new-spun thread and rose stiffly to go. The Kalevide's head whirled with her directions.

"Wait," he called as she hobbled away. "Where am I to sleep tonight? And tomorrow? The nights are cold. Are there houses on the way, people who will offer shelter?"

"Sleep in the nests of the birds who fostered you," she said coldly, her mission accomplished. "In the meadows sleep among the grasses. In the woods sleep with the grouse under a willow." With that she hopped away into the nightfall.

The journey was easier than the Kalevide expected. Although it was long, as the strange woman had said, the road was clearly marked and had no real hazards. Where it branched to bypass the wooded hill, he blithely took the left-hand fork. "Always to the left," he repeated confidently to himself. The words of the crone had been precise; they left him none of the choices and doubts which had stymied him at the crossroads. He did not ever stop to consider whether what the woman had told him was true; it was much easier to follow the prescribed course without question.

He sang. Bold songs of glory helped dispel some of the gloom that had clouded his thinking. Although the days were still cold and the sky still overcast, the Kalevide's heart grew lighter as he swung along the road. Soon he would see swords, and one of them would be his. He made up a song about swords of gold.

The river, when he reached it, was not the steep, tumbling cataract he had expected. It flowed slow and shallow and was gray, not white, the color of milk and mud. The waterfalls were low and coarse, mere remains where rocks had given way under ages' weight of ice and water. As directed, the Kalevide walked the bank southward until he came to a headland where he looked

[85]

down on a small, perfectly round lake. A gray, weathered hut stood deserted on the beach.

Beyond the lake, around the base of a higher mountain, a circle of cones marked the foundry of the smith. The cones were ashes. A gaping black hole in the side of the hill led into the workshop. Through cracks in the mountain's cover, columns of black smoke from many hearths and forges rose to the sky like a raven's plumes. The sound of hammers pounding carried faintly across the water to summon the Kalevide closer.

Walking slowly around the left side of the lake, he eyed the black mouth of the cave with a growing dread. He could not enter there, he thought, he could not go underground, not again. To the Kalevide, to be beneath the earth meant to be dead, and that was something he could not face.

For a long while he lingered on the shore, gathering courage. He tried to play, ducks and drakes, skimming flat stones across the water. He even swam, heedless of who might be watching him from the other side, but the clang of iron on anvils still pounded in his head, and the acrid stench of burning ore stung his nose and eyes. He could not escape them, and he could not escape his fear. Nonetheless, his need for a sword outweighed all dread and discomfort. The sights and sounds and smells would not last—he could leave them behind, but he could not abandon the sword, not when it was so close. So he told himself as he sidled unwillingly around the lake.

When he reached the opposite shore, however, his resolve crumbled. He could go no farther. The noise rose, roaring out of the earth. To the sound of hammers was added the scream of metal being tortured. Furnaces bellowed, iron groaned, and over all the noise growled the deep-voiced chants of the smiths themselves as they sang and beat their commands into their works. The Kalevide sank miserably to the ground. Sitting on his heels, he stared at the entrance to the mountain. He could not flee; he could not go forward. The clang and clamor hammered at his wits no less than the metal.

A youth, perhaps the Kalevide's age, perhaps younger, walked past him from the cave and ducked into one of the small, round workmen's huts built against the hill. The Kalevide looked up blankly as he passed but could not speak. He thought this boy might have been himself if he had stayed with his teacher. With a shudder he noticed that the youth walked with a slight limp.

The young smith barely glanced at the Kalevide as he went by on his errand, and only when he returned, some time later, and saw him still crouched in the same place did he speak.

"You, boy," he said roughly. "What are you doing here? What do you want?"

The Kalevide put his hands over his ears and forced himself to stand. He searched for words.

"Where is the swordsmith?" he finally asked, shouting to be heard over the din. The other laughed.

"And what do you want of the smith? Have you come to learn the trade? You look strong enough. But do you have the will?"

The Kalevide groaned and shook his head. "I have come for a sword," he said. "I want a sword, the best there is."

"Oh, is that all? Another brave commander. All right, come with me. I'll show you what we have."

"Are you the smith?" The Kalevide was incredulous.

Again the young man laughed, but friendlier. "That is my father," he said. "I must be apprenticed three more years before I join my brothers beside him. It will be long before I am truly a smith, but then I shall take his place and support him in his age, when he is too old to wield his hammer. Come, I'll show you the workshop."

"No, I can't. I can't go in—not there—" The Kalevide could not explain; words fled from him.

"But that is where the swords are."

"Bring it—them—bring them out—here. Will you? So I can see them by daylight."

"By daylight or dark, the work is the same. Oh, all right, I'll bring you some to see. Wait here." The Kalevide could not have moved.

When he returned, the young smith was carrying an armload of gleaming weapons, swords of all sizes and fashion, all with brightly polished blades and gaudy scabbards. Behind him hobbled a crippled old man, his father, the master swordwright. The youth laid the swords, one by one, on a cloth of soft, black velvet. They rested in a half-circle, each one with its point aimed at the Kalevide's heart.

He forgot his terror. Even the sounds of the foundry faded into the background of his mind as he reached eagerly, for a long, thin-bladed sword and whirled it around his head. It was lighter than he had expected, or else he was stronger. He looked at it closely as he imagined a man would; he felt its point with his thumb. Once he had seen one of his mother's suitors bend a swordblade into a hoop. He tried it. When he let it go, the blade straightened with a musical note. The Kalevide smiled. The tone was pure. Finally, to test its strength, he raised the sword again and slashed it down on a stone. The blade shattered. With a look of scorn he tossed the hilt away.

"You call these swords?" he laughed. "They're toys, children's toys."

Before they could stop him, he snatched up two more and smashed them both over the stone. The two smiths swore. The Kalevide began to laugh foolishly. Seizing another pair, he whirled them both over his head while doing a little dance, but before he could break them as well, the elder smith reached up and caught his arms and brought them down by sheer strength.

"You boy, you stop," he shouted. "No more breaking good swords. You, boy, showing off. What for?"

The Kalevide merely grinned and wagged his head. "These aren't swords. What good are they? Broken blades. I wanted to see your best."

"You pay, boy. You pay for all good swords you break."

"I'll pay, don't you worry about that."

"How you pay? You got gold, boy? Got grain, horses, huh?"

"I've got enough; you can take my word for that. You'll get your money when I find a sword I like. Now bring me some more."

"You pay plenty, boy. You see," the smith muttered. Nevertheless, he sent his son to bring out some of their first-quality stock. He hadn't expected the Kalevide to recognize the difference.

"You sure some warrior, huh, boy," he said to the Kalevide while they were waiting for the youth to return. "You sure know your weapons, hey." Flattery to charm, and disarm, a customer. He would recover his losses.

The Kalevide, wanting to impress the smith with his knowledge of arms and his right to bear the best there were, boasted of his wealth and power in his own land. No price was too high, he exclaimed, not if he could find a worthy blade. The smith nodded. He would recover his losses.

The next swords brought by the smith's son were of a much finer workmanship. Although cased in plain wooden scabbards, when they were drawn their true quality was obvious. Though not so gaudy as the first lot, their blades were of harder steel and held a keener edge. The Kalevide grasped the largest and whipped it from its sheath. It felt like a reed in his hand. He balanced it; he brandished it. He leaped back and forth, feinting and dodging as though in some fantastic combat. Then, with all his might, he swung it against the granite block which had been the ruin of the others. Sparks leaped off the stone as the steel bit deep, but the

[88]

blade did not break. It merely dulled slightly, and the granite split. The Kalevide beamed.

"Better," he said to the smith. "Much better. Let's see how the next one is."

"What for, hey? Why you hurt good swords anyway? You showing off, is all. What for? Why you want to break good work? My work."

"I have to see how strong they are, don't I? I want the strongest sword in the world. How can I tell if these are any good if I don't try them out? They don't seem much use to me, though; they're toys. Are they really the best you have?"

"Those good weapons, boy," said the smith harshly.

"Better than you'll ever need," added his son. "Toys to children, perhaps, but tools to men, even if they are for a bloody work."

"Let me see some more," insisted the Kalevide. "I still want a sword."

"You want to see good sword, boy? I show you sword. I show you best sword ever forged. Sword not even you can break. Not for sale, this sword, but I show it to you. I not sell it, too good for you, boy. You come, you see. You think my work no good, huh? I show you some sword. You want to see, you come." Abruptly, the old smith turned his back and hobbled off toward the cave.

"I can't go in there," said the Kalevide softly.

"Why not? Afraid?" teased the youth. "Come, the metals won't hurt you. Not yet, not here. If you want to see this sword, you'll have to go in. He won't bring it out. And you ought to see it. Pa doesn't speak words so good, but he is a master of the songs for iron. He can shape swords finer than any man alive, and this is his masterpiece. You'll never see one better, not in this world. It will more than match your strength. I don't even know why he wants to show it to you; he won't sell it. He can't. Are you coming, boy?"

Something called to the Kalevide, commanding him to enter the foundry, something dark, beyond his power to know. His hands still tingled from holding the other swords, and he lusted for more. He forgot his worries and followed the young smith through the workshop. Inside, the unrelenting noise and roar of madness assailed him once again. This was much larger than the smithy where he had suffered as a child. The cavern was huge, and many shafts led to unknown depths where ores were dug. The darkness was broken only by circles of light around each of the half-dozen hearths set about the perimeter of the cave. At each one, nearly hidden in the gloomy twilight, a smith was toiling at his anvil.

"My brothers," shouted the youth, indicating two of the craftsmen. "The others are my father's workmen and servants. One day I will have one of these forges for my own. That's where my father works." They passed a large anvil set in the very center of the floor.

The Kalevide hardly heard him. He had closed his ears to the constant clamor of the metalwork. Afraid to look around him, he followed his guide blindly through the foundry, scarcely drawing a breath lest he smother on the smoke-filled, reeking air. The cavern's walls and roof seemed to be closing around him; he felt himself being buried beneath the vast weight of the mountain. Ahead, the master smith limped through the shadows toward an iron door mounted in the wall of stone.

"Here, you look here, see this one, boy," he bellowed as the Kalevide came up with him. "This some sword, I tell you."

The room was only a small closet for storage, bare except for a few boxes of odds and ends, the clutter of the smithing trade, and a single naked bed. On the mattress lay the sword, long and straight, as though waiting for a lover.

"You see, boy, you see how good I do. Not for sale; I not selling you any swords, no more. But you look at it, you see it, look hard. You believe me, I good swordwright. Yes, sir. You not breaking this one."

Shyly the Kalevide approached the waiting sword. For once he felt himself overcome with awe. The blade was perfectly bare, unmarked by any of the elaborate designs he had expected to see etched into its metal, and in its simplicity it impressed him more. Whatever spells lay on this sword needed no base inscription. They were bound inside its spirit. In the manner of the native swords of Soome, the blade was straight and double-edged, wide at the hilt and tapered to a sharp point. The blue metal gleamed in the faint light that reached the storeroom from beyond. It smiled with an evil glint.

"Go on, boy, you touch it. You not hurt this one, no, sir. Pick it up. You feel it. Don't cut yourself, ho, ho."

The hilt, too, was plain, a solid grip of steel encased in snakeskin. Only the pommel and the guard were adorned with gold. Reverently, the Kalevide closed his hand around the sturdy hilt; it fit him perfectly. He felt a shudder tremble through him, as though he had tapped a deep source of power. He ran his finger along the double groove in the side of the blade, but did not dare to touch its edges or the needle-like point. It was enough just to caress the blue-veined metal.

"This best sword ever," the smith was saying behind him. "Ilmarine, great master smith, him even could not shape better. Seven years, seven years shaping. I and my sons, we working on this blade. Seven years. By the ores, some work! Seven years, seven metals, seven kinds from seven lands. Seven years we are heating irons in fires, burning seven woods. How you like that, boy, huh? Seven years we hammer bar to shape blade, hammer, pound, bang, bang, seven times seven times we bend it over and beat it flat again like blade. Fold it over, hammer. Seven times seven times uncounted sevens the layers hammered into blade. Invisible to eyes. Not even I am seeing layers, only seven souls of sword know shape in metal.

"Seven years, boy, we quench and temper metal in seven kinds water. Sea water, fresh water coming from Lake Peipus in your country, boy, and rain water, dew water, tear water, sweat water, and life-water, blood. This a weapon, boy, meant to cut and kill. You watch out, you touching it.

"Seven years, by Ilmarine, my sons, I, we cast seven charms of mastery on blade; speak seven unspoken spells. Seven years, boy, we work hard. Hey, you know what songs we beat in steel?—Oh, it was good work we do. Yes, sir, by all metals, nobody anyplace shape another sword like this one."

"I want it," whispered the Kalevide. Even in the foundry's roar, he whispered. "Let me have it, please. I must have it, I must. I need this."

"You like it, huh, boy? You like feeling it in your hand. No. Cost too much and not for sale. You not need it, what for? I only show it so you see a good sword once and maybe you feel not so great a little. Not for you, boy. We do this for another man. It is his; cannot sell it. Seven years we shape it, twelve years it wait. Sleep alone on bed, you see. Someday man come for it, take it away. Or maybe he not, maybe he dead. Who knows? So maybe his heir come for sword. Cannot sell it to you."

"Please. You must. This is the only sword I want. The others are no good, not for me. This one, please. I've never felt like this about anything. It burns in my middle, I want it so."

The smith laughed out loud. "Not for sale, boy. I tell you. Cost too much. If I sell it to you, you could not pay so much."

"How much? Tell me."

"Not selling sword. You understand? But if I would, would cost you nine strong horses."

"You shall have them."

"Not for sale, boy, but would also cost four pair ponies."

"Yes—what else?"

"Have to have twenty milk cows, ten yoke oxen, fifty fat calves, hundred ton wheat, two loads barley, one load rye, thousand gold pieces, hundred pair gold bracelets, two hundred gold rings, one lapful silver brooches. You got so much?"

"Yes, and more."

"Also wanting third part of kingdom for youngest son and dowries of three maidens for all three sons. By the ores, if I were selling sword, I want all this, I say, but sword not for sale. Too bad."

The Kalevide cradled the long blade in his arms. He stared blankly at the smith who returned his gaze with a smile.

"I will pay you all you ask. I must have this sword."

"It pretty good weapon, yes, sir, boy. Cost a lot, but you get good sword, best ever. You want to pay so much? Why not? Okay, you." The Kalevide could have wept. "You pretty strong fellow, you and sword go good together. Yes, sir. You buy best sword. I shape that sword for man called Kalev; he promise to pay me, but he never come. So you get sword. He comes, I tell him you got it. Maybe you have to fight him for sword. Okay, you not worry, you got it now. With this sword you beat anybody. Boy, you treat sword good."

"Kalev was my father," whispered the Kalevide. "His wealth is what I use to pay you. He is dead, and I am his heir."

"Oh, ho, that funny joke. Lucky for you you come or maybe I sell sword to somebody else and you have to fight him to get it back. Sword maybe kill you then."

Taking a belt and scabbard, unadorned but covered with snakehide, from an iron cabinet, the elder smith fitted them over the Kalevide's shoulder so that the sword would hang by his hip, but the Kalevide was not yet ready to let his cherished prize go from his hand.

He carried it proudly into the main foundry where the noise and darkness, stench and heat no longer disturbed him. He had gained a strength beyond them all. The assembled smiths dutifully admired his purchase and praised his wisdom in winning it. Everyone said it was the best sword ever. While they were watching, he flourished it over his head. The sword seemed to become a part of his arm as he waved it around. The cold steel blade glared in the red light of the forges, but now it smiled with fierce joy to serve its appointed master. Slicing through the thick, smoky air, it sang aloud its high, shrill cry. At the

Kalevide's touch it had awakened, become alive, quick to work the will of the hands that held it.

Around and around the Kalevide whirled. The sword roared louder. It raised a wind which, rushing from the cave, would rend an oak and tear roofs off houses. With a mighty shout, he rose high on his toes and swung the sharp-honed blade down with a lightning flash upon the great master anvil standing alone in the center of the mountain. Passing through the hardened iron, the sword clove the anvil to the ground, and never marred its own edge. The smiths winced. The severed anvil tottered, then crashed. Thick clouds of ash and dust filled the cavern.

"Does it have a name?" the Kalevide cried. He was exultant. "Tell me its name."

"All good swords got names, boy. How else you talk to them? You call name, sword talk back, maybe, be good friend. Listen, boy, sword do anything you want in your hands, even cut good anvils, got no hands of its own, so it follow yours. You understand me? It do what you want, but good sword got mind of its own in metal, and you got to know how to talk to it, tell it what to do, to be sure it understand and make no mistake. Only with name you sure it listen and obey. Only you know name, know origins, of sword you got all control on it. Till then it got spirit of its own, and you not trust it wholly. So, I keep name. I keep name till you pay me. You understand me, boy? You pay, you get name, you get control, sword all yours then."

"I'll pay you. I said I would. I don't have it all with me now, but I have it, at home, and I'll send it to you as soon as I get back. I promise. I swear I will."

"Sure, boy, you promise. But maybe you forget, huh? No, you pay me now, or I go with you till you pay."

"All right, if that's what you want. I'm ready, I have what I came for."

"Hurry, hurry, what for, boy? You got something you got to do? You stay; we drink some. Celebrate your sword. Have supper. In morning we go and I get wages, okay? I get wealth; you get sword, get glory. Some sword, huh, boy?"

In the joy of the sword all else was forgotten. At their master's command the lesser smith dragged the broken anvil away and cleared a space in the center of the forge room. They brought out iron benches and tables and laid them with bowls and cups of copper, iron, and silver. Golden barrels were rolled in from hidden cellars, and in a moment ale was flowing freely. Songs

and laughter replaced the din of hammers as the workmen rev-
elled in their unexpected holiday.

With the sword in its snakeskin sheath standing between his
knees, the Kalevide sat stiff and uncomfortably erect. The foundry
still intimidated him. The smiths' songs were frightful, filled
with metal lore. To his ears they sounded harsh and inhuman.
The smith's youngest son, seated next to him, offered him cups
of ale. Little by little, as he drank more and more, the Kalevide
relaxed. He even began to stamp his feet with the others in the
rhythms of the songs and to laugh when those around him
laughed, although their stories were of ore and metal, which he
did not understand.

"This sure is one fine sword," he boasted to the smith's son.
"Yes, sir. Lucky chance I found it. Boy, if I'd only had this
sword a few days ago, I could've killed that sorcerer for sure."

"You fought a sorcerer?" The youth was amazed.

"Sure, fought him and vanquished him, and if I'd had this
sword, he wouldn't've got away so fast, let me tell you. I'd have
killed him for sure." The Kalevide then recounted the quest
which had brought him to Soome. He mentioned his search for
his mother, but mostly he bragged of his meeting with the
sorcerer.

"I didn't think a sorcerer could be killed," said the young
smith dubiously. "For that matter, I didn't think a man could
ever escape from one. From the tales we know, no one gets
away. He would destroy you, boy, you or any mortal man. He'd
eat you for dinner or enslave you forever."

The Kalevide shrugged and refilled his cup.

"I don't know. Maybe I'm stronger than other men. Maybe
I'm not mortal. Maybe I'm more. Let me tell you, this one had
no power on me. I wiped out his demons, then I clubbed him
cold. That's the way to treat a sorcerer." He downed another
drink. "If I'd had this sword, I'd have killed him. Indubit—
indu—no doubt about it. Cut off his head. Would have been
easy, one two, snick, snick, cut, slice, so long, sorcerer—hee,
hee—so short sorcerer."

The youth beside him grimaced. Sorcerer or not, the image
was too grisly.

More kegs were tapped. Huge cauldrons overflowing with
fresh brewed ale were carried in by burly men from the bathhouse outside. The workmen drank until they were silly. They
laughed, shouted, danced, threw their caps in the air, rolled on
the floor, wrestled between the anvils. Apprentices bragged to
each other about their strength and crushed iron goblets in their

hands to prove it. Their elders gloated in the glory of their craft and the high value of their work. The master smith himself straddled an anvil and bellowed louder than the rest. The Kalevide was shocked to see how much shorter his left leg was than his right. A dusty journeyman limped by the bench, and the Kalevide snatched the bowl out of his hands before he could protest. Not knowing any of the songs of these people, he drank to show his strength.

"I hate this country," he said, leaning on the youth. "How can you live here? It's so cold. Come home with me; nicer in Viru. Nothing here but sorcerers. Sorcerers, that's all. Oh, I forgot, and smiths. Is that all there are here, sorcerers and smiths?"

"Oh, there are others," replied the boy, trying to shift the Kalevide's weight off his shoulder. "Farmers and hunters, the usual sorts. There used to be more, but the tribes have been driven away by the cold and storms, which have been getting worse with every year. Crops no longer thrive here, and grain is scarce. Some say the weather has been changed by the sorcerers and wind-enchanters to drive the men away, so the land will be exclusively theirs. I don't know. It doesn't matter to us here. We are smiths; it is always warm beside the forges. Our ores are here in Soome, so here we stay, and no one bothers us."

"What about your women though? Hey, where are your women?" The Kalevide looked quickly across the room. "You don't even have serving-girls to pour your ale." He drank deeply from the youth's own cup.

"We are smiths. We have no women. This is a workshop, a place for men only. Women are for farmers, not for us. They are not allowed to see our arts."

"But don't you ever want to . . . you know? Don't you get the urge . . . to lie with a woman? Hey, listen, let me tell you about this girl I met on an island where I stopped to rest when I swam over here. . . ."

"You swam? Across the ocean?"

"Sure, why not? It wasn't very far, and anyway, I stopped at this island. And, listen, there was this maiden there. I didn't even know her name but we . . ." In his drunkenness, the Kalevide described Kaare and all that happened on her island. He concluded with a giggle, "And then she jumped."

The youth pulled away in horror; the Kalevide fell over sideways on the bench. He sat up, then added, "Just like that. Not even a splash. What a thing to do. Up and jump."

"I see, you're jesting," said the young smith, trying to smile.

"But you shouldn't abuse a maiden's virtue by telling lies about her."

"No, listen, it's true, all of it. I swear!"

"You're serious?"

The Kalevide looked up at him. "She was my sister."

"Ilmarine and iron! What kind of man are you? How can you tell this? Without shame! Without guilt!"

"It's all over now; I can't do anything. She's dead."

"No sorrow? No remorse?"

"It won't happen again, I tell you. I swear I'll never touch another woman." He meant what he said.

"I don't believe you even understand what you did. How can you just sit there and make light of it."

"I didn't do anything."

"You rape a woman, your sister. You kill her, and you say you didn't do anything?"

"I never killed her. She jumped."

"You were responsible. Don't you feel any regret for your crime?"

The Kalevide lurched to his feet; he towered over the youth.

"Stop it. Stop saying those things, you. I never killed her. I never killed anyone."

"No grief? No guilt?"

"Stop it!"

"You rape; you kill."

The Kalevide, unable to answer, shoved hard against the boy and sent him sprawling in the dust, then he turned and tried to explain himself to another man seated nearby. The young smith rose from the dirt and charged. Butting with his head, he toppled the Kalevide over backward across the bench. The other smiths roared their approval. With his hands on his hips the youth waited for the Kalevide to get up and exchange fair blows. Awkwardly he staggered to his feet. In his left hand he still gripped the sheathed sword. Black clouds of soot swirled around him; he could not see. The laughter of the others roared in his ears. They began to pound the tables with their iron cups. The master smith beat his hammer against the anvil. The sound drove the Kalevide crazy. It was the clang of iron on iron all over again. Everyone was shouting for him to come on, fight like a man.

The anger exploding in his head was unbearable. His face twisted, his eyes bleared red, his mouth worked in uncontrolled spasms. With his right hand he swept the enchanted blade out of its scabbard, and before anyone could move or cry out, he struck off the youth's head. The grim trophy rolled across the floor to the feet of its father.

The other smiths shouted for revenge.

"To hammers, boys, to tongs," cried their master. "Break bones of him. Pound him, crush him. Murderer, you, make you into dust."

The Kalevide stumbled back against the cavern's wall, waving the polished, red-stained sword wildly at the circle of men closing in.

"You kill my son, you, boy," the smith was shouting. "Innocent boy, harmless boy. Son of mine was going to support me in old age. Sweet boy, he never hurt nobody. Why you do that? What for? What sort of man are you to do that?"

"Be quiet, you, smith," shouted the Kalevide in return. "Who are you to talk to me? You're not my father; you can't touch me. I have the sword. I have power in my hands." He lunged recklessly from side to side, but the workmen easily dodged away.

"You let him go, boys," the smith commanded. "Nobody more get hurt. No more sons get killed by crazy man. He is like crazy, mad dog. Let gods take care of him. Let gods strike vengeance down."

The Kalevide reeled through the doorway into the open air. The bright light of daylight hurt his eyes and blinded him. Stumbling away from the cave, he entered the shade of the wood behind the mountain. As he disappeared between the trees, the last angry words of the smith pursued him.

"You go good, boy. You go away, get out of here, you die, too, someday. Listen, sword, you hear me? I know your name, I say to you: avenge my son. Someday when he not expecting it, you strike him. You cut head off him. Head go one way, feet go another. You cut him for my son. You hear me, sword? You remember." He turned away and spat.

Following a small stream flowing southward out of the lake, the Kalevide blundered through the forest until he came to a high waterfall. There he slipped and crashed down the rocky slope to land in a nest of bracken where he fell asleep, the naked sword clutched tightly in his arms.

11   F_{og}, spawned on the waves and raised by sorcerers, smothered the lifeless shore. Giant shapes loomed through the gray mist. The Kalevide reeled away. Another phantom took form behind him. He whirled around. Wherever he turned, another silent fiend reached for him. With a cry of madness he slashed at a giant's arm with his sword. The enchanted blade roared as it struck. He leaped at one after another, hacking them to pieces, but his foes were only stones. The Kalevide left their bodies in piles of rubble as a warning to all who would oppose him.

Engulfed in the constant fog, he could not remember who he was, where he was, or how he had gotten there, or what had happened to him. The sorcerer was only a dream in the back of his mind, the smith's son not even that. The only thing real to him was the sword in his hands. Blood stained its blade, but he could not remember whose.

An old man, clad only in a ragged gray tunic and bark sandals, stood at the edge of the wood, watching the phantom battle with amusement. The Kalevide rushed at him, whirling his sword over his head, then suddenly stopped. High in the air, a bridge arched across the sea. He stared at it stupidly. His sword drooped to the ground. This was unlike any bridge he had ever seen. He and his brothers had often laid logs across small streams and called them bridges, but they were nothing compared to this soaring span which seemed to float in the sky, reaching across the ocean to disappear in the drifting mists of distance.

Suspended on cables so thin they looked like threads of silk, the bridge was supported by a spire-like tower fashioned, like the span, of wood so finely worked and carved it looked like lace, as ethereal as a spider's web stretched between the clouds. People passed to and fro on the high highway. Some drove carriages, some rode, most strolled along the sky-borne promenade, their bright clothing splashed with sunlight, spilling splendid colors, rainbows, over the world's dreary banks of fog and cloud. At first the Kalevide thought they were gods, but the more he looked the more they seemed no different from mortal men and women. Their laughter floated like gossamer to earth. They were happy.

The small old man bowed, then turned and stepped through a door in the base of the tower. The Kalevide followed without question.

They stood in a tiny room cluttered with odds and ends, shells, bits of driftwood, polished stones gathered from the beach, bunches of dried herbs and seaweeds. It was only an antechamber, however. Another open door revealed a magnificent palace beyond. Its walls were hung with tapestries of trees lit with golden threads of sunlight. Where the ceiling should have been, the filaments of the bridge gracefully spanned the sky's own vault.

"Are you a wizard, then?" the Kalevide asked, awed by it all.

The old man raised one finger. "No wizard am I, nor sorcerer. Only a poor man am I, betimes a fisherman. What you see is merely my poor hut."

"It's a castle, a city! Look, marble walls, and that highway overhead! How can I get to it? I would cross that bridge if I could."

"I am a chanter, a singer of songs. I have no need of castles or cities. There is nothing here, young man, nothing but a poor man and his hut. What you see is merely the light of my songs reflected from the clouds."

As soon as he said it, it was so. The bridge, the tower, the palace dissolved into the mist, disappearing as though they had never been. The room became a miserable shack thrown together haphazardly out of sea-washed branches and tree stumps. It stank of fish. The Kalevide rushed outside in dismay. The old man remained alone in his hovel.

A long log, the trunk of an oak tree beached in a recent storm, lay on the shore half in, half out of the sea. The Kalevide scrambled along it to the water's edge, but there was nothing there to see. The bridge was forever gone.

"Damned sorcerer," he swore, disgusted at himself for being gulled so easily by the vision. Nevertheless, the image of the high bridge and the castle built of stone remained embedded in the deep recesses of his memory to affect his future dreams.

The old man's small fishing boat was beached in the shelter of the tree. The Kalevide leaped down and shoved it into the waves. Here was transportation away from that land filled with sorcerers and fogs. If the bridge was lost, at least he would not have to swim to get away. He raised the ragged sail and let the wind draw him southward across the sea. To drive the boat faster, he paddled with his hands. In the sharper wind away from shore he slashed at the waves with his sword to make them yield a smooth passage.

Beyond the guardian reefs of Soome the fog banks dwindled. In the cleaner air of the sea-born breeze, the Kalevide's mind too began to clear. As the mists blew away, he sang a boasting song:

> Kalev's son—never weary,
> Kalev's son—never tired,
> his back—like an oak tree,
> his shoulders—gnarled and knotted,
> his arms—twin oak trees,
> his elbows—two elm trees,
> his fingers—spread like branches,
> his fingernails—like boxwood,
> his loins—like hardened iron.

Twilight fell across the sea. The Kalevide slept. In the erotic rocking of his small boat, so like a cradle, he dreamt of voyaging across a wide water. Three ships passed his, each filled with witches, enchantresses, sorceresses, old and young, each one more beautiful than the one before. They opened their arms beckoning to him. They enticed, invited, lured, spun spells on him.

With a start, he wrenched himself out of the dream before any of the witch-maidens could trap him irretrievably in their wiles. His body shaking, he earnestly renewed his vow to renounce all women. As the cold wind blew him farther across the sea, it swept away the last of the clouds covering his memory. The bloodstains on his shirt and sword spoke aloud in brutal witness of the young smith's murder. The Kalevide cringed in horror to recall the deed.

In the deep midnight he passed near the island where he had seen Kaare. The sails lost wind. He drifted. The scene of him betraying her replayed in his imagination to fix itself so indelibly that he would never again forget the crime he did to her. Too well remembered, he saw himself coming upon her in the early morning twilight. He heard again the mystery of her song. He saw himself tearing her clothes off her body and forcing her thighs apart with his fist. He felt himself once more thrusting himself violently into her, and he wept. What had she felt, he wondered, why hadn't she cried out? He did not understand. Once more he heard himself trying to talk with her; he spoke his name. Even as he remembered, he spoke it again, ''Kalevide.'' Again he watched her leap to her death in the hungry sea.

The sad, slow sound of a maiden singing rose from the deeps in a lamentation for her fate and the far sadder fate of her brother who had slain the innocent. Her cheeks blushed with the blood of his sword, she sang, but he must suffer fearsome penance.

The Kalevide groaned. He could no longer hide in forgetfulness or use madness for a shield. His crimes cried before his eyes. He expected at any moment to see the maiden floating, ghostly white, on top of the waves, but there was nothing there. The boat drifted slowly away from the island as he mourned for Kaare, whom he had loved.

His grief for her mingled with his sadness at his mother's fate. He had lost them both. Rocked gently by the water, he sang a quiet lament:

> Where do they grow, the alders
> weeping, the gentle aspen
> mourning, the crying pines?
> Where grow the sighing birches?
> Where I sorrow, spring
> alders, where I tremble,
> aspen, where I weep,
> pine trees, and where I suffer,
> the birches sigh.

Only with the dawn did he begin to rise out of his gloom.

The sun rose to reveal the shores of Viru. He landed in the cove beneath Kalev's knoll where, for a moment before he went home, he knelt on the beach, his sword held out in front of him, in token of his return. He realized now how terribly fruitless his quest had been; he should never have left. Warm breezes wrapped around him. He imagined he heard his mother's voice borne on the wind. She sang of a young eagle which had soared from its nest in innocence, only to return stained with blood and scarred by crime. The Kalevide bowed his head before her words.

A flock of golden finches fluttered around a rock high on the knoll. They looked like a cloud of sunlight, tiny flashing specks of morning, bright darts of new spring. As he walked up the path from the cove, they swarmed around him, then swirled away across the grassy meadows. Their light chirruping cheered him for a moment, but he could not completely cast off his regret. Strident sea gulls screamed at him from overhead.

The Kalevide's brothers greeted him joyfully at the gates in front of the hall.

"We thought you were dead," said Paari, taking him in his arms and weeping openly.

"Look at his bright new sword," exclaimed Jaani. "Our little brother's going to be a man."

The Kalevide drew the sword from its scabbard to hide his embarrassment behind pride. The sight of his brothers, their honest joy, the thrill of being home again and safe, all brought him close to happiness.

"Where is mother?" he asked. "I heard her singing."

"She is not here," Paari said sadly.

"Not here?"

"She is probably dead."

"No! I heard her."

"You must have heard the wind, or the birds."

"No, she isn't dead. I won't let you say it. You just couldn't find her, that's all. Did you even look, or did you just sit around here eating and getting fat like you were when I left?"

"We looked. Of course we did. And we did not find her. We do not know she is dead, but she probably . . ."

"Stop!"

". . . is. Come inside. We will tell you everything, but you must want something to eat yourself. There is time enough for tales later on."

The Kalevide grudgingly let them lead him indoors. He had been so sure his mother would be there when he got back that he didn't quite know what to do now that she wasn't.

"Not much of a breakfast for you, I know," said Paari laying several round, flat loaves of bread, and some cheese and dried fish on the table. Jaani filled three bowls with fresh goat's milk. "We have not had much time for hunting since you went away. Remember the game we caught the day Linda disappeared, the bear and elk and ox? We gave it to the people of the hamlet. They were hungry, and we had no need for it."

The Kalevide tore at a piece of bread, waiting for them to tell him more. He wasn't interested in kitchen accounts.

"Well?" he demanded impatiently when they said nothing further. "Tell me what you've been doing to find mother. If you've done anything."

"That is unkind. We searched for her, even as you searched, and we will tell you all about it later, when you have eaten, when you have rested. Would you like to bathe? The fires are lit in the bathhouse."

"You look a mess," Jaani remarked.

[102]

The Kalevide glanced at his bloodstained shirt and torn trousers. "I fell," was all he would say.

Paari leaned back on the bench, relaxed and content. Jaani sat across from him, smoking a long-stemmed, foreign-looking pipe. Smoke rings drifted lazily in the room's still air. The Kalevide glanced at both of them.

"Why won't you tell me?" he insisted. "Tell me now."

Paari sighed. "All right, little brother, always in a hurry. We will tell you."

"If you will listen."

"Well?"

"We searched through the great world," Paari began. "Wherever you did not go, we went. We saw some things and learned some things, but we saw and learned nothing of our mother, Linda."

"But she must be somewhere. If you really looked, you would have found her."

"The world is very wide, little brother. I followed the ocean's shore to the west. I journeyed southward, and then west again through lands where I knew men dwelled."

"I went eastward," Jaani said. "Far to the east. I sought paths in the trackless waste. Neither of us found one sign of our mother."

"I walked beyond the forest," Paari said. For his brother's sake he would make a tale of his adventure. "I crossed many lands. For three days and a fourth I wandered. I cannot tell you all the villages and outposts I saw. Yes, and great cities built of stone. I walked through western Viru, through Harju and Laane both. I braved the dread lands of Lati and Leedu. Farther yet I crossed the borders of Poolu and even Saksaland. In Taani I stopped and went no farther, but I spoke with men from other lands beyond the sea. None had news to tell of Linda.

"On my way I met five maidens. The first was formed of tin, the second copper, the third was silver, and the fourth one gold. Of these four, only the daughter of the Gold King would speak to me. She told me of a path to follow if I would find another who would answer my questions. For a long time I walked that narrow, winding way through a land strange to me. Around and around it led, until at last I met a rosy-cheeked young maiden of flesh and bone, as fair a maid as ever mortal man could long to see.

"I asked her to tell me news of my mother. Had she seen her, I asked, did she know where she was? In a voice as sweet as summer's dew, she answered that she knew nothing at all of Linda, but supposed a hawk could have flown away with her. 'Come with me,' the maiden said then. 'If you seek a woman, come with me. In my village we have many handsome maids and wives.' But I replied that I had come to seek a mother, and not a wife."

He paused and gazed fixedly at the Kalevide, who was listening to the story as rapt as a child.

"What happened then?"

"Nothing. She smiled; I said farewell. We each went our separate ways. I came back here to see what you were up to. The maiden did invite me to return, though, if I ever wanted other company. And perhaps I shall."

The Kalevide was disappointed. A tale should be more definite and exciting, he thought, not realizing that this was no mere story but real, and the world was not constructed like a fairy tale. He turned to Jaani to hear his account.

Jaani leaned forward thoughtfully, as though reluctant to begin. Smoke drifted slowly through his half-pursed lips while he considered his pipe. It was a delay directed solely at his brother's impatience. Only when the pipe was finished would he speak.

"My search for Linda was long," he said at last. His voice was gentle, like his smoke. "And if I did not find her, it was only because she was not in the places where I looked. I went to the east, as I said, I made my way through forests and crossed wide steppes, until I left the lands of men far behind. I sought her in the wildways. In marshlands and valleys, deep woods and grassy plains, I searched for her. Where I went I looked for signs, for the faintest of traces which she might have left, but there were none, always none. Do you know what it is to search so far, so long, for something, farther and farther, yet never find the smallest clue?

"I traveled for seven nights, and an eighth, a ninth, a tenth. I lost track of time while I wandered in the waste. I crossed mountains and swift rivers. I went through woods and deeper forests. Now and then I saw the signs of living men, tribes dwelling in the wilderness, but I shunned them. I wanted to find Linda in the pure, untrammeled country, alone.

"Then one day I came upon a tiny clearing where a little hut stood on a plot of green grass. Here dwelled an aged man, a woodcutter, and his woman. I could not pass them by without a word, so I bowed to the man and woman, and paid them the honor due their age. I prayed them to tell me news of my mother, but both were mute. Only the cat could speak, and she merely mewed.

"I went on, farther on. In the dark forest I met a gray-haired wolf. When I asked it where my mother was, it only grimaced. Again I went on. I found a grizzled bear, but it, too, would tell me nothing. It only growled. Do you know what it is to meet with silence? To hear no speech when you long desperately for words?

"At last, when I had passed beyond the darkest wood and come to the verge of a wide, green world bright with spring, I saw a cuckoo balanced on a thorn-bush. 'Tell me, cuckoo,' said I, 'Tell me where I should go.' 'Cross this meadow and the next,' it sang. 'Wend the winding path to meet a one who will tell you all you want to know.'

"With a leap I followed the bird's directions. I skipped over the grasslands, and when I found the place described, I saw a bubbling spring ringed with buttercups and daisies and, in the background, roses. The water from the well was pure and silver; it flowed across the lawn in a sparkling stream. Around the fountain sat four lovely maidens. They were clad in snowy smocks of linen.

" 'Shall I find my mother here?' I asked them, but they answered that they knew her not. 'Every day we walk the forests and the glens,' said one of the maids. 'Every day we wander through the woods and meadows,' said another. 'Never have we seen your mother,' said the third. 'She must have flown away,' said the fourth one last.

"They laughed. Their laughter was like water. They said that I should stay with them and help them keep the well. Leave off searching for my mother, they said, they would love me tenderly. I answered that I had not come there seeking marriage, and that I must return to my homeland to see how my brothers were faring. But I said I might return another day. When I left them, they were laughing, and their laughter was the spring."

"Who were they?" asked the Kalevide in awe. Never had he heard such tales. "Were they water sprites?"

"Who knows?" laughed Jaani. "I'll have to go back and find out."

Silence followed. The Kalevide brooded on his brother's reports. After the first wonder wore away, he was unsure whether to believe them or not. If they were true, if his brothers really had searched the world as they said, what hope was there for finding Linda anywhere?

Paari insisted he tell them of his own quest. The Kalevide told them what he could, but he deliberately did not mention the maiden on the island or the brawl at the smith's workshop, or even the song he heard in the wind when he stepped ashore in Viru. Following his brother's lead, he tried to make his story brave, a tale of hero's deeds.

Of his meeting with the sorcerer, he said, "There were a thousand armored demons at the fiend's command. Both on foot and horse, but I hewed them down like drops of rain or hailstones."

"Are you sure this was a sorcerer?" interrupted Jaani.

"Of course, didn't I just say it? You were the one who told me about the sorcerer's hat."

"But was it the same sorcerer?"

"Why wouldn't it be? He had no hat."

The Kalevide went on, telling them of finding the smith and discovering Kalev's sword, which he drew once again so they could admire his success. He did not explain the blood on the blade.

He tried to tell them about the bridge, too, but words failed him. Its mystery was far too deep for his dull tongue to describe. All he could say, lamely, was that he wanted someday to build such a bridge across the sea between Viru and Soome.

"Then people could travel easily from one land to the other," he explained. "We could send settlers over there. There's land for the taking. I can drive all the sorcerers out, now that I have my sword; then our people can live there in peace. We can double the size of our country."

"You're dreaming," said Jaani. "Dreaming the way our father used to dream long ago. It will never happen, no more than Kalev's kingdom. Kingdom indeed!"

"Do you remember," said Paari, "when we were very young—before you were born," he added to the Kalevide, "—how Kalev used to talk about his plans for the future? On and on and on, without end, late at night when we were supposed to be sleeping. He used to tell mother all his hopes and schemes for glory, dreams for power. I do not think she understood, though. I never heard her answer."

"I was too little to remember," said Jaani. "I don't really have any true memories of Kalev at all, except maybe the sound of his voice and a sense of him towering over me. But I was only two when he died, after all. What I do remember, though, is how the elders in the village used to laugh at the stories of his dreams and all he was going to do. That's all they were, dreams and fantasies, like our little brother's bridge."

"It could be true some day," the Kalevide said stubbornly.
Linda had told him such tales, too, and laughed at them and said
she didn't understand, but he believed they were true nonetheless. "The three of us could carry out our father's plans if we
tried. Kalev's kingdom can be real!"

"You're dreaming," teased Jaani. "Spinning songs of air just
like the bridge you saw."

The Kalevide frowned. "Yes, I suppose I am dreaming, and
Kalev dreamed. But dreams can come true. We shall build a city
here, and then another and another. Walled cities, built of stone,
like the castle I saw. Merchants will seek our land with goods
from around the world. We'll be rich and famous. We'll ride
horses, raise armies. My sword, the sword of Kalev, the sword
of Viru, will lead them!"

"And you will be king?" said Jaani.

"Yes, I'll be king, why not? We can march across the earth,
all of us, together."

For a moment a vision formed in his mind. As if he saw the
future clearly, he saw what must become if Viru were to fulfill
its promise and reap the glory it deserved. He saw himself,
astride a great white horse, standing like a stone. It was his
father's dream, of course, but in that moment he took it for his
own.

"For myself," Jaani said softly, "I would rather walk the
forests quiet."

"You are a king already, though we have never hailed you
so," said Paari. His words stunned the Kalevide. Suddenly it
was no longer a dream but real and terrifying. "It was Kalev's
will. You are his heir. Since our mother is gone and probably
dead . . ."

"Not dead! She can't be."

". . . we are orphans now, and it is time for us to decide
what we will do."

"I know what I'll do," said Jaani. "In the morning I'll start
out for the east. I know where four maidens wait for me beside a
well."

"Yes, no doubt it is time for us to go. I know a village where
I will find the loveliest of wives."

"Stop it, both of you! Stop teasing me."

"We are not teasing. This was Kalev's will. His last words in
this world were that his youngest son should inherit everything.
You are now the king of Viru."

All his life the Kalevide had longed to hear those words. He had dreamed of ruling men. He had seen himself standing at the head of armies, leading them into battle with a great sword in his hand. Yet, with the reality of Jaani's words, the dreams whirled in his head, became blurred, distorted, confused. He felt sick. What Viru needed now, he suddenly saw, was not the golden prince which he had dreamed marching to victory, but a man to oversee the land, someone to supervise the ploughing and see that crops were sowed, someone who could keep the fields clear and fertile. This was what his brothers meant when they spoke of a king for Viru, and he knew they were right.

"I can't," he said weakly. "I'm not ready." The words hurt, but he went on. "I don't know how to rule the land. I'm not fit to run the farm. You remember the time I tried to plough the field. I ploughed one furrow, just one, then I fell asleep and lost the ox. Everything I do ends like that. I'm always falling asleep."

Jaani interrupted. "A moment ago you were eager to lead armies across the world. A moment ago you wanted to raise great cities, build a bridge across the ocean. You were going to forge a vast empire. And now you tremble at the thought of managing one small farm in a remote corner of the world."

"It's not the same!"

He wanted to explain, but could not. The words would not come. His brothers sat looking at him, so comfortable, so care-free; they would not understand. He could rule, he knew he could, a farm or a kingdom, but not alone. That was why it was so important for him to find Linda. She could guide him; Jaani and Paari must help him. Then he could be king. Alone—the prospect was terrifying.

"Stay," he pleaded. "Stay with me. We can rule together, all of us." It seemed so easy.

"We would soon quarrel," said Paari. "You would want one thing, and I another, Jaani a third. Kalev anticipated this when he designated you his heir. Other nations have been destroyed when brothers fought for control."

"But what will I do?"

"Oh, you will get on well enough without us. The people here will work for you, men will plough and herd, women will weave and brew your ale. All you need do is ask them and tell them what to do. They are simple people."

"That's the problem," the Kalevide groaned. "I don't know how to tell them. I don't know anything about anything."

"Perhaps two brothers will come," Jaani said with a smile. "Two strangers from a foreign land like us out to seek their fortunes."

"But what if they don't?"

"Well, what if they don't? What if the worst of your fears is true and nothing is done, the fields are not cleared and the fences not kept? What then? The world moves in and eventually overruns the land. Viru was once the earth's, and the earth will reclaim it one day. It will happen whatever we do, so what is the harm if it happens now? Why not let the forest return? Our people once dwelt happily in the wildwood, let them do so again. They would not suffer. It might even be better for them."

The Kalevide slammed his fist down on the table. "No! Whatever we do, we can't allow that to happen. Viru must become great. That was Kalev's one desire, and it is my desire. He would have built a kingdom to last a thousand years. That was his legacy to me—to us—"

"You see how quickly we would quarrel," said Paari. "You still dream of kingdoms; your brother would have us all return to the forest life from which our people came. We all have different visions for the future. I, for one, am content to let Viru pass to you, for no other reason than that it was our father's wish. If you do not care to abide by his will, well, that, too, is agreeable to me. We will put it in the hands of Taara who should rule the kingdom."

"I don't understand."

"I propose a contest," said Jaani. "First we'll walk across the country our father founded; we'll greet all the forests, groves, rivers, streams, lakes, bogs, and marshes until we're steeped in the sap of the land. Then we'll have a contest to see who has absorbed that spirit most deeply. Viru will choose its own king. What I propose is," here he winked at Paari, "a trial of strength. When we reach the last lake in Viru, whoever throws a stone the farthest across it, with the gods' help, wins. He'll be the king of Viru and the other two will fend for themselves."

"It is fair," said Paari. "It is right to let the gods and the land decide."

For a long while the Kalevide sat silently brooding on Jaani's proposal. "All right," he said eventually. "I agree, too. Let the gods decide." In the moment of speaking he made a strange decision.

He rose to go. Jaani groaned out loud.

"Oh, Taara, can't we wait till tomorrow morning, at least?"

The Kalevide mumbled something and rushed out the door.

Later that evening, his handkerchief still wet with tears, the Kalevide wound his way to the knoll to speak once more to his father's tomb. He walked slowly, thinking sadly that this might be the last time he would ever walk this way. Sorrowful mists closed over him; the night was dark and heavy. He wished he could read the future, an art he had never had, for he longed to know what was going to happen to him and whether he was doing the right thing. Tonight there was no one alive to tell him. No birds called through the foggy darkness.

On the summit of the knoll, he climbed the rocky cairn itself and knelt on its top with his head bowed to touch the mound's rough earth.

"Speak to me, Father," he prayed. "Kalev, come, speak to your son. Tell me what to do. Tomorrow I'm going away, and I might never return, and I don't know what to do. We're going to have a contest to see who should be king, and I'm going to let one of my brothers win. They think the gods will decide, but I already have. I have to let them win. I'm not ready to rule everything alone. I need Mother with me. I have to go away to find her, Isn't that right? Isn't that what I have to do? Tell me. I know you wanted me to be king; I know I'm going to fail you again, and I'm sorry. I don't want to be a disappointment to you, but I can't stay here. I can't. Not alone. If I failed with the kingdom, that would disappoint you even more. Paari or Jaani can be king. They can keep Viru alive. I have to find Linda, wherever she is. Do you understand? She was your wife; you know how important she is to everything. That's why I have to go away. Speak to me, Father, please. Tell me it's all right, because I don't know what's going to happen."

Far below the rocks and soil, far underground, deep within the center of the earth, sand trickled between brittle bones; gravel dislodged by the Kalevide's boots ground against a skull.

"Speak to me, Father," he cried. "It is your son. Do you hear me? Rise up from your tomb, now, Father. Come up and counsel me. Tell me I am right. Please, Father. Stroke my hair. Comfort me."

From the grave the dead do not rise. Grass and moss grow over the earth and bury flesh long decayed. Only the sun and moon can caress a lonely son; only the wind can comb his hair. And the lights will only shine sometimes, and the wind does not always blow.

"Speak to me, Father," he moaned. "Help me, your son."

No answer comes from the tomb.

12   In the first faint light before dawn the three brothers and their dogs set out from Kalev's hall to walk the land. In that hour before morning the world around them seemed wide and empty of everything mortal. It was too early for the herds to be stirring in the pastures; the workfolk were still asleep in the hamlet. Only the songbirds were just beginning to wake. Dew lay heavy on the meadow grasses.

They walked southward through the dark pine forest dedicated to men and the leafy rowan wood beloved by women and the hazel thickets that were the last refuge for maidens, orphans, and the sick. Paari and Jaani slipped between the trees with the feet of deer. The Kalevide shuffled, bear-like, behind them. The sun rose and touched the oaks' new leaves with gold. Wildflowers blinked in the morning light.

For three days and a fourth they followed the winding ways which led them back and forth across the width of Viru, through mournful willow woods and alder groves, down hillsides green with fir, along river banks lined with slender birches, past the white-flowered may, through tangles of brake and briar. The boughs and branches of all the shrubs and saplings were lithe and alive with the buds of beginning leaves. The ground was moist, soft with moss and mould, and it, too, was alive.

Everywhere in Viru water flowed. Unnumbered small streams wove webs across the country. Most were the merest trickles; a few required fallen tree trunks or stepping stones to cross; some were true rivers, difficult to ford. The brothers passed countless small lakes and ponds and many wet marshes. Only the hills were dry, and even these were traced with silver streamlets like veins. The flatlands seeped with moisture. The earth itself exuded the sap of springtime. Paari said Viru was blessed, that water spirits dwelt everywhere in the land. The Kalevide prattled about bridges, pointing out places they could be built, describing their fancied designs. Gradually he forgot the purpose of their journey.

In the heat of the day they lunched on bread crusts and dried fish in the shade of high elms and wide beech trees. When they were weary, they rested beside the singing springs which flowed out of the ground wherever they walked. At night they slept in the arms of the forest they loved. They met few men along the way, for they had left the trails of travelers. Occasionally a lone hunter or woodsman appeared, exchanged a few words, then slipped away. In the woods men prefer to be alone.

From time to time Paari and Jaani stopped to greet a place they knew. They spoke mostly to trees, which they believed were their kin, and to streams, but also at times to hillsides, and occasionally stones, anywhere they had found shelter or a resting place or a cool drink. The Kalevide was less intimate with the hidden clefts and hollows of the world, yet, he, too, paused to speak a word with the forest groves and green meadows, to share the companionship of the trees and grass and fertile waters. This was his home.

On the fourth night of their wandering, long after the sun had slipped away to the western lands and left their world in shadow, they discovered a lonely house in a clearing in the deep wood. Orange light spilled out of the open doorway, drawing a path through the trees.

"It might be dwarves," Paari said cautiously. "Or demons."

"The dogs would know," Jaani replied.

The Kalevide did not care. Demon or dwarf, no uncouth fiend would dwell in his land unchallenged. Drawing his sword, he rushed the house.

"Wait!" his brothers shouted running after him, but he thought he was invincible.

A man and a woman came to the door. The Kalevide bore down on them, his sword held high. They bobbed their heads.

"No!" cried Paari. "They are men, men of our kind."

"We were expecting you," said the old man, bobbing his head again.

"Now you are here," said his wife.

"Come inside," said her husband.

"Come in," said she.

The Kalevide lowered his sword in confusion and followed his brothers into the house, carefully closing the door behind him to conserve the light that was pouring outside so wastefully. A score of pine torches blazed in copper holders. The hall was draped with bright colored ribbons and banners and decorated with garlands of the first spring flowers and budding branches borrowed from the forest, as if it were dressed for a great celebration. Huge logs were roaring on the hearth, where copper cauldrons sang. The air was rich with fragrant smokes and the smells of cakes baking. Both the man and woman were dressed in the fashion of their people, the old ones, the man in his best long smock and trousers, the woman in vest and blouse and skirts. Threads of gold and silver embroidery, stitched in patterns of leaves and birds and strange beasts, glinted in the firelight. The man wore boots of golden leather; she wore saffron slippers.

Without another word, the old woman showed the three brothers to their places at the table and served them from heavy platters spilling over with rich meats and baked fish, diverse cheeses and many cakes. She brought them honey loaves and butter, puddings and thick cream, and bowls of mead and ale. Tired and hungry from their travel through the forest, all three welcomed the service, and welcomed more the food.

While they gorged themselves, the old man stood across from them with his back to the fire, dancing up and down like a wood grouse, bobbing first on one foot and then another. It seemed almost to be a ritual. Like his wife, he said nothing more after his first words of greeting. No one else was there.

The warmth of the cottage, the sweet honey, the smooth ale, flowed into the brothers. They felt themselves glow.

"Father," said Paari, pushing his plate away at last, "all was good and more than good. We are grateful for your gifts. But tell us one thing: where are all the others? This feast cannot be meant just for us."

"All of you," said the old man, still dancing.

"The three of you," echoed his wife. She remained at the far end of the table, beside the Kalevide.

"You said you were expecting us. How did you know we were coming, or when we would get here? We told no one; we did not even know ourselves."

"We were expecting someone," said the man.

"You were the ones to come," said she.

"We were expecting you," he concluded.

The Kalevide refilled his plate.

"Your house looks ready for a wedding," observed Jaani. "Is someone courting here? Have we intruded? Where are the others?"

"There are no others," said the woman. "You are the only ones to come."

"You live alone, then?"

"Alone?" The old man continued dancing.

"We are two," explained his wife. "How could we be alone?"

"Yes, the two of you, I understand. I mean, are there any more besides you two? A moment ago I thought I heard some maidens gossiping."

"Our daughters," said the woman stoutly.

"We have three daughters," said the man.

"Three," she repeated.

[113]

Jaanie smiled. "Three daughters, and there are just three of us; how appropriate. Where are they? Or are they daughters of the air that we cannot see them?"

"They are in their storehouse."

"Sleeping."

"Certainly sleeping."

"Oh, I doubt that." Jaani laughed. "I can hear them giggling. Don't they want to see the men who have come to call? Bring them in, we could all dance a while."

"In the morning," said the man.

"In the morning," said his wife.

A loud snore from the Kalevide suddenly startled them all. While Paari and Jaani were talking, he had been eating, devouring all the cakes and sweetmeats, and filling himself with ale, until quite suddenly his head fell forward onto the table. He was asleep. He snored. With the woodwife leading the way, his brothers carried him to a closet bed built behind the hearth, where they dropped him, lost in a deep, dreamless sleep. The others would have gossiped more, but the sound of his snoring was too loud to ignore. It rocked the very rooftrees.

In the clear light of morning a cuckoo sang on a hawthorn limb, a thrush on a willow, and a bluebird on a rose bush. Three nymph-like maidens, scarcely grown from girlhood, yet old enough to wed, stood in the sunlight to greet the three strangers as they came, bleary-eyed, out of doors. All three maids wore dark skirts of wool, one brown, one red, one blue, and richly embroidered woolen overshirts. Their stockings, too, were wool, red and blue and gold. Silver shoes sparkled on their feet. Scarlet ribbons were tied around their knees, and more were plaited in their honey-colored hair.

Curtseying shyly, they put bowls of fruit and cups of fresh milk into the brothers' hands, then backed demurely away. Bunched together they bobbed their heads and scratched at the ground with their feet like chicks. All at once they scurried away in a flutter, to sit in their bower swing, giggling together.

"You see our daughters," the old man said, stepping outdoors, followed by his dour-faced wife.

"Three daughters," she said.

"Exactly so, exactly three. Each one a beauty."

"You can see how beautiful."

"And handy with housework."

"Certainly handy."

"So each of you will choose the one he wants to be his

bride." Unconsciously, the man fell into his odd hopping dance of the night before.

"Certainly a bride," said his wife. "What lovely wives."

"Lovely indeed."

"Our daughters."

The brothers laughed, two of them.

"Dear people, good people," said Paari, putting down his bowl and cup untouched. "Kind people, we thank you for your friendship and the hospitality of the night. We thank you for your trust and for your offer. But we did not come here seeking wives. We have no thoughts to marry. Not even your three lovely daughters."

"Certainly lovely," said Jaani.

The smile on the old man's face melted into a frown. His shoulders slumped; his feet grew heavy. Why dance any longer?

"We were waiting for husbands for our daughters," he said sadly. "We were expecting three men to come. Why else would we decorate our house so brightly, burn so many torches, prepare so much good food, or give it to you? Do you think we can offer such fare to every passing stranger? It was for our daughters' husbands. We were told they would come. Three men who would make our daughters wives."

"A regrettable mistake," said Paari. "If you had told us sooner, we would not have troubled you. Some other men must be coming. Perhaps they will come tonight, or later."

"Or later," echoed the man.

Jaani interrupted his disappointment. "We don't have to rush away. We could stay awhile and play. Maybe we can't marry now, but why not be merry? The sun is bright, the sky blue. Listen to the birds. For myself, I'd like to try the swing with these three lovely maids."

The Kalevide blushed for his brother, and for himself as, for a moment, he thought of Kaare on the island. Embarrassed, in the flush of shyness, he gripped Jaani's arm and pulled him back roughly. The high-pitched, twittering voices of the girls across the yard chattered in his ears like the chirping of small birds.

"We must go," he said brusquely, uncomfortable in the presence of the old man and his wife, so like Kaare's father and mother. "My brother doesn't know what he's saying. We cannot sport with women."

Shouting sharply to the dogs, who had been rummaging underneath the cottage, he set off sternly down the path leading southward. Reluctantly, Paari and Jaani went after him. They had to hurry.

"Are you angry?" asked Jaani. "I only wanted to play a little while. What harm there, little brother? It meant nothing."

The Kalevide did not want to listen, however, and only strode more firmly along the trail. He could not explain his shame. Jaani let him go a little ahead, waited to see if he would say anything, then turned and ran back to the clearing where the old ones still stood in front of their lonely outpost in the wood. The three maidens in the swing were silent. Tears slipped down their red, round cheeks.

"Sometimes one may love; sometimes one must leave," Jaani said to the old man. "Today I leave. Perhaps tomorrow, or another day, I may return to live and laugh." With a quick wave to the maids, he caught up his cloak and raced after Paari and the Kalevide, who were now far ahead. The old one shook his head and danced forlornly on one foot.

Late in the day, the day after they left the last house in Viru, they came to a small hidden lake, the Saad Jarv. The low afternoon sun was settling behind the treetops, and the clear sky overhead was darkening. The water reflected the sky's deep blue and made it seem more blue. The surface of the lake was utterly still, unruffled by any breeze in that calm hour. Waterfowl floated motionless in the twilight, with not even a ripple around them. Along the farther shore, tall oaks were reflected in the polished mirror of the pool. In the great silence it seemed very deep, although it was not.

Rushing out of the woods, the three dogs threw themselves into the water after the ducks. Their raucous barking destroyed the stillness. Their splashes broke the serenity which had sheltered the lake. With great leaping bounds, they chased the terrified birds until they finally escaped, flying away in a fury of squawks and beating wings. Their feathers, for a moment, flashed patches of blue more brilliant and pure than the water. Across the lake a heron, disturbed from its slumber, rose out of the reeds and rowed majestically over the chaotically rocking water to perch on the high, thin branch of a tree, where it remained to watch the men walking across the wide, grassy bank to the shore.

"This is the last pure lake in Viru," Paari said solemnly. "Farther on we will find only marsh and stagnant water. The gods rule here; you can feel them near."

The Kalevide idly tossed a pebble into the pool to watch it splash. Yet even he was impressed with the power of the place.

"Let's throw stones before it gets too dark to see," Jaani said clapping his hands. "Whoever throws the farthest wins."

The brothers separated to select their stones. Paari walked along the lakeside to seek his from the water. He handled many and cast them aside until one seemed to fit into his hand of its own accord. It was smooth in his palm, round and heavy. Only an old, gray stone, well worn by time and water, nevertheless, it raised its voice to call him and he heard. Speaking softly in return, Paari took it from its bed and thanked it for choosing him, and thanked the lake for letting him have its child.

Jaani walked back to the edge of the woods where he chose his stone from the forest soil. Covered with a mantle of moss and moist earth, it was nestled in a bed of matted leaves. Tenderly he pried the sleeping stone loose. He peeled back its cover to reveal its naked body, then with a gentle kiss, he breathed his warmth upon its cold flesh to wake it, while whispering gentle words of greeting and listening in turn to the stone's own slow slumberous thought.

The Kalevide went farther than his brothers, following the rocky channel of a small stream trickling into the lake from the deep fold of the forest. Although many stones lay along the creek bed, most were unsuitable round cobblestones. The Kalevide needed a flat disc, such as he had played with as a child. While searching for the perfect one, he saw for a brief moment a picture of himself as a boy, standing by the waterside, a stream, a pond, the cove of the sea, playing at ducks and drakes, passing the long hours of loneliness. Of all the skills he had ever tried, hurling stones was the one he had mastered. He knew what kind flew well; he knew how to give them flight. Today he would show his brothers what he could do; he would prove he could excel.

In a flash of white and green and black a magpie flew out of the wood, landed just in front of him, bent his head, tapped a stone, then, with a raucous, rattling, laughing cry, leaped into the air again to light on the limb of a small oak tree. Enchanted, the Kalevide picked up the magpie's stone. It was perfectly suited to his hand, ideally shaped, the best size and weight. Eagerly, he raced back through the forest to rejoin his brothers. His sword clattered at his side. The magpie flew away.

"As the eldest, I have the right to go first," said Paari. All three were ready, all excited and anxious to begin.

Without waiting for an answer, Paari stooped, spoke a quick word to his stone, then straightened swiftly, setting the full

[117]

weight of his body behind his throw. The heavy stone flew from his hand like a bird, or a sudden storm. It rose high, higher than Paari had believed it could fly. Called by the sky, he thought, and with that thought it soared still higher, summoned by the gods. Then it paused in its flight; it turned and dived. Like a hawk it plunged into the middle of the lake, only to be lost, as water foamed up and covered it from view.

With an easy grin, Jaani pushed his brothers back and took his place to throw. Three times he whirled in a circle with his stone. Three times, while he spun, he chanted a song aloud, so that his words would clear a pathway through the air for the stone to follow. When he released it, it flew like an arrow. It rose high, not so high or so steep as Paari's, but it went farther, so far it was nearly lost to sight in the twilight. When at last it fell, it landed close to the far shore and buried itself in the mud below the water's edge.

"Well thrown!" cried Paari. Jaani smiled.

"You don't know anything about anything," said the Kalevide. "Neither of you. Stand back and I'll show you how to throw stones." For once he knew he could outshine his brothers.

"Won't you take off your sword?" urged Jaani.

"I'll never take off this sword. I don't need to now. Watch this."

Without another word he leaned back. The smooth, flat stone, given to him by the forest, was cupped in the bend of his finger. From the corner of his eye he checked to see that his brothers were watching him; today they would learn something. He would show them that he was master of at least one feat. The stone felt good in his hand, and he felt good. He knew he was strong—he had discovered that when he killed the ox—and he was lithe and young. He had power; he need never suffer defeat. The drive to win was supreme. He was a man. A great laugh rippled through his body, and he let himself be carried by its wave. Here was victory. In a moment he snapped his arm forward sharply. The stone sang out of his hand like a bird, like a ship in a storm.

It did not soar as his brothers' stones had soared, lofting themselves to the heights of the sky, rather it skimmed close to the surface of the water. Not a hawk, but a tern. It dipped once to kiss the pond, farther than Paari's had gone but short of Jaani's stone. His brothers sighed. "Wait," he said. The stone launched itself once more, and flew on across the lake. Again it stooped, then skimmed beyond, making countless ducks and drakes over the water until it had passed his brother's throw. It continued, finally leaving the lake behind to fall at last on the firm ground among the trees on the opposite shore. When the Kalevide stepped back, a broad grin was spread across his face. Victory!

Paari held up his hand. "Let no one speak," he said. "Let us find our stones first, to decide for certain who truly wins. There must be no complaints later of trickery or deceit. Besides, it is getting dark. Soon it will be impossible to find them."

Since the quickest way to the other side was through the water, all three pulled off their boots and waded across the lake. At its deepest place, the Saad was no deeper than their knees. Such are the lakes of Viru. Lunging through their own waves, the dogs romped among themselves, caught in their own foolish play. Paari's stone was lost forever. He felt for it for a while with his toes but had to leave it hidden in the gravel. Jaani's stone was found, half-sunken in the mud near the bank.

On dry ground again, the elder two waited while the Kalevide searched the shore for his own. Eventually he found it, nestled in thick grass at the foot of an ancient oak. He recognized it easily by its markings.

"You see," he said proudly, showing it to the other two. "Now do you see how stones are thrown? Always use a flat stone."

"Oh, it wasn't the stone," cried Jaani embracing him. "It was you! You won the victory. What strength! I'm proud of you, little brother. Indeed I am."

"A god or some power must have guided your hand," said Paari. "I have never seen you throw so well before. The gods have smiled on you; they have given you their gift."

"It is just as our father wished," said Jaani. "Kalev's will could not be denied, no matter how we tried. He knew you for his heir, the king of Viru."

"What?" Confusion and terror collided in the Kalevide. Jaani's words struck him like a thunderclap.

"Have you forgotten, little brother? Whoever won today was to be hailed as Viru's king. You yourself claimed victory. Congratulations, little king brother."

Bewildered, the Kalevide backed away as Jaani tried to embrace him again. He had forgotten. In the pleasure of the long trek south, in the beauty of the lake, in his own desire to impress his older brothers, he had completely forgotten the purpose of the contest and his own vow not to win. Caught up in the excitement of the sport, he had thought only of victory and felt only pride in his strength. It was so like him, he realized for once, to undertake a venture and then, at the crucial moment, forget his purpose.

All his resolutions dissolved unrealized in the air. It would have been so easy to have let Jaani win and given him the kingdom; instead his own folly had trapped him forever.

"We must bathe him now," sand Paari, "and crown him king before Taara."

In the middle of his dismay, the Kalevide was seized by his brothers and dragged back into the lake. The sword caught between his legs, tripping him. All three fell over with a splash. Three times Paari and Jaani struggled to hold his head under water, but each time he rose up, sputtering and coughing and cursing. Barking loudly, the dogs jumped around their masters to join the romp. Somewhere in the forest a raven cried. The heron left its perch. Finally the Kalevide broke free from his brothers and scrambled ashore. Climbing the bank, he tripped over his scabbard again. He caught himself, and came up holding his blade drawn in anger.

"Peace!" cried Paari and Jaani together.

Still smiling, despite their brother's anger, they followed him onto the firm, dry ground, where they stripped off their clothes and wrung out what water they could. Although the wool would never dry in the cool of the evening, they spread the wet clothing on the grass while they went into the forest to gather oak boughs from Taara's holy trees, to fasten into a wreath along with what wildflowers they could find in the last of the twilight. Thus they fashioned a crown for the king of Viru.

"Now we must depart," said Paari soberly as he pulled on his boots. He and Jaani had brought a change of clothing in their bags; the Kalevide was forced to suffer the cold of wet woolen garments.

"Where will you go?" The Kalevide glowered at them. He was angry that they could deceive him as they had, and distressed that they would leave him. The oak wreath, still on his head though he did not want it, had fallen askew and begun to unravel. The leaves were tangled in his hair.

"I am going to the east," said Jaani. "When I walked the wildlands in search of Linda, I felt at home within the unending forests. I will go there again; perhaps I'll find my fortune too." He winked and added slyly, "Besides, I know where four maidens dwell."

Without another word, he whistled to his dog, Armi, and stepped away between the trees. At once he vanished from view, absorbed by darkness. The Kalevide would never see him again.

"It's too soon," he moaned to Paari. "Too soon for you to be going. Look, it's night now. You can't go yet. Stay here a while. Tonight, tomorrow, longer. You don't have to leave. Stay with me, help me begin with Viru. Show me the things I need to know. You're my brother. Help me.''

"Dear brother, I must go. I no longer belong to Viru; my place is not here anymore. Already Jaani and I remained far longer than we should have.''

"Do you know where you are going?''

"To the west.''

"To that mountain? That village?''

"I think so.''

It was so easy for them, the Kalevide thought. They knew where they were going; they were walking readily into new lives waiting for them. Why couldn't it be as easy for him?

"You should return to that house where we stopped two nights ago,'' he said. "The maidens there seemed bright and willing, if that is what you want. It's close enough that you could help me when I needed help.''

"It is too close. If I stayed in Viru, there would be strife between us. I must go.''

"What am I going to do?'' It was not a question; it was a plea.

For a moment Paari squatted on the grass beside him. "I will tell you this much; then I will leave, for you are the king and a king must rule for himself. Hear me well, my brother, this is what you must do: keep your country. This is the one duty of a king. You must plough it; you must defend it. Those are your tasks. Reap the bounty of your land, and protect it from loss. Listen well, it is springtime now, a time of growing, the time to plough and sow. Already it is late, but not too late. Begin by turning the earth.''

Then he stood and called to Irmi, his black companion. "Oh, yes,'' he added, as they moved away. "I have one more bit of advice.''

"What?''

"Put on your boots.''

Man and dog then walked together around the southern shore of the lake. For a long while the Kalevide could watch them, until at last they turned westward and were hidden in the trees. Now he was left completely alone, seated on the soft grass on the far side of a lake where no men walked. At his back rose the wide, unbroken woods of Taara, sacred beyond belief. Before him, across the shallow water, lay the land of Viru that now was his.

The sun had long since departed, along with its afterglow, and only the dark and the still remained. The lake returned to its deep, untroubled calm. The Kalevide pulled his knees up under his chin and rocked sadly back and forth, holding his sword close to his breast. A few tears came to his eyes, but he wiped them away and withheld the rest. He was not completely alone; one friend remained. Mustukene came out of the woods and, sensing his master's sadness, lay down with his black nose burrowed into the soft earth beside the Kalevide's bare feet. The Kalevide thought of his mother and his brothers and how he had lost them all. Although it had been scarcely two weeks since Linda had disappeared, it seemed far, far longer. He missed her more than anyone could know. Now, in a single day, both his brothers were gone. They left and he was forced to stay, to rule Viru when he would rather be out in the world searching for his mother. What was the kingdom compared to that quest? What was the kingdom if he could not share it?

The moon rose over the forest. It was round and pale and bathed the land and lake in its melancholy light. The Kalevide reflected sadly on the lost joys of his childhood, although his childhood had not seemed a happy time. In a single day his youth was ended; begun was the time that must prove a burden and a trial to him. Now he must depend on his own unaided efforts, and he did not see how that could be. He lamented. His reign should have a bright beginning. Greatness and glory should burn like lights for Viru, or so he had always dreamed. Power and wealth should shine on his kingdom. "Kingdom," he thought wryly. "Am I a king?" How could he accomplish what he dreamed, if he knew nothing of kingship? Where was Linda? She would have guided him, but she was gone. His brothers, too, were gone, and both so quickly. His only living companion was a dog. Musti was faithful, but what help could he be? The Kalevide clutched the sword to him and rocked. "Father, Mother," he moaned over and over again, though they could not hear. Once, in a custom now long forgotten, he tossed a piece of silver into the lake as an offering to the gods who watched him, and he vowed that since they had made him be a king, he would heed his brother's words: he would see to the ploughing and the keeping of Viru. He would try; it was all he could do. A night wind ruffled the crowns of the great oak trees in the forest behind him.

The eyes of the night watched the Kalevide. So did one pair of eyes that had ňo place in that serene world. Across the lake a sorcerer stepped out from his hiding place among the trees and approached the water's edge. There, opposite the Kalevide, he, too, squatted on his heels. He, too, stared through the darkness. His secret haunts left behind, he had returned to Viru to wreak his revenge. Linda had spurned him and escaped. If he could not strike her, he would strike her son, the son who had stolen his cap of spells, the son who was his mother's blood, whose blood he had vowed would flow on Viru's soil. The shape of vengeance has no bounds. Pain and sorrow were his to call. Cloaked in darkness, the sorcerer waited. Already he had summoned his first visitation; now he waited for it to come. Retribution was his to work. Soon the king must come home.

13   The white mare emerged from the black, night-draped forest of the unknown south. For a long while she lingered, motionless, between two dark trees as she cautiously scanned the still waters of the lake. Looking like a spirit in the waning moonlight which lit the shrouded world, the mare then stepped daintily to the waterside to drink. Dew drops and mist sparkled like crystals in her mane, curling over her shoulders like a fall of water or a stream of fresh, new snow. All of her was the color of ice. Her coat was as white as first frost; her tail was the wind. Even her cycs were white. A thin fog floated lightly on the ground and over the water's skin, and as the white mare stepped delicately through the grass, the mist swirled, as though alive, around her pure white hooves. Pale clouds of steam coiled from her nostrils with each calm breath. Silently, she dipped her head to drink from the icy pool.

The Kalevide secretly watched her coming closer. Though cramped and aching from his long night's vigil crouched in the cold, he dared not move, lest he frighten this apparition and send her back again into the woods. Perhaps during the night he had dozed; perhaps this was a dream. He did not know. If it was a dream, it was an enchantment too beautiful to lose. Beside him Mustukene stirred. The young dog's muscles grew tense and quivered as it, too, became aware of the approaching mare. Carefully, the Kalevide closed his hand over its muzzle to keep it still. The pup was still too young to endure silence and long waiting, too young to know patience. Slowly, ever so slowly, the white mare came nearer, walking through the water along the edge of the lake, her head held high and alert. On every side the forest was poised, utterly still and silent. The only sounds were from the gentle wavelets lapping around her ivory feet.

"She is the queen of horses," thought the Kalevide, completely awestruck. "She is sent to me by the gods."

The mare was the grandmother of the Sarvik and of the wife of Tuhja who is Emptiness, but he took her to be a sign sent by the gods and powers who had chosen him to hold the kingdom of Viru. Through the long, dark night he had been beleaguered by doubts about his fitness to rule, yet now this token came to him, the signal of promise, of fortune, of glory for him and for his nation.

"I shall capture her," he vowed silently. "I shall capture her and lead her to my kingdom. I shall harness her to plough the fields of Viru. She shall sow her fortune in the earth." In his mind he heard again his brother's words, that this was the time to plough and plant. "Yes, Paari, it is the time. The sign has come. The mare is Viru and she is mine."

He envisioned himself stepping behind those ice-white flanks to plough furrows in fields as yet untouched. He foresaw great harvests born, and his fancy soared. Visions came to him of vast herds stampeding across the plains.

"I shall breed her to the best of studs, and raise a race of horses that will sweep the world with Viru's name."

Beneath the deep blue sky before morning, underneath the western falling moon, against the background of dark oak trees, the white mare seemed made of living silver. Closer, closer she came, slowly. She dazzled the Kalevide with the brilliance of her coat. No such steed had ever walked the earth of Viru, nor any mortal realm. With each graceful step he beheld the supple movement of her flesh; it rippled like the water. She radiated fertility and strength.

"I shall ride you," he said under his breath. "Oh, sweet mare, I shall ride you, and none but me shall ever mount you."

He did not move; he dared not, even though the ache of flame was growing in his groin. His fingers tightened on the dog, although he was already more tense than it was. The mare had walked half the distance toward him, yet she never noticed him as he sat, a huddled black shadow, looming on the shore like a giant stone. They were alone, the white mare and the man. The sorcerer across the lake had departed long before the dawn had begun to lighten. He had done the deed he wanted; his vengeance was begun. He slipped away to hide again in the depths of the forest so he would not be caught by sunlight.

The Kalevide watched the mare's every step intently. She seemed so innocent and pure as she approached him. Then, when she was nearly in his grasp, she stopped. Again she bent her head to drink. He could hear the soft, lapping sounds of her mouth in the water. He could see the ripples spreading from her lips. He ached to touch her. When she raised her head, silver droplets clung to the soft hairs around her mouth. Now she came no nearer, as if she were being deliberately coy. She did not move, but fixed her white eye on the place where he crouched waiting, anxious, yearning for her. The distance between them was no more than twice the height of a tall man, and it was a torment to him. He felt now as he had felt when he first beheld Kaare, or when he first saw his father's sword.

Suddenly he could hold himself no longer. His body shook; he was bursting with need for her. With a cry of anguish, he leaped to his feet and lunged at the she-horse, but she was gone. Although a single step was all that separated them, his hand passed vainly through the liquid of her mane. A flash of light, she turned and ran. With a shrill scream of terror, she plunged straight across the lake. The stream of moonlight drew a path through the mist on the black water; along that silver road she raced toward the western shore and Viru's land. Each lunging, bucking stride flung high waves into the air so that it seemed the waters parted. Each splash rose in an outward-spreading arch, colored silver by the calling moon, to spill over an unseen cascade, to fall again into the wildly churning lake.

Mere steps behind the mare, the Kalevide followed, but she was faster than he. Charging through the waves, he cursed his impatience. If he had waited, she might have walked into his hands. Now, as she fled, it seemed as though all his high hopes were fleeing with her. He saw his dreams of Viru escaping. She might have been a cloud, a creature of mist, striding across the water away from him. Again and again he swore he would capture her. She was not lost yet. He would bind her and bring her to Viru to serve him. He would chase her until she dropped, or until he died. Yet she was drawing away from him rapidly. Before he reached the center of the lake, she had gained the bank and climbed onto firm ground.

Across the open meadow the white mare flew, seeking the north and west where she was destined to escape. She would have disappeared into the forest, but brave Mustukene streaked out of the darkness to turn her back. While his master had taken the shorter, but slower, path through the water, the dog had sped along the shore, northward around the lake, a black shadow skirting the edge of the trees. Trapped between the dog on her flank and the man behind her, the mare could do nothing but turn to the wood that went west. As Musti flung himself at her heels, she swerved; she dug her hooves in the soft turf, nearly fell, caught herself, then charged up a narrow trail. The earth echoed the pounding of her feet. Far away, a sorcerer smiled.

The narrow track, barely visible, dodged between the alder trees and entered the deep forest. It was a path made by animals, not men. The white mare pulled herself up a slight rise, then ran forward with all speed. Barking behind her, the black dog followed, but soon fell farther and farther back as she lengthened her stride. Accustomed to running in the wood, now she flew with the speed and desperation of a wildwind.

Farther back, the Kalevide ran, following Musti's faint bark. The woods grew darker. Now and then a shaft of moonlight pierced the branches to make the trees seem black demons' silhouettes, but the moon was setting and the sun had not yet come. Blindly, he stumbled over fallen trees and into standing trunks, but still he ran, driven by his frenzied need to catch the flying mare. His sword banged against his hip and often threatened to trip him, until he clutched it firmly with one hand. With the other arm he pumped hard to add power to his stride.

He ran. The outlines of the trees became indistinct, blurred images bent by speed. The path plunged down one slope and up another. Ahead it crossed an open glade where the Kalevide could just see the white flash of the horse ahead of him, a splash of light, a wraith, before she disappeared once more amongst the darker trees. Well behind her, Mustukene seemed a black shape only, running low against the ground, losing speed. He lacked the strength for an extended chase. The Kalevide himself seemed no more than a shadow as he ducked between unseen tree trunks and plunged across the clearing.

Soon he overtook his dog, now utterly weary, nearly broken by the effort of the run, yet valiant to go on, loping, staggering, struggling to breathe. The puppy watched his master pass, then let himself collapse at last. For a moment he lay on the wet, spongy earth in a small meadow, panting furiously, tongue swollen too large for his mouth, but he could not hold still for long. He had done his part; he had saved the quarry, yet he could not quit, not yet. Too eager for the hunt, too faithful to the Kalevide, Mustukene dragged himself along the trail. Sometimes able to trot a little, more often he walked in pain. He limped with exhaustion, but he would not die.

The white mare led the Kalevide ever westward, far from the heart of Viru and the land where his people dwelled. She left the forest behind and galloped straight across a wide moorland. Dawn came slowly over her; golden light suffused the thick air of morning. Out of the gray and blue and silver, which had been the tones of moon and night, new colors arose, light greens and browns and yellows. The meadows grew from dark to drab to green as the leaves of grass awoke and clad themselves in daylight's hues. Out of the emptiness that clothes the night bushes emerged. The stems of gorse and broom were so dark they seemed black, yet they were touched by the light of gold as the swelling sun struck their first young blossoms. Distant hillsides became aflame with yellow mustard flowers.

The Kalevide was close enough now to keep the white horse in view, and with every effort of strength and will he held pace with her. Her mane streamed over her back with the wind she made; her tail flew behind her. Where her feet touched the softness of the ground, springs began to flow out of the earth. The Kalevide splashed behind her in a thin, golden ribbon of water that trickled through the meadow grass. The streamlet washed the blood from his feet, cut and punctured on sharp stones and sticks in the forest. Somewhere he had left his boots, though he could not remember where. The cold water bit, but he put the hurt behind him. He had always been proud that he could control the pains of his body.

The white mare and the Kalevide ran far across the wildness of the country, the two of them alone in the vast, untouched region. The downlands rang with the sounds of her hoofbeats and the feet of the Kalevide, but there was no one to hear them. No one except one. Far behind Mustukene was someone whose ears could hear any sound that carried on the wind, someone who had no need to run because he had conjured a steed out of a fallen log: the sorcerer. On the back of his unlikely mount, he rode in comfort with his bow and bolts of pain.

The sun overhead sucked the last wisps of fog from the land. It drank them as it drank the dark and left a day bright and clear. Horse and man ran together through the morning and through the afternoon. The sun turned and they raced into the disc of its single burning eye.

The Kalevide's legs grew heavier; he knew he was slowing. A pain cut into his side like a knife. Breathing was difficult. When he sucked for air, his lungs were burned with molten iron. He longed to fall down and sleep, but he knew that if he did, everything was lost. He would have failed yet another time.

"Let me catch this mare," he prayed to himself. "Let me just do one good thing. It will make up for everything before. If I can accomplish something once, I can do it again. And again. Then I can achieve anything I wish. Only let me do this now."

To give himself strength while he ran, he rehearsed in his mind all his past feats of glory. There were only two. He had wrestled with the wild aurochs and killed it with the strength of his arms, and he had vanquished the sorcerer in Soome and all his enchanted horde. To these two deeds he would add the capture of the mare as a third. A third to outweigh the two deeds of dishonor he had also done.

In the anguish of his mind and body, he longed not to think of those two things, but they returned to him unbidden; they would not be forgot.

"When I have caught this mare," he thought, "then they will leave me in peace. With her I will win forgiveness. The gods declare. She is their sign." For him, the white mare was redemption.

Neither man nor mare flew any longer as they had flown. The white horse plodded slowly toward the setting sun, her head drooping, no longer proud, no longer alert. She was no longer the dazzling creature seen by moonlight before dawn. Her coat was plastered with thick lather; her mane was matted and torn, her tail tangled. She limped. White spume dripped from her gaping mouth. Behind her, the Kalevide staggered. Now and then he slipped to his knees, but always stumbled up again. He sobbed and cried out hoarsely, mumbling incomprehensible words. He cursed her.

"I will drive you," he tried to say through the thickness of his mouth. "Drive you—Drive you—I—to the gates of—Pōrgu—Ride you—I—I—will catch—you—ride you—I—"

Again he stumbled. This time he fell and struck his face and could not stand. He had lost everything, he thought, but when he looked up, the mare stood near. She too, could no longer move. Or was she teasing him, toying with him? Anger drove him to rise. Painfully, as though he were torn apart inside, he stood. She did not flee, even as he came closer to her. Only when he reached out his hand to grasp her did she turn her head. Slightly, subtly, just enough to slide from his grasp. He groped for her, but again she slipped away. Together they staggered around the plain, drawn into a long, grotesque dance.

"Damn you, damn you," he gasped. "Damn—"

Back and forth they wove, until he could endure it no longer. Finally, as was foreseen, he flung himself across her neck. She did not move; she could not. Lost in the emptiness of his own exhaustion, he leaned against her side and held her.

"I—caught you—I—" He could hardly speak, but he needed to claim his triumph. "I—caught—you—Mare! You could not—escape—me. We—destined for—each—other—you—Mare—me—"

Her flanks heaved against his as she, too, gasped for breath. The deep sweat that caked her sides soaked through his shirt and mixed with his own.

"I—caught—you—I will—ride—you—ride you—Mare—Ride—a thousand years—you, I—will ride—you, forever—"

A cold wind swept from the forest nearby and cut through his clothes. In a fit of uncontrollable shivering, from the wind, from fatigue, the Kalevide clung to the white mare's neck and hugged her for warmth and comfort. He wanted to vomit.

"Tomorrow—tomorrow—ride—you, then—you—not now—rest—now—sleep—ride you—tomorrow, horse."

With a shudder he straightened. Then, keeping one hand twisted in her mane lest she escape him in the end, he fitted the rope belt from his shirt into a hobble to keep her from straying. It was inadequate, he knew, but it was the best he could do. He had no other rope, and he had no strength to bind her properly. The white mare did not struggle; she, too, lacked the power. All the force left within her burned as hate from her eyes. Once, while he was bending over to tie the hobble, she tried to bite him with her pointed teeth. Clumsily and off balance, he swung and struck her across the nose, then fell over on the ground.

The Kalevide lay where he collapsed, sprawled on the rise of a slight knoll, with his legs stretching downhill toward a hollow. With a few clumps of grass and heather for a blanket, he slipped into a depthless sleep. The white mare, though hobbled, grazed free. While the Kalevide slept, the sweat that poured off his forehead and from his arms sank into the ground to form a spring that afterwards became known for its wondrous healing virtues. All who drank from it were strengthened. Weak children grew straight and strong; the sick and feeble became hale again. The water was used to heal sore eyes, and even the blind were cured. So it was said in later days. The weary were restored, and maidens who came to taste the well went away from it with rosy cheeks to last their lifetimes.

*　　*　　*

Deep in sleep, the Kalevide was haunted by dreams. The white mare strayed. He saw her walking slowly toward the forest, the dark forest from which came an endless stream of wolves and bears and foxes. All were starving. All were so lean and wasted that they seemed more creatures of death than living beings. Underneath coats of scurf and mange, their skin was dry and yellow. They growled with wicked malice as they stalked the white mare mercilessly. She tried to flee, the beautiful pure horse, but, hobbled, she could not run. Bravely, she tried to defend herself. With hoof and tooth she fought and killed many, even as more and more of the demon beasts poured out of the wood. They overwhelmed her. They bore her down and savagely tore her to pieces.

The white mare fell into a shallow depression at the edge of the forest. The blood that flowed from the wounds in her chaste, white flesh formed a small pool of clear, red water. Her liver, torn from her belly, became a rising hill, red with crimson clover. Entrails, dragged across the earth by howling beasts, became a trembling marsh. Her bones were scattered over the field; covered with moss, they formed soft hummocks. Her hair grew into reeds; her mane became the bulrush. Her tail that once had streamed like the wind was changed into a hazel bush, decorated with light, downy catkins. All around the hollow and the lake that nestled there, stood a ring of low, hump-like mounds, the bodies of the wolves and other animals the white mare slew before she fell.

The Kalevide woke shivering in the midst of a fog that clouded daylight. It was morning, well past dawn, yet the sky brooded and the day was dark. The sun seemed to be the moon hiding behind the overcast. His body ached. It hurt even to raise his head, but he had to look for the mare. The sight of her would drive away all the dread and oppression left by the dream. For once, he thought, he had completed a worthy deed; he had captured his prize, and he had done it alone, unaided. She had proved his strength.

Where was she? Anxiously, he sat up to look. She should have been grazing in the field nearby but there was no sign of her. Hidden, he told himself, concealed behind a mound, or in a cloud of mist. He tried to convince himself that her ice-white coat would blend perfectly with the fog, so that she became invisible, but his anxiety would not let him believe it. Near the wood he found scraps of the rope he had used to hobble her. The ends were frayed, gnawed through by pointed teeth. Although the mare herself had bitten the cord, he thought immediately of wolves and believed his dark night's dream was true.

He called aloud for her, but there was no answer, there never was, not even an echo in that lonely field. He cursed his folly which had let him leave the mare alone and unprotected. He had never even considered the possibility of attack—from beasts, from outlaws, from demons, from all the dangers of the world. "You never think," he moaned, "Sleep, sleep, sleep, that's all you ever do." Why hadn't he watched her more carefully? Why hadn't he waited for Mustukene and set him to watch? For that matter, he wondered, where was the dog? Had Musti deserted him, as everything seemed to do in the end? "Damn the dog," he said aloud. "Damn me, damn the horse, damn all the beasts of forest and field."

As the Kalevide stumbled along the treeline toward the east, the ground beneath his feet quivered with the tremors of wet marshland. Red, oily waters oozed over his sore and naked feet. The forest behind him loomed like a wall, dark and forbidding, unlike the woods near his home. He was loath to enter there; it seemed ripe with power, a demon's haunt, or a god's.

A great silence hovered everywhere, as though the world were deserted. The Kalevide halted. Into the quiet came terrible sounds of death, their source hidden behind a blackthorn bush. With dark foreboding he listened; the voices spoke only of the dead; the nightmarish whine of flies, the flat croak of ravens. What they said was a mystery to mortal man. From nowhere another black raven appeared and flapped to the ground behind the bush. Although he was afraid, and the thought of seeing the white mare's mangled carcass made him sick, the Kalevide had to look, if only to be certain she was dead. Steeling himself for the worst, he stepped around the tree. His heart beat wildly, his bowels trembled.

Muttering among themselves, the carrion eaters climbed off the corpse and hopped to one side to show him the body of their meal. They did not go far; they would not leave their feast for long. The Kalevide bent in horror over the body of his dog, Mustukene, lying on its side, half-hidden by the tall tufts of marsh-grass, impaled through the neck by a sorcerer's bolt.

A few moments before, in his distress, he had cursed the pup. Now, seeing its long, lifeless body, the dark stain of dried blood from the holes in its throat, the torn flesh where the ravens had pecked at dead meat, the insane swarms of flies around its half-open, frozen mouth locked in death's grin and around its fouled tail, the yellow worms crawling out of its once-quick eyes, the Kalevide could only groan in misery.

Kneeling beside the body, he tried vainly to brush the flies and maggots away, but he could not bear to touch them, and finally just threw a few clumps of grass and sod over his friend. He laid a cluster of yellow flowers by Musti's side.

"Who did this?" he asked the earth. "Who? Who could kill a harmless dog? He was just a puppy, just a big, silly, happy puppy who never hurt anybody, an innocent living being. Who could be so cruel?"

There was no need to ask. He knew who had fired the shot. Even if he had not known already, the markings on the arrow would have told him. It was the sorcerer, unquestionably the same sorcerer who had ravished Linda. Defeated once in his homeland, the Kalevide thought, he had returned to Viru for revenge and wrought it by killing the dog. Unaware of the true reason for his enemy's wrath, and unable to guess its limits, the Kalevide believed the sorcerer had come merely to repay him for the beating in Soome, but he wondered nonetheless if he would be satisfied with Mustukene's death, or would he follow him and haunt him seeking more vicious vengeance? Did he lurk near even now? It was a horrible thought. The Kalevide tried to draw the arrow from his dog's body, but it burned his hand. In pain he ran.

He plunged, raging, into the forest, screaming aloud his anger and madness. He damned the sorcerer and his servants, the wolves which had come out of the night to destroy the white mare while their lord struck Mustukene down. Sorcerer and wolves, wolves and sorcerer, inseparable, together they had worked to wreck his brightest hopes. The sorcerer had stolen his mother, the wolves had ruined the mare. All his dreams were torn apart, and fiends would come for more. They would never be satisfied.

"Come out! Cowards!" he cried again and again. "Cowards! You! Curse you! Come out. Fight me! Do you only strike at night? Come out, damn you. Face my sword!" He weaved through the trees, circling backward so no one could sneak behind him. "Come out, cowards! Where are you? I can't see you!" He was frantic.

No one answered. He reeled, and crashed back into a tree. Lashing out in rage, he felled it with a blow. Then he charged in a frenzy through the forest, striking at anything he could reach. Young saplings fell before his onslaught. He tore through shrubs and bushes and hacked at every tree with the sword whose blade was sharp enough and strong enough to slice through any wood. He lopped off great branches; he cut down full trees.

In a crevice between two high stones a half-grown wolf was sleepily gnawing on the thighbone of a rabbit it had caught and eaten days ago. The Kalevide came upon it too suddenly. His face twisted, burning red, and distorted with rage, he leaped at the wolf with his sword high. He shrieked one word, "Demon!" and struck. The blade cut the cub in two and cleaved both rocks. With a roar, the Kalevide pulled the massive boulders down over the body of the harmless beast.

His rampage carried him farther to the south. He found bears and foxes, even as he had seen them in the dream, and he killed them all. He slaughtered wolves and lynxes, weasels, minks, and boars. Even simple hares and squirrels fell, for he was blinded by his fury and struck wildly everywhere. A storm of fire had been released in him which could not be checked or controlled. All animals fled in panic before him. They scurried through the underbrush and thickets toward the boundless marsh that lay beyond the wood. There was no refuge there, but there they might find a more peaceful death. Any beast he caught, he destroyed. He would have exterminated the races of the wolves and bears completely if the dark of night had not come up and overwhelmed him.

Behind him stretched a swath mowed through the forest like a road. Before him spread the vastness of the dreadful swamp. In the darkness the Kalevide was suddenly overtaken by weariness. The fire that had burned in him was spent, extinguished, replaced only by an awful sense of emptiness. His body felt drained, worn out and empty, as though purged. In his weakness, the point of his sword drooped to the earth. Blood dripped from its point onto the marshy soil. His hands and arms ran with the gore of animals. The signs of his rape dyed his shirt and trousers and even masked the stains left from slaying the smith's young son. The Kalevide collapsed. Heedless of where he was, or who he was, or what he had done, he rolled over onto his back with his arms spread apart. The blood-stained sword was locked in the grip of his right hand as he fell into a trance-like sleep.

The dreams that came to him were nightmare's dreams. First only the sounds were sensed, wrenching sounds, sounds of pain, sounds that congealed into a slowly revolving wheel of nauseous, viscous, dead-yellow light. In the light he saw the faces of the animals he had slain. He saw their grisly, grinning jaws, and saw them cleft in two. He saw their blood flow into the thick, pulsating light. The dream of beasts then faded and was replaced by a dream of war. The war marched inexorably across the country. From the vantage of a hill or knoll he saw dark men ride dark horses, dark men who were the war, men who had no faces. Bemused, he watched them rape a maiden. A messenger arrived to tell him of the war's disaster, but he upbraided the foolish old man for disturbing him and sent him home again, even while the war walked on. In his dream he fell asleep to sleep without a dream.

The Kalevide woke once, or dreamed he woke, in the dead of night. With a groan he tried to rise, but something held him back, an unseen pressure, binding him, pushing him deeper into the depths of sleep before he could truly wake. What he saw in that sleep now came so clearly he could not tell if it were another dream or if it were true. Even in after days he never knew.

An old man came out of the forest. Small and dark, weathered by long ages, he looked like a peasant clad in simple, homespun clothes. His hair was entirely white, his beard long and unkempt. If this were a dream, then the old man stepped directly out of an ancient oak. If it were real, the Kalevide reasoned later, then he must merely have stepped from between two trees.

Approaching the Kalevide, the old one bowed humbly and saluted him as a king.

"Forgive me, sir, for disturbing your rest," he said without a hint of mockery. "I mean no disrespect, young lord, I know you wish to sleep, the great ones always do, but there are things to be done, young king, and no time left for ease. When I was young, long, long ago, lord, the birds sang to me once that a king can never know true rest."

In a voice as dry and rough as oak bark, he began to chant. Bent in a crouch, swaying back and forth in the manner of the bards, he sang:

> Heavy care the ruler
> carries; weighty loads
> he bears. A hero
> has the greatest burden.
> A thousand duties await
> the mighty; thousands more
> beset the son of Kalev.

The Kalevide stirred restlessly. Suddenly the old man's tone changed. His voice rolled with power.

"Already you have devastated the countryside. You have

hacked your way wantonly through the woods. You have felled proud trees and torn up tender shrubs; you have trampled fragile seedlings beneath your heedless feet. You have crushed the infant woodland flowers. Can you repair such damage? Already you have slept too late. You have slain the beasts and gentle beings who live among the trees. You have slaughtered helpless wolves and bears and foxes, hares and deer. Can you restore the lives of innocents? Already you have slept too long. All the forces and powers which guide this world avert their faces from this ruin. Can anything prosper without the favor of the gods?''

Then the elder's voice changed once more; it grew hoarse, but gentler, almost a whisper, but not without hope. He told the Kalevide how he could atone for all the wrong he had done now and before. Despite all the death and destruction, he and his country still could prosper, if only he would work for the benefit of his people and regain the blessing of the gods. It would not be easy. Great labors awaited him; he must begin. Although he had sent his messenger away, a war was on his borders. He must see to the defense of his land. He must, moreover, provide for his people and maintain them from want. If he would only strive for the good of all, then Viru would indeed gain its destined glory. These were words the Kalevide longed to hear.

"Yet beware the sword, young king," the old one warned. "Most of all, beware the sword with blood on its blade. A sword that has tasted life, lord, thirsts to drink again. Murder begets murder; a man who sheds the blood of innocents can never be secure."

His voice faded away with the wind, and through the rest of the night deep silence hung everywhere over the wood and marsh. The Kalevide sank once more into the refuge of dreamless sleep. The old one, who was Taara, held the young king's head in his lap and stroked his brow to comfort him.

PART II

14 The son of Alev, the Alevide, looked down curiously at the body of a man lying half-concealed in the high grass at the edge of an unbounded marsh. The man was coarsely clad, like a ploughman or cowherd, although, the Alevide knew, clothes could conceal as well as reveal a person's station, and he was covered with blood. His shirt and trousers were caked with it, his hands black with gore, even his long, golden hair was streaked. In his hand he gripped a mighty sword.

"Are you dead?" the Alevide asked, prodding the inert body with his toe. "Murdered perhaps?"

The body lay on its back, legs spread, arms flung open, as though to bare itself to the world's eye.

"How unafraid is death, how unashamed," he mused, "but it's a dreadful way to die. Alone, in such an unfriendly place as this. No man would walk in this swamp, much less come here to die. It must be terrible to die bleeding to death, alone, to feel the life flowing out of your body and know you cannot stop it. I wonder what a man feels then. What did you feel, my silent friend? What did you do? Did you watch your blood running out of your veins and sinking into the soft earth until your eyes closed? Did you know you were dying?" The Alevide shuddered. He wanted to leave this man but could not, not yet.

"If I should ever die," he thought, "I would not want it to be like this. I'd rather be lying on my own couch in my own house in the warmth of my own hearth surrounded by my friends and family." A bitter smile twisted his mouth. "Of course, I have no couch, no home, no hearth, no family, no longer a friend. I suppose then if I should get my wish, I shall never die. That's logic."

The Alevide turned to face the forest. A breath of wind blew across his lips. "If I should die," he cried aloud to the wood and to the clouds above the wood, "may I not die as this man died, lost, in such a forsaken swamp. May I not bleed to death, and may I not be alone. Let me have at least one mourner, for this is not a fit death for any man.''

Again he gazed down at the man on the ground. ''Shall I take your sword, lost friend? You don't need it, not anymore. Shall I? You have nothing else worth taking, it seems. No, a man's sword is his own. I'll take no man's arms. What would I do with them, except end the way you've ended? Shall I bury you, then? Or would you rather have demons gnaw your bones? They will, you know. It's a pity you can't talk; what tale would you tell? Would you tell me who you are and how you perished? Was it a war, or was it a more personal affair? Were you struck down in vengeance for some crime? Would you boast of your fall; would you claim you died bravely, or would you be ashamed to tell? No answer?'' Again he prodded the body with his boot.

There was a flicker in the dead man's eyes. They opened wide.

''Are you dead?'' the Alevide politely asked again.

For some time the man on his back could not speak. He could not find his tongue or control his mouth. He had been too deep, wherever he had been, and had returned too soon. Words eluded him. When he tried to focus his eyes, he could only see the vague outline of the stranger's shape looming over him, a tall figure silhouetted against a sky that was too bright for his bleary eyes. He groaned heavily.

''Who are you?'' he muttered finally, his voice thick with sleep.

''Well, well, if the dead can speak, what can they say?''

''Who are you?'' the Kalevide asked again. He tried to rise, but still lacked the strength.

''Not dead, then?'' the son of Alev said with a smile. ''How lucky for you. When I saw you lying there all covered with blood, I thought surely you had met a tragic end.''

''Who are you?'' The Kalevide almost shouted in his frustration. If he could not raise his body, he could raise his arm. The Alevide quickly kicked the sword aside and pinned the Kalevide's wrist to the ground with his heel.

''Would you kill a man who never did you harm?''

The Kalevide groaned again. ''Who are you?'' he said weakly. Despair crawled into his voice. Too many memories came upon him too quickly. He recalled what had brought him to this mire, remembered running the white mare across the wilderness, and all the horror that had followed. His brothers had left him; he had become the sole king of Viru. His mother was lost and he could not leave to rescue her. There had been the maiden on the

[140]

island, and the smith's son. It was too much; he wanted it done. "Will you kill me?" he asked miserably.

The Alevide did not answer but only stared at him in disbelief.

"Are you going to kill me?" the Kalevide repeated. "Are you my death?"

"Don't be silly. I don't even know you, why would I want to kill you?"

"I don't know. It doesn't matter. Nothing matters. Will you let me up?"

"If you promise not to raise your sword against me again, now or ever, for good cause or none."

"Why not? It doesn't make any difference. This sword won't serve me very well, anyway."

Once released, the Kalevide heaved himself awkwardly to his feet, and shuffled like a bear to the small stream trickling slowly along the edge of the swamp. The Alevide watched amused while he washed himself haphazardly, wincing as the cold water touched his scratches.

With his head a little clearer, if not cleaner, the Kalevide ambled back to the stranger. Thrusting his sword into the soft earth, he threw himself to the ground beside it.

"Are you a wizard?" he asked.

"A wizard?"

"Yes—or a sorcerer?"

The Alevide smiled at his boyish questions. "I am no sorcerer," he said after a moment. "What makes you think I might be a wizard?"

"Your hat. All the holes in it. It's very strange. And you wouldn't tell me your name."

"If I told you I had made a great quantity of silver vanish inside this hat, would you believe me?"

"You are a wizard, then."

"Alas, no. No wizard, no sorcerer, not even a wind-enchanter. Just a wanderer."

"How, then? The silver."

"Ah, that's a tale long in the telling; you wouldn't care for it."

"I might. Tell me, please."

"You're a strange one, aren't you? I should be the one asking you for tales. Here I find you in this dismal swamp, looking quite dead, bathed in blood. Isn't that something to wonder at? But do I press you with questions, and if I did, would you answer? And yet you're pleased to ask about so small a thing as a hat."

"Who are you?"

"Now that is a far better question. Simply said, I am the Alevide, the son of Alev. I come from a country behind the Golden Mountains that stand between East and West in the world. I lost my father's inheritance there, and now I hope to find my fortune in a foreign land."

"What happened?"

"Another tale long in telling. Shall I give it to you?"

"Please."

The Alevide studied the other's face then laughed out loud. "I don't know why I should, except that I'm alone and have no one else to tell, and you look gullible enough. This is the truth, then, if you will believe a stranger's words: I am the Alevide, the son of Alev the War Trader. He died not long ago, and soon after his death the Riders appeared in our village. They claimed to be my father's henchmen and hence his heirs. They took everything he had owned."

"Were they? His heirs, I mean."

"I don't know. I never rode with my father or met any of his comrades. He traded arms over the mountain passes to the tribes at war. Perhaps these men were his partners, perhaps that made them his kin, perhaps that was the custom among those clans, perhaps they were only pirates. I don't know. It didn't matter. I couldn't fight them. All I could do was flee.

"They seized my father's house and sacked the hamlets nearby. They robbed what they could and raped whom they would, and when they were satisfied with what they had, they put the torch to the rest. One night of fire destroyed it all. I can still see, I'll never forget, the flames, orange rage, exploding over the blackness of that night. Houses, barns, fire, heat, horror. Animals trapped in their stalls, screaming in terror. People suffering more. They ran in panic across their fields, only to be ridden down like hares by the howling horsemen who hacked at them with their sabers and hewed them to the ground for sport. I saw a woman's belly slit open, a man set afire. Children watched their parents die, and died themselves. I escaped to the forest. I hope some of the others did, too.

"After that, well, I wandered. I walked across the width of the world to find another home for myself and the people who survived. I crossed the high Golden Mountains and the Central Plains, I skirted wide lands of steppe and prairie, I measured the boundless forest. It was a long and lonely journey. Few people dwell in the far wilderness. Traders never venture there and trappers rarely seek it. I forged new trails. I crossed six rivers, and a seventh. I climbed the ninth steep range of hills, and the tenth.

"Here and there, in the forest and on the edge of the grassland, I found people dwelling in remote homesteads and hamlets. They were kin to me, they spoke a tongue related to my own, and they were kind. They gave food, shelter, hospitality, simple fare, but fair. I traded songs for my livelihood. Some thought, as you thought, I was a wizard, and sought my skills to cure a stitch or quell a fever, to break a drought or banish a witch. I helped them the best I could, though I confess I have more wit than wisdom.

"Often enough, the folk were mean, they gave few gifts or were not impressed by a traveler's tale. Then I toiled in the fields to earn my keep. I learned a little of husbandry and herding flocks, but I never stayed very long in any settlement. Everywhere I went the people of the tribes dwelling between the forest and the steppe told of other countries farther west, paradises, where riches were and wealth was won. I wandered in search of them."

The Kalevide listened, spellbound; he, too, had lost much. The Alevide drew a deep breath.

"I don't know if you will understand this, but it is important. The burning of my village was the victory of war, which was my father's trade, but it was only the final phase of a process that began when he first came into the country. Before that the people dwelt comfortably in the deep forest, and knew the trees to be their friends, but when my father settled there at the foot of the mountain and began to build, they quickly left their woodland haunts and crowded into the hamlets that sprang up around his estate. He gave them gifts, goods they grew to want and then to need, and in return they worked for him and did his will. He gave them tools and taught them to till and toil while he reaped the service of their lives.

"My father committed many crimes, but this, I think, was the worst. He destroyed the people. The fire only finished it. Through his efforts their way of life disappeared. Only the very old ones remember how to dwell alone among the wild trees; the rest have forsaken their lore for a life of ease. They became dependent when they could have been free.

"They never saw it, of course. They thought Alev was their benefactor because he brought them the new ways, the world's ways. They believed in him, so when he died, naturally they turned to me, his son, to lead them and protect them. A lot of protection I gave. The Riders came and all I could do was tell them to flee, as I fled, and pray they could survive in the great forest that once had been their friend.

"Somehow, though, I mean to make up for what my father did to them. Somewhere I'll find a land where they can live safe lives and feel secure. They're dispersed now, but I know they're waiting for me to return, bringing bounty, even as Alev did when he first came. I might be gone for years, but they'll tell tales and sing songs and create legends to keep the memory alive, and I do not want to disappoint them. It's too late to reclaim their forest life, I know, but I will find a place somewhere, in the uttermost west if necessary, where they may settle and know peace and not have to fear the horror of the horsemen ever again."

"Viru is safe," the Kalevide said simply. He did not understand much of the stranger's story, but he was touched by his loss and by his longing.

"Is it?" said the Alevide. "I hope so, for your sake, but I fear. I fear for myself, and for the world. In my wandering west I often walked in the wake of pillage and plunder. The Riders of the Golden Khan are marching across the steppes. I saw their stallions; I heard their baggage wains; I felt the earth tremble at their advance. Already they rule all the eastern lands; how long before they overrun the west?"

"They won't come this far."

"You think not? I hope not, for if they do, I fear there is no haven anywhere. My goodness, you do bring out the melancholy in a man. That's not usually my way. You don't have any food with you, do you? I'm quite hungry."

"No." The Kalevide had long since lost his wallet, along with his boots. It would have been empty anyway.

"Ah, well, we'll have to find something, that's all."

Foraging together along the edge of the forest, they discovered the crisp curled sprouts of bracken breaking through the sleeping sod. Thrushes' eggs rested in tufts of grass. Along the stream, the Kalevide pried sticky roots of marsh arum loose with his sword. The Alevide caught crayfish in the pools. They warmed more to each other's company and shared their meager treasures. The Kalevide boasted of the bounty of Viru, beyond the forest, where he was king.

"Were you always alone?" he asked later after they had eaten.

The Alevide hesitated. "No," he said slowly. "No, I had a companion, a boy, my cup-bearer. I found him the morning after the fire standing at the edge of the wood, staring at the embers of the last building burned, spellbound by the spectacle. He looked like a calf caught outside the pen at slaughtertime. I called him my cup-bearer to give him status in the world. He was my friend.''

"Where is he now? What happened to him?"

For a long while the Alevide would not answer. He stared at the ground sunk in a pool of recollection. It took a concerted act of will to pull himself out again.

"Suppose I tell you the tale of this hat and the holes, and how I hid a hoard of silver within its brim," he said glibly. The Kalevide could not see how that answered his question about the cup-bearer, but he could accept anything the other chose to tell. He enjoyed listening to stories.

"I told you how we crossed mountains and hills, plains and prairies, rivers and streams," the Alevide began, "and how we left the grasslands for the forest. Beyond the forest, as we wandered westward, we, the cup-bearer and myself, came upon a vast, unbounded swamp, the most foul, fetid, noxious, noisome marsh and mire I have ever seen in all my days, a sewer seeping through the very walls between this world and the deadly, dreadful world under earth.

"Vapors rose out of scum-covered sinks. Fog and mist writhed out of the slough to hang like palls in stagnant air. It was a horrid land, decayed, dead. No birds flew there, no ducks paddled on the ponds, no herons stood vigil in the reeds. No choirs of frogs sang in chorus to the spring. Snakes slipped silently through mossy shadows; vipers and adders undulated in black pools. It was, in short, this very swamp you see before you.

"The boy and I skirted around it as best we could. Once I climbed a small hill to scout a drier path. Two men were standing in the middle of the stream below me, arguing about something, pointing, gesturing, jabbering away in the most awful, uncouth language I have ever heard. Nor had I ever seen men like these. They had thick, tangled, light-colored hair caked with dung-yellow mud, long, straight noses, eyes too pale to see. They were wearing short shirts of some coarse animal hair and were naked below the waist.''

"Demons! Someday I'm going to rid this land of all of them and their kind.''

"That may be, but they looked more like mortal men to me, though who can say for sure? I offered to settle their dispute for them. The boy, my cup-bearer, thought I was crazy, but I saw a chance to make a little silver, perhaps, and to promote peace. Their argument seemed to be about property lines.''

"How could you tell, if you couldn't understand their language?"

"Well, yes, it was difficult. We pantomimed a good bit. I told them I would survey the swamp for them while they went to fetch my fee. It was all a sham, of course. I didn't have the least idea how the lines were supposed to run, or even what the quarrel was really about, but it didn't seem to matter. What was important, I thought, was that a verdict be rendered, not what it was, so long as it was accepted. So I put on an elaborate display of learning, performing sacred rituals, chanting songs of power, summoning wisdom from the sky. I danced. I measured distances between landmarks, I laid out lines up and down the marsh, I set flags at all the corners, anything to make the marshmen think I knew what I was doing. They watched a while, then left, I thought to bring me the silver I'd requested for my fee, but they never returned.

"We kept working, the boy and I, through the twilight, in case they did come back, when suddenly a water demon emerged from the stream. It rose like the fog itself, solidified. It's gray hair blended into the damp grayness of the air and water. His face and body were gray, too, and he was wearing a gray smock and white silk apron. But he seemed real enough.

"The demon asked what we were doing. He could speak our tongue, a little. So long as the gray one was there I thought it very unlikely the two brothers, if they were brothers, would return, so I decided to see what I could get out of this one. I told him we were damming the river to put in a lake, develop it for cabin sites, drain the marsh, set up farms. It was the first thing I could think of; I thought I might sell him a lot or two.

"The demon became very upset, however, insisted he liked the swamp the way it was, and why didn't we go away. So I suggested, very subtly of course, that we might take our project elsewhere if he would pay us a little something for our trouble. He promised to fill my hat with silver, which seemed fair. I told him we had a proverb in my homeland:

'By the horns the ox we wrestle,
     by his word the man is bound.'

and so bound the demon to return with sufficient money in the morning."

"I once wrestled an ox," said the Kalevide. "A moor ox, actually, an aurochs, which is bigger. I killed it."

"Is that so? Well, that night the cup-bearer and I dug a deep

[146]

pit near the edge of the swamp. We made it wide at the bottom, very narrow at the top, then I cut these slits in my hat and fit it into the mouth of the hole. When the demon found us next morning he poured an apron full of silver coins, one by one, into the hat. You should have seen his look when they disappeared. He went back for a second and third load, but still couldn't fill it. He poured chests and purses, pouches and pockets full of silver into my hat. and when it remained empty, he finally begged for more time. To raise some more money, I suppose. Naturally, I refused. He tried to persuade me to accompany him to his home to help him bring up more silver, but I knew it for a trick to get me away from my hat.

"Unfortunately, the boy piped up and volunteered to go in my place, and I couldn't stop him. He had come with me in search of adventure, he said, and this was his best chance, to walk where no man of earth had ever walked before. When the demon returned to the water, my cup-bearer followed him.

"After a while, when he did not return, I dug out my silver, a fair lot, I might say, removed it to a hiding place, and set out westward again, hoping to find a happier land. And so I met you."

The Kalevide frowned. At the beginning of the story he had been inclined to laugh at the foolishness of the demon and the audacity of the Alevide, although he could not follow all the twists and turns of his plan. By the end of the tale, however, he was less sure of the rightness of it.

"What happened to the boy, your cup-bearer?"

"I don't know. He disappeared under the water, as I said."

"And you let him go?"

"What could I do? He wanted to go. He'll make it back, I'm sure. I've taught him to be tricky. If he doesn't, well, there's nothing I can do, is there?"

"You didn't wait for him, though."

"I couldn't very well, could I? Who knows what beings dwell in the mire? The illusion of wizardry would not protect me long from anyone unfriendly."

"No, but you shouldn't have abandoned him. Friends don't abandon their friends, not in any stories I know."

"It is done. This is not a child's fable."

"You shouldn't have let him go in the first place."

"How else could I have got rid of the water demon without arousing his suspicion?"

The Kalevide shook his head. It was too much for him. "I don't know," he said.

15   The boy followed the ancient demon across an endless plain, barren and void, without features to mark one place from another. Everywhere was the same, colored the same drab gray, without variation or relief. Gray light suffused the atmosphere like fog, yet less substantial than mist, as though the air could not endure the intensity of clear light or complete dark. No sun or moon or stars shone here, nor ever would in this world beneath the living world; no clouds covered the sky, for even clouds will show some gradation of shade, stripes and swirls in a darker gray. Here nothing eased the sense of emptiness.

The air hung lifeless and still. No sounds disturbed the silence. The boy deliberately scuffed his boots in the dry, gray dust, hoping to hear even a whisper but there was none. He tried to call to the demon, to beg him to slow his pace a little, but the words died stillborn in his mouth; they failed and fell, a muffled sob, like an infant born but deprived of breath. The air was too thin to sustain even the weight of sound, and yet it sustained his mortal life.

The world of underearth was without time. The farther the boy ventured from the lands he knew, the less he felt a part of the patterns and rhythms of living men. He passed over the plain without knowing how long he had traveled or how far. His only point of reference was the ghostly demon ever ahead of him, and that moving point referred him to nothing he could understand.

With a growing dread he recalled stories the old ones of his village had told him long ago of children who were stolen by dwarves and carried underground, of youths in search of adventure who went willingly beneath the earth to play with golden toys, of heroes who delved the deep underworld to rescue maidens doomed to be prisoners of dark princes. In all the songs and tales, when the child or youth or hero returned to his homeland, he discovered his world had spun through untold years in the short time he spent underground. Was that what was happening to him? When he volunteered to accompany the demon to his lair, had he put himself into such a story? When he came out of this adventure, would he find ages had elapsed in his absence? Would the Alevide, his only friend, be gone?

The old demon drifted across the gray earth like a wraith,

turning neither left nor right, nor ever looking back to see that the cup-bearer followed. In the distance a meager light glimmered, a thin orange beam in the vast desert waste, cheerless and cold, but a break in the endless, empty gray. The boy ran toward it, to discover a lamppost holding a small iron pot in which oil was burning. Farther on there was another lamp, and another. They were placed randomly on the open plain and marked no meaningful road.

Beyond the lamps the land gradually changed. At first it was only a slight rise and dip in otherwise level ground. Then a tree appeared, then a small clump of grass. Here there was a tiny rivulet, there a single boulder pushing out of barren soil. The world slowly assumed the shape of a normal world where life could grow. Coming out of that nether space lying between his earth and the spirit's, the cup-bearer lost a little of the fear that had come over him. Nevertheless, everything around him was strange. The grass was not quite like the grass he had known in his life, nor were the trees. The differences were small and indescribable, but something had changed the look of each blade, each leaf and twig, something in the shape or color, something unnameable, something wrong. The birds in the bushes were like no birds he knew. The small animals that skittered away in the brush had never run beneath the open sun. Every creature, every plant was a travesty, a misshapen image of those that lived on earth, even as the demon was a mockery of man.

Silence still reigned everywhere. The narrow stream they were following tumbled soundlessly over its rocky bed. Its water bubbled and eddied around polished stones, but with no rippling song. No wind rustled in the branches or whispered in the grass. A gray-brown-coated thrush-like bird perched on a stunted tree arched its neck to sing, but no thrilling warble poured from its breast. A bullock in a browsing herd of cattle raised its horned head to low, but no bellow welled from its throbbing throat. The boy tried again to speak to his guide, and again words failed him. Even the flies and mosquitoes swarmed noiselessly.

Leaving the desolate plain far behind, the demon led the cup-bearer across a series of small hills and into a wide valley where horses grazed. After a time without meaning, they came to a gate set in the middle of the pasture. It marked no boundary. No fence or wall stretched from either side of it. There was no other structure anywhere on the meadow, only the simple gate of post and poles, but the demon halted, nonetheless, carefully unlatched the gate, swung it open and stepped through. The boy followed quickly, before he could be shut out.

The land on the other side looked the same as the land they had left. The grasses were the same, there was the same dreary shrubbery, the horses looked exactly like the others, but there was a profound difference, which astounded the boy and made him rejoice.

They were crossing a wide quagmire where more horses were feeding when he first noticed the change. The ground was soft, heavily trampled into a bed of mud by the ponies' hooves. Earth which should have been rich and black remained gray clay smelling of sulphur, but there were sounds when the horses stepped. All at once the boy could hear the delicious squelch of mud sucking hoof. He could hear the animals' chewing. He could hear the chuckling laughter of the demon just in front of him. He could hear his own heart beating.

"Djuva mugu jar," the old one said in his own language, then seeing the befuddlement on the boy's face, he translated awkwardly. "Home is being near. I hearing sounds now of porridge cooking being in kitchen. Oh, ho. Family is all waiting for us. Supper eating soon. You are coming, following me more please. Zakhad muz. We hurrying now."

The boy could not reply.

Looking down on the demon's farm from a ridge, it looked at first glance like any other farm, but even as the cup-bearer gazed at it, it seemed to change. It, too, was a mockery of what should have been. The house became a puzzle of wings and sections, some straight and narrow, some curved, with gables and arches, galleries and vaults, courts and quadrangles, high pointed roofs, peculiar domes. Doors opened everywhere, and nowhere, without regard for passageways or walls. It was a building built for a nightmare.

They passed over a low wooden fence, past an empty kennel, and so came into the demon's keep. The boy gazed in amazement at the maze of outbuildings and sheds, which seemed to spring out of the earth, displacing others, piling one atop another without plan or purpose. The more he tried to understand their arrangement, the more complicated it became. Nevertheless, the demon threaded his way through the twists and turns without hesitation. Suddenly he stepped through an invisible door jerking the boy in after him. Just as the door closed, the cup-bearer thought he saw two men, humans, standing guard outside. They were in chains.

Marching along one hallway after another, crossing empty courtyards, climbing stairs, turning down countless corridors divided by unnumbered doors, the boy's head whirled. The hall seemed larger and more confused inside than it had outdoors. Never in his life had he seen such a building, and he prayed he would never see a second. As they wound their way upstairs and down, out one door, in another, around a tower, into a cellar, out again, he began to fear he would never come out alive.

"Where do you keep your silver?" he shouted to the demon. The silver was, after all, his reason for being there.

"No silver. Not being any silver, not now. Thinking only of supper. That good. You are liking supper. Then we are talking of silver some."

As if it did not matter where they were, the demon opened one of the thousand doors and pushed the cup-bearer inside.

"You eating now. Having supper with sons of mine. Good boys, oh, ho."

It was a large, windowless room, with bare gray walls and no comfortable furnishings, only a few rough-hewn chairs scattered, or thrown, about on the floor. In the middle of the room, a long wooden table was set for an elaborate feast, as if the richness of the fare might make up for the poverty of the room. The demon's three sons sat on one of the benches built into the table. They all looked alike, with the same lank, gray hair, the same colorless skin, the same drab clothes, like smaller copies of their father.

"You are staying here," the elder demon told the cup-bearer. "I going seeing my only mother," he muttered as much to himself as to the boy as he closed the door. If he were to fulfill his oath to the Alevide, he must somehow persuade the old bitch, his mother, to help him and that, he feared, would be very difficult. Perhaps he could give her the boy in exchange for the silver he would need.

As soon as their father was gone, the three young demons leaped for the cup-bearer. They pulled and pushed at him; they pinched his arms and ribs and thighs. They grabbed at his hair and bit his ears, all the while twittering and squealing in their own outlandish tongue. He tried to push them off, but they squirmed around too much. They were too quick and too strong. They ducked under his hands and dodged his kicking feet then came at him again from behind or below.

"Dju zbaljizja gar muzz," they screamed.

"Un zubhanazu muzu ljozu," they shrieked.

They were working themselves into a frenzy. One forced himself under the boy and began tickling him. The others poked and prodded. Although it was all in play and they meant no harm, the cup-bearer cringed at their affection.

When they saw he was not going to join their fun, the young

demons allowed him to sit on one of the benches while they sat on the one opposite. With a great clatter, they pushed plates and platters in front of him, dishes wrought of gold and silver and copper. The cup-bearer supposed they were stolen from the burial mounds of men, robbed from the barrows of kings. Here was wealth at last, he thought, and with a little luck he could win himself some, if with a little more luck he managed to escape.

The demon's sons poured a viscous liquid into his cup, a silver goblet set with amber, jade, and gems such as he had never seen. They scooped some jellied meat into his gilded plate and ladled gray, cold porridge into his copper bowl. Although the boy was truly hungry—he could not even remember when he had last eaten—when he contemplated the food set before him, his belly rose in anguish. Was it true, he wondered, that demons ate the flesh of men? Better not to know, he decided as with a shudder he reached for a golden knife.

Blue sparks leaped along its blade. The children tittered and whispered to each other as he jerked his hand back in surprise. He reached again, now for the plate itself, but flames spread over all the dishes. Tongues of blue fire leaped from the beakers; more flames played around the edges of the platters. Although it was a cool fire which consumed nothing, the boy could not bring himself to test it to see if it would burn him. Whenever he withdrew his hand, the flames subsided; when he reached out again, they shot up. He could not bear to touch that blue fire. Tears stood out in his eyes. In terror, he sat utterly still and stared at the useless feast that had tempted him bitterly.

"Zhurjada khi zjem," whispered one of the demons.

"Zjus jar bazjus," said his brother.

"Zhurjada, zjus berjus."

"Zjus drabhaz."

"Zjus jar ljubu bhasu."

One reached across the table and took a handful of the boy's porridge and crammed it into his own mouth. The others laughed.

"Khubak zjus nje azdjaz?"

"Zjus nje ulkhunjuz."

"Bhad zjus jar dajb djabz."

"Zhurezum zjem duvkhe."

"Azdju!" They cried at him all together. The boy cowered where he sat.

At once, all three grabbed across the table to steal the rest of the meat and drink. Snatching the gray, fatty flesh off his plate, they tore it to pieces before they finished with it. One spilled the boy's cup over the table. A burst of flame shot up from the liquid and raced toward him, only to flicker out just before reaching his body.

The cup-bearer held himself very still, fighting to control his fear. He did not look at his tormentors, not even when they reached over to fondle him, nor did he listen to their foolish talk, which might have been gibberish for all he knew. He knew, nevertheless, they were talking about him, laughing at him, and likely planning more devilment, and he could do nothing about it. What had possessed him to undertake this venture, he wondered. The lure of silver and lust for adventure were certainly glamorous in prospect, but even if he gained the greatest glory, it could not compensate for the humiliation and horror he suffered. The Alevide must have known, he thought; why, then, did he let him go?

"Maz zabljizum duljuz bhujrukh!" the demons screamed in his ear.

They had left their seats and were racing around the room. One stood on the table to dance; the others started a hideous chant. Suddenly the cup-bearer felt one of them pawing at his legs under the bench. He was fumbling with the thongs of his boots; cold hands touched his skin beneath his breeches. It was cruel. The creature scratched and pinched his calf and reached higher up his leg. The boy writhed away to escape, but the other two gripped him from behind and held him fast.

He squirmed and twisted desperately, and for once their hold broke. He fell over backwards onto the floor. All three pounced on him simultaneously. They pressed him down beneath their sprawling bodies, and he felt their wet mouths on his skin. They were sucking him like leeches. He lurched to his feet, but they clung fast. One, gripping him around the neck, hung down his back. Another had somehow caught himself beneath his arm. The third was fastened upside down to his breast, his feet locked around his chest and shoulders, his face between his thighs. Awkwardly, the boy staggered around the room. The demons had no weight, but he could not shake them off.

Eventually, they let go of their own accord. He prayed they were done, but they bounced back and began pulling him this way and that, tossing him back and forth until he fairly careened around the chamber. They whirled him across the width of the room, then tossed him up to the ceiling, catching him in their arms as he came down. Three times they tossed him up. The third time they let him land on the hard stone floor.

Groaning miserably, the boy staggered up and begged them to

leave him alone. Although they could not understand his words, the note of pain in them was universal. They led him to the bench to rest and regain his breath. His body ached from the fall; his skin itched and burned where they had scratched him. He shuddered at the memory of their touch. He had to escape; it was the only thing he knew.

What would the Alevide do if he were here, he asked himself. He wouldn't be here, he replied bitterly. Well then?

The cup-bearer looked around the room for a way out. There were no windows, only the door, and the demons were sitting on the floor between him and it. Their mouths hung open, hungry. Gaping stupidly, they began to rub themselves obscenely beneath their smocks.

The Alevide always said be tricky, he reminded himself. Imagining he were the Alevide, the boy rose and held up his hands in a sign of power. The demons licked their lips with cold gray tongues and wiped their noses. Wondering what he was doing himself, the cup-bearer pulled a length of string out of his pouch. The Alevide had always told him to carry string. Stepping to the wall away from the door, in order not to arouse suspicion, he set about measuring the length and breadth of the room, using the string for a unit length. The demons watched curiously, supposing this were a new sort of play, as it was. From time to time the boy wrote figures on the floor with a stub of charcoal he also found in his pouch. The marks were meaningless, but he trusted the demons would not know that and would take them for inscriptions of deep lore. How easy it was, he realized, to pass nonsense off as sense to the unwitting.

The first wall measured six-and-a-half cord-lengths long and three high. The latter was only an estimate, since he could not quite reach the ceiling, even by standing on one of the chairs. Moreover, one end of the room seemed higher than the other, and not quite the same from side to side. Estimate or not, the cup-bearer was satisfied with the measurement; it gave him a figure to work with.

The back wall was somewhat less than four cords wide, again of variable height. The third wall was slightly less than six cords long. He measured it twice, and then again to be sure there was no mistake, but it was true, the room was not rectangular. While he strode confidently about the chamber, standing, kneeling, marking off the distances, adding up his tallies, the demons watched with growing amusement; they remained crouched on their heels in the middle of the floor, well out of his way. When he moved from one wall to the next, first one and then another and finally the third turned with him, so that in the end each of the demons was facing in a different direction, and none faced the door.

The boy supposed the fourth wall would have measured less than four cords wide, but he never stopped to check. When he reached the door, he bolted. Dropping string and charcoal, wrenching the unlocked door open, he ran headlong down the outside corridor without ever looking back. He turned a corner, fled down another hallway, and ducked into the first closet he saw, only to flee again as soon as he realized it offered no sure hiding place. Desperately, he doubled back, running up some stairs, down some others, through another part of the tangled building.

Pursuit, he knew, could not be far behind. Often he was sure he heard loud shouts behind him in one of the nearby passages. At other times there was only the soft slapping of naked feet on the boards as a single searcher advanced unerringly. Demons darted along the corridors and hallways, looking for him in every room of the confused house. Now and then he would catch a glimpse of them across a courtyard or through a window. They ran in one direction, he ran in the other, yet he never escaped them for long. Sometimes, when they were very close, he would crouch in a cupboard or closet or tiny vault, holding his breath till they passed by, but there was no rest. No place gave hiding he could trust, even in the small, dark rooms, he felt exposed and vulnerable. What if they should look in? Terrorized by the thought, he would duck out of his hole and dash back the way he had come, knowing they would soon be after him.

In one corner after another in countless chambers he hid, only to flee again each time he heard the demons near. Always he kept ahead of them, but never far ahead. That was a part of his nightmare. He ran in panic, without a plan, until he was exhausted and lost in the maze. He could not count the turnings he made, nor the stairs he climbed, nor the doors he passed, nor the rooms where he paused. His pursuers were always there, always close to him, running as he ran, yet never quite catching up. Always they were one room behind, peering into it, then rushing off on a false trail even as he slipped out and doubled back, but always their paths converged again. They were close on his heels. He dived into a hidden nook, or climbed a chimney. They passed by. For a moment. Again he ran. He crossed and recrossed his path. He sped down corridors and galleries, ducked through arches and vaults, climbed over half-walls and barricades, clattered down stairs while the demons raced up the opposite flights.

The cup-bearer now felt inextricably caught in the web of his own fearful fantasy.

He knew he was lost. Inside that crazy building there was no chance of his finding his way out again. He could stay there forever, dodging around, eluding capture, remaining always one step ahead of the fiends. But what was the point, if he never got out again? He was weary now and ready to yield. Let them take him, he thought, but he could not make himself stop running. He could not make himself give in. On and on and on. There was no release.

He slipped into a cupboard for a moment. Gasping for breath, then afraid to breathe, he listened intently for any sound. Once again he heard the unmistakable padding of the single pursuer who did not run with the others. He was in the next room now; only one wall separated them. The boy immediately ducked out of the cupboard and raced down yet another long, dark, sloping hallway. It offered no protection; there were no connecting passages here, no side rooms. If his secret foe found him there, he was trapped, and he would welcome it. Yet he ran. He could not help himself. Surely the enemy was behind him. He did not dare to look. He ran.

At the end of the hall stood one small door. The cup-bearer wrenched it open and flung himself through, fully expecting to find himself at last in a closed room with no escape, the room where he would die.

Instead he fell into daylight, such daylight as there was in the demon's realm. Outside, the chase was the same, madly scrambling through a maze of paths and alleys, merely trying to find a way around the house, constantly striving to elude capture. Once, by surprise, he found himself face to face with two men chained to a wall.

"Pass to the right," one said.

"Avoid danger," said the other.

No sooner had they spoken than the house turned on its own legs and the boy was lost and alone again. Three small dogs, a bitch and two puppies, were trotting down the path toward him; each had a linen cloth around its neck and a willow whisk in its teeth. The queen of Pōrgu, the dog of hell, the demon's old mother, and the mother of more, was returning from the bathhouse with two of her sons. The cup-bearer, desperate to avoid being seen, followed the guards' advice and ducked down a narrow walkway to his right.

Where it crossed another he turned again to the right, recklessly charging down the passage. He turned again, to avoid

[156]

danger. The high walls of disordered structures leaned precariously over his head. For once he felt protected in that crazy array. Pursuit seemed far away; no sounds of the chase found their way through the convolutions of the maze. He allowed himself to walk.

Coming upon a tiered wall of wood and stone, he mounted the steps of a broken stile and so left the domain of torment behind. In the open and exposed to view, he ran once more, but now he knew it did not matter where he ran. He was so completely lost he had lost all hope of finding the path which had brought him into this land. He ran, wanting no more than to leave the castle of madness behind. He raced across a meadow and into the far uplands where he had never been. There were no horse pastures here, no grazing fields, no line of hills like those he had crossed before, only unkempt gardens of onions and turnips. He stubbed his toe on the wooden stems of parsnips unharvested for years.

After an unmeasured time, after crossing uncounted fields, he came to a solitary gate set in the middle of a wide valley. Knowing it was impossible, he knew it was the same gate he had passed when entering this realm with the demon. He had come by a different route, he had come to a different field, but the gate was surely the same, as if it were the focus of every direction in the underworld.

"This is madness," he cried to himself even as he stopped, carefully unlatched the gate, stepped through, and closed it behind him.

Beyond the gate he was engulfed once again in the silence of the land. The boy shouted out all his pain and rage, knowing he could not be heard, and so released much of the terror which had grown in him and gnawed in his bowels. A strong man may go wherever he will, like the birds; an ordinary person must endure thousands of fears.

Again he lost his sense of time in that gray-shrouded world. He went out of the lands where the herd-beasts grazed, beyond the eerie moors and meadows cloaked in their awful stillness. The trees became scarce once more, the bushes rare. A solitary bird, too maimed to fly, hopped ahead of him then turned aside. Once more he was the only thing alive. He entered the gray plain that was without feature, without hope, but also without harm.

Some time later, though whether it was much later or not he could not say, the boy came to the mouth of the tunnel he knew would lead him to the marsh in the upper world where he had left the Alevide. How, after drifting aimlessly over that unmarked plain without a guide, he came to that very tunnel was as great a mystery as how he found the lonely gate in the meadow. The boy did not care; he was too relieved by the thought that he would soon see the living earth again. The last of his fears slipped away. He thought of the tale he would have to tell his friend. True, he had won no silver, but he had had an adventure for all of that.

At the end of the tunnel he dived into the murky pool of gray water that was the exit from the underworld and the gateway to the world above. Streaks of light showed in the water where the living sun touched the stream. The boy pulled himself eagerly up toward the light.

"Master!" he cried sputtering in the open air. "My Alevide!" It was a joy just to hear sounds after the silence of the plain. The sky was overcast and gray, but it was the gray of clouds that could be blown away, not the colorless gloom of Pōrgu.

"Master," he cried again. "I have returned."

There was no answer. He was alone in the stillness of the swamp. The Alevide was gone, leaving behind only the wreckage of the pit they had dug to catch the demon's silver. The cup-bearer stared at it in dismay. Its message was clear enough. He was abandoned. His smile faded. The laugh that had lit his lips for a moment died. Nausea rose in his stomach. Behind him there was a faint ripple and a splash, an obscene laugh. The boy turned to see the ancient water demon emerging from the stream and coming toward him.

16   "What will you do now?" the Kalevide asked the Alevide.

"As I told you, I'm searching for my fortune. I'm looking for a place that's comfortable and safe, where my people can live in peace. I will keep on until I find it."

The Kalevide clasped his knees and rocked back and forth on the ground. An idea was ripening in his mind, but it was a difficult birth.

"Bring them to Viru," he blurted. "The forests here are rich and there's room enough for everyone."

"Well, that's an offer, isn't it? I have to be sure the land is secure, though. I owe my people a life without fear. I don't mind a demon or two, they're easily outwitted, but I will not have them suffer the pillage of the Khan's riders ever again."

"There's nothing like that here. I'll make you my land steward." That was what he wanted to say. The words came out of his mouth like a rush of water breaking through a dam. Here was the answer to so many worries burdening his mind.

The Alevide looked at him with a glint of amusement.

"I mean it. You'll be governor of all my lands. Viru is a good country, as good as many, better than most. Someday it will be greater than all. You say you're looking for your fortune. Here you can make your own. You know the ways of farming; you know how to plough, you said . . ."

"Yes," the Alevide said cautiously. He thought the Kalevide was mad.

". . . and you know how to keep sheep and cattle. You can herd horses."

"Yes."

"Then you must come with me and be my steward. Say you will. I have inherited everything that was my father's. My brothers have gone and there is no one else. I need someone to oversee the farms of Viru, someone who will guide the villagers and tell them what to do, see to the tilling and sowing and reaping and all that, you know, and make sure the fields are ploughed. I need someone who will breed my animals and build my herds. This is how Viru will achieve the greatness it deserves. It's more important to me than anything else. I want the glory my father foresaw. I want herds of horses. I need a man who will get them for me. Say you'll be the one."

The son of Alev searched the Kalevide's face for signs of trickery, but there were none, not a trace of guile. The king of Viru was incapable of deceit.

"When I first saw you lying there, unconscious and covered with blood, I thought you were dead," he said slowly. "I said to myself, 'Here a people has lost its king,' and I asked myself why. But you were not dead. You lived. You lived to give away your kingship. Again I must ask why."

Now it was the Kalevide's turn to smile. "I'm not giving anything away. I shall still be king. Once, it is true, I thought I had to renounce my father's inheritance, but I see now that I cannot. It isn't permitted me. I must keep Kalev's kingdom as he wished. You'll only be my steward, the manager of my lands. You will see to the building, the fencing, the ploughing, the reaping, the milking, and the herding, all that is required for the country to thrive and to hold back the wild. But you will do it for me, in my name. I will still be ruler of Viru, and as long as I live, I will not resign that rule."

"You say you will be the ruler; yet you ask me to rule. The things you say I will do, these are the duties of a king. If his land is to prosper, how can he delegate them? Will the seeds sprout for another man? Will the cattle bear calves for any but the king? I don't know. But I do know that if I were king, I would not want someone else to stand between me and my land or between me and my people. I would trust no other man so well."

"There is something else I must do," the Kalevide said softly. As much as he trusted his new friend, he still could not tell him everything. What the Alevide had said was true, but he had no alternative. How could he say to another man that he was unprepared for the tasks described? How could he reveal the doubts that numbed him whenever he thought of his responsibilities? How could he confess such impotence? Instead, he said he needed to search for his mother.

He explained how she had been seized by the sorcerer and carried off to an unknown land and how she depended on him alone to save her. He recounted his adventure in the north, and how, although he had found no sign of his mother there, he had won his father's sword. He did not mention the smith's son or the maiden, Kaare.

"Now my brothers have left me," he concluded, "And I am the only one who can find her."

"It's not for me to say," said the Alevide, "but have you considered that she is probably dead by now?"

"No! I do not, I will not believe that. Not until I see her with my own eyes and know her fate for certain."

"Then I wish you good fortune in your quest."

"Then you will accept my offer?"

The Alevide hesitated no longer. He was used to winning by his wits and earning his way by devious craft, but when such easy fortune falls from the sky, who was he not to seize it quickly before it was lost forever in the all-absorbing earth?

"Yes, I will accept. I will be your steward and oversee your lands, provided my people may settle here if it is to their liking. That is all I ask."

"You have my word. The folk of Viru will embrace the tribe of Alev."

The Alevide laughed. "By his horns the ox we wrestle, by his word the man is bound."

"My word is good."

"I'm sure it is."

If the Alevide had any doubts, it was how he would reconcile this young man's dreams of glory and pride in a sword with his own vision of how a nation should be ruled, but he was confident, that, with one ruse or another, he could lead his new king in almost any direction.

They were walking toward the true forest when they saw two figures approaching from the marsh, where no man should have been. The Kalevide and the Alevide both froze. For the Alevide it was a habit he had learned in his trek across the steppes, when any man in the distance was likely to be his enemy. The Kalevide thought first of the sorcerer who had wrought him such woe. He had vanquished him once, only to have him return for further ill. Had he come back again? Were these his servants?

"It's my friend," the Alevide said quietly. A light flash that was both joy and sorrow fluttered in his heart. "It's the boy, my cup-bearer. I thought he was lost."

"Who is that outlandish fellow with him?"

"What, have you never seen a true water demon? This is the one I told you about, who was supposed to fill my hat with silver but broke his promise."

The boy and the demon walked slowly, unaware that they had been seen. To anyone watching, they looked like boon companions strolling arm in arm, but the boy was being held firmly by the demon and nearly dragged along. Every time he tripped or stumbled on the uneven, muddy ground along the stream, the old one tightened his hold, to keep him from falling, to keep him from running away.

When they were quite near, the Alevide slipped silently out of the trees and called a greeting to his friend. The boy looked away; he stepped instead closer to the golden-haired stranger he did not know, anyone to put between himself and the demon and the Alevide both.

"Where are you going?" the Kalevide asked.

"We have to have a contest," the boy said miserably. He still avoided the Alevide's eyes. "I have to wrestle with this old man."

"Wrestling, yes. Being good contest-sport. Boy and me," the demon bubbled.

The Kalevide looked at them both and laughed. "You'd better grow a little first, my lad. You're small for such serious games."

Putting the cup-bearer behind him, he told the water demon that if he wished to wrestle he would be glad to oblige. It was the king's perogative, he said. The demon agreed reluctantly, although this was not at all part of his plan. He had thought that if he could overcome the boy by strength where craft had failed, perhaps he could still recover his precious silver from the Alevide, or at least free himself of his promise. What wrestling this other person could accomplish was more than he could see.

"How did it go with you?" the Alevide asked the boy as the Kalevide led the demon off to find a site suitable for their match. The cup-bearer kept his distance and would not answer.

"Did you trick the old man out of any more money? How was the adventure?" Still no reply. "Was it bad for you?" he asked with concern. The boy shrugged. "Tell me about this wrestling. Why do you have to fight this creature who's so much bigger than you? Won't you answer me?"

How could he answer? What could he say? Could he tell his friend, who had deserted him, that he had fainted from fear when he had seen the demon rising out of the pool and coming toward him after his long flight from the underworld? Should he tell him of the terrible disappointment he had felt that moment when he had come out of the water, so filled with joy and excitement, only to find himself alone? He had escaped safely; he had expected to be met with rejoicing. Instead he had found himself abandoned by his only comrade in a horrible land. Were there words to express that hurt? Or should he tell him instead of the love and pain he had felt just now, seeing him again? Was it all something he should laugh off lightly? Should he pretend to be brave and bold, and boast of the demon's concern when he fainted? Could he describe how foolish he had felt when he came to with the sloppy old man bending over him, waving the flat of his hand like a fan and muttering uncouth words in his demon's tongue, prayers perhaps to the healing powers of his own people? How relieved the demon had been when he recovered; he had laughed out loud with his ugly demon's laugh and poked at him with his fat fingers while making rude jests.

"What you are running away so fast for?" he had said, struggling with the human speech. "Not helping me carrying silver money bags." There had never been any silver for him to carry, the boy was certain. "No, no, not helping with heavy sacks and boxes—oh-ho, oh-ho—" that awful laugh. "You burning yourself, maybe, or being bit by gadfly? Oh-ho, oh-ho. Being maybe stung by bumbling bee? You running away so fast, you, oh-ho, oh-ho." He had pinched and poked and tweaked till it hurt.

He didn't know why the demon had proposed the wrestling.

Perhaps it was part of his plan to cheer him up after he fainted, perhaps it was a plan to take him back to Põrgu. All the cup-bearer knew was that he had been caught unconscious and defenseless at the demon's feet and had had no choice but to agree. To the Alevide he said only that he had promised.

The Kalevide led the others a short way back along the swamp toward a hill overlooking the surrounding countryside. Since the demon was loath to walk far from water, they followed a small stream until they reached its source, a spring close to the crown of the hill. There they could gaze southward across the vast reach of the marshland, desolate, devoid of moving life. Here and there clusters of small, shrouded trees huddled together in common fear, and in their shadows silent pools of stagnant water slept beneath thick palls of moss. Beyond were only clumps of briar bushes and endless mats of marshgrass which concealed the swamp's quaking mire. As it stretched beyond their view, the wasted land became more and more void and gray; it took its color from the gloom of ever-clouded days until, in the far distance, swamp and sky merged into a single, joyless field. The demon looked fondly on his homeland; the men turned away.

In the other direction lay the darker mass of the deep forest, darker, yet less forbidding, for the fresh-leaved birch and alder sparkled amongst the near-black fir and pine. In the west the woods joined open downlands, where broom and roses flowered. In the east the trees were thicker; there, too, was the wide water of Lake Virts and, farther east, the silver shadow that was the great Lake Peipus on the border of Viru. The Kalevide declared that this hill was the place where they should wage their contest. It stood between two worlds.

While the Alevide and the cup-bearer found seats from which to watch in safety, the Kalevide and the demon tried to impress each other with feats of strength. They began by hurling stones. First the demon grasped a gigantic rock and hoisted it cumbrously to his waist. For more than an hour, it seemed, he stood thus, with the stone balanced precariously in his hands and against his belly while he staggered back and forth under its weight. At last he turned ten times around, gathering strength, and swung the rock up around his head. Then with a mighty shove he heaved it. The stone fell heavily, ten paces from the shore of Lake Virts, where it remains, a monument as large as a bathhouse.

The Kalevide did not listen to the demon's proud boasting about his strength. Choosing his own stone quickly, he hurled it away without a moment's pause. He did not need to strain or gather strength; his power was within him. Although his was smaller than the demon's stone, it flew much farther. Leaving his hands like a hawk, the rock rose and disappeared from view, although for a long while all four could hear the roaring of its flight, but eventually it fell to earth beside Lake Peipus, where anyone could have seen it who cared to look. The Kalevide smiled smugly at the demon as he wiped his hands on his trousers, and they prepared to wrestle.

Expecting them to come together with a rush, the Alevide braced himself for whatever dire thing must come when these two strong forces met. Would the power of their clash split the very hill where he sat? The cup-bearer stared at the Kalevide in open awe and admiration; he was very much relieved that he did not have to face the demon himself. That was all the two combatants did, however; they faced each other. A stream of sunlight shot through the clouds to light the Kalevide's golden hair with its divine glow. The shadow of the cloud crossed the demon, who was wishing he were in his own world, underearth, where his true strength dwelled and no sunlight fell.

They grimaced at each other and made faces to weaken the other with fright. For a while they stood rigid and stared. Then they strutted back and forth across the hilltop and stamped the earth in rage. It seemed a dreadful dance. After an hour, suddenly they charged together, and before anyone knew it had begun, the bout was over.

A spasm seized the Kalevide. His face twisted; his eyes stood out of his head. An unholy, obscene cry burst from his lips as he seized the demon by the neck and groin and lifted him off the earth. The weightless spirit came off the ground as lightly as a wisp of fog. With the roar still filling his mouth, the son of Kalev whirled once around and hurled the demon away, into the far swampland where he was spawned.

When the old one struck the ground, he rolled for seven leagues, ploughing a trench through the muddy earth, then slid down a barren mound until he caught finally among some dead bramble bushes. For six days he lay there, stunned and unable to move leg or limb, barely able to breathe or to raise his head or open an eye. After the seventh day, when the others had forgotten him, he sank quietly into the ever-engulfing ooze of the bog, and so vanished forever from the world of living men.

The Kalevide stood very still, amazed that the match was over so quickly, and that he had won. He was astonished that he had so easily overcome a member of the race which, like all his people, he had dreaded all his years. His body twitched slightly from the spell which had come over him so suddenly and as quickly gone, but he felt pleased and proud. The cup-bearer was gazing at him with complete devotion. The Alevide laughed as the Kalevide embraced them both. His sudden fit of strength, now released, had left him happier than he had felt for days. He hoped, by this unblemished victory, to win redemption.

Together they built a fire on the hilltop and laughed and sang and were merry through the waning day. The cup-bearer told the Kalevide the tale he could not tell the Alevide, of his adventure in the demon's kingdom. The Kalevide replied with a story of his own about his victory over the northern sorcerer. The Alevide, meanwhile, sat silently watching the patterns in the fire while the other two drew closer together. Though the sounds of their pride and pleasure rippled in his ears, he ignored them. His mind was too much awhirl with plans and schemes for the stewardship of Viru.

While the boy listened avidly, the Kalevide boasted of his defeat of the moor ox.

"What was that saying of yours?" he called to the Alevide. "You know, about the ox."

The Alevide smiled secretly. "This? 'By the horns the ox we wrestle; by his word the man is bound.' "

"By his neck the demon we wrestle," laughed the boy.

"And you see how true it is?" said the Alevide. "Look what has become of the demon who did not keep his promise to me."

"By his crotch the demon we grapple," giggled the boy.

"Is that why I beat him easily?" joked the Kalevide. "Because he would not keep his word? And all this time I thought it was my strength that defeated him."

He paused, however, and his smile faded. He spoke more seriously, "Suppose a man did not keep his promise; what would happen to him then? Suppose he promised to pay a certain price for something, but then didn't pay it—not because he didn't mean to pay, but just because he forgot?"

The Alevide looked at him through the firelight, but it was impossible for him to read what was on the other's mind. "It's not for me to say," he said with a shrug, "but I should think the man would not be lucky. He would not thrive if he left his debt unpaid." The Kalevide considered this but did not reply.

"Why do you ask? You're not thinking of breaking your pledge to me, are you? For then certainly you would lose your luck."

"No, no, it isn't that. But when you repeated your proverb just now, I was reminded of something I was supposed to do. I never paid the smith what I promised for this sword, that's all. I wanted it very badly, you see, and I swore to send him a great deal in return for it."

Briefly, he described his bargain with the smith. As he spoke, however, he often had to grope for words; he was unsure quite what he should say. There was so much he could not reveal to anyone. When the Alevide heard what had been promised for payment, he was astonished that anyone could own so much, and even more amazed that he would spend it all for a single sword.

"It was worth it to me," the Kalevide said simply. "And I would have paid even more. The sword was designed for my father, and it is no ordinary blade. It holds the very fate of Viru bound within its steel."

"Since you already have the sword, I don't see why you worry about the payment."

"But my promise."

"Oh, that. Well, if you really care, I suppose it's not too late to take the smith what you owe him. If you think you should. How long has it been? A few days? A week or two? It shouldn't matter much. Your luck won't have changed yet." The Kalevide was not convinced.

"Will you go? Now that you are my steward, you can deliver the goods to the smith in my name. He must be paid; I don't dare risk his curse."

"I will do what you tell me, of course, but I wonder that you don't want to take charge of this treasure yourself. It must be most of the wealth of Viru. Don't you want to deliver it yourself?"

The Kalevide was stretched out on the ground, away from the fire; now he turned his face away from the others as well. He could not say he feared the smith or that he could not face him again. To do so he would have to tell his tale of murder.

"I must search for my mother," he said deliberately. He spoke into the ground so that the others could hardly hear him. His eyes were closed.

The fire burned low and the darkness of the night enclosed the hill. There were no stars. The Alevide lay down opposite the Kalevide, and the cup-bearer lay between them, feeling quite small beside these two great men. All the excitement of the day now made him restless and unable to relax. Beside him the Alevide was very still, his breathing slow and peaceful, though he, too, was still awake, and would be for a long time absorbed in the deep calm of the night, and one with the forest and the sky. Fretfully, the boy twisted on the rocky ground and rolled a little, finally coming to rest against the Kalevide's back. He felt more secure next to this simple giant who was already fast asleep.

17 For a long while the Alevide pretended to be asleep. He even prayed to return to the untroubled peace of his dreams. It was better than confronting the man who was crouched across the clearing. The stranger was so well concealed in the shelter of an overhanging stone that if he had not moved slightly the Alevide might never have seen him at all. He watched suspiciously through half-shut eyes, wishing the man would go away. It was not polite to surprise a person before dawn. The Kalevide and the boy were still deep in sleep, however, and the stranger did not seem inclined to leave, so, he supposed, it was up to him to learn who he was and what he wanted. Why had he approached so secretly? What was he hiding from? Whom did he fear?

Even as the Alevide groaned, shrugged out of sleep, and sat up, the man did not move, but waited, watchful, unafraid, yet obviously wary and ready to strike quickly and without question. A long, slim knife was poised in his right hand; a crossbow, primed to fire, rested by his knee. He offered no greeting to the Alevide, but merely studied him coldly with fixed, blue eyes.

"If I had wanted to, I could have killed all three of you," the stranger said at last. His voice was clear, his tone neither threatening nor friendly.

The words were unsettling; the Alevide gazed back at the stranger. The man's suit was entirely of deerskin, his tunic fastened at the throat by a single clasp of bone, his only ornament. Thongs were tied around his ankles so his leggings would not catch on twigs or briars as he trod woodland paths in stealth. On his feet were soft leather shoes which would walk with a whisper. The stranger's brown hair was cropped close to his head; his small, black beard was neatly trimmed. All this the Alevide noted in a glance. He noted, too, the pack filled with provisions beside him. Since he was hungry, he smiled broadly, prepared to counter any threat with sly goodwill.

"And why would you be wanting to kill the three of us?" he

asked innocently. His eyes fastened on the piece of roasted meat in the man's left hand.

"I do not want to slay you," replied the stranger. "But there are others who do. There are always others. The world is filled with enemies. They are everywhere; you should be constantly on guard. But look at this camp: in the open, exposed to any attack." His words curled with derision. "You were wise to choose a hilltop; this site could be defended. But then you post no watch. One of you should have remained on guard, better two, while the other slept. If you were going to sleep, you should have hidden yourselves in these rocks; easier to protect; harder to be surprised. You should never have built so large a fire, nor left it to smolder. By day the smoke summons your foes; by night the coals reveal your location. How do you think I found you so easily? You were lucky I did, and not the others. I stood sentry for you; it is likely I saved your lives. Dangers are everywhere. You must always be vigilant."

The Alevide thought that staying awake all night, alert, on guard, without a friendly fire, was a cold, uncomfortable way to spend a night. This was no time to argue defensive strategy with a stranger, however. Instead he yawned.

"Did you just happen by?" he asked casually, "Or were you looking for us? Is there something you need? Or did you just come to share your food with us?"

"If you are the one they call the Kalevide, I have come with news for you. Dire news."

There was a stirring on the ground across the clearing as the other two woke up. The Kalevide stretched noisily.

"I am Kalev's son," he said thickly.

"Then I must tell you I bring news of war," said the stranger. "There is a war approaching Viru, and your country is ill-prepared for it. What are you staring at, boy?"

The cup-bearer was gaping at him, with wide eyes and open mouth.

"I'm hungry," he said shyly.

"Then eat." The man tossed him the slice of meat he was holding. The boy caught it with outstretched arms and pressed it silently into his mouth with both hands. The newcomer then settled back and dug in his pack for more for himself. He had delivered his message. The Alevide watched him anxiously.

"We have not eaten for days," he said at last. "We have no stores. All we had is lost."

"You have no stores? You came into this wilderness without provisions? That was very foolish." Though his words were

[168]

sharp and critical, nevertheless he drew two flat loaves of bread out of his pack and put them into the eager hands of the hungry men. "Even if you did lose your supplies, the wood abounds in beasts and birds which you could have trapped or shot for your meat. There is no excuse for hunger; you could have provided for yourselves." While he spoke, the stranger carefully wiped the blade of his knife, first with grass and then a linen rag. Then he began to hone it gently with a whetstone. Soon it gleamed like a needle of steel.

Neither the Kalevide nor the Alevide could answer. Their mouths were too full of crumbled bread. While they ate, the man spoke more of his mission and the duty that had brought him there. He addressed only the Kalevide, however, and ignored the other two completely. His message was for the king himself; the others were not important.

"The war is not yet in Viru," he said. "But it comes. Every day it comes closer. A well armed army of men and horse is at your borders. I have seen its head myself, as it marched the road along the coast between the forest and the sea. The war comes slowly, but with a weighty force.

"My scouts report that foreign knights are well established in the lands to the south, in Lati and Leedu. Already they march on Laane and may have touched western Harju. Soon, there can be no doubt, they will strike the heart of Viru itself. I cannot say accurately how strong this invader is. The troop I observed was merely an expeditionary party, the vanguard of a far greater army. I do not know how large the main force is, or even who they are, but they are more than you can believe, and they are bent on complete conquest."

The Alevide put his food aside. His languor was cast off; he was alert to every word. "What were these riders like?" he asked. "Have they ridden from the eastern lands? Are they mounted like the wind? Do they wear their hair in topknots that stream like the tails of their swift horses? Do they sear the very air with their shrill cries of war? Do they carry small, round wooden shields and wield curved sabers that can cut the sunlight?" Too well, he remembered such men; too often he had fled such savage horsemen in fear. Too great was his horror of the hordes that swept the plains like fire in the grasses.

"I do not know the men you describe," the stranger said thoughtfully. "Apparently more than one enemy is abroad. Sooner or later they must come together. The knights I saw were of another race, coming from the west. They ride their horses slowly, but with a ponderous tread. At a walk they are able to ride inexorably over anyone opposed to them; at a gallop they are the thunder itself. Even their horses are clad in heavy armor beneath their flowing draperies. The men bear lances and wield broadswords, not sabers. One blow could cut a man in two. Their long shields are emblazoned with a cross-like device, a sword, black, the color of dried blood. They march always in silence, without war cries or songs, only the heavy beating of a drum. You could not see their faces for the iron helmets they wore.''

"These are not the ones I know," replied the son of Alev.

"In this world there is war on every side."

"I saw them once in a dream," the Kalevide remarked.

"My men are well-trained, and eager to fight," the man went on, "but they do not have the strength to stand alone against such weight as this. Hence I have come to seek you. Our peoples are kindred, yours and mine, young son of Kalev. We must be allies in this struggle. The enemy that comes is a threat to us all; it will destroy our nation and our way of life, unless together we can mount a force sufficient to turn it back and defeat it. As soon as I saw the war ride into the land, I left my people in a place of safety, to watch and gather what intelligence they can, while I went to alert all the people of the countryside, to warn them of the danger so they would have time to prepare their defenses and muster their men-at-arms.

"Your folk, I must say, were confused by my message, and unprepared for any threat. When I asked to see their headman, they said he was somewhere in the southern reaches of the land, doing they knew not what. Fortunately, for me, your trail was easy to find and easier to follow. That is the cost of your lack of caution. Suppose I had been one of your enemies, what would have become of you then?''

The Kalevide shook his sword in the man's face. "I have this," he boasted. "You wouldn't have stood against it for long."

This man did not laugh. "You would never have had a chance to lift it. You would have been killed while you slept, unguarded, exposed. A crossbow bolt in the back, a knife across the throat; it would have been easy enough. I tell you this not to threaten you, but to impress you once more with the need for vigilance. That is a handsome blade, however. May I see it?" he asked with respect.

The Kalevide passed his treasure across to him. Pride and caution warred in his breast, and pride prevailed. He was pleased to have his sword admired, and the stranger seemed to mean no harm.

"Yes, a very handsome blade," said the other almost with awe. "Much finer than I imagined when I first saw it lying in the dirt beside you. Of northern craft, I see. I know the man who shaped it, and there is none more skilled, unless it be his sons. You should be very proud to own this." Delicately, he stroked the polished steel; he touched its edge with reverence. "I can sense its spirit. It must have a name, so you can speak with it and command it well."

"Not yet," the Kalevide said simply. "I wield it with the strength of my arm."

"I see. Nevertheless, it is a worthy blade. If you are worthy of it, you might be more formidable than I supposed. How will it fare, I wonder, against the invader's iron mail? We shall see, no doubt, and I believe it might prevail. Yes, it might prevail, if you have courage to stand firm yourself. Keep this sword by you always, young king. You shall need it when you meet your enemy. Your country's fortune may rest on this single edge."

"I know. It was my father's."

"Then how can you treat it so?"

"What do you mean?" The Kalevide looked at the stranger suspiciously. The man's tone was too caustic.

"Steel must be kept well-polished and honed, but see how soiled it is. There is blood on the blade that should have been wiped away days ago. Do you want your father's sword to rust? You must protect it from damp weather. Look, sand in the scabbard. Do you leave it lying around on the ground? Do you want to dull the edge? No weapon should be treated this way. If you want your sword to protect you, you must protect it as well. If you want it to serve you, you must treat it as your dearest friend. It lives, no less than you."

Before he could say more, the cup-bearer suddenly interrupted. "Who are you?" he cried. "Who are you to come here saying these things to the king?"

The man turned and stared at him coldly. "I have told you why I am here."

"Why should we believe you?" the Alevide said. "It might be a trick. Before we can weight the words, we must know who brings them."

"Who I am, and what brought me to Viru, is a long tale for telling."

"One can never be too cautious," mimicked the Alevide. "One must be ever vigilant."

"That is so. Then hear this: I am no spy, I am Sulev's son. I do not hide it. Sulev is dead, and I lead his clan now. We have been driven from our homes in Karjala in the north by forces we could not combat. It was not war and arms, such as now threaten Viru, but the power of sorcerers and wind-enchanters which was raised against us. Cold came, and hostile weather. The winters turned too harsh; the summers too brief, until we could no longer survive in our homeland. Such forces are changing the north into a wasteland and driving all mortal men away. Even the reindeer and bear have begun to move southward. How could we remain? Only the wizards, hidden in their enclaves, are not touched, but they would not help us. We were forced to flee.

"We traveled southward on sledges while snow lay on the ground. In Soome we searched for a place where we might settle, but we found nothing there but fens and mist-hidden valleys. And always the threat of more trouble hung over us. Not long ago, a few days, a week or two, no more, we built rafts and barges and crossed the arm of the sea. Thus we came into your country. We landed in the west, where there were few people, and thought we had found a new home—only to discover fresh threats confronting us.

"At least these are threats we can understand and combat. We could have fought an ordinary enemy in Karjala; no invader would have forced us from our homes. But what use were our arms against the powers that pursued us in the north? We had no defense but flight, so like cowards we fled. Our chanters could not withstand the winds propelled against us; our healers could not control the plagues. So, like the others, like the deer and bear, like the other tribes who have gone I know not where, we left our homes. We abandoned them to the sorcerers, the enchanters, and those who shape the deep forces of the world."

For a moment he paused in sad reflection. The Sulevide had been fond of his father's lands, with their wild, lonely fells and fog-shrouded forests and white-spilling streams more lively than any he had seen in this land. He was bitter at his exile.

"I hope that the evil that works in the north will remain there and not spread across the sea to this Viru of yours. I hope the sorcerers, once they have driven men away from Soome, will be content with what they have. I do not believe their malice is associated with the danger that threatens here. The knights of the sword come from the west, and are probably not in league with sorcerers. Nevertheless, there is an uneasiness that grows in the world." He turned to the Alevide. "You report another menace approaching from the east. There is danger on every side. Every-where is unsettled, and times troubled.''

He turned back to confront the king of Viru. ''Now you have heard the story of Sulev's son. You may believe it or not; it does not matter. For you it is not important. What is important is the enemy that is threatening your country and the lives of all your people. What will you do?''

It was the Alevide, however, who first spoke in the silence following the Sulevide's long narration. ''Since I was a small boy,'' he said lightly, ''I have heard songs sung—and sung them myself—of the sons of Kalev, Alev, and Sulev.'' He hummed:

> ''. . . the golden sword
> of Kalevide, the silver spear
> of Alevide, a crossbow
> of copper for Sulev's son.

But I never believed the songs were true, or that I would live to become a part of them.''

''This is no time for idle banter,'' the Sulevide said harshly. ''Mortal dangers are at your door. Are you still unable to believe that?'' He appealed to the son of Kalev. ''You are the king of Viru; this rests with you. What will you do?''

''What?'' The Kalevide had been dozing, daydreaming.

''What will you do for your people?''

In his dream he imagined himself at the head of his great army on a hill overlooking the sea. In his outstretched hand he held his sword, flashing in the sun, pointed at the sky. He saw himself clad in golden armor with a golden helm, inlaid with gems, ivory and jade, and carrying a shield of gold like the sun. He was mounted on a great war charger, its caparisons embroidered with gold and silver and pearls. All the maidens of the country stood around him, staring with admiration. At his back were the Alevide, with silver shield and spear, and the Sulevide, tall and straight, armed with his shining crossbow. For some reason the cup-bearer was nowhere in the dream. With all the vast hosts of Viru he, the Kalevide, would drive the invader into the sea. He would crush the enemy, then march forward to claim an empire in Kalev's name.

''What will you do?''

The question nagged. It dragged him back to the reality of the present time. The Kalevide blinked his eyes and realized every-one was watching him, waiting for an answer. Suddenly he felt very young. In the shock of awakening, he realized that the figure he had seen in his dream was not himself but Kalev. Once again he understood that he was not yet ready to step into his father's place. This was all coming too quickly. No sooner had he settled the problem of how to manage the farms, by appointing the Alevide his steward, than this new problem arose. He needed more time. What would he do? He asked it of himself. The truth was, he did not know, and he knew it.

"There is no time for delay," warned the Sulevide. "With every moment the danger advances. What will you do? Will you lead your armies yourself in these wars? Do you want me to deploy my people with yours or on a separate flank? Where will you engage the battle? When will you march? You must decide."

With an effort, the Kalevide controlled his voice so his words would carry confidence and command. He was learning to be a king. "You say that you are skilled in warfare and leading men in battle. I ask you then, son of Sulev, to be my captain. Will you serve me and be my war-master, as the Alevide is the steward and governor of my land? Muster my people; train them, teach them to fight. Do whatever you must do to defend Viru from this attack."

The Sulevide nodded. "I will do this. My men will instruct yours; we will teach them to be warriors."

"No!" cried the Alevide, "Do not allow this! It is an unholy charge you give him. Your folk are not fighters; they never have been. They are farmers and foresters, like my own, people of the earth and woods. You must let them live in peace."

"There can be no peace," said the son of Sulev. "There can never be peace. Not when armies march and war is a constant threat. Even now the war is at your threshold, and you are not armed or ready."

The Alevide ignored him; his eyes were fixed firmly on the Kalevide. "And what will you be doing while your men learn lives of death?" he asked rudely. "Will you stand in front of the army to meet the first of the enemy? That is the duty of a king. A leader cannot ask men to fight for him, fight and die, while he lives far away in comfort."

"When I am needed, I'll be there. I will lead my people. Never doubt that. But now I have some other things to do. Do you understand that?" He wanted their understanding; he needed that support. The Alevide did not answer. "The Sulevide can lead them now. If he acts in my name, and with my authority, it's the same as if I were there in person, isn't it?"

"It is not quite the same," said the Sulevide. "Men follow their king and expect him to stand in front and lead them himself. That cannot be denied. Nevertheless, for now it will suffice if I command. For a while there will only be skirmishing; the true war will come later.''

"You see? There is nothing to worry about. The Sulevide has control of everything. I trust him; he will do whatever is necessary.'' Then the Kalevide added boldly, "Of course, if the battle should spread, or your needs grow greater, you must tell me. Then I'll come at once with my sword, to lead Viru to victory.''

With his authority assured, the Sulevide prepared to depart immediately. Already he had stayed and talked too long. He knew, from what he had seen of the villages, that he had much to do before the war arrived.

While dividing his provisions with the others, he said, almost casually, "If I have complete authority in matters of the war, then I make my first command now in your name, my king,'' and, standing as straight as a fir tree and pointing at the Alevide, he declared, "This man must come with me.'' The cup-bearer laughed out loud.

"I? Whatever for?''

"I need an aide and messenger, and you will do. You have wit, if not discipline. You have a good eye and an able tongue. Your first task will be to carry my orders to my kinsmen where I left them. I myself go to muster all the people.''

"Don't be ridiculous!'' The Alevide was astounded. "I am no warrior. I have no place in any army. Marching, marching, off to war. Hear the horn, now the drum. No, thank you!''

"Every man will fight for his country. It is his duty.''

The son of Alev appealed to the Kalevide. "You can't send me off with him. I have other things to do. After all, I have your mission to attend to.''

"What mission?''

"Don't you remember? You asked me to deliver your shipment to the smith, to settle your debt with him. You don't want your luck to turn at a time like this, do you? Then there's the matter of getting the crops in order. The fields must be prepared, seed sowed, songs sung. You don't want anyone to go hungry, do you?''

"In time of war,'' the Sulevide said, "the defense of the nation has priority over every other thing.''

The Kalevide nodded; so it seemed to him. "Defense comes first. You can settle with the smith later, when you have done whatever the Sulevide wants. He'll understand. And then afterwards there will be lots of time for growing things. You go with him now, as he commands.''

The cup-bearer curled into a ball and laid his head on the Kalevide's knee.

"Be tricky," he giggled to his former friend.

For the first time the Alevide felt the flick of anger. Pointing at the boy, he said in exasperation, "If there must be a messenger of war, send this cub."

"No, I want him here with me," the Kalevide answered simply. "I may need him."

"Come," commanded the Sulevide. "There is no more time for delay." With that he checked his crossbow to see that it was ready to fire and scanned the forest toward the north to read the signs of wind and birds, to ensure that no enemy warrior lurked nearby. Then he marched bravely down the hill toward the wood and the path that would lead him to the heart of Viru once again.

The Alevide sighed with resignation. Nothing was left now but to follow unwillingly and let the time for his extrication come later. Tugging his cloak close around him, he glided after the Sulevide. Although he would do nothing to harm his new-found homeland, he vowed in his heart to make this master of war rue his command.

18

When the Alevide and the Sulevide were gone, and even the sounds of their passing had been swallowed by the forest, the Kalevide stretched out on the ground again to rest while the morning revolved overhead.

"What are you going to do now?" the cup-bearer asked playfully.

"I shall sleep a little to rebuild my strength. Then, I think, I will take up my search for my mother."

"I thought you said that defense was first, before everything else."

"So?"

"Then don't you think," the boy was teasing, "don't you think you should do something to provide for your people? Something to protect them in this trouble? You are their king."

"What else can I do?"

"Oh, I don't know. But I don't like to see you miss all the glory. Couldn't you fortify the villages or something? The cities in Vene have high walls around them. Couldn't you build something like that around your towns while the Sulevide takes the troops out to battle? Then if a real war is really going to come, as he says, your walls would save many lives, wouldn't they? You would be honored for that.''

Walls of defense! Fortification! Why hadn't he thought of this himself! It fit so well with his visions of Viru; it would be a lasting monument to his fame, like his father's cairn.

"Stone walls!" the Kalevide cried enthusiastically. "A city! Strong buildings of polished rock. Yes!"

"It will take a long time to build them out of stone."

"Will it? Oh I've never built anything before."

"You could build with wood now, then rebuild with stone later, when there is peace."

"I will need strong timber to make stout walls, as stout as I want. But I know where there are good trees for the taking. In Pihkva. It's all virgin forest there, never touched by a woodsman's axe. And I can look for Mother at the same time; I can hunt for clues while I gather lumber. What a smart boy you are! What an excellent idea!"

"Pihkva? Is it far?"

"East of here; the other side of Lake Peipus. You must have passed through it, or near it, before you entered the swamp."

The cup-bearer shuddered. "Why do we have to go so far away? Aren't there good trees right here? These oaks look strong enough to me."

The Kalevide was shocked. "These are the trees of Taara. It would be blasphemy to cut them."

"Can't you give this Taara the trees in Pihkva in trade for these? As the Alevide says, be tricky."

"Taara is our god."

"The woods of Pihkva must belong to some god too."

"But that's outside Viru, so it doesn't matter. Besides, only sorcerers and Letts dwell there, and they have no gods. Why do you think I want to go to Pihkva? Because if there are sorcerers there, my mother might be held prisoner. Maybe I can find her."

"I understand. I don't like the idea of sorcerers, but I'm sure I'll be safe with you."

"I'll leave at once, but you, my lad, I'm afraid you must stay here." The boy's bright smile faded. "You have to stay, in case any messengers come with news of the war. What if I'm needed in battle? Only you will know where I've gone. Only you can send them to me. It is important."

The cup-bearer withdrew in upon himself. Huddled on the ground, shaking, he seemed very small.

"You'll be safe here, don't worry."

The boy said nothing.

"I'll return soon."

Still no answer.

"You don't want me to go, do you?"

He shook his head a fraction.

"Don't be afraid," the Kalevide said. "Nothing will happen to me. I have my sword." But the boy continued to shiver, despite all his efforts to control himself. "You will be safe, too; stay here and wait for me. I will return, don't worry. I'll come back for you soon. I'm not the Alevide, I won't abandon you."

Girding on his great sword again, and slinging the pack with the Sulevide's provisions over his shoulder, the Kalevide loped down the hill toward the east. He never once looked back at the boy who wept behind him.

In the shelter and shadows of the forest, he walked along paths made by deer and other wild beasts, tangled woodland trails winding under arched branches and low undergrowth. Often he had to stoop and scramble and, at times, even crawl on all fours to make his way through. Soon the Kalevide began to pretend he was an animal himself.

The path to the east led him first to the muddy waters of Lake Virts, a shallow lake spreading southward till it was absorbed into the vast swampland. On the sandy bank stood the water demon's stone, but the Kalevide passed it without a glance. He was already looking ahead too eagerly to notice the signs of the past, even when they marked his own moments of triumph. The morning sun was still shining on the lake when he came out of the forest. With a feeling of rising jubilation, he ran wildly to the waterside and splashed across the full width of the pond. Here and there cold springs bubbled through the mud and tickled his naked toes as he kicked happily through the water. Lake Virts, when undisturbed, was so still that the flow from the springs formed narrow channels which never mixed with the warmer, brackish water of the lake. When the Kalevide raised his waves, however, they roiled the striped waters together so much that they were joined ever afterward. He did not have to wade, he could well have walked around the northern shore, but he was like a yearling bear cub wanting to play. The Kalevide plunged through the lake as though it were a puddle.

"It's going to work!" he shouted to the treetops. "It's all going to work!" In the joy that comes with sunlight the vision of Viru blossomed in his mind. Everything became possible, possibilities became true. "The Alevide's my land steward, the Sulevide's my war-leader, the cup-bearer's my friend. And I'm

still the king! Everything is right. We'll build my father's kingdom. Viru! An empire to last a thousand years!''

A small muddy brook ran out of the eastern end of Lake Virts,
passed through the forest and soon joined the River Ema, which
flowed slowly eastward until it entered Lake Peipus itself. Between
the lakes the trees grew taller and straighter. They formed long
corridors where the Kalevide could walk with a longer stride.

Once he spied the small figure of a man alone off among the
oaks. Not a demon, not a sorcerer, no evil wight, nothing from
his dreams or fears, this was merely a simple peasant gathering
firewood for his neighbors' hearths, someone to remind the
Kalevide that even in this remote corner of the land he could
meet men of his own kind.

Shouting cheerful hellos, the Kalevide turned off the trail to
greet the woodcutter. Blackberries and brambles snagged at his
clothing and scratched his legs. Drawing his sword, he hacked a
path through the snarl of underbrush. The small old man cast one
hasty glance over his shoulder and fled. One look was enough. It
showed a giant figure crashing through the woods, wielding a
mighty sword, bellowing. In a panic, the forester disappeared
into the dark protection of the trees.

The Kalevide laughed. He would have enjoyed chatting with
the man a while, to hear the news and learn what lay ahead in
the land of Pihkva, but just then the forest was friend enough.
Swinging back onto the main path, he began to sing. Although it
was a song to chant when embarking on a journey, he sang it
now not as a prayer or charm, but for the simple gladness in its
music:

> Land's old wife, primeval
> mother, from the earth
> arise, from the field
> awaken, in the woodland
> come, aid an only son,
> a grand warrior, travel
> gaily with me, join
> in my journey, keep,
> the trailways open, drive
> dangers from me, make
> the forest friendly, mother.

Birds fluttered among the treetops, singing songs too quick for
his ears to hear. A tomtit, no bigger than his thumb, darted past
his shoulder, crying, ''Flee, flee, flee,'' in its high shrill voice.

[179]

It reminded the Kalevide of the small birds Linda had always kept and called her messengers. "Flee, flee, flee." He stopped to listen to the other subtle sounds in the woods. Was the forest giving him a warning? His mother had always told him to listen to the birds; did they now bring him a message? He looked behind him but saw nothing.

Shadows filled the wood. The forest world was caught in a pale darkness where not even the sky showed clearly through the thick branches of the oaks. A small cloud of mist rose off the damp ground; it meant nothing to the Kalevide. Perhaps there was a slight movement, a shadow within the shadows, slipping off the path to hide amongst the trees. He was not sure. "Perhaps a weasel," he said to reassure himself. "Yes, probably a weasel. That would frighten birds, but not me." He was mistaken.

Later he stopped from time to time to listen to the faint sounds behind him. After that first warning, however, there was never anything loud enough to make him linger long, nothing he could not say was the chirp of a bird or the drip of water from an unseen spring. Soon he forgot dangers. His tension slipped away; he let himself feel at home again among the trees, lost in the easy hours of walking. Here and there the bright eyes of wildflowers winked at him through the trees. The air was warm. The songs he sang became simple tuneless chants without words. He ceased to be conscious; he forgot his dreams for Viru, even his quest for Linda. He was content. He was one with the wood.

Before the sun set that day, the Kalevide came into a hidden meadow nestled between two gentle hills. It was the hour of utter peace that is a prelude to dusk and the dangers of the night, the hour when the forest sighs to itself for the ending of its day and prepares to sleep. A thin silver stream skipped through the meadow-grass and watered the ground, lit in the late afternoon with golden glowing star-flowers and sweet white cresses. It flowed out of a well at the far end of the glade. By the well stood a golden-haired maiden, thinly clad in a shift of silver gauze. A girdle fashioned of anemones and speedwell clasped her waist. She was a nymph, a spirit of the air, a fosterling of Pikne, the thunder-lord.

When the Kalevide saw her standing alone beside the fountain, more beautiful in the twilight than any woman he had ever seen, he was reminded of the stories his brothers had told of meeting fair maidens in wild places, and of the love and allurements they offered. Such tales were true. Here was a sign that fortune smiled; this was the time for him to atone for what he had done to Kaare on the island. Although, like a boy, he longed to run to the maiden, he was afraid of frightening her and so forced himself to walk toward her slowly, with only a hint of a kingly swagger. His left hand held the hilt of his sword erect so she could see him for a man of power.

When he was quite close, he saw she was weeping. Gently, he reached out to brush the tear from her cheek, but she pulled back shyly from his touch. His fingers felt only a whisper of hair, a curl as light as mist. The silver streams of her teardrops made her seem even more innocent and beautiful. Reverently, he knelt on the ground before her; he bowed his head.

"How shall I help you?" he asked. In that moment, touched by her beauty, he was prepared to do anything for this pure maiden. He would have fought for her; he would have traveled to far places. He was ready to wrestle with the wildest beasts, or to brave the very fiends of Pōrgu. If she had asked, in that moment, he would have sacrificed his kingdom, even his life, on her behalf. He had become a king; he needed now to be her champion.

With long, pale, delicate fingers, she wiped the tears from her soft blue eyes and folded her light golden hair off her ivory face, then touched him once on the shoulder to be certain of his strength.

"My ring," she sighed; the sound was a gentle breath of air. "I have lost it in the well. I dipped my hands in its water that I might drink, and the well stole my ring from my finger. So deep and dark it is within the well I could neither catch my ring nor call it forth. And now the well will keep my golden ring, my father's ring, oh, my beloved father who gave it to me."

A single sob shook her slender form. As she drew her shoulders together, her body seemed even thinner in sorrow, more frail, more vulnerable.

Gallantly, the Kalevide rose and without hesitation plunged into the icy water to recover her lost jewel. Suddenly, three young sons of a sorcerer rushed out of the woods carrying a millstone over their heads. The delicate traitoress stepped aside, and, certain that the mouse was in their trap, the evil ones flung their granite stone into the well on top of the Kalevide.

It was long before he came to the surface again. Within the well it was dark indeed, black enough that he had to grope blindly in the muck and mire on the bottom. While he was searching vainly for the ring, the millstone sank slowly past his head. When at last he sprang from the water, he flung it down at the girl's feet.

"This is all I could find," he said in disgust. "I doubt you'll need a larger finger-ring."

With a loud, derisive laugh, the maiden disappeared into the air. The young sorcerers had already run away into the woods. The Kalevide was left wet and desolate, alone in the meadow as the sun sank behind the world.

"This is not the tale my brothers told," he moaned.

19

To a mortal eye the lake looked black overlaid with a fabric of lighter blue, the reflection of the sunlit sky of afternoon. Filaments of mist floated over its smooth, unruffled water. Lake Peipus lay like a sleeping woman, still in deep slumber, until the Kalevide stepped into her bed with his clumsy feet and broke that majestic calm.

He waded knee-deep through the icy water, enraptured in the beauty of that moment, oblivious to the spell he disturbed. His steps were buoyant. He was filled with pride. If it were not for his need to return to Viru quickly, he would have lain on his back and drifted through the afternoon. Instead he spread his arms and sang exalted songs to the sky. He was alone, in the middle of a vast lake, beyond the view of surrounding forests, in the eye of the sun alone.

Red crayfish scurried away from his feet; small fish fled in fear. Only the trout and pickerel dared to linger near. Now and then one brushed against his calves before gliding away into the deep darkness. The tip of his sword trailed in the water. He towed a raft of timbers behind him.

That morning the Kalevide had risen with the sun and crossed to the wildlands of Pihkva beyond Lake Peipus's eastern shore and cleared trees with the sword of Viru until he had levelled the land. Having cut more timber than even he could carry, he left half on the beach and lashed the rest into a raft to take across the water to his home.

The lake, where he entered, was so wide he could not see the farther shore. In the distance, water mingled with the sky, and from their union clouds arose in the north, rolling out of the water to cast a grim shadow the color of iron over half the lake. Soon there would be a storm.

The Kalevide was unconcerned. He was too filled with the

glory of his work well done to worry about future danger. Where he stood the sun still shined.

The rippling waters of Peipus swirled around his thighs, grabbed at his genitals, gripped his buttocks. Beneath his feet the bottom was sand and mud. It felt like flesh. The Kalevide imagined himself walking across a woman's breast. He curled his toes and pressed his heels into the mud as if to squeeze the earth, to touch the nerves lying beneath the silt.

Remnants of a tale passed through his memory, bits of a story his mother had sung, about the origins of Lake Peipus and the one who drowned beneath its first waves, and about the Princess Rannapuura, daughter of the king of Karkus in the age before this age in the lands of Viru. She was a child with golden hair and eyes like harebells, and she had been taken and made a thrall—for reasons he could not recall—to the old witch named Peipa. Through all the years of her girlhood Rannapuura had had to live in the hag's castle high on a rock in Ingrija far from the plains of Karkus. There she had grown more fair with every passing year, until finally, with the aid of the white gods of the forest, she escaped. Peipa had ridden forth one night at midnight, as witches do, and gave the princess a moment to steal away. Taking the magic tokens given her by the white gods to thwart the witch, she ran for her father's kingdom, only to be pursued too soon by Peipa. Mounted on a fierce red cock, the hag wielded a bar of iron like a sword. Whenever she came too close, Rannapuura cast down one of the magical gifts, which then became an obstacle to impede the witch's steed. A silver comb became a jagged river, now called Pliha, with its shining waters. A wool-carder became a forest; an apple, by the power of the gods, became a granite mountain too steep for the witch to climb.

Again and again, however, despite all barriers, Piepa returned and nearly captured the princess. Rannapuura fled in terror. Then, at the extremity of her strength, faint from want of food and lack of sleep, she came within sight of her father's castle on the plains of Karkus, but then the witch seemed so close to her that she lost the last hope of escape. In her final moment of fear, the maiden flung down her white linen robe, her last gift from the gods. The cloth tripped the vicious red cock, his feet entangled in its liquid folds. As steed and rider fell, the robe rushed forth, transformed into a vast lake with high, raging waves which engulfed the evil witch. The princess ran to her father's embrace.

Howling storms raged over Peipa; they flung waves at her back and hurled water in her face. Nor could the cock escape the flood. He arched his neck and raised his beak; he crowed. He beat his wings against the waves but could not fly, and so drowned wretchedly. The witch called on all the dark forces and evil spirits she knew, but none would help her. She, too, sank howling into the depths of the water. There she lies in pain and torment, forever covered by Rannapuura's linen robe. Pike and sturgeon and other demons of deep water gnaw at her flesh and limbs to torture her. As she writhes in agony, storms sweep across the lake, now named for her. Great billows and waves, impelled by her wrath, wash over her tomb. At times she sleeps, as all things must, and the lake is calm. The water is still and serene; whispers of mist float beneath blue sky, for the robe had belonged to a princess. The calm cannot last, however, the tempests cannot remain still for long. The witch must wake, and when she wakes, the storms return.

The Kalevide began to walk more cautiously and with a lighter tread. He had far to go.

Across the lake a sorcerer waited for him hungrily. He opened his arms and muttered obscene chants to summon his quarry into his grasp. For once, with victory near, he dared to come out of the forest's shadows, to stand in open daylight. He danced on the shingle. He stamped the earth and beat his heels on the sand and sharp stones. The oblique slits that were his eyes wandered over a face distorted by frenzy; yellow tusks jutted from his swollen, hate-filled mouth. Already he had cast off his tunic of untanned skins; he wore only his belt of power and his shoes, since he no longer had his hat. His hands were clutching the arrow-bolts that were his spells, his pains, his griefs, his gifts to give.

For long distances and many days, he had followed the Kalevide. Through forests and meadows and marshlands he had dogged him patiently, always on his trail, always near, yet always willing to wait until the time was fixed to strike, the time when he would loose all his powers on this man and be avenged. At times he had toyed with him, played small games, just enough to let his victim know he was pursued, yet never so much to warn him how deadly the danger was. He had freed the white mare and allowed her to return to her dwelling place in the underworld, from which he had summoned her. He had set his sons to ambush him by the well. He had haunted his footsteps. For a moment's sport he had shot the dog.

Now, however, the time had come to crush the Kalevide. He would shape his evil humors to wreck final vengeance on this mortal who was the spawn of despised Linda and who, to spite him, had destroyed his sorcerer's cap and so destroyed so many powers unknown to men. For that there was no reward save torture and torment. The sorcerer drew his short bow and fired his bolts into the dark lake water. He released his curses to wake the sleeping power that had been Peipa.

With the wind-enchanters and wizards, a sorcerer can call a storm. This one now summoned the strongest that was in his power to bring. In a moment the waters seemed to draw away from the middle of the lake where the Kalevide walked, and as they sank, they turned gray. Then they roared back in fury. The sun fled from the sky, and deep billows marched from the north. The sorcerer raised high winds that howled in a gale. Sharp rains lashed the Kalevide's face. The waters rose and rolled their high waves down on him, waves building power as they swept unchecked along the length of the lake. They broke over his back, but the son of Kalev only laughed at the madness of the storm.

"You nasty little puddle," he shouted to the lake, "you've wet my shirt!"

Tightening his grip on the towline to his raft with one hand to hold it against the churning waters, he drew his sword with the other. Like the hero he was, he flourished his blade, and with a long, sweeping stroke, which he fancied could mow down even a running foe, he lopped the heads off the waves that were rolling around him.

The sorcerer watched in dismay while his storm was vanquished. He cried more charms, and beat his drum in fiercer rhythms to raise more winds and drive more waves, but to no avail. The gales were overcome, and soon they died, calm returned. The lake subsided once again for a while, but the rage that he had unleashed upon the world now spawned a storm in the sorcerer's mind. All black thoughts and visions boiled behind his evil eyes as he cursed the Kalevide, who, unaccountably, could defeat his most dreadful powers. No mortal man could be protected from such wrath unless he were beloved by the higher gods, and that, the sorcerer thought, was surely impossible. He slunk away into the woods to recover his spent strength.

The Kalevide came out of the water like an ox emerging from a pool, snorting to blow the wind from his lungs. For a moment all the world paused, as though it waited for him to bellow. Free of Lake Peipus's grip, he dragged his load of wood up the beach, where he danced proudly, laughing and shouting taunts at the water.

"Rage on, Peipa," he cried. "Blow your guts out. You can't hurt me."

He strutted back and forth, home once again in Viru where he was king. A stone offered itself to his hand. He skimmed it out of sight over the lake. The water heaved once in its bed, but it had used all its strength for the time, and was obliged now to rest and endure his insults.

His sword flashing in the air, the Kalevide trimmed his timbers, lopping off branches, hewing planks. When he saw the naked blade, the sorcerer hiding in the forest longed to possess it. With every stroke his desire grew until it burned through his body, ready to explode. This, he thought, must be the secret of the man's great power. Since he bore no other shield, this must be the strength that enabled him to withstand his spells, and this, the sorcerer knew, he could steal.

In the twilight, the Kalevide soon tired of his task. Leaving it half unfinished, he gathered up a bed of sand and shingle near the shore, where he quickly fell asleep, pleased with himself, pleased with his good day's labor, pleased to have beaten the storm. Lying with his head to the west and his feet to the east, he hoped to wake early with the sun's first rays on his eyes. He held his sword close to his side.

The winds of evening rose; waves surged again on the lake and dashed angrily against its banks. The ground shook, and the forest echoed with the sound of the Kalevide's snoring, which filled the world around him with a roar like the thunder-lord driving three-in-hand down the iron bridge between the clouds.

In the dead of night, when the last birds are still and only wolves prowl the forest, the sorcerer crawled out of his dark lair to strike his enemy. Afraid to wake the sleeping man, however, he merely crouched by his head and glared malevolently on the face that assumed, in the moments of sleep, the softened outlines and blush of peace. The sorcerer spat. The sand beside the Kalevide's golden hair congealed into a yellow lump, as though struck by venom. It might have been amber. Unaware, the Kalevide groaned without waking and rolled onto his side, revealing the sword the sorcerer craved.

His slanted eyes gleamed lewdly when they spied the length of the weapon. With a clawed hand he reached out to seize it, only to draw back with a hiss when he realized the Kalevide still lay on its hilt. Moonlight through the broken clouds touched the ground with chilling light. In the gloom of madness the sorcerer began to work enchantments on the sword to draw it safely to him without disturbing its master. He spoke to the spirit welded in its steel. He called on its origin, and invoked the powers of iron. He chanted the names of the fires that had shaped it, and of the waters that had quenched its heat. It was to no avail; he could not command it. He tried supplication, begging it to come to him, imploring, entreating, enticing, cajoling, promising more glory, if it would only consent to hang by his side rather than the Kalevide's. The sword would not be persuaded; it would not forsake its true commander for another. When neither charms nor enchantments, chants or incantations, flattery or praise would move the blade and bend it to the sorcerer's will, he was forced to delve for deeper spells to bind it to him. Taking herbs and powders from the pouches on his belt, he scattered rowan leaves and thyme, fern and meadowsweet over the reluctant sword. Being careful not to touch the Kalevide with a single grain, he spread seven kinds of dust on the scabbard and sang dark songs to summon magic from the earth with threats of vengeance and violence such as iron should know and understand. He raised the rhythm of his fevered chants, and just as he began to fear he would not have enough strength to complete the spell, the sword inclined toward him. He called it again and commanded it with foul words. And it came. It came just enough for him to touch it and draw it closer. The Kalevide moved restlessly but slept on in blissful ignorance. A smile was on his face. He sighed. The sorcerer grasped the sword and wrenched it from his side.

The blade, however, had not been wrought for common hands. It was heavy. And it was still loath to leave its appointed owner. Had the spells not confused it, it would have cried out for rescue, but it could not think of the words. Having no hands of its own, it could not turn to attack the thief. Its only weapon was its weight, and with that weight it fought.

The sorcerer had intended to take the sword in his arms and run with it to some dark hole of safety, where he could caress it and in time turn its great power to his own use and against the Kalevide, but the sword was too heavy, and he could not hold it. Desperately afraid of being caught, he finally dragged it along the ground. Although the sword held back and struggled, still he drew it away, step by step, into the refuge of the wood. Cold sweat poured down his face and sides; his arms felt as though they were being pulled from his body, but the sorcerer would not let go of his captive. He had been denied the woman, Linda, when he wanted her; he would not be denied this prize in her stead.

The brook Kapa flowed sluggishly through a clearing in the forest on its way to join Lake Peipus. The sorcerer leaped across it but the reluctant sword slipped from his grasp and sank to the bottom of a deep pool. Unwilling to enter the water, which was loathsome to his race, he renewed his enchantments and blandishments, but too late. The sword had felt the sorcerer's soiled hands and would not return to them. It resolved to remain where it was, and no power he could summon could dissuade it.

Dawn began to glow around the rim of the world. The sky over Lake Peipus awoke; tormented clouds screamed pink and purple as if in pain. The lake's bleak waters swelled and rolled high waves against the banks in prelude to another storm. The sorcerer's mouth curled in a mask of madness as he was compelled to quit his incantations and flee. Still weakened by his night-long struggle and his battle of the day before, he did not dare to face the Kalevide's vengeance by daylight. Before he crawled back into the forest, however, he spoke parting words over the sword. Although he could not make it rise and come to him, he could, and did, cast a spell to addle its poor wits forever.

No welcome smile of sunlight warmed the Kalevide's eyes to bid him wake, only a sky dark and ominous, filled with omens of imminent wrath. He reached unconsciously to touch the sword. Its hard shaft would assure him he had strength to overcome all evil and dread. The sword was gone. Gone! The shock of discovery shot through him like a sorcerer's arrow. Suddenly he felt very sick. He had lost the dearest thing he had.

The Kalevide knelt on the ground. As far as he could tell, the sword had deserted him on its own. The sorcerer, in his escape, had left no footprints, but the sword had. As it was being dragged through the mud, it had contrived to gouge a deep track, like a scar, in the soft earth. He followed it, calling frantically for it to return to him, calling to it as a brother, begging it to come back. There was no reply. He sang a song said to restore lost property; he prayed to the powers of the forest. Still no answer came. The clouds of morning lowered, enfolding the land in a deep mist. It muffled the sounds of his pleas. Far away, a cuckoo cried with a call like a wounded dog in pain. To the Kalevide it sounded like the echo of his loss.

He followed the wandering trail through the trees and across a meadow's grass and reeds to the bank of a small brook. There it ended. The track did not resume on the other side; it did not turn upstream or down. It vanished as if a hawk had stooped out of the sky and borne the sword away to unknown lands. The Kalevide groaned. This was too much like the time he had lost the ox, too much like the loss of Linda, too much like the white mare's disappearance. Once more something he loved was lost in mystery. Once more, he feared, he faced an endless, fruitless quest. Sadly, he cried to the sword that had been his strength.

As though summoned, the blade appeared suddenly, shining on the bottom of the pool. Through the water, it looked even larger than it had on land. In the first flashing moment of recognition the Kalevide forgot his grief. Heedless of the mud, he flung himself to the ground beside the stream to speak, through its reflection, to his straying friend.

"Why did you leave me?" he cried. "Weren't you happy with me? Was there someone else's hand you wanted to hold you? I missed you. Won't you come back to me? Come out of that pool; it looks so deep and cold. Tell me why you left me, why you hurt me." Accusation and recrimination were not on his mind, he only wanted the sword to know that it was important to him that he still wanted it, needed it, yearned for it, and that he, too, had suffered.

From the bottom of the stream the sword sang in reply; its voice was giddy, drunk on adventure and hard-won freedom. Its words rose like bubbles in the water.

"Against my will, against my will," it sang merrily. "I did not choose to go. Oh, no, not me. Another hand compelled me, another hand impelled me, another hand enspelled me, the hand repelled me, but I did go. Oh, woe. He lured me, he held me. The sorcerer, oh, the sorcerer. He charmed me, he alarmed me, he harmed me. He forced me to go."

The Kalevide listened as if to a lost friend. His heart went out to it for its suffering. He ached to take it in his arms and rock it against his breast like a frightened child. In his relief at finding his treasure again, not even the news of the sorcerer disturbed him. He was confident of his strength now and feared no one. As soon as he recovered the blade from the water he would be invincible again.

"He dragged me, he gagged me, what could I do?" the sword sang on. "I could escape, I should escape, I would escape. I did escape. No hands can hold me long against my will. Oh, no, not me. No evil hands, no wicked hands, no hands command, no hands demand when evil is their plan. Not me, oh no, not me. I have no hands, no hands have me. I'm free. Into the stream I leaped. A fish, I wish."

"Come," the Kalevide said, "I'll take you home now."

Stretching his arm under the water, he could just barely grasp the end of the scabbard. At the touch, the sword slipped wantonly out of the sheath and slithered to the deepest part of the pool. There, naked on a bed of dark green mosses, it lay, glistening bright silver and wreathed with garlands of marsh marigolds and the delicately cut leaves of water-crowfoot.

The Kalevide grew angry. Shaking the empty scabbard in frustration, he cried, "Will you come up? Or must I come down there after you?"

"I'll not come up. I can't come up. Oh, no, not me. I'm free. You'll see. No, don't come down, oh, no, unless you want to drown. I'm in the arms of a water nymph, and I'll not leave the one I love. Oh, no, not me. She holds me tenderly."

"What? Does a sword prefer a maiden's arms to a mighty hero's hand? Does it choose a woman's caress before the glory of going into battle with men?"

"Ha, ha, ho, ho, a hug, a kiss, for me, for me. What bliss. Battles I have known, of battles I'll have none. I've felt the hero's hand; I know what hands have held me. Who should know them more than me? Do you? We'll see. Do you recall your first great fight? Do you recall the swift stroke you struck? The cut that slew the smith's last son, the one, the son of the one who won me from the fire? Have you forgot? I've not forgot. Not I. Not that murder. Oh no. You made me do it, I did not want to kill. What could I do? I have no hands, oh no, not me. Your hands compelled, your hands repelled. Your hands held poor me. Against my will, against my will, I kill. No more, no more for me. I'm free."

The Kalevide bowed his head. What the sword said was true, too true, nor was the young smith's murder the end of the slaughter he had wrought unnecessarily with the sword in his hand.

"So be it." The words, though difficult, must be spoken. "You are free, as free as a sword can be. Keep your soft repose." He swallowed his pain. It was a bitter moment, it hurt, but never again would the blood of innocents be on his hands. He loved that sword and now he gave it up; it was an atonement.

"I still have the strength of my own arms," he said. "I will depend on them alone to overcome my enemies." He was speaking more to himself than to the sword.

When he turned sadly to go, it was the hardest step he had ever taken. His truest friend was forsaking him, and he was letting it, and he knew that once he walked away, the separation would be complete. There could be no returning, they could never be one again, the pain would be too great. The ache in his heart cried out to him to stay, to linger at least a moment more, to plead some more before leaving forever. He turned back, but not to beg.

"If any people of my race, if any of the kin of the Kalevide or of the Alevide or of the Sulevide come by this place, speak to them in words," he said. "Tell them you were once the sword of Kalev and of Kalev's son. And if ever a great singer should pass by, sing to him. If a hero who is strong, as strong as I, should come, rise up to greet him. You will do these things for me."

The Kalevide paused briefly to be certain the sword would understand and remember his words. He knew its blade was keener than its wits, and now it was obviously mad as well, but it was vital, he thought, that it know clearly how he felt and what he wished. He forgave it its faults and forgave it even its final hurt to him, although the pain of that parting cut very deep. The only anger in him now was aimed entirely at the sorcerer who had wrought this and so much other woe on him, and that anger burned with a flame that consumed even his sorrow until it flared out of him in a final curse. Buckling the belt and empty scabbard around his waist, the Kalevide spat words like venom, and by them bound the sword to his unshakeable command.

"Sword, I do not know your name, but I bind you by the name you bear, sword, if ever the man should come who brought you here and left you, sword, you will strike that man, and with your stroke you will cut off both legs of that man. So be it!"

He spoke at last with the voice of a king, although he little understood the import of his own words.

20   **W**hile the son of Sulev strode through the ancient forests of Taara on his way to arouse the people of Viru to the dangers of war, his mind marched over the myriad preparations he must make and the commands he must issue before the battle came.

"There is not enough time," he said to the Alevide. "My men will have to hold off the enemy by themselves until I can muster an army, and there is too much to do. I fear they will be overcome."

The Alevide walked lightly beside him. He accompanied the Sulevide only because he had been commanded; had he been free, he would have stopped often to admire the depth and beauty of the land they were crossing. There was no need to hurry that he could see. Here in the forest were the riches he had

[191]

sought so long across the world. Here he might find a new homeland, a place to dream once again of peace. In the Sulevide's mind there was no room for such fancies.

"I will have to train the troops in the very first fundamentals of warfare," he continued. "They have no skills whatsoever. I have seen them; I have seen the extent of their preparations. But I will teach them myself. They will learn the drills and maneuvers to use against a horse-mounted foe and the rudiments of tactics. If my men, who are not without skills, can just hold the iron knights long enough for me to raise two small companies, or even one strong troop, we should be able to drive them from the land. The cost will be high, but that is unavoidable. Afterwards, we can build for the future on the foundation and experience they have acquired, so that when the final war comes Viru will have an effective fighting force able to stand against any foe and prevail."

His voice droned monotonously, like wasps swarming around dead meat. The Alevide reflected how he had known such men before. His father and his father's henchmen had been like the Sulevide, traders in war, stern men who found their strength in combat and proved themselves with feats of arms. Nor were they all brigands and raiders, like those who had burned him out of his home and driven him from his land. Some believed in honor and fought their wars in the name of peace, or justice, or mercy. Underneath, however, they were the same, living for the battle that would bring their death. Of such men were heroes made. For himself, the Alevide preferred words and barbs of wit to swords and crossbow bolts.

"We will have to mobilize everyone," the Sulevide was saying. "The women as well as the men. They can gather supplies and provide food and forage for the fighters. They can build barricades to block the horses. If necessary, they can take up arms and fight beside their husbands and sons in the last defense of their homes. I have known many women who were as fierce as any men.

"The men I will divide into small, mobile squadrons to meet the knights. It will be easier to train them so. Arming them will be difficult. I understand there are a few swords and spears and shields, even a little armor, which Kalev collected years ago but never used. Of course, the hunters will have their crossbows, and everyone has a knife. But for the rest? Well, there are always fish spears, scythes, hayrakes, cattle prods and the like. Even posts and poles can serve, although they make poor weapons against a mail-clad knight. That is the price to pay for being so poorly prepared, I fear. Still, such weapons are better than none. A man must have something in his hands, no matter how rude. He must be armed, even if he falls.''

"It is a grave mistake," the Alevide said bitterly, no longer able to hold his peace.

"A mistake? You would have them die defenseless?"

"I would not have them die at all. To give them pitchforks to fight against knights is a mistake; to divide them into squadrons is a mistake; it is a mistake for women to fight beside their men; it is a mistake for you to worry about armaments and supply. Everything you say is wrong. These people are not warriors. They are peaceful folk, used to tilling their fields and foraging in their woods. Don't change them, don't destroy them. Let them slip away into the forest, as their kind have always done when danger threatened.''

"You would have them run away? Run and hide like cowards? If they are men they will not be afraid to stand on the battlefield and face the enemy. Their honor demands it.''

"You don't understand. They aren't cowards, but they aren't fighters, either. I know these people who dwell in the forests. I have lived with them, and I know how they feel. They will not understand what you ask of them. They only want to live. Isn't it better for them to survive as they wish than to succumb as you require?''

"I? I require them to succumb? On the contrary, I offer them their only hope of survival. I do not want anyone to die; I have no desire to see folk suffer, and war is suffering. Nevertheless, if they want to live, then they must fight, and fight bravely, for their lives. It is possible, no, it is inevitable, that some will die. But if they die on the field of battle, then they will have died for a worthy cause, for the sake of their country, their people, that the rest might live. They will have died honorably and will always be remembered. Their names will be sung in songs and told in tales, and so they will live forever.''

"Nonsense. You know they will die. The rest is a fairy tale. You expect these poor men to stand in a line against the march of knights just so they can be ridden down. What fun is there in such sad songs?''

"They need not die, not all, not if they learn the arts of war. I will teach them how to fight against the iron knights. I, too, know these people. The tribe of Sulev and the tribe of Kalev are close kin. My men have learned to be warriors; the others can learn, too.''

"If they do, they will become something they are not now.

You will have made them like the knights who have come into the country and brought the war with them, the very ones they must fight. You will have changed them, corrupted them, destroyed them. They will no longer be free men, living at peace with the forest and the land, and so their spirits will die. They will become pieces in the blind machine of the war, brothers to the knights, and their lives will end. Whichever happens, if they fall to the invader's lance or if your lessons are learned, they must succumb. And that, I say, is wrong."

"You have wit, and you have imagination, which is why I chose you for this mission and why I listen to you. Nevertheless, the words you speak ring with treachery and defeat. You do not—"

"What defeat?"

"—understand that the threat is here, now. The danger is real and grows stronger daily. It is too late to pretend that all is safe and people may live at peace in the forest, for peace no longer exists. The war is here; we are at war. The iron knights are marching on the borders of this land. What you speak of is no longer possible, if—I say, if—it ever was. If the people do not wish to live as conquered men, worse than beasts, certainly less than men, then they must fight. It is as simple as that. They must fight actively and eagerly to protect their homes. And they must be prepared to die; that is what it means to fight bravely. There are worse things than death.

"The invader is now at Viru's threshold; soon he will be in the door. He must be struck now, and struck swiftly, before it is too late to strike at all. How can the people preserve their freedom, their lives, if the enemy is free to march across the land. If everyone hides behind trees as you suggest, how will they keep the wolves out of their sheepfolds? Hiding and hoping will not drive the enemy away.

"This need not have happened. It would not have if the people here had been prepared. If they had been strong and armed and ready to fight, the knights would not have dared to attack. This will be a painful lesson to them, but it is only a small war we face now. It will teach the men how to fight, so they will be prepared in the future. I say it must be faced squarely and fought now, for if it is not, a greater war will surely come, drawn by our weakness. What do you suggest instead?"

"If I were a wizard, I'd sing down a fog upon the horsemen, wrap them in mists and clouds and hide the country from their eyes. I'd deceive them with phantoms, confuse them with smokes.

I'd lead them from the land with luring songs of enchantment. I would trick them, but I would cause no one pain."

The Sulevide laughed out loud. "Sing them away with wizardry! What a dream. There is no glory there; who can sing of heroes in a fog? Besides," he added soberly, "you are no wizard; you have no such songs to sing."

At the crossroads they parted, the Sulevide taking the path to the right, to the Kalevide's hold, where he would muster as many men as he could from the nearby hamlets, the Alevide turning to the left, toward the western sea. Before they separated, the Sulevide gave him a scroll of parchment to take to his kinsmen hiding in Harju.

"Give this to Laino, my lieutenant," he said. "In my absence, he acts for me. It is the command to engage the knights and hold them until I can come with reinforcements. Without these orders he will do nothing, only wait. I do not know where the war would go then. Much depends on your mission."

"You trust me with it? After what I said?"

"I must; I have no other messenger. But, yes, I trust you, for if you do not obey my command, you will never be able to return to Viru. It is that simple."

"It is that difficult," thought the Alevide.

"I believe, moreover, that you have the intelligence to see that what I have said is true. The future of Viru depends on this war, and I believe you will do nothing to harm the land you serve."

With a disconsolate shrug the Alevide accepted the scroll and slipped it into his pouch. There was nothing more to say. They parted, each to do what he must.

The Alevide's path led him through the forest to the shore of the open sea. With his first glimpse of the water he felt his breath flow out of him to behold this wonder, the like of which he had never seen. There were islands there, some small, some quite large, so large it was difficult to tell at a glance that they were islands, but it was the sea beyond the land that bewildered his eye, with its vast, gray, endless emptiness. Such distance, such force were beyond all he had ever known. He had walked the wide, unbroken prairies with their grasses that rippled in the wind like water—or so one said, until one saw the sea—but the steppes were as nothing next to this unending ocean which went on and on, until it must pass the very end of the world. The prairie held no power like the ebb and flow of the water and the rise and fall of waves. When abroad on the plains, a man could stop in the tall, nodding grass and know where he stood. There might not be a tree or hill to break the evenness of the land for as far as he could see, yet still he could plant his feet firmly on the ground and say, "This is where I am." Where could a man plant his foot when on the sea? What must it be like, the Alevide wondered, to be on the other side of that great distance and to look back from beyond all sight of land, to be upon the sea where the waters were never still and there was no way for one to say, "Here I am"?

Heedless of his awe, the water rolled unceasing waves against the shore, gray breakers that gnawed the shingle, then flowed back again into the womb of their mother sea. Overhead the sky was troubled. A line of storms marched out of the east, even as troops of horsemen trod the boundaries of the land on every side. Squalls drew black curtains of rain over the coast to wash both sea and country clean. Between these short-lived storms the sun cut through the black-silver clouds and struck the earth and sky with golden fire. Where the Kalevide had once seen a bridge suspended over the sound, a rainbow arched, a span of copper, linking the lands of north and south.

A dark shadow took shape in the air like a wing across the sun. The phantom settled among the rocks ahead of the Alevide to wait for him. Fear closed over the shore.

"Am I dreaming," he wondered, "or am I mad? What is it?"

It was only an ancient crow, however, a wretched creature, battered by uncounted years. Its tailfeathers were broken, its wingtip crippled. One eye was blind. With its head cocked awry, it hopped in a clumsy circle around the bewildered Alevide, closing in on him until at last its filthy wings brushed his legs. It clawed at his trousers. An awful stench of carrion clung to the bird. When it glanced up at him with its one good eye, it was so close he could see the flared nostrils of its time-worn beak. The creature sniffed the air noisily; it snuffled around his pouch to discover the message hidden there. It had smelled the war; the scent of blood had lured it there.

The Alevide kicked the foul thing aside and rushed down the shore on the pathway of the wind, desperate to escape death's messenger. In his pouch he carried the Sulevide's orders; on his tongue he held the secret passwords. He knew the commands of his captain: banners shall fly and lance heads strike in battle in the cause of righteousness! Behind him, like a broken heap of coal, the crumpled body of the crow lay among the stones. It was not dead. Soon it would rise, and limp away along another path. It would call its friends.

More clouds masked the sun, and with the clouds came another apparition. An eagle swooped out of the highest air to land with a great spread of wings in front of the Alevide, who was too afraid to move. It glared at him through hard, jeweled eyes. The feathers of its neck rose in a fearful crest. It clutched at its astonished prey with a golden talon. Its cruel, hooked beak gaped as it breathed the mist. With its head thrust forward, it weaved and bobbed, searching for the scent. It sought by smell to detect the message concealed within the Alevide's wallet. Already it had found the stench of battle; the reek of blood had brought it. Now it would know where and when the war would be. The eagle released the Alevide from the grip of fear and left to call its comrades.

"Is this what men must suffer?" he groaned as the great bird soared away to disappear, a small black spot lost in the farthest reach of the sky beyond the world. He knew too well the mandate he carried, the cry to arms, the call to strife: flags waved, trumpets blown, spears sharpened, axes honed, swords polished!

In a small meadow above a cove waited a raven's son. Unlike the crow, this one was young and sleek. As it came through the gray grass, it preened and strutted. The feathers of its wings and back glistened with color, as though oiled with blue and brown and green to make them black. Its bill was strong and heavy; its eyes were bright, carved from jet. Its eager beak opened; its black tongue became a thing alive as it croaked. The Alevide could not run; he could only stand, staring in dread fascination as the raven came toward him. It held its head alert; it sniffed the air. It caught the odor in the wind and recognized at once the meaning of the scent. The dark bird jabbed its sharp beak at the man and breathed the message bound within the mandate on the scroll. It, too, had smelled the war; it, too, had been drawn by the stench of blood. It, too, left to call its comrades.

Next, from the woods, bounded a young wolf cub accompanied by a lumbering yearling bear. They romped across the meadow, dodged around the thorny tufts of gorse, raced playfully past rosebushes, like children playing tag, the bear cub trying to catch the young wolf's tail, the wolf too nimble to be caught. The Alevide watched their frolic, but could not laugh as they ran tumultuously toward him. Drawing his cloak tight for protection, he shuddered when they sprawled breathlessly at his feet.

The animals rubbed against his legs; they licked his hands happily, as though he were their master and they his hounds. The sun, pouring across the sea, brought the meadow alive with its long golden light while the cubs rolled on their backs in front of the lonely man. They sniffed and panted; the wolf thrust its nose into his pants leg; the bear burrowed its muzzle between his thighs. They sought the message he had hidden. They tried to read its secrets in the scents. They pawed at the wallet he wore by his side. The bear raked his ribs with a sharp claw. The smell of war had lured them; the stink of blood had aroused their lust. When they found the word they wanted, they rushed away to spread the tidings.

The Alevide nursed his injured side, but the wound was far less serious than the hurt inside his heart. This was no mission for him; he, of all men, should not have to bear the message he bore. What he had seen so far was just the beginning, he knew. Once the words were delivered, the war would be released and all horrors freed: the flags would be unfurled, spears and lances aimed. Men would wield their axes, fire arrows. Sword blades would flash in the sun, and peace would be destroyed. All would die.

The Alevide's path led him away from the downs and wound across a wide, soft marsh as level as the sea which shaped it. The flats were overgrown with rank, matted sedge; beneath his feet the soil was thick, slippery mud, blue and oily, that stuck too much to his boots. All around was the stink of salt and decay. Out of the clinging mist emerged the shape of a woman.

She stumbled toward him, chewing on garbage, limping on legs so bowed they could barely support her tiny body. Her arms and legs were as thin as willow wands, mere bones with no soft layers of flesh. She wore a grimy, ragged shift that could not hide her shriveled breasts or her belly swollen with hunger. The Alevide forced himself to look at her face. Her eyes were empty; her cheeks were white, empty folds and wrinkles. Her mouth had forgotten how to smile. Thin hair, drained of color, was tied in a knot tight on her head; it made her look bald, and all the more horrible.

This was Famine. When they met, she embraced him. Wrapping her spindled arms around his waist, she pressed her face against his belly. Heavy, mewling sobs, "uh—uh—uh," poured like slime from her mouth as she fumbled at his belt, trying to reach beneath his shirt to find his pouch. She looked up at him hungrily with her friendless eyes. Her nose was wasted and shrunken into her face so that it seemed no more than two small holes which snuffled as she tried to breathe. She sniffed for his message. She sobbed for his words. "Uh—uh—uh." She mumbled with her face against his trousers that she might discover the mandate he had hidden. She had smelled the war approaching; the reek of blood had called her. She was hungry for the battle. With loathing, the Alevide pushed her off him. She staggered, but did not fall. Tottering away into the fog, still mewling, she went to call her kindred.

Beyond the salt marsh lay a strand where nothing grew. In a ceaseless churning, gray, white-topped waves ground the naked shingle. Banks of mist were closing on the shore. The Alevide ran along the water's edge, where foam lay like rancid cream. In his madness he wanted to shout to the sea, "I have the war-master's orders. In my wallet I bear his mandate and the decree of my king: Flags and banners shall fly unfurled, snapped by battle's winds. Horns shall be sounded. Spear points and lances do their duty, axes and fish-spears perform new labors. Cross-bows be drawn, arrows shot. Swords shall cut the flesh of men. Knives shall stab and draw men's blood!"

The ocean roared in his ears, and he ached to roar back to it, but he could not. His tongue froze with fear. He could not move. He was arrested by a single man standing in front of him. Solitary, tall and silent, wrapped in the gloom of nightfall, with one arm pointing, he summoned the Alevide. He was standing on a shelf of gray stone, robed in a cowled black cloak which hung like a shroud to his feet and concealed all of him but his face and the single beckoning hand. He was hideous in his silence. His eyes were two burned-out holes. On one side of his face the skin was falling away from the bone; the other side was so pocked and scarred it no longer looked like living flesh. The hand that pointed was a leper's hand. As the Alevide, compelled against his will, came closer, the specter raised its head still higher to smell the air. He shook off his hood to bare his yellowed, hairless scalp. This was Plague, the dire murderer of all people. Of all the seven-fold curses of war, this was the most dreadful. Ever mute, he sniffed the wind; he smiled with a death's head grin. He had smelled the war. The scent of blood had drawn him. He disappeared to call his comrades.

The Alevide staggered to the water's edge, where he was violently sick.

"This is the meaning of the mandate," he declared. "War and murder, death and disease. Men made into meat for beasts, corpses to be carrion for crows. Scraps of flesh in the claw of righteous nobility."

Taking shelter in a nest of boulders, he let the night close over him while he pondered what he should do next.

"If I carry this message for the Sulevide, his cause will be served. His men will fight, and the men of Viru will fight, and likely the invader will be driven away for a while. I will have done my duty to the Kalevide and ought to get some gratitude for that. I wouldn't mind that; a little gratitude may well be turned into a larger gain. On the other hand—" In his heart another decision had already been made. "—it's no gain for you, my friend, not set against the greater evil. War breeds wounds; what is gained is bloodshed. War has the throat of a serpent; it swallows its victims whole. The battle the Sulevide wants and my king allows will bring nothing but pain and sorrow, suffering and despair. How can I carry that message to peaceful home-steads and hamlets?"

As the decision which had germinated in his breast now blossomed, he felt light-headed and silly, as though intoxicated by the scent of flowers. The Alevide crawled along a long ledge of rock jutting into the surf. Groping through the darkness more by touch than sight, he found a nook at the very end where he could sit with his legs swinging over the sea. Waves broke below him flinging refreshing sheets of spray into his face.

"Let this message be damned," he shouted as he took the parchment scroll from his pouch. "Let its words be cursed." He drew his sheath knife. "May it be sunk in the depths of the water, lost among the spawn of fishes, drowned among the seed of eels." With the knife he hacked the parchment to shreds, then scattered the scraps over the waves. "Let it sleep in endless sleep; let it rest locked in deep caverns. May it find repose buried by the sea's blue stones, rather than that I should carry it anymore, rather than that I should keep it. Let it be strewn along the coastlines and spread between hamlets."

Thin white strips of parchment spilled from his fingers. Some floated on the rocking waves; some sank at once. Fish fled in terror from their message. Before morning all were gone, taken and torn by the foam, sunken and lost in the mud. Thus the Alevide stilled the clash of battle. Thus he solved the threat of war.

21   Towing his load of timber, which he had lashed into a rude sledge with vines and withes, the Kalevide passed through deep pine forests and a young wood of birch and willow, dressed like maidens in fresh green-yellow

leaves. In a hazel copse, where orphans and the sick often sought refuge, he stumbled over something soft lying half-hidden in the dark green bracken. Distracted by his sadness, it took a moment for him to realize it was a man lying at his feet.

The man, a peasant clad in a long, embroidered smock, red stockings, and bast sandals, was quaking with fear and prayed for protection. The Kalevide lifted him clumsily to his feet by his hair and tried to brush some of the leaves and twigs and bits of earth off his smock, but one glance at his benefactor, and the man rolled over and curled up in fright.

The Kalevide laughed out loud, his own troubles forgotten. This fellow was so small in stature, so timid, so fragile, quivering so, with his small round face and tiny dark eyes, he looked like a little woodland animal.

"Don't be afraid," the Kalevide said gently. "I won't hurt you."

"You won't? You're sure? You promise?" The thin trembling voice came from between the man's curled up knees. "Please don't hurt me."

"Of course I won't hurt you. Why should I? I'll help you if I can." Slowly the little man unwound. "Now, tell me what frightened you."

"Oh, master, I couldn't. No, it's a long and fearful tale and I couldn't bear to go through it all again, no sir, and what if it frightened you, too? So please don't ask me, no."

"But I do ask. How can I protect you if I don't know what dangers are hiding in my forest?"

"If you say so, sir, only it frightens me so. It was yesterday, it was, and I was wandering along the lake, keeping to my own affairs as I do, sir, not bothering a soul, for what can a poor woodcutter like me do to anyone? I am a woodcutter, you see, though I have been a fisherman, and truth to tell, my lord, I'm not really anything at all, just a poor man, making a living the best he can, foraging for food in the woods and by the lakes and sometimes in folks' fields, but not meaning any harm, and when I can't find anything anywhere, well, I beg a little, but I trouble no one, it's what I do, that's all, and it's what I was doing yesterday when the storms came and I lost my way and wandered around and around for a long time and it grew darker and colder and, I tell you, sir, I began to be afraid, but then I found a little footpath and I said to myself, I said, 'This will take me to someone's house,' and it did, sir, though truth to tell it was a poor and lonely hut I found, and if I had known what I would

[201]

find there I would have thrown myself off a cliff first or drowned myself in the lake.''

''Why? What did you find?''

''It was a big, empty room inside the hut, sir, and one old woman standing by the hearth-place cooking soup, and I thought it would be all right, for I was mightily hungry then, so I sat right down and asked for a bowl of that there soup she was fixing, and what a soup it was, with half a great pig in the pot and peas and barley and onions and the smell of it so sweet it drove away all my fears. She was friendly enough, the old woman was, she brought me her very own cup of that soup, saying, 'Eat it quickly,' that's what she said, 'Eat it quickly before my sons return,' and how was I to know she had any sons when I thought she was all alone? Soon as I had finished, she whisked me off under the table and told me to hide in the straw which was laid all over the floor there the way some people do, and she told me to lie as still as ever a mouse, her very words, 'As still as ever a mouse,' for if her sons found me they'd kill me quick as that and likely eat me, too. Well, I knew then she was a good woman, so I gave her a wink and thanked her once and burrowed deep into that straw where I thought I might just sleep a little, for I was mightily tired, but before I could even close my eyes I heard footsteps, and what footsteps! I tell you sir, although it is a terrible thing to tell, it was the footsteps of her sons and, forgive me for saying so, great son of Kalev, I don't think even your strong feet could make so much noise or shake the earth as much as they did when they rushed into the hut, like bears they were, two great giants of men. They stood in the middle of the room and smelled the air and then one of them roared, 'Who is he?' and the other shouted, 'I smell man sweat,' but the old woman only answered that anything they smelled they'd brought in with them and no one had been there but her. That's what she told them and there I was hiding underneath the table in the straw. But then those two giants, her sons, lay down next to me and set to snoring, and I may tell you, I never slept a wink at all that night I felt so trapped, I never dared close my eyes, and when the old woman opened the doors at dawn, this morning that was, and went out to do her chores, I crept out behind her and escaped while her sons were still asleep on the floor, and then I fled away from that place. I ran, how I ran, I ran as fast as my little legs would carry me, through one wood and another, but I never saw them I was running so fast. I ran into the third woods but my strength gave out and I threw myself into the fern patch to hide, your worship, and there I lay until you found me, I'm pleased to say, although I did take you for one of the giant sons at first, come after me, and that is the end of my tale, may it please you, sir."

The Kalevide chuckled at the man's simplicity. "Is that all? Didn't you steal their treasure or take a magic egg or anything? Didn't they bite your toes or tweak your nose? Just a little? Didn't they even pull your hair?"

"Oh, no, noble sir, you see, I was hiding in the straw and they never saw me, though perhaps you didn't understand when I said I . . ."

"Yes, yes, I understand, I just thought your story should have more to it, that's all. Well, little man, you needn't be afraid anymore, I'll protect you from all dangers in the wood."

"You say so, sir, but how? Meaning no disrespect, great lord, but you don't have so much as a sword with you so how can you defend me who am only a poor man and small and useless in battle?"

"I have my own strong arms. They're more reliable than any sword."

"If you say so, though frankly, a sword can cut and kill and what can empty hands do if the giants come, or worse?"

"Well, then. I'll make a club, if that'll make you happier."

Breaking off a young pine tree, the Kalevide peeled off its branches to form a stout staff. Once he had defeated a sorcerer's conjured horde with such a weapon. The small man had nothing to worry about now.

"How's that?" he said. "Will you come along with me now?"

Before he could say another word, the man of small stature scrambled like a squirrel onto his back and clung there with one arm around the Kalevide's throat and his feet wedged into his belt. The man was so small the Kalevide hardly noticed his weight. Taking up his tow rope, he set off along the path once more.

"You need never fear again, my friend," he said. "The Kalevide, Kalev's son, will protect you. I will protect all the poor people in my realm. Let anyone distressed summon me, and I will rescue him. Let anyone who is poor and hungry or weary from toil seek the son of Kalev, and I will give him shelter and food, a haven, a refuge. This is my promise, small friend, this is the word of a king, for a king can do no less."

Before he had a chance to redeem his pledge, however, the Kalevide was beset.

The trap was laid in a small, marshy clearing blocked on one side by a cliff down which tumbled a high waterfall, a white, cascading turmoil leaping from the steep rocks to run away across the meadow in a meandering stream. Where the water ran, thick beds of golden moss were lit with flowering white cresses which made the wall of stone and the brookside look touched by frost and snow.

As soon as the Kalevide stepped into the open space, the sorcerer's three sons leaped from their ambush and struck him from behind. Forcing him back against the cliff, they surrounded him. Escape was impossible. All three were armed with staves of slender young birchwood and dried pine boughs. The elder two also carried long whips, with handles of polished beechwood and lashes tipped with millstones. The black coils of rawhide looked like evil snakes on the ground as they were loosed to strike.

"What do you want?" the Kalevide shouted. The sorcerer's sons did not reply even as he dropped the tow-line to his sledge and took a step toward them, his staff raised, ready to defend himself from these leathercoated youths. They only circled menacingly, now and then flicking their whips at his shins and ankles.

"What do you want?" he demanded again. "I haven't done anything to you. Let me pass in peace." Their silent stares burned with hatred. It did not matter to them who he was, how powerful he might be, or whether he had ever done them ill or good. "Let me go before someone gets hurt," he said, brandishing his club. "This is my country. You have no business here." They only grinned malevolently.

Suddenly the youngest of the three darted under the Kalevide's outstretched arm, and tried to push him off balance, to trip him with his stick so his brothers would have their moment to pounce. The Kalevide just barely evaded his charge; the youngster ducked away before being caught.

"I think you should get down," the Kalevide said quietly to the small man clinging tightly to his back. "They mean to fight." The man of small stature only shook his head and moaned softly. His body was frozen with fear; he could not move.

The sorcerers continued to worry their victim with their whips until he could no longer contain his anger. With a roar of rage, the Kalevide rushed them with his club. They dodged away, but he caught one with a hefty swipe across the back. The pine club shattered, leaving only a useless stub in his hand. The boy he struck rolled away unhurt and bounced back onto his feet. The other two closed again, to pommel the Kalevide with their own staves.

"Get down," he hissed urgently to the small man. The poor fellow was incapable of moving.

The Kalevide, his hands empty, tried to ward off the sorcerers' sticks with his arms, but too many strokes broke through his guard, and they hurt. Without a weapon, he knew, he could not stand against all three for long. Now he wished for his sword, but wishes cannot cut, and the sword was far away. Fighting desperately through the howling pack to his sledge, he broke the ropes holding the planks together and, catching up one of the timbers, he swung it full in the face of one of the sorcerers. The long plank broke. He reached for another, and another, and began dealing blows left and right against all three.

Lost in the flurry of assault, the Kalevide swung blindly, sometimes striking his foe, sometimes the ground instead. The boards were unwieldy weapons, but his rage had been released, and he fought without bound or control. His face twisted into a distorted mask of anger, nor would his madness be released until the battle was done. He whirled and struck again. He stopped and thrust upward. Again and again. The small weight of the man on his back no longer troubled him; his burden was forgotten. He spun around while he struck and dodged. He hit; he blocked the sorcerers' own swinging clubs and vicious lashes. The meadow rang with the crash of wood against wood and stone. He bent to duck a blow and came back battling, hitting back harder each time, driving his own violent assault. The wooden boards he used for weapons roared in the air, and he roared with them with his own exalted cry. With every stroke he smashed another plank on someone's back. Splinters and shattered scraps of wood piled up all across the clearing.

It could only last a little while. Soon his supply of timber would be gone, and he had not yet done any damage to any of his assailants. Although he had hit them repeatedly, these sorcerers were tougher than he had expected; they were far more powerful and enduring than the phantom horde he had whelmed in Soome, and now that they saw his load of planks diminishing, they pressed their onslaught still harder in hopes of easy victory. Already he could count on one hand the boards remaining to him, and all three of his opponents continued to push at him. Then, from somewhere in the bushes, he heard a small voice.

"Strike with the edges, Kalev's son," it cried. "Strike them with the edges."

He did not stop to wonder. Turning the plank in his hands, he began to hit with its sharp edge, instead of the wide, flat side he had been using. Now the weapon whistled, rather than roaring. It cut the air like a sword slicing through the sorcerers' thin staves. Their lashes wound around the plank and were wrenched from their hands. All three began to cry in pain as he struck them again and again. With a shout of victory he ran at them, laying swift strokes on every side, beating them. One he hit squarely in the ribs, another across the side of the head. The third ran away before he, too, could be felled. Limping and howling like wolves, the sorcerer's three sons fled away into the forest. If they had not been savages, well tempered by long exposure to the heat and cold of day and night, the Kalevide's blows would have left all three lying dead on the field.

When they were defeated and gone, a last wave of excitement washed through the Kalevide. He leaned back against the cliff to catch his breath and savor the pleasure of victory, only to discover something stuck to his back. At first, feeling the lump, he though of desperate wounds or broken bones or a weapon somehow left embedded in his flesh, but there was no pain. His back was one part of his body that did not ache. Reaching tentatively behind him, he touched the body of the man of small stature whom he had completely forgotten in the frenzy of battle. The Kalevide shuddered. He unhooked the lifeless hands, still clutching his shirt, and freed the small feet from his waist. Some stroke early in the fight must have killed him, but the Kalevide had never known it. The man had been his shield; he had saved his back from uncounted blows, and he had never known that, either. Tenderly, he laid him on the ground beside the stream to straighten his arms and legs. Bent as they were, the man seemed even smaller than he was. He looked like a helpless child.

He was interrupted by a soft, whimpering cry coming from the bushes nearby. It reminded him of the voice that had saved him during the fight.

"Come out, little brother," he called hoarsely. "Come and show yourself to Kalev's son."

"I cannot, no," the small voice sniffed. "No, I dare not. I have no clothes."

The Kalevide chuckled. "If that's all, come out and I will clothe you. I owe you a reward for helping me."

From underneath a briar bush crept a hedgehog, naked and shivering and small. Its tiny, hairless, pink body trembled so it could scarcely walk. The Kalevide cupped his hand and let the creature sniff his fingers. He tried to touch its tender skin, and would have picked it up in the palm of his hand, but the hedgehog backed away, shy and afraid.

"I promised you a shirt," he said, "and a shirt you shall have." From the tail of his tunic he tore a square of cloth which he tossed to the urchin. "There, little friend, that should keep you warm."

The hedgehog pounced on it, curling tightly around the scrap of cloth. The piece was a bit too small; it left the little one's legs and belly as bare as before, but before the Kalevide could cut another, the hedgehog had scuttled away into the undergrowth, content with its small reward.

When the small animal had vanished, wrapped forever in ragged warmth, the Kalevide was left alone in the meadow void of moving life. The wind died, and everything grew still. Only the stream beside him rippled, and even that was calm. Now, in the quiet evening, he was moved to mourn for the man, dead on the ground, whom he had promised to protect and had failed. All he could do now was grieve. It was the final act of the battle.

In the long twilight, beneath the joyless sky, he dug a shallow grave with his hands, and gently laid the small body of his friend inside it. This was the protection he could give. He piled earth and stone over him to keep him safe from rats and wolves and all more dreadful scavengers. Now the little man would no longer need to fear the terrors of the wood. In a ring around the gravesite the Kalevide planted berry-bearing bushes which were just beginning to come alive with bright white blossoms. In the dawn they would catch the dew and the mist of the waterfall and would sparkle in the early morning sunlight. Perhaps then this man would feel secure.

His sad duty done, the Kalevide gazed dully about him at the destruction left from the battle. The devastation was complete. The field which once had been a green-golden meadow was now a trampled mire. The wreckage of his lumber lay everywhere, broken boards, shattered planks, all scraps now, scattered as though some wanton godling had played at tipcat there and then run wild.

The Kalevide sighed; in the morning he would have to go back to Pihkva to gather the timber he had left behind on the shore, but for the time being, he was too tired and sore to think about it. Bringing sand from a nearby hill to build a dry bed on the swampy battlefield, he threw himself down beneath the naked, moonless, starless sky and welcomed sleep.

He trusted sleep. It had the power not only to restore his strength, but to wash away all sadness and to brighten all care. In the night he would dream again the day gone by. He was young. He could still hope for dreams that would relive the glory of the struggle just won, and spare him sorrow.

While the Kalevide slept, in the dark hour of deep midnight, the master sorcerer emerged from the forest. Crouching over his prey, once more he glared, with malice and malevolence, on the face wrapped in innocent repose. With dark spells and incantations, he took the Kalevide's sleep and shaped it to his evil will. He scattered his leaves and herbs, nightshade and hemp and poppy, over the man in slumber. He breathed foul words and chanted black charms of power to cast the son of Kalev into a trance from which he would not emerge for many days and nights. Weeks and months would pass before he would be allowed to wake in the living world.

22   On the sacred hill of Taara people gathered quietly in twilight. Youths and maidens, men and women, elders and children, all clad in white linen, came together and stood in respectful silence while the old man kindled fire with a whirling wheel in the manner of the ancients. Soon the first quick flame curled alive in its soft bed of tinder. At once, loud shouts of gladness burst from every mouth to greet the infant fire, born as if by magic out of the torchwood. It was Midsummer's Eve. The people had gathered to sing and dance in celebration. Torches were quickly lit from the first flame and cast into waiting piles of logs and brushwood to ignite the holy bonfires. On every hilltop and high place the ritual was repeated. Red-golden flames appeared everywhere against the darkness. Tongues of fire licked at the sky; the night came alive with light and dancing shadows. Shouts of "Summer! Summer!" resounded through the villages and forests of Viru as everyone rejoiced.

The people, wreathed with garlands and bouquets of cornflowers and daisies, the amber-herb and yarrow, danced in circles around the fires. Hand in hand, laughing couples leaped through the lapping flames to cleanse themselves of all disease and ill-fortune. In the groves boy and girl, young and old, took turns on the swings suspended from the high branches of Taara's oaks. Beneath long ropes twined with sweet honey-vines, they swung as high, as fast, as far, as they could fly, for however high they soared, so they believed, so high their flax would grow that year, and as many times as they swung, so thick would grow their corn.

Late in the night, lovers slipped away into the deep forest to seek in secret, so they said, the sweet-scented, sacred sonaialg-blossom, the magic herb that bloomed that one night only in all the year.

On the morrow every household rekindled its hearth with the embers of yesternight's bonfires. A charred stick was buried beside each threshold for luck. The flowers and bouquets, satu-rated with the holy smoke, were hung about the houses and barns to ward off the spells and afflictions of sorcerers and wicked spirits and all ill-wishing persons. In their huts and hamlets, people spent the day in feasting. They drank heartily of the ale brewed since spring but only tapped that morning. They sang; they danced. Tomorrow the festival would be over, and they would return to their toil in the fields or in the woods or on the sea, but for one day they were free, and since they had been promised abundant harvests, plentiful game, and good fishing, they had cause to celebrate that day, so celebrate they did, the joy of summertime and the turning of the year.

The Alevide, having completed the errands of others, had finally put Viru's farms in order. Now, on Midsummer's Day, he could look forward to bounteous crops, for the earth of the land was fertile and blessed by fortune. Corn was ripening richly in the fields. By autumn the sheds and granaries should be swollen with golden oats and rye and barley. The acres of blue-flowered flax shone like lakes in the summer light. Flocks of sheep and herds of cattle browsed in their lush green pastures. Lambs trotted beside ewes; calves sucked greedily at cows. All were thriving. The future looked so favorable that the Alevide had even begun to clear a piece of land for himself close to the wood where he would build his house and soon a settlement for his people, if they should wish to follow him to Viru from the east.

Already the Sulevide had raised a small fortress to keep his clan enclosed and protected. It was surrounded by a palisade of pointed timbers and equipped for siege. Now, in the weeks of summer, he was busy preparing an army for Viru.

One by one the iron knights of Saksaland withdrew from Harju and Laane, where they had found no war. They returned to their stone citadels along the marches of Lati and Leedu; there they began to incite the native Letts and Vends with hatred for their neighbors and with the need for war.

Saber-wielding horsemen swept like wildfire across the eastern plains. Reports were heard in Viru of savage riders overrunning the wide steppes and prairielands. Already, rumor said, they held the principalities and governments of Vene and had even entered the nearer provinces of Polotsk and Vitebsk in forays of rape and plunder.

No one in Viru knew the fate of the king. He seemed to have vanished from the earth. From time to time messengers were sent to summon him home again, but they always returned without word of his whereabouts. From his lonely outpost on the hill the cup-bearer directed all who sought the Kalevide to search the neighborhoods of Lake Peipus and Pihkva, but even there they found no sign or trace of him.

The boy himself grew weary with his waiting. The Kalevide had promised to return; he had said he would come back to take him to Viru. He had sworn he would never be left alone again. He had promised; he had given his word, but where was he now? There was no report, not even a rumor to say what had become of him. At last the cup-bearer could bear it no longer. He left his station one day and trudged unhappily northward by himself. The journey, which would have been delightful if made with a companion, was dreary and depressing instead. He did not see the beauties along the way; he felt no joy in the forest. With no one to share these moments, beauty held no joy.

Once in Viru, the boy hid himself in the Kalevide's empty house, where he was surrounded by mementos of his short-lived friend and the memories of his dreams for happy days to come. Occasionally the Alevide looked in to see how he was or if he needed anything, but there was little he could do now to help him. The boy would not forgive. He became embittered; the clothes he donned were dark, his words grew sullen. His once-quick smile became a sneer, his wink a frown, but it was only a mask for his sadness.

In its watery bed, the sword of Kalev began to brood over all the commands enjoined on it.

Somewhere in the forest lurked a sorcerer bent on evil.

The bright white petals have fallen from the blossoms on berry bushes in a ring around a grave. Hard, red jewels of fruit swell where the flowers had been. Summer has turned toward autumn while for seven weeks the Kalevide has lain in his enchanted sleep on his couch of sand.

Out of the innocent depth of that sleep was shaped the single dream that filled that long span of time:

[210]

From the center of the world a mountain peak towered so high that its summit was lost in the clouds of heaven. The mountain was hollow, and in his dream the Kalevide stood inside the peak on a high shelf of stone, a gallery circling the immense cavern. From that vantage point he gazed in anguish upon the workshop of the world's first smith.

Far below him, so far they seemed dwarfed by the distance, dark men scurried everywhere over the hard stone floor of the mountain, busy in the turmoil of their labor, never resting. They seemed so small that to the Kalevide's eyes they looked like insects, not men. They all looked the same. They wore uniform clothing, not the smocks and aprons he would have expected in a smithy, but strange single-pieced garments that were both trousers and shirts, all of the same dark cloth, blue so deep it seemed to be black. On their heads they wore round, silver helmets for protection.

The foundry was so vast no one ever walked from side to side. Instead, the workmen rode on wheeled vehicles not drawn by animals, but powered by some unknown force hidden inside them. Some rode from place to place on small three-wheeled cars. Others drove huge, lumbering wains, larger than any ox could haul, wagons weighted under gigantic loads of charcoal or ore or limestone, destined for the gaping mouths of huge furnaces set around the perimeter of the mountain. Here men with shovels fed roaring fires or charged tremendous vats with metal, metal which dissolved to molten iron that was like liquid pain.

The dream contained all the dread of all the smithies the Kalevide had ever known, but magnified now a thousandfold. The heat in that cavern was unbearably intense and the smoky air stifling; far worse was the noise, the constant raging of machines which knew no peace. The hollow of the mountain roared and bellowed, shrieked and muttered in endless turmoil out of the center of the earth. Gates of furnaces opened with ringing clangs; fires thundered, blown by jets of gaseous wind from the utter bowels of the world. Huge quantities of ore and stone rumbled down iron chutes. Molten metal seethed and fumed with venom. Above the heads of the workmen, monstrous ladles rocked on iron rails; their wheels screamed with the screech of hard metal on metal. Their cups plunged hungrily into the molten broth and came forth filled with running fire. Here the very spirit of the iron was formed. As they trundled, swaying and shrieking, beneath his eyes, the Kalevide gazed horrified into pools of red-white searing hate. Across the hall the ladles were tipped, and vomits of fire gushed from their lips into endless rows of molds, the casting ingots which later smiths would shape into metalware. The streams were like blazing waterfalls. The spew of sparks erupted like fountains to the mountain's height. In the dimly-lit cavern the blast of light was staggering.

Hammers pounded constantly. Across the foundry the weights of graypainted presses, larger than men, rose and fell, rose and fell, rose and fell, beating sheets of metal into forms for unknown purposes. High speed drills bored countless holes in heavy plate; the iron screamed in pain. Iron bars, larger than trees, thundered across series of rollers. Ejected from the entrails of gigantic presses, one and then another, and another crashed against the sidewall. Again, again. The chaos of noise grew more violent. All around the workshop machines were cutting, grinding, bending, wrenching, turning, shaving, honing, stretching, crushing; wheels, blades, drills, hammers became instruments of torture. The air was too filled with metals' tormented screams rising above the drumming, the clanging, the rumbling. The vibration became a part of the earth and rose through the stone. It passed through the Kalevide's feet into his body; he wanted to scream. The very rock of the mountain seemed to tremble from the onslaught of sound.

A whistle blew. A single high, shrill cry that reached above all the roaring clamor. For a moment everything fell silent and all activity stopped. Around the smithy the machines were still as the workers streamed like ants out of the hall. They hurried through the doors set somewhere in the walls beneath the gallery to seek deep, hidden chambers where they would feed or sleep or drink themselves into a stupor, their only relief from their sunless lives.

It was only a pause; the quiet could not endure. The men who left were as quickly replaced by other teams pouring in through other doors. Another whistle sounded; levers were thrown, switches turned, and the dread machines resumed their tireless, insane rant.

The only ones who did not leave when the first signal blew, the ones who could not be replaced, were the master smiths. In the very center of the foundry, a circle was cleared of all the giant devices which filled the rest of the mountain. Into this circle no beastless carts careened, no dark-uniformed workmen walked. This was the true heart of the workshop; here metal craft was born. Here there were no thundering furnaces, no crashing presses, only one small forge, with gently glowing coals fanned by an ancient leather bellows, and a single anvil set in the very center of the circle. Around this anvil worked nine smiths, the nine masters of metalwork. No others were allowed near.

Seven sat in a ring on the floor, for the anvil was built low to the ground. In their hands they held copper hammers with handles wrought of silver. The eighth, junior to the rest, hobbled between anvil and forge, and back again, carrying the iron bar they were shaping. He held it with a pair of silver tongs, and when he laid the gleaming ingot gently on the anvil, each of the smiths struck it in his turn. The ninth was the master of them all, the master of all smithcraft, Ilmarine himself.

He was clad, like the other eight, in a long white linen smock that reached to his ankles. A white leather apron protected the cloth from sparks. Both were spotless. Below the hems, the Kalevide could see, his shins shined like silver. So, too, did his wrists and arms. As flesh had withered with wretched age, this master of smiths had replaced it with undying plate. His legs, his arms, his chest, his loins, all his parts now were wrought of enduring metal. When he paused to wipe his brow, his wrist rang against his forehead with the pure tone of a silver bell.

Ilmarine did not walk. He rolled around the circle of the seven seated smiths on the silver wheels which had replaced his crippled feet. Each of the seven struck once at the shining bar of iron, then, when the cycle was complete, Ilmarine lightly tapped the work with a golden hammer to impress his mark upon it before it felt the fire's wrath once more. Then he rolled to the next position and the rite was repeated. Around the circle the series of hammer strokes rang with the clear notes of music, sometimes fast, sometimes slow, often heavy, often easy, whatever the ritual required, while above their hammering the smiths sang the strident songs of iron. Thus they toiled unceasingly through time. They were shaping the blade of a sword, a sword far mightier than the sword smith of Soome had wrought for Kalev, far mightier than any on the mortal earth.

The Kalevide gazed down on their work and yearned for that sword. His eyes were riveted to the blade of his dream. Even the noise and clamor of the foundry, although continuing unabated, seemed to fade, forgotten as his attention fixed on that central circle. Around went the cycle of shaping strokes, around again, around like a wheel that turned forever without end. Each blow was a caress. Once Ilmarine took the silver tongs from his assistant then gripped the gleaming blade in his own two silver hands. The air around him shimmered in the aura of its heat. Ilmarine raised his arms and held the sword before him. He held it out to the Kalevide as though presenting it to a king.

At that moment a young man broke into the workshop and ran across the floor toward the middle of the room, shouting as loud as he could to be heard above the din of the machines. All at once all other sounds inside the mountain ceased. The presses and rollers continued to work, the furnaces still blazed, but in awesome silence. As the youth ran by below the Kalevide, he looked up. His face was ghastly pale; his clothes were stained with blood. He gripped his head as though he had to hold it in place on his neck.

"Stop!" the young man shouted. "Stop, stop, stop, stop." The word, cried only once, seemed to go on forever, echoing in the hollow cavern.

"Waste no more labor on the son of Kalev, Do not waste this sword on the son of Kalev! He will only use it to slay his friends or slaughter helpless innocents. Waste no more of your power on this man who is a murderer!"

"It is not true," the Kalevide wanted to cry out in return. "Not true!" He wanted to shout so that his words, too, would ring off the walls, but at that moment the son of old Tuhja, the Contemptible One, that is Emptiness, used the nightmare to strangle him so he could not utter one word in his defense. The Kalevide felt as though he were smothering under unbounded pressure. A mountain lay on his breast; it forced him down deeper into his dream. The roaring in his ears now came from inside him. He no longer saw the foundry or the smiths. He was blind. He knew that he was dying if he did not wake and fought desperately to pull himself out of the grip of that engulfing sleep. It felt as though he were swimming upward through a pit of thick liquid iron, but cold and gray, not molten with white heat. He could not breathe, and all his thrashing was to no avail. Then for one moment he let himself float suspended in the viscous liquid. For an instant he stopped struggling and rested from his inner torment. In that instant he opened his eyes and found himself in daylight and awake.

23   For a long while the Kalevide could not move. He lay, stupefied, on his back, with his eyes gazing blankly into the distance of the pale blue sky, but after the darkness of deep sleep, the bright light of morning was too bright, and he was forced to close his eyes again while he composed himself from the effects of his nightmare.

He could not keep them closed for long. The dream had been

too deep; in the night behind his eyes he sank into the echo of his horror. With a loud groan, the Kalevide forced himself to look at the day again. A magpie was perched on the tip of a long branch of a bramble bush which arched over him like an arm. "Wake, wake, wake," the black-and-white bird shouted raucously. He must rise, it cried, he must hasten to his home, he had lain asleep for seven weeks, entangled in the sorcerer's snare.

The birds spoke truly when they spoke, so the Kalevide believed, because Linda had told him so, and so he believed the magpie's cry. For a moment more he lay immobilized on the ground, breathing deeply, thinking he must get up, wondering if it were possible, then with a curse for the sorcerer, he leaped to his feet, frightening the messenger away in a burst of iridescence.

Seven weeks! How could he have lost so much time without knowing it? Seven—there was no time to think about it, no time to stop, no time for breakfast, no time for anything at all. Seven weeks! His people were waiting for him. They would need him. He was going to build walls around their villages. He was going to protect them from the war. The war? The Kalevide groaned. What had happened in seven weeks? Was it over? Had it begun? Had he failed his people as he always feared he would? Bitterly, he cursed himself for falling asleep in the first place.

The shattered remains of his timber lay scattered over the meadow, a reminder of his battle with the sorcerer's sons, but all he could think of was reaching Viru and building walls for his people. There was no time to return to Pihkva for more lumber. Without his sword he could not cut any close to home. The scraps and fragments would have to serve. Some might be useful. He might still help the people.

Anxious to hurry, and slowing himself by hurrying too much, the Kalevide spun in distracted circles, picking up bits of broken board, lashing them into a sledge, checking the knots, checking them again, retying them all, untying them to add another plank, looking for provisions he no longer had, tightening the tow rope, thinking about shaping himself another staff, deciding not to, changing his mind, changing it again, checking his knots, looking around, trying to decide what direction to go, setting out, starting over. It was impossible to go back by way of the hill where he had left the cup-bearer, even if the boy were still waiting for him. That route was too long, there was no time, he must head directly home. His planks would be needed; he would be needed. Seven weeks! He plunged into the forest, not quite certain of the direction he was going, but desperate to be gone.

An uncertain trail led him into a wilderness wilder than he had known to be in Viru. It wound through groves broken by great boulders heaved upward through the ground in ages gone. Granite shelves lay exposed to the air like gray scars on the earth. Here and there streambeds trickled with muddy water the color of old blood. Hillsides were barren, stripped of trees as though raked by savage claws. Here the air was unnaturally close and still, the sky leaden, laden with foul fumes. Slowly, the track drew the Kalevide into a narrow stone-bound canyon wedged between two steep-walled mountains. Toward evening, smothered in gloom and shadow, he came to the black hole of a cave gaping like a voracious mouth in the naked rock face of the cliff. It was the entranceway, one of many in every land, to the dreaded realm of Põrgu.

A large fire was burning in front of the cave; black and smoky flames blazed out of a pile of tar-soaked timbers. Three small men were clustered around an iron cauldron hung over the fire on thick chains. As they stirred whatever mix was seething inside the kettle, they chanted obscene songs.

"What are you cooking there?" the Kalevide called. He had suddenly realized he hadn't eaten at all that day, indeed not for seven weeks, and he was famished. "Can you spare some of your soup for a traveler?"

"Eh? What does he say? What?" The eldest of the three cupped his hand behind his ear as if he were deaf. "What does he want?"

"He says, 'What's cooking?'" shouted the second suppressing a smile. "He says he wants some."

"He says he's hungry," shouted the third.

"Hungry? Hungry, is he? Aye, some men are. Some are."

"What's in your pot?" The Kalevide shouted, too. "Is it for a feast or wedding, or can I have some?"

"Eh? You don't have to shout, young man. Not to me. For a feast, is it? No, no feast. For a feast we boil an ox so great it takes a hundred men to kill it. Five hundred men to bleed it. A thousand men to clean and cut its meat. Today we are only three. We cook only the poor folk's fare. No feast today. Sorry."

"It's all right. I don't mind." He still shouted. "I'll take whatever you have. I'm hungry."

"What's that? What does he say?"

"He says he's hungry," repeated the other two in turn.

"Aye, some men are."

The Kalevide was becoming exasperated. Once more he demanded to know what was cooking in the cauldron.

"Good enough fare," replied the elder testily. "Good enough

for most. Half an elk it is, and a boar's ribs. The lights and liver of a bear.''

"Suet of a wolf," added the second, as if it were a litany. "The hide of an old sow-bear."

"And an egg," intoned the third. "One egg from an abandoned eagle's nest."

"Good enough, good enough," the first returned. "Good enough for most. This kettle cooks for all men; all men taste our stock at one time or another. Tonight the pot cooks for the Sarvik and his old mother. The cat and the dog both have a portion. The rest will be divided among the workmen; all will have an ample share. I warrant we can feed enough. Are you hungry, youngling? Give the child some soup."

The Kalevide gagged in disgust. "That is the worst-looking mess I have ever seen. Don't you have any bread?"

"Eh? What's that? What does he say?"

"He says he doesn't want any."

"Doesn't want any? Well, it's good enough. Good enough for sorcerers and witches. Maybe he's too fine and fancy. Maybe he'd like the oaten cakes the old mother bakes for the dainty folks, for the maidens. They're not for us, not for the likes of us, no. And not for him, neither, I warrant."

"But a man would die if he ate that."

The old man cupped his ear.

"He says he would die."

"Aye. Some men do. Some do."

"Where is your master?" demanded the Kalevide. "I'll speak to him about this. Perhaps he knows how to treat a stranger with some courtesy and respect. And don't think I won't tell him how his servants have mocked me."

"Eh? Eh?"

"He says he wants to see the master."

"He wants to see the Sarvik."

"Well, let him. I don't care." The old one rudely turned his back on the Kalevide and refused to have anything more to do with him. "Let him go," he mumbled over the steaming cauldron. "If he wants to, let him. I don't care. Who is he? Let him see the Sarvik. So what? Won't taste my soup. Who cares? Who is he, anyhow?"

Nevertheless, the younger two pleaded with the Kalevide not to go. "Please, sir, you mustn't disturb the master," said the second. "Please, not the Sarvik. You won't come back again. No, not easily."

"You'll be sorry if you go," warned the third. "You won't come back at all."

The Kalevide would not be dissuaded. He was angry now and determined to see this lord, this Sarvik, whoever he was, and teach him better hospitality. This was his land; he was responsible for the behavior of all who dwelled in it.

"Show me where to find him," he insisted. "I'm not afraid of any man."

Since it was, after all, his own request, the demons ushered him into the cave and directed him to follow the tunnel. It would lead him into Põrgu underground.

As soon as he had disappeared into the utter darkness of the pit, the three suddenly burst out laughing. They clapped their hands and danced around the fire.

"The lion's in the net," sang one.

"And the bear is in the trap," returned another.

"Oh, he takes his hide to market now for nothing," wheezed the elder, well satisfied.

From a gaping mouth at the cavern's entrance, the passage tapered to a hole so narrow that the Kalevide was compelled to crawl if he wanted to get through. It was totally dark inside the earth; he had to grope cautiously, afraid of hidden traps or pitfalls. The tunnel continued to close around him; it grew so tight that the walls scraped his back and sides. Through the twisted passageway he writhed, on his belly now, turning this way and that until he lost all sense of direction. He no longer knew which way was left, which right, which up, which down. In the underworld all directions are reversed.

In the absolute darkness he felt as though he were in a tomb, his own grave, pressed in on all sides by the silent weight of stone. All his life he had feared to think of being underground; it had always seemed too much like being dead. Yet here he was, crawling like a worm, passing into another world, a world that some said was the land of death itself. Perhaps he would not even get that far. Perhaps he would be caught in the tunnel, wedged in the rock, unable to move. Perhaps that was all Põrgu was, a slow and silent death.

Ahead of him he saw a piece of jutting rock. He reached for it to pull himself forward, and then realized excitedly that, indeed, he could see it. He was no longer blind. A thin, faint light had come into the cave to touch the walls around him. The tunnel looked as though it were cut through the stone, but cut for smaller men than he, or men less substantial. Although it took a long while before he reached the source of that light, eventually he came into a chamber illuminated by a single lamp suspended from the ceiling by an iron chain.

The room was small, but large enough that he could stand with ease. Except for the lamp and two large urns, it was bare. One jar held liquid as white as milk, the other something as black as pitch. Between them was a large folding door. The Kalevide pushed on it, but it was securely barred on the other side. He had come to the end of his journey. Sliding miserably to the floor, he leaned back against the doorframe. He was alone in a vault hollowed from the earth.

While he sat, sadly musing on his fate and the folly which had brought him to this end, he heard faint sounds through the wall. Maidens spinning thread were singing songs in soft, plaintive voices. Their song seemed a lament for lost happiness and the hard life they were forced to live. It was a prayer for a savior to come and rescue them from the cruelty of their lot.

Eagerly, the Kalevide pounded on the door. He would be their deliverer. He braced himself and strained against the latch, but the door would not open. No strength of his could break the lock. Still the sound of the maidens' singing called to him. Listening to their mournful song, he was reminded of the air maiden by the well and supposed he was being duped again. These spirits, or whatever dwelled behind the wall, must have sapped his strength for it had never failed him before. Had they barred the door to make him seem a fool? Did they mock him in the moments of his death?

He almost kicked the door in anger, but checked his rage so they would not have the satisfaction of hearing him complain. Instead he began to sing a song of his own, a song of four fair maidens who went gathering flowers in the woods and what happened to them there. He sang it gently, to tease them, in tones just loud enough to carry through the wall. There was a sudden sound of scurrying, and then someone spoke directly to him.

"Hurry! Open the door," she said. "Everyone is gone; the family is away. You can free us safely. Let us out. Please."

"Open the door yourselves," the Kalevide replied coldly. "Then maybe I'll see about your safety. I won't be fooled again."

"We can't." This was a second voice, softer and more plaintive than the first.

"It's locked; it's always locked," said a third. "Can't you break the door down? We're all alone here."

"No, I can't break the door down, as you no doubt know already."

"If you're not strong enough, dip your hands in the liquid by the door. The darker water. It will give you great power. But, listen to me, before you enter, dip your hands into the white to moderate your strength or you'll break everything to pieces."

The Kalevide demurred. "I have never needed help before," he said.

"Do as I say," the voice said sternly, "and don't be so proud. This place is different from the lands you've known before."

Although he feared another trap, the Kalevide did as he was bid, and plunged his arms into the urn of black liquid. Despite looking thick and oily, it was so thin he could scarcely feel it. When he drew his hands out, they were dry. The liquid was cold, however, a more deathly cold than he had ever experienced, and he felt no stronger. No great power surged through his body, nothing like the force that had swept through him when he wrestled the aurochs, or again when he grappled with the water demon. Was this just another jest? When he faced the door, it was almost with loathing. The Kalevide was certain he still could not move it, and if not, then he would leave the maidens where they were.

Yet when he pushed lightly on the panels, his strength doubled and doubled again, unfolding like a flower. Springing open, the door crashed to the floor. The posts, broken from the wall of stone, fell over with a roar of thunder. Boldly the Kalevide strode into the next room, only to find it empty.

For an instant his eye caught a fleeting glimpse of skirts and slippers as maidens fled in terror through another door. He followed them.

"Stop!" one shrieked. "Go back. Use the milk-white water. Wash off the enchantment."

He merely laughed, however, and pursued them down the hall. At the end he came into a large chamber whose walls, floor, and ceiling were hewn from stone. It was sparsely furnished, with only a large stone couch in the middle and a stone cupboard set against one wall. Lamps of oil burning in stone pots hung on chains with links of stone. They cast a dreary light across the room. In the corner, thrown aside, were three spindles, looking like disused children's tops. Two of the maidens disappeared down another of the many hallways leading out of the chamber. The third lingered in the doorway to see what manner of man their rescuer might be.

A quick glance at the maid showed her to be well fashioned,

young and fair, with strands of honey-colored hair spilling wantonly from her kerchief. This the Kalevide noticed in an instant, but he had no eyes for the fashion of her blue and crimson skirts or her scarlet stockings or silken slippers stitched with silver threads, and he never saw the delicately embroidered birds and flowers on her white linen overblouse. His gaze was drawn aside, instead, to the stone cupboard beside her. There on pegs were an old ragged hat, a slim willow wand, and a naked sword.

"It is the sword of my dream," he exclaimed. "Ilmarine's sword!" He was about to take it when the maiden clutched his arm.

"Beware this sword," she said. "It belongs to the Sarvik, lord of this realm, and to him alone. Touch it at your peril."

"It was meant for me!"

"Take the hat and rod, if you like. They are yours and will do you many wonders if you wish, more wonders than steel ever could. A sword can serve only one master truly, and it must be obtained from the smith who shaped it, or it will bring no luck."

"That is so," the Kalevide said with regret, then added boldly, "you may keep your hat and rod though. I don't want them. They're only fit for sorcerers and wizards, not for Kalev's son. I have the strength of my two hands, and that is strength enough."

"Don't be so proud," she said saucily. "You don't even know what you can do with these. Watch." She took the cap from its peg. "They say it's made from the parings of old fingernails, but I don't know. It looks like felt to me. There isn't another hat like it in the world, though. With a wish it will satisfy any desire. Look." Pulling it down over her ears, she chanted:

> Raise her, raise the maiden,
> the golden maiden, raise her,
> raise her like the son of Kalev,
> like her friend in stature.

With the words she began to grow. Her head rose an ell in height, and her body broadened and filled out accordingly. In a moment she was as large as he was. She laughed. Her voice boomed deeply to match her size.

The Kalevide laughed foolishly with her. Unable to resist, he snatched the hat from her head and clapped it on his own, singing:

Shrink me, shrink the hero,
the son of Kalev, shrink me,
shrink me like the maiden,
like the honey maiden was.

Immediately he sank in stature. He felt his flesh and bones contracting as he dwindled in size until he stood no taller than the maiden's chest. A singing sensation hummed through his body as his spirit seemed to flow faster, compressed in the smaller frame, as the shorter string of a kantele vibrates more quickly than the longer strings and holds a higher tone. His tunic fell like a skirt around his ankles. His empty scabbard scraped the floor. Everything around him suddenly looked strange and outsized. The angles of things were changed; shadows fell differently. From his new perspective he noticed details he never would have seen before; he missed as many that he had known. He could not see the tops of things so well. The maiden herself now seemed huge, even grotesque, as she towered over him. Her body was too large. Her swollen breasts strained the fabric of her blouse. Suddenly he too laughed, and scarcely recognized his voice; it was high-pitched, like a little boy's. He felt giddy, as though newly come into the world. He was a child again.

The maiden took back the hat saying, as she resumed her normal size, "There. Didn't I promise you a wonder?" Since they were now a match, she kissed him quickly on the cheek. "But I don't see how you can stand to be so big," she added playfully. "I didn't like it. I felt so fat!"

"Then today I'll stay a little boy. I'll be your little brother. But let me have the hat, in case there's trouble." The Kalevide slipped it into the folds of his shirt where it would be handy if danger threatened.

While they were sporting together, the other two maidens returned. The eldest strode directly across the room to bolt a door leading down another passageway. The other maid merely stood and gazed shyly at the floor.

"These are my sisters," explained the maiden. "This one is the eldest, and she keeps the geese that feed on the common. While that one—see how bashful she is—has to polish all the gold- and silver- and copperware."

"Yes, but you, you baby, have to sweep the floors and haul out the ashes," said the eldest.

"We have a hard life," observed the second girl sadly.

"Why did you lock that door?" The Kalevide asked. Were there more traps planned for him?

"It leads to the kitchen, where the old mother is at work with her baking. If she heard your noise, she would soon investigate, to our peril. We should be safe now."

Safe. The meaning of the word suddenly struck the maidens, who had never felt safe in Põrgu before. It meant new joy. The youngest caught the Kalevide's hand and whirled him in an excited dance. The eldest joined their circle and drew the second sister in with her. All four reeled in a spinning ring. The Kalevide's scabbard swung beside him like a third leg. They sang, running through all the songs they knew, and when they could no longer sing, they were content to laugh. In their sheer delight, they ignored the scratching and growling noises coming from behind the bolted door.

Out of breath at last, all four fell back on the couch of stone and giggled foolishly. The Kalevide spread his arms and drew the sisters close, the eldest on one side, the youngest on the other, while the second sat demurely on the floor by his feet. Immersed in their breathless excitement, he was both proud and happy and, because he could forget where he was, he felt for once a part of the way that things should be.

"Tell me about yourselves," he said when he had caught his breath. "Tell me who you are and how you came here. I don't believe you're demons."

"Demons indeed," sniffed the eldest. The youngest laughed; the second sister shivered.

"We came from a country far from here," said the eldest. "As far from here as can be. A thousand leagues or more. A land where the sun was always shining and where all men lived in wealth and happiness. Now we must live where the sun will never shine and men only suffer. When we were children, we were stolen from our home by sorcerers, who sold us to the Sarvik for slaves. Now we must do his bidding day and night, early and late. Whatever he demands we do. We have lived in Põrgu a long, long time. Longer than you would think. A thousand years? Longer? Even we no longer know. To spare us tormet, Ukko, in his mercy, gave us our youth and beauty to keep for as long as we kept our virginity. When that is lost, we shall age as other women do."

"But what good is it?" moaned the youngest, "What good to be forever young and beautiful when we are hidden away here, and denied all happiness and pleasure?"

"It was the most Ukko could do; he could not set us free."

"In all that time, couldn't you ever escape?" he asked. "What about this wishing hat? Wouldn't it take you out of here? It's

[223]

sorcery, I know, but you're women; you don't have the strength of men.''

"Where would we go?" whispered the second sister.

"No one in our homeland would remember us," said the eldest. "We have no family any more, no one to welcome us. Sometimes it is easier to remain in a situation that is hard, even intolerable, but familiar than it is to embark into an unknown life."

"Then before tomorrow's day is done, I will do what Ukko could not. I will take you all away from here. If you need a place to go, I will take you to Viru. If you want families, I'll give you each a husband."

The Kalevide promised to wed the eldest sister to his general, the Sulevide, since she seemed more sure, more hard, than the others; she was sensible and she smiled less. The youngest would wed the Alevide, because she liked to laugh. The second sister, the prettiest, but also the quietest, should have the cup-bearer.

"Three of you for my three men," he said. "You will found the three noble lines of Viru."

"No wife for yourself?" teased the youngest.

"No, I cannot marry. Not now."

She touched the empty scabbard between his legs. "Is it because you have no sword?"

"I took a vow," was all he would say.

"Without a sword how will you free us?" asked the eldest, ever practical. "How will you defend us against the Sarvik? The way out of here is not easy; you may find yourself trapped here with us."

"I'll fight him with my hands if I have to. I'm strong enough."

"Use the wishing hat and rod," urged the youngest.

"No, that's sorcery, and I won't use it in a good cause. I'm sorry I even played the hat game with you. It was wrong."

"It was only play."

"You would be wise to employ whatever devices come to hand," said the eldest. "You are not in your country now but in Põrgu, where simple strength and bravery are not enough. The Sarvik has a thousand sorcerers in his service and a thousand demons at his command. He is the lord of winds and spells of evil more dreadful than you can dream."

"And a rod is as good as a sword," said the youngest.

The Kalevide only laughed. "I'm not worried. I once vanquished a host of sorcerers bare-handed. I once slew a horde of conjured spirits. I've wrestled with a demon and grappled a mighty ox to the ground. I've never been defeated in battle."

"Are you so strong?" asked the second sister in awe.

"When I have my right size I am. Right now I feel more like a girl. Maybe I should wear a skirt," he added with a giggle.

They all laughed.

Their fears forgotten for a while, they began to play again. Through the rest of the evening and long into the night they danced and sang and were merry in many games. They played the falcon game, where he was the falcon and they the doves. They played kiss-in-the-ring, blindman's buff, hide-and-seek, and many more, some of which they made up themselves. Whatever they played, even the most foolish game, the Kalevide always won. The sisters let him.

When at last they were weary, they retired to the couch and extinguished all the lights. A dog was whimpering behind the kitchen door.

24   In the first hours of morning all three maidens were desperately anxious to leave Põrgu behind. It had been fine to sport in the night, it was exciting to think their savior had come, but that thrill of freedom could not last long if they remained inside their prison. Their master, the Sarvik, was due to return at any moment. If he found them playing, their fate would be too terrible to contemplate. Yet the Kalevide showed no inclination to leave.

While the sisters paced nervously around the stone-walled room, he lounged back on the rough-hewn couch as if he were expecting someone important to come or something momentous to occur, although he did not know who or what.

"Let's go," pleaded the second sister.

Sounds continued behind the kitchen door, constant reminders of their danger. If the creature trapped there ever escaped to raise the alarm, the wrath of Põrgu would crash down harder than any fist.

The eldest sister examined the bolt on the door. "It is still secure," she said to reassure them. "The old woman will not interfere with us, but there are others."

"Please!"

"The Sarvik," said the youngest. "You promised to take us out of here, away from him."

"All right, we'll go," said the Kalevide finally, "but only if you show me around this palace first."

For the maidens it was such a relief to be moving at all that they immediately agreed, although their danger remained, and would remain as long as they were underearth.

Quickly leaving the cold room of stone behind, they pulled the Kalevide through a stone doorway and down a gallery hewn from stone. The passage was long and unbroken except for a few niches carved in the smooth walls to hold stone lamps. At the end of the gray hallway they entered a large room whose walls and furnishings were wrought entirely out of iron. The air itself vibrated with the venomous spirit of the angry metal. Even the bolts and rivets glared with malice.

"This is one of the Sarvik's rooms," the eldest sister said. "Here his male servants meet and work or perhaps amuse themselves if they are able. Here, too, he sometimes tortures them in ways too terrible to describe."

"Come along," the Kalevide said in an anguished tone. "I don't like it here." The chamber reminded him too much of the workshops of smiths and their atmospheres seething with the spite of violent ores.

Through an iron doorway they entered a long gallery of iron. Safely beyond that grim passage, they came to a second room furnished entirely in copper.

"This room is for the maidservants," the eldest was explaining. "Here they come together to work or relax as best they can. And here, too, the Sarvik torments them and punishes them in ways not fit for you to hear."

The Kalevide, however, was listening with one ear only. His attention was caught more by a large box of jewelry and ornaments in the corner. Eagerly he pawed through the intricately designed bracelets and brooches, choosing finally, as the maidens pulled him away, several copper rings for his fingers, a band for his wrist, and a long copper chain to hang around his neck.

Through the copper archway and beyond the copper gallery, they came into a room of silver, filled with gleaming silver furnishings and fittings. A bright silver table and a single silver chair dominated the chamber. Chests of silver treasure were placed in each corner. The Kalevide knelt by one and then another to dig through them.

"This is one of the Sarvik's own rooms," the second sister said. "Here he often spends his time relaxing in this chair and planning his business for the coming day."

The Kalevide held an embossed arm-ring up to the light, liked what he saw, and slipped it onto his wrist. Then he took another, and a necklace adorned with small silver bells. More rings glittered on his fingers. To the maiden's comments he merely nodded.

They went through a gate of silver and along a silver hallway into a room of gold.

"This is another of the Sarvik's rooms," said the second maiden, reciting her words. "Here he feasts and revels when feeling merry. Yesterday I spent long hours polishing all the goldware here, preparing for his next high banquet."

"Uh-huh," mumbled the Kalevide, more interested in the many caskets of glittering jewelry. He offered her a chain of gold, saying, "Here, take this; it's nice;" but she shook her head. Her sisters, too, declined his gift. In the lands of men the necklace would have been worth a great fortune; in Põrgu it was tawdry. The Kalevide draped it around his own neck. Like a child loosed in his mother's jewelry case, he began to deck himself with more and more ornaments. He pinned clasps and brooches to his shirt and fastened gleaming rings to his arms. His copper rings were cast aside, replaced by more precious bands of gold. Soon every finger gleamed with at least one, some with two or more. Several lengths of gold-linked chain tied around his waist became his belt. Golden collars adorned his neck. At last he discovered a suit of golden armor. He donned the gleaming breastplate of gold and the matching gauntlets and greaves, all embossed with whorls of golden wire. The spirals captured light and cast it wheeling forth to dazzle all beholders' eyes. After that he could take no more.

Walking out of that chamber and along the corridor of gold, the eldest and youngest sisters lagged a few paces behind while the second hurried the Kalevide on.

"What kind of man is this?" whispered the eldest. "I have never seen anyone act this way; he has so little concern for the danger. What is he thinking of, or is he mad? Gathering gold instead of fleeing as far and as fast as he can. Is he going to rescue us or not?"

The youngest sister shrugged her shoulders. "I hope so," was all she could say.

The fifth chamber was decorated entirely with silk. Silken tapestries draped the walls, silken carpets covered the floors. From the chest in the corners silken raiment overflowed. This was the room where the Sarvik's women decked themselves in silk array for festive days. Beyond the silk gallery was the chamber of satin, where the Sarvik's maidens dressed themselves; beyond that was the room of lace, designed for little girls. The Kalevide passed through them without interest; he had no eye for the treasures there.

A curtain of lace, a film as light and delicate as spiders' webs, covered the last archway. He swept it aside and strolled down the gallery of lace until he left the palace behind and entered a wide courtyard where, instead of grass, silver coins covered the ground.

Seven storehouses stood in a ring around the yard. The first was built of heavy granite blocks so finely carved and joined, the seams between them were invisible. It was filled with rye. The second, overflowing with barley, was fashioned of steel plate. The third, for oats, was constructed of hens' eggs joined by invisible cement. The fourth was similarly formed of goose eggs; it held wheat. The fifth, containing stores of millet, was of polished quartz; the sixth, full of vegetables and root crops, had been built of the finest eagles' eggs.

It was the seventh, however, which was the wonder of them all. It could not have been seen in the lands where men dwelled, or anywhere else on earth. That it should exist in Põrgu was sacrilege. This small storehouse had been fashioned entirely from the fragile eggs, inconceivably rare, of the Siuru, the mystic blue bird, Ukko's daughter, of whom legends were told and songs sung. It was filled with lumps of lard and tallow, unrefined, yellow, and rancid with age. Thus the Sarvik kept his goods.

The Kalevide was bored. He hardly glanced in the storehouses and completely ignored the cow barns, built entirely of bones woven like wattlework, behind the courtyard. Whatever he was looking for, he would not find it here. Slowly the party meandered back to the palace, where they strolled through more of its maze of corridors.

"Tell me about this Sarvik," the Kalevide asked at last as they turned into the last hallway. "Who is he, and what does he do?"

"We do not know very much," replied the eldest, hoping that the more he learned, the more he would be inclined to leave. "Much about the Sarvik is a mystery, and he keeps it so. He will not speak his true name. I cannot tell you his origin or his lineage. I do not know if his father was a bear and his mother a wolf, or if it was a mare that suckled him and a goat who rocked the cradle.

"I do know this, however: he rules a vast dominion. What you see here is only one of his estates, and only a portion of one at that. He has countless other holdings which occupy much of his time. That is a blessing for us, since he is often away. He takes long journeys from one place to the next, but always he makes them in secret and incredibly short times, so no one ever knows when he will appear or where. No one ever sees or hears which way he goes, or what lands he visits. No one even knows how he travels, or the vehicle he rides. We see him going out or coming in, but when he is away, we know nothing of what he does, except that what he does is not good.''

"It has been said, and it may be true," interposed the youngest sister, "that at the center of the world floats a vast open space where the Sarvik rules seven worlds, seven islands surrounded by seven streams, seven islands thronged by the spirits of the dead, seven lands where the shades must live in crowded villages with no hope ever to escape. He is the lord over all, and they are his subjects, as Ukko in his wisdom has decreed since the world was born.''

"He is a heartless master," continued the eldest. "He rules with terrible severity, and knows no mercy, although it is said, as you know, that on the Night of the Wandering Dead, his subjects are allowed to visit the houses where they once lived. On that day they flee their islands in shoals. Through the caves and caverns of the earth they fly with a rush of wind to reach the places where they once knew joy or grief. But when that day is done and the feasts are completed, they are compelled to return, each to his hut within the kingdom of Pörgu; then there is a great sighing in the caves. No one dares to linger in the lands above longer than the time allowed. They fear the Sarvik's wrath. There is no escape.''

The second sister added, "The Sarvik takes his servants, his workers and his maids, from the folk of those lands. He forces them to follow him to the palace and do as he bids in the iron and copper chambers you just saw. If they fail in anything, any task at all, he beats them with bars of iron and with copper rods.''

The Kalevide recoiled. "Don't draw away like that," laughed the youngest sister. "We aren't dead, not yet. We haven't been rowed across the river. We haven't even seen the seven islands, nor do we ever care to, thank you, for we have seen those who have. No, the Sarvik sometimes takes servants from the sunlit world; sometimes he has a taste for living flesh. That is why he brought us here.''

By this time they had passed beyond the seven open galleries they had walked before, past the seven chambers of stone to lace, and come to the very end of the last long hallway. Here they found a pair of wide wooden doors studded with nails. The Kalevide flung them apart, expecting to see another room fashioned from other strange and precious substance, crystal, perhaps, or amber or ivory.

Instead he stepped into a small, plainly furnished closet containing nothing but one wide canopied bed, two straight-backed wooden chairs, and a small table against the wall beside the bed. The walls were bare; there were no chests of treasure. Two glasses stood on the table.

"What room is this?" he asked in consternation.

"This is the Sarvik's own room," said the eldest. "Here he sleeps with his wife. And sometimes, too, he comes here alone to rest and relax after a journey. In recent days his trips seem to tire him more and more. Then the old woman comes with boiling water for his bath. She beats his back with bath whisks, and soon he recovers."

"We're not allowed in this room," warned the second sister. "We shouldn't even be here now." But the Kalevide had already stretched out comfortably on the soft pillows on the bed.

"Don't worry," he said, beckoning them to sit by him. "No one knows we're here. Tell me some more."

Cautiously, the youngest took the cushion beside him; the other two took the chairs.

"What more can we say?" said the eldest, "His brother-in-law is Tuhja, whose mother is the bitch of Põrgu. Sometimes they come here together to have a small feast with some of their other friends and family. Then they act like pigs. They all get into this bed together and drink beer and shout and sing, until they fall out onto the floor in a stupor."

"And they snore," added the youngest.

"How would you know, if you're not allowed in here?"

"You can hear them—everywhere."

"Is this beer left from one of those feasts," asked the Kalevide, picking up one of the two goblets on the table.

"Don't touch that!" cried the sisters together.

"Why? What is it?"

"Enchanted liquor, meant only for sorcerers and the Sarvik. One beaker, that one, gives the one who drinks the strength of ten oxen. The other takes away the same amount of strength. When the Sarvik is weary, or when he is going out in the morning, he drinks the beer of strength for a tonic. At night, or if he wants to restrain his power, he sips the ale of weakness."

The Kalevide frowned at the goblets, muttering, "Potions for strength, liquors of weakness. Like the two jars of liquid by the doors outside." He put the glass down where it had been. "All enchantment, all sorcery. Is nothing real here?"

"The Sarvik is real, that is enough," said the eldest soberly. An uneasy chill fell over all three maidens.

"If you are lucky, you will never meet him to see how real he is. In fact, we would be wise to leave right now. Already we have waited too long. At any moment the Sarvik might return from his journey. When he travels in his own dominions underearth, he is often gone for a long time, days or even weeks, but he does not care to stay for long above, not where the sun shines by day and the moon and stars by night. Since we do not know where he is, we cannot know when he will return. We would do well to be cautious."

"Let's go!" pleaded the second sister. More timid than the others, she was trembling visibly with fright. "If he catches you here, son of Kalev, it will mean your death surely. No one ever sees the sun again once *he* has his hands on him.

Once more the Kalevide merely laughed at their worry. "I can't believe he's as terrible as you say," he said. "I'll have to stay here, I think, just to meet him. I'll speak to him about how he's treated you, and maybe I'll teach him some manners. Somebody has to show him he's not as powerful as he thinks."

"Are you mad?" exclaimed the eldest.

"He's coming!" shrieked the second.

"I hear him," cried the third sister.

From far away came the sound of a heavy door closing solidly. Hollow footsteps resounded along the corridors.

"Quick now," pleaded the youngest, "use the wishing hat! Take us out of here, before it's too late!"

The Kalevide sat up on the bed. "I thought we were done with that kind of talk," he said sharply. "No enchantments. None of that, not for me. I'll use this hat once, and only once—to get my own size back. Then I'll match your Sarvik with my own honest strength that I was born with."

Another door clanged shut somewhere in the palace. The maidens paced frantically around the room, begging him to move. He would not listen. The eldest two sisters struggled to close the massive door and bar it. The youngest just glared at the Kalevide.

The sound of heavy footsteps grew louder as the Sarvik came nearer. One by one, the great doors in the corridors closed behind him.

"Hurry!" they pleaded. The Kalevide was imperturbable.

The noise swelled in the halls. It was the thunder of a hundred horses pounding across an iron bridge. It was a thousand wagons trundling over a copper roadway on bronze wheels. The entire cavern, the very interior of the world, seemed about to crumble under the violent onslaught of noise. The earth quaked. The floor of the palace shook under the Sarvik's footsteps as he turned down the last gallery leading to his bedroom. The first two sisters pulled the Kalevide to his feet. The youngest quickly switched the two goblets on the table beside the bed.

Despite the dreadful clamor ringing around him and despite the maidens' fears, the Kalevide drew himself up to face the doorway proudly, ready to meet whatever monster might appear. To bolster his courage he recalled his former feats of strength and bravery. To bring himself victory, silently he recited the chant:

> Like the oak tree in storms
> of summer, the red glow
> above showers, the rock
> amid hailstones, the tower
> against wild gales of wind.

So he would stand, fearing nothing.

With a final thunderclap the Sarvik dashed the closet door open with his fists, revealing the four small figures trapped inside. The maidens cowered together in one corner whimpering with fear. The Kalevide stood in front of them, as their shield. Though still immovable, he did finger the enchanted hat concealed in his shirt. He looked like a boy, no taller than the girls.

Whatever the Kalevide had expected when the Sarvik came through the door, it was not what he saw. Here was no monster, no giant ogre, no hideous demon. Why were the maids so terrified? He was only one small man, smaller indeed than many, elderly, perhaps handsome, with neat gray hair and a trim moustache. He wore a well tailored suit of plain gray wool over a white silk shirt, and in his hand he carried no weapon, no brutal iron club, no threatening copper spear, no biting lash, only a small square leather traveling case. A man might even welcome him for an uncle. Certainly the water demon had looked more imposing, the ox had been more powerful. What the Kalevide did not see, however, was the awful hollowness in the Sarvik's eyes. There he held all horror, but the son of Kalev did not meet the master's eye.

"Who are you?" the Sarvik asked, amazed to find anyone in his room. "What are you doing here?" His voice was soft, with just a hint of a foreign accent.

"I came to wrestle," replied the Kalevide.

"With my girls?"

"With you."

"Are you crazy? Why would you want to fight me, an old man, somebody you never saw?"

"Are you afraid? Do you refuse my challenge?" The Kalevide felt only contempt for this coward. The Sarvik sighed.

"You are a fool, boy, but if you wish to fight, I will fight you. What ideas the young men have these days! Would you like some refreshment first? Some beer, perhaps? He crossed the room to the small table and, unaware that the cups had been reversed, took the one on the right while offering the other to the Kalevide.

"No, thank you."

"You are certain? It's quite good; my mother brews it herself. No? You don't mind if I have some, do you? I've had a long, hard day today." So saying, he drained the goblet in his hand.

"Do you want to do this now, or would you rather wait till after dinner? The old woman usually brings me something about now."

"Let's wrestle now. Then you won't want any supper."

"So, as you wish. You, girl," the Sarvik said to the eldest sister, "run down to the iron room and fetch the double chain, you know the one I mean, so the victor can bind the loser when we're done. You understand, of course," he added to the Kalevide, "there is a forfeit when you lose." The Kalevide only snorted.

They went out to the courtyard, where there would be more room for them to fight. The two younger sisters followed fearfully after them, not knowing what else to do. The eldest brought the chain as commanded. While waiting for her, the Sarvik and the Kalevide marked off an area and set posts at the corners, so their battle would be fair. Casually, with no great concern and certainly not so much concentration as to be rude, the Sarvik studied his opponent. He was amused by the weight of golden jewelry hanging on him.

"You found my treasure chests, I see," he remarked. "Are you a thief, then?"

"If you want it back you'll have to take it," sneered the Kalevide. He did not mean to return to Viru empty-handed, as the cup-bearer had done.

"Yes," said the Sarvik, "I suppose I shall."

Suddenly his hand shot out, like a snake striking, and caught the Kalevide's golden hair in a painful, inexorable grip. At the same time his left hand clamped down on the Kalevide's neck to bend him over, force him to his knees. The Kalevide reached up, grasped the Sarvik's shoulder, and pulled him over similarly. And there they stood, both bent double, both staring down at the ground, whose silver coins winked up at them and mocked their proud struggle. Each was caught in the other's hold, and neither was strong enough to force the other off his feet. They strained and shoved, but could not move.

As soon as he felt the Sarvik's grip on him, the Kalevide knew that this foe was not at all like the water demon, whom he had defeated so easily, nor even like the sorcerer's sons he had routed. Beneath that dapper suit of gray, within his slight gentleman's body, there was hidden an awesome, unshakable power. The sinews and muscles in the Sarvik's neck and arms were drawn as tight as knots of iron, and the Kalevide could not break the fiendish hold that held him.

For his own part, the Sarvik was astounded that his own strength was not greater. He had expected to make short work of this youthful intruder who dallied with his servants. He meant to throw the upstart down, bind him up, and cart him off to an iron cell before he ever knew what struck him. Yet he was locked in this frozen dance instead. Either the mortal was far stronger than he had imagined a man could be, or else he himself had been more fatigued by his last journey than he had realized. The draught he had drunk had given him little strength; indeed, he felt his power slipping away.

From time to time the two of them would turn a little. One or the other would shuffle his feet and try to catch his opponent off guard. That was their only movement. Behind them, beyond the boundary of the ring, the three maidens, trembling in terror, waited, horrified, for the outcome. When the wrestlers turned or stamped their feet, the ground itself rumbled and heaved like waves in a storm, awakened by the stress and pressure of the battle. The entire kingdom underearth was rocked. Walls of the palace cracked as its foundations weakened. The arches bowed, the roof tottered. In the lands of men, tales were told of mountains about to explode, and songs were sung of two dragons locked in deadly combat in the bowels of the earth.

"That is time enough," the Sarvik panted. "Let us rest a while."

Relaxing his hold on the Kalevide's hair, he stepped away.

Painfully, the Kalevide straightened. Side by side they leaned against the granite wall of the first granary. Both gasped for breath.

"Would you like something to drink now?" The Sarvik offered, hoping once again to entice the other to drink some of the water of weakness. It was a thin trick, but all he could think of.

"No."

"Nor I. You're fairly strong, did you know that? Where did you get such strength?"

"I'm stronger than you think," said the Kalevide thickly as they squared off for another round. Then, before the Sarvik could regain his hold, he whipped the wishing hat out of his shirt and clapped it on his head while wishing to resume his natural size and strength. At once he grew up as strong as an oak tree, tall as a pine. He towered over the lord of Põrgu. The Kalevide's face twisted in a ferocious spasm of rage; all his hair stood straight out from his head.

Mercilessly seizing the Sarvik's head, he lifted him completely off his feet and high into the air. Then he slammed him down, driving him deep into the ground like a stake. First to his calves, then to his knees, then to his loins he rammed him until at last, embedded to the waist, the master of the underworld could not move.

"Quick, the chain!" the Kalevide called to the sisters, but before he could bind his enemy, the Sarvik began to shrink in size. Smaller and smaller he grew, finally sinking into the ground, disappearing like a stone in a quaking swamp.

"Come back here," the Kalevide shouted angrily. "Come back, coward, you," although no trace of the Sarvik remained to reply.

"Hurry," cried the maidens, tugging on his arms. "Let's get away from here."

"I shall return," the Kalevide cried to the spot where the Sarvik had vanished. There was not even a hole there. "I shall return to put you in chains someday. You'll see, you coward."

"Come on," said the youngest sister urgently. "He's gone; he can't hear you. Don't waste your time. He's gone to raise an army. Hurry."

They ran through the palace, down the hallways and galleries and through the Sarvik's seven rooms. Racing through the halls of satin and silk, the sisters hurriedly swept up armloads of gowns and dresses, shifts and blouses. Stockings and kerchiefs and ribbons streamed behind them as they ran. Bows spilled through their fingers like flowers. In the gold and silver rooms the Kalevide scooped more trinkets and treasure into a golden helm to carry away. Desperately they sped through the rooms of copper and iron. In the final chamber of stone the youngest maiden paused just long enough to conceal the enchanted willow wand in her sleeve.

Behind them the palace was coming alive as the Sarvik's hordes mustered for pursuit. From all the remote corners of the castle came shrieking cries ringing alarm. Screaming chants howled through the passageways. Footsteps like hoofbeats clattered over the floors. Demons were coming nearer from every direction. The Kalevide stood in the broken doorway leading from the first anteroom to the tunnel.

"This way, hurry!"

"There's no time," cried the youngest sister. "Use it now! Use the hat to take us out of here!"

"I will not. I'll take you out myself."

"Fool," she shrieked, "Someone's coming down the tunnel. We're trapped."

"There's no one. Come, follow me."

"Yes, the demons! The watchmen! Hurry, use the hat. Do it now!"

Without thinking any more, the Kalevide donned the wishing cap and, putting his arms around all three maidens, cried, "Hat, hat, to the entrance gateway take us; take us now to the gate where my timber lies."

At once they were spilled out of the mountain at the mouth of the cave. Head over heels they fell, for the hat had not thought to reverse their positions in the transition from the upside-down world of Põrgu to the upright lands of men.

No one was there. The three cooks had long since disappeared, taking with them the cauldron and its chains. Only the ashes of their fire remained, and a few glowing embers. While the sisters collected themselves and their bundles of clothing and the Kalevide's gold, the Kalevide fanned the coals into a small flame, and contemptuously tossed the hat onto the little blaze. It flared once, then vanished in a gasp of black, greasy smoke.

25   "No! Don't!" the sisters cried simultaneously, but it was too late. The hat was destroyed.

"Why? Why did you do that?" The youngest was nearly in tears. "Why did you have to burn it?"

"You tricked me," accused the Kalevide. "You made me use the hat when you knew I wouldn't. There wasn't anybody coming, but you still made me use it. I don't know why you did it, but I've fixed it so you won't trick me again."

"You fool, don't you know there will never be another gift like that on earth again?"

"And a good thing, too."

"You don't know the things you could have done with it. How much you could have done for your people, for all people."

"It isn't any good to do things that way. Every sorrow I've ever known was because of sorcerers and sorcery, and I won't have any more. In my land everyone must rely on himself and his own strength, his natural strength, as I do. I will do what I can for my people, but by myself."

"The hat saved us," moaned the second sister. "How could you destroy it? What will we do now? What hope is there for us?"

"Why are you all crying?" The Kalevide could not understand their sorrow, or cope with their tears. "I meant no harm. You should be rejoicing now, not weeping. Look, you're free."

"Free?" The voice of the eldest was cold. "Free? Not yet. We are not safe. We have not begun to get away. Do you think they will not come after us? Do you believe the Sarvik lets mortals escape so easily from Põrgu? He will come for us; do not be deceived. The hat saved us once. It would have saved us again. We would have been at your house by now, we could have been with your people, if it were not for your foolish pride. You might wish well you had kept that hat."

"Nonsense. I'll save you yet, and we'll be home soon enough. If you'll just stop crying. Please. Don't cry. Here, look around you. See how pretty everything is? Look, the sun is shining, the sky is clear. It's the nicest day of summer. How can you weep on a day like this? Can you even remember when you last felt the sunshine? You're in my kingdom now, in Viru, and it will get even nicer. So don't be sad any more, please. You'll soon be home; you'll see your husbands. You're about to receive life's greatest pleasures, the things you were denied so long underground. You'll see, as soon as we reach home. So, cheer up, will you? Be happy. Stop crying. Please.''

His words were true. The day was too lovely for them to mourn for long, and no amount of grieving would restore what was lost. The three sisters helped the Kalevide tie his sacks of stolen treasure and their own hastily gathered bundles of clothing on top of his sledge of lumber, then followed him gladly down the trail through the barren canyon.

The Kalevide led them northward, not along the track by which he had come. Although this route was more difficult, he was reluctant to show them the desolation he had seen before. For their first look at Viru they should see its beauty, not be struck so brutally by an unnatural ugliness that could only remind them of the unhappy life they were leaving behind.

The maidens were simply glad to be going away from the cave and its gate into the underworld. To them any land, no matter how harsh, if it was under the sun and open sky, was better than the desolation of spirit that was Põrgu's.

''That Sarvik wasn't very strong,'' the Kalevide remarked when the sisters caught up with him. ''From what you said I expected him to be much more trouble but I beat him easily. He was nothing.''

''So it seems,'' said the eldest, who knew her sister's trick. ''That is how it is with demons, and sorcerers, and their kindred races, easy to defeat, easy to outwit, until you find yourself caught in their power. Then pray to the gods for mercy.''

''Well, you needn't worry about that anymore. None of them will dare come near me.''

''You think not.''

Shadows flitted out of the mouth of the cave. At first they came one at a time, then in pairs and threes, until a great swarm ascended and poured into the air like a column of smoke. They flew high over the mountains, spirits without shape or substance, but sentient and cold. They coiled across the sky, the hordes of Põrgu, a long, dark serpent, ethereal, and, in its silence, immeasurably menacing.

They quartered the forest, searching for the fugitives. A chill came into the air. The fresh wind died, then rose again with a foul, bitter breath. In other valleys and distant lands bird songs were stilled, men were afraid. Soon the seekers sensed the tracks they sought. They streamed down the length of the canyon on black, soundless wings. The smile went out of the daylight.

"Something's wrong!" cried the youngest sister, first to feel the change in the air.

"There, look!" The eldest sister pointed. Where the sky had been clear and unmarred blue, a single, dark, smoke-like plume crossed the face of the sun. The edges of the cloud were tinged with red; the rest was brown and gray.

"What is it?" asked the Kalevide, also chilled by what he saw.

They could not tell him. It might have been an unnaturally large flock of jackdaws or bats, or smoke from a fire, yet all knew, though they could not say, it was surely something far more terrible. At once they quickened their pace. The sledge lurched and bounded over ruts and broken stones. The Kalevide pulled as though his heels were on fire. The sisters pushed. The trail grew steeper. Nothing grew here except a few stunted alders struggling to survive in the barren, drought-stricken dust. Their leaves were as white as bones. The canyon narrowed. The sides of the mountains were closing together as if to form a gateway, or a wall. Somewhere ahead a river roared in rage. Behind, the silence boded fear.

From the open mouth of the cave stepped the Tuhja, pale and corpulent. The one called Emptiness, the Contemptible One, cousin and brother-in-law to the Sarvik, steward of the lands of the dead. He was fat beyond reason. Vast folds of flesh rolled at his belly and his breast and his hips and sagged loosely from his thighs and his short, round arms, and in that soft fat was his horror. Any souls fool enough to let him come upon them or to enter his embrace must surely smother there. The Tuhja wore a white, tall, pointed hat, and a single shapeless garment of white cloth hanging from his shoulders to his feet. It did nothing to conceal his obscene shape. He might have seemed robust and jolly, rolling along the valley pathway, if only he had laughed a little, or winked, but the pale white flesh of his face never once rose in a smile. His mouth was no more than a round, meaningless hole, something pushed into dough by a hasty thumb.

The river rushed headlong past the hidden entrance to the ravine. Elsewhere it flowed slowly and serenely around the feet of the hills, joined now and then by brooks and streamlets springing from wells within the mountains. Elsewhere it wandered peacefully across the plain and restful meadows and sought lakes to wed before rambling onward toward the sea. Here, however, where the cliffs rose sheer above its southern bank, here where the hillsides were bare of green trees and growing plants, here it raced tumbling and churning treacherously over rocks and boulders in a desperate need to escape the neighborhood of the approach to the Sarvik's realm. Once a pleasant stream had spilled out of that narrow gorge, skipping through the valley, leaping from the high shelf of rock to mingle its white waters with the greater river, but that creek had long since dried, however, or else it had crawled underground to hide its face from living eyes in shame for its place of origin, and now the river, too, longed to run away.

The Kalevide burst through the cleft between the mountainsides and froze on the edge of the precipice. A white and hungry flood raged below him. On the other side above the river lay gentle slopes and open lands, offering easy paths to safety, but the water was too deep and too wild here to wade and too wide to step over. Amid the jagged rocks the river bared its teeth at them as surely as the river of death. There was no escape. To the left and right no path was possible; the hills were far too steep to climb. The Kalevide, feeling trapped and angry, whirled on the maidens.

"What can we do now?" he cried.

Behind them the flitting shadows had clustered around the Tuhja. To the Kalevide and the sisters looking back anxiously, there seemed to be an enormous, oppressive, whirling, murky gloom bearing down on them, a mist that was no more than empty fear, but fear made manifest to the eye.

"Get behind me," he told them sharply, putting the girls on the edge of the cliff so that he could stand between them and the approaching horde. "I will fight them as long as I can, but there are too many. If I fall, try the river. Maybe you can live. But if not, death is better than capture. Don't let them take you!"

"Don't you wish you had the wishing hat?" teased the youngest sister.

He wanted to hit her, but there wasn't time. The shadow of menace was too near. He turned to watch it in awe; at the same moment, she slipped the willow wand from her sleeve and shaped it in a way that he could never know. The supple stem bent into a graceful curve and then unfolded in her hands, and with her wish it became an arch that spanned the rushing river.

"Look what's here," she announced, as though she had just chanced upon it. Merrily, she led her sisters across the bridge, then called to the Kalevide to follow. Although he did not understand what had happened, he obeyed, hoping the slender bridge could support his heavy load of timber and treasure. There was never any danger. When all were across, the maiden raised the arch, and it became a rod once more.

"How did you do that?" he demanded; his voice was scolding. "Let me see that."

"Oh—it's just a stick."

Before he could insist, the Tuhja and his followers arrived on the spot they had just left. The spirits, unable to cross water, streamed through the gap between the hills and gathered in awesome silence on the small shelf of stone. The Tuhja, squatting on his fat haunches and removing his hat, wiped his brow with a soiled handkerchief. His head was bald. Seventy of the shadows formed a somber cloud around him, a shape alive with motion, yet not alive.

"Are you there, little brother?" the Tuhja called across the river. He was breathing hard after his chase, and his voice was little more than a whisper. Yet all four on the other side of the thundering river heard him easily. The Tuhja's words entered their minds not through their ears as sound, but through the deeper well-spring of understanding where dreams are formed.

"I am here," the Kalevide shouted back.

"Good, that is good. Is it hot enough for you? Whoooee, me, too."

"What do you want?"

"I will tell you, dear brother. Yes, I will tell you. It is my daughters. Are you eloping with them? I ask you fairly, is that a way for a man to behave?"

The maidens shook their heads earnestly; they would not be claimed by such a loathsome creature.

The Kalevide did not doubt them. "These are not your daughters," he shouted across the river.

"My fosterlings then, yes. I love them as my own true children. Does that not make them mine? Are you stealing them away from me?"

"It looks like I am, unless you come get them."

"Dear brother of mine, have you been wrestling with my friend and sister's husband? Did you drive him into the ground like a post?"

"If you mean that weak old man, I suppose I did, though I'd hoped for a stronger foe. If his bones aren't broken, I'm not to blame."

"Dear little friend, did you lock our old mother in the kitchen and treat her like a mouse in a trap when she was baking oatcakes for the little girls?"

"It could be. And it could be she roared and howled all night long and had to make her bed, finally, in a bin of peas. For all I know she sleeps there still, if a flea hasn't bit her."

"You did take the Sarvik's little cap, did you not? Do you want him to walk bare-headed in the rain?"

"I think I did. But your Sarvik will never wear that hat again, for I gave it to the fire, and it burned to ashes which blew away with the wind."

"Ah-h-h-" The Tuhja sighed. The spirits behind him stirred, but the deed was done. After a while he spoke again. "Dear little brother, did you take some of our treasure, perhaps?"

"Indeed, a little, not much. Some gold, some silver. No more than ten horses could carry and maybe twenty oxen. You may be sure I didn't take much copper."

"Good son of Kalev, my friend, did you also steal the bridge builder, the wishing wand?"

"Now there is something I did not take. It may be some brown-eyed maiden borrowed it, but certainly no stronger person would have bothered with such a little thing."

"Have you been treating my girls well? You have been nice? You haven't done anything wrong or nasty?"

"That I'll tell you another time."

"Yes, my little friend, I expect I shall see you once again. Yes? You will come again soon, I hope. You have debts to pay us."

"I'll come back, dear brother," said the Kalevide with a sneer. "If I'm ever short of money, I'll stop by for some more of yours. I'll even repay my debts—with more."

Nothing could be gained by banter and, since he could not cross the river, the fat Tuhja rose cumbrously to his feet and moved to leave.

"I hear your promise," he said in parting. "You will come back, and we shall look for you soon."

His followers leaped to the air, forming a long, dark spiral streaming toward the black gateway leading underground. They flew as though on fire, or else pursued by gadflies. More slowly, the Tuhja struggled up the slope of the gorge to return to Pōrgu. He would have to report the result of his pursuit to the Sarvik, who would not be pleased with the failure. Oily sweat poured off his body as the contemptible one clutched at the withered trees and pulled himself uphill toward the cave. He had obtained the Kalevide's promise to return, but that was slight consolation for what had been lost.

When all were gone, not to return, the Kalevide hitched the rope of his sledge around his waist once more and hurried off on the trail that would take him home. From here on the way would be easier, with only gentle slopes and open meadows and stately forests to traverse. Now that he was free of danger from the Sarvik, the urge to see his people returned in force. He longed to see the Alevide, the Sulevide, and the cup-bearer again and was anxious to learn how all his people had fared in his absence.

The sisters felt none of his concern or need to hurry. They were only glad, even giddy, to be released at last from Pōrgu's grip. Since the Tuhja himself had failed to recapture them, it was unlikely that any other would try. So they linked their arms together and danced and skipped gaily down the trails the Kalevide chose. They sang songs of green things growing and the summer seasons of the year, only to stop time after time when they would have to study a fir bough, to feel its rough texture or smell its nearly forgotten fragrance, or else to bend and pluck wildflowers, to tuck them in their hair or between their breasts. Then they would race to catch up with the Kalevide to shower him playfully with daisies and wild pea-flowers. In their hands they carried leafy boughs of birch and willow which they waved foolishly at each other as though they were flags.

"Listen!" cried the second sister, deeply moved.

It was a turtledove calling softly to its mate. To the maidens it sounded like spring after their long winter underneath the earth.

Their party crossed one stream, and then another. Both were easy to ford, for both were small and gentle, languorous and slow in the heat of the summer, making no more than a slender trickle in the middle of their much wider beds. While crossing the third such stream, the Kalevide surprised the maidens by announcing that he had to rest there. Strong as he was, he said, his back was weary and chafed from hauling the sledge.

While he prepared a bed of sand beside the shallow, rippling water, the sisters wandered wantonly across the grassy meadow toward the next rising hills. With skirts raised above their knees, they danced like nymphs among the cornflowers and poppies. Here and there thick berry bushes rose in mounds above the lush grass. They gathered sweet fruit in handfuls and crushed it into their mouths so that the juice gushed forth and stained their lips bright red. Far behind them, the Kalevide was already fast asleep, snoring lustily to the wind.

A fierce rumbling in the earth shook him out of his stupor. A thundering wall of white water was rushing down on him, a turbulent flood meant to sweep him away without a care. Born in the mountains, spawned by a sorceress in spite, it crashed down the gullies and ravines in quest of the Kalevide alone. The wrath of the underworld was not yet spent.

The wall of water was only paces away when he rose and

scrambled hastily onto a slight rise of higher ground. Failing to catch its quarry, the flood seized the sledge to tear it from his grasp. The timbers bucked; the raft rolled on the tumbling waves. The ropes groaned, but the lashings held firm and the towline did not break. None of the treasures were lost.

Where the meadow had been was now a river, wide, roiled, and muddy like a troubled lake. The higher bushes were round islands. Fish fed on berries; crayfish walked among the flowers. Bewildered by what had happened, the Kalevide gazed around him stupidly. He was alone. There was neither sight nor sign of the sisters. Alone, he cried; he was always being left alone. Just as he was becoming reconciled to the loss of his sword and the greater loss of his mother, helped by the distraction of the maidens, he was doomed to loneliness again. Was there no end to sorrow?

In an hour the river would return to its former size. The flood would recede, the meadows return. The grasses would dry, and wildflowers would show their washed faces to the sun. The Kalevide could not wait an hour, the urge to run away was too strong. Running masks grief; it hides pain. What a fool he had been to rest, he thought miserably. It had cost him his companions; it had nearly cost him his life. He was vulnerable. He must not rest anymore. Time and danger loomed too urgently. He must return to Viru at once. There was no time to wait for the flood to subside, no time to look for the maidens' bodies. He must return to his people. At that very moment they were probably locked in the grip of war. They would need him. They would need his timbers. He must hurry.

The Kalevide plunged into the muddy water and waded across the remainder of the river, disconsolately dragging his raft behind him. The sledge had become his ever-increasing burden. Although it tired him and slowed him down, he could not leave it. He must draw it back to Viru. This became more important than the desolation in his heart. It was his duty. He was the king.

Resuming his northward march alone, he entered a family of hills beyond the meadows. A high fluting sound, like the calling of a bird but happier, rose over the forest. It was the laughter of young maidens. His maidens. They were not drowned, not lost. He was not alone. The joy of knowing they were still alive made him run down the trail. Around the second bend he found all three seated in a circle, looking dishevelled, their clothes rumpled, and their garlands of flowers awry. They were telling riddles to test each other's wit, laughing gaily, oblivious of the danger he had just encountered or the hurt he had suffered. With them was a fourth person whom he did not know.

"Look who we found," called the youngest sister, who saw the Kalevide first.

"He says he is the son of Olev," added the second, by way of explanation.

The young man rose and humbly saluted the Kalevide. He was wearing the white, though somewhat dusty and travel-worn, smock of an artisan. On the ground beside him was a leather pouch filled with tools. The Kalevide hardly looked at him in his eagerness to greet the girls. Speechless for joy, all his sorrow fled, he embraced them all and nearly embraced the man as well.

Later, as they walked along the forest trail, the Olevide explained who he was.

"I have come from the west," he said. "From lands beyond Saksaland. I wasn't sure where I was going until I met these lovely girls and they told me who you were and suggested that you might help me. At least, they told me to wait and speak to you, if you didn't mind. I'm looking for work, you see."

"What do you do?" The two men were walking together while the sisters trailed not far behind and tried to overhear.

"I am a builder." The Olevide's voice was soft and sure. "A mason, primarily. I prefer to work in stone, but I can also build with wood or metal, or whatever might be needed for a job."

"Are you a smith, then?" The Kalevide would have nothing to do with a smith, but he was not averse to having someone with him who would deal with the metalworkers.

"Not a smith, no. Although, as I say, I can work with metal well enough. I can keep my own tools sharp and in good order, and I can fashion fittings when they are needed, but that is only by the way. I much prefer larger works, such as bridge construction or boat building. I will raise cities for you, if you give me the men and materials to work with."

"Yes, there is some work to be done in Viru," the Kalevide boasted. "Right now and for a long time to come, because I'm going to build my city into a great capital and my land into a mighty nation. So there might be a place for you. I had rather thought to do it myself; it seemed the proper work for a king. But I could use an assistant, I'm sure. Of course, there's the cup-bearer, too. You'd have to work under him as well. Would you mind?"

Politely, the Olevide ignored the question. "Is that what these timbers are for?" he asked instead. "Your buildings?"

"Yes. You see, I'm going to put walls around all the hamlets so my people will be protected. There have been threats of war. Already it may be too late, I don't know."

"Have you built much before?"

"Why do you ask?"

"Forgive me for saying so, but I was noticing your sledge."

"What about it?"

"It's—interesting."

"What's wrong with it?"

"Nothing, if it suits you, but look here." They stopped so the Olevide could explain what he had in mind. The sisters discreetly said nothing. "You see how you've made your lashings? Fewer turns and fewer knots would hold the planks more securely and more efficiently with less waste and effort. I'll show you." He rearranged the timbers and deftly retied the lines so that a single knot did the work of the Kalevide's many. "Isn't that much neater now? Not only is it stronger, but the sledge takes on the appearance of being designed rather than merely thrown together." While the Kalevide considered this, the Olevide continued to readjust the loads of gold and silver and clothing so that the weight would be evenly distributed.

"You left out two planks," said the Kalevide, pleased to have caught him out in a mistake. Too much competence is sometimes hard to take.

"I know," the Olevide replied. Taking a draw knife from his tool kit, he began swiftly shaping the two boards into sharp-edged rails. While he worked he continued to speak, seriously but not intensely, merely with the voice of one who knows his craft well.

"If there were more time, I would fashion wheels for you. Even a pair of wheels on a single axle would make this load so much easier to pull, don't you think?" Seeing the look on the Kalevide's face, he added quickly, "You do know what wheels are, don't you?"

"Of course, I know what wheels are. I'm not a fool. But in these lands only the gods drive on wheels. Sledges are good enough for men."

The Olevide shrugged but said nothing. He would show what he could do, enough to impress this new master of his, but he knew that he could do more.

He quickly drilled a series of holes through the finished runners and laced them to the underside of the carriage with rawhide thongs. "There, see how that is. Not wheels, but they should make your load a little easier." Then, as they resumed their walk, he added lightly, "You understand, these rails are very makeshift. They won't last long. Just long enough, I should think, for you to reach your destination."

Although the sledge was still very cumbersome and heavy, it now seemed, to the Kalevide, to glide along as easily as a sleigh in winter. Why had he never thought of putting runners underneath, he wondered. Then, with a strong, fast pace, he marched out ahead of the others. Behind him walked two of the maidens, the eldest and the youngest, still merry and laughing together and telling each other stories, though beginning to grow eager to reach their new home.

Farther back, the Olevide walked in company with the second sister. Softly, so that none of the others could hear, she told him of their terrible life in Põrgu as the handmaidens of the Sarvik. She told the story simply, but it was not a happy tale she told. Their steps slowed, and they fell even farther behind the others. The Olevide listened carefully and let her talk without troubling her with questions or asking for explanations. After a while, he took her hand and held it in his.

On the brow of the last hill, the Kalevide halted. The two sisters came up and joined him, and soon the Olevide and the second maiden also. Ahead of them lay the coastal plain of Viru. In the light of the long afternoon the grasslands were the color of green jade where hay, ripened under summer's burning sun, had just begun to dry. Even now, reapers stood in the fields with scythes. Slowly they mowed the high, rich grass and laid it in swathes. To the watchers on the hilltop far away, the men and women seemed very small, like toys, the caricatures of folk who work without care in the sun. Elsewhere golden-white fields of corn, bright rye and oats and barley were laid in neat rectangles between the hayfields. On the slope just below them, a small flock of sheep was browsing. A large, curl-horned ram led his three ewes and their lambs slowly across the hillside. They drifted like clouds over the pasture, looking for the end of the day. In other meadows more sheep were grazing peacefully, and herds of red cattle.

The hamlet, where most of the people who worked in Viru's fields lived, was located at the edge of the dark green wood spreading far to their left, small round huts of bark arranged in a half-ring. Farther off was the circular stockade erected by the Sulevide.

"Is that the kind of palisade you intend to build?" asked the Olevide, pointing to the structure. The Kalevide nodded. "Good enough for a quick defense, I suppose," the builder remarked. "But if you want your building to last, it should be stone. Your country is rich with both granite and limestone, I notice. You should have cities of stone for your people." Again the Kalevide nodded; that was his dream. For the moment, however, he was awed by the brilliance of the scene displayed before him, silenced by the sight of his home.

Far to the right was the clearing where the settlement of the Alevide was slowly taking form, but directly in front of his gaze stood the long, gabled hall his father had built, the house that now was his. A thin whisper of smoke streamed up from the roof to show that someone was inside, that it was not deserted, that there would be welcome there. In the distance behind the house rose the knoll where Kalev was buried. It looked stark and blue-gray set against the haze far away. Beyond the knoll, out of view, lay the endless sweep of the sea. Suddenly the Kalevide shouted.

One word. "Viru!"

Abandoning his sledge, he charged headlong down the hill toward his home. The sheep streamed away from him in fright. Hearing his cry and seeing him rushing down on them, the people in the fields panicked. They dropped their tools and caught up their children and fled for their houses or for the safety of the woods. Dogs barked and snapped at his heels as he raced through the village crying the name.

When they realized who it was, however, when they saw it was no demon, no giant, but their own king and chief returned from his long absence, the villagers, somewhat abashed, flocked around him and accompanied him on the final moments of his journey. They quickly lost their embarrassment and began to cheer and sing as they formed themselves into a triumphant parade leading him to the gates of his great house.

From his fortress the Sulevide marched with a company of men across the fallow ground to greet his commander. Armed with spears and swords and iron helmets, his troops were an unlikely sight in the midst of Viru's beauty.

The Alevide came hastily across the fields where he had been working with the reapers, helping them finish their first cutting before a storm could come. In his hand he still carried his hay rake, which he raised to wave in friendly salute to them all.

Behind the Kalevide and the stream of people followed the three sisters and the Olevide, all four pulling the forgotten sledge of timber and treasure.

Finally the Kalevide arrived at his house, the dwelling place of his father, the heart of his land of Viru. How proud he was! He was home, and his people were gathered about him. Everything was good. The folk looked happy, even prosperous, and they were obviously glad to see him. The fields were flourishing, the livestock fat. He smiled at everyone and everything, even the broken skull above the gate. The Alevide came up and embraced him exuberantly. The Sulevide shook hands.

"Where is the war? Is all well? How is the harvest? And the herds? Where are the knights? What has been happening? Have we any horses?" A tumble of questions following the first greetings.

"The war has been delayed," the Sulevide replied dourly. "For a while there is peace. The worst will come later."

"The best is happening now," laughed the Alevide. "Your lands are thriving. Indeed, it would be a sorry thing if the crops didn't grow, for the earth here is very rich. But don't look for horses quite yet. Come inside; you must have much to tell us. You've been away for a long, long time."

"In a moment. Look, I want to show you something." The Kalevide pushed his way back through the flock of people pressing around and peering for a glimpse of their king, straining to hear a word that he said. He waved, and they fell back a small pace to let him through to his sledge. There he opened the sacks and bundles piled on top of the timber. Gold, silver, jewelry, rings, all the bright things he had taken spilled out in a shower. "Look at that," he cried, "and that, and that," holding aloft glittering chains of precious metal. "Look!" displaying the golden armor.

The cup-bearer stood alone on the porch of the house, leaning moodily against the doorpost, hidden in shadow.

"Here, look at this. And there's more." The Kalevide opened more bundles. A torrent of silken dresses and underwear gushed from one sack. He blushed and stuffed them back hastily, then opened more of his plunder. "Lots more. And still more where this came from. When we need it, I'll go back. Viru will never want again." He was singing with joy as he showed off the last of his prizes from Põrgu.

"And then, of course, we have these," he said finally, bringing forward the three sisters. Through all the excitement they had stayed behind the crowd with the Olevide. This was not, after all, their homecoming. All four felt awkward and out of place among these people who were strange to them, but the Kalevide took the maidens by the arms and led them through the throng. Here was the gift he truly wished to give his nation. He had lamented his long absence from his land and people, time lost by the sorcerer's enchantment; now with the maidens as brides to his companions, Viru would never again be lonely.

Towing the sisters behind him, he drew the Alevide and the Sulevide to one side. Vainly he looked around for his cup-bearer but, not finding him, proceeded to present the maids as he had promised.

The Sulevide and the eldest sister greeted each other with dignity and then withdrew to discuss the terms of their marriage, so that both would clearly understand their respective duties and responsibilities.

The youngest sister and the Alevide never heard the crowd's shouts of congratulation or their songs of praise. They were locked in the trance of each other's gaze and lost to the world around them. For them, the look between their eyes had opened a span of time that was not a part of others' time. Their hands touched; they knew no more than that. She owned the wishing rod. Now it formed a bridge between their hearts, a rainbow for their love, a bond they both would share for all their lives. Whether the joy the Alevide and the maiden felt in that unmeasured moment was born because of who he was and who she was alone, or if it was that with their hands both cast webs of trickery to weave the other's life with his, this was not for anyone to know. It was the world's own smile.

Standing with his arm around the second sister's shoulder, the Kalevide beamed majestically over both couples and the rest of his people. Only the cup-bearer was missing, and not until he, too, had received his promised bride could the happiness of all be complete.

26   "No," said the cup-bearer one more time. "I don't have to, and I won't."

"You're being a spoiled child."

"Say what you like."

"Well then?"

"I'm not going to marry her."

"She looks pretty enough to me."

"It has nothing to do with that. I just don't want to marry her."

"That's ridiculous."

"No, it's not."

"It is."

"I don't want to marry anyone."

"Even if I ask you?"

"It makes no difference."

"Well, I'm not asking. I'm telling you what to do."

"You can't force me. Not even you."

The Kalevide and his cup-bearer were arguing, as they had been, it seemed, interminably, about whether the latter would marry the second sister. The young king of Viru was rapidly losing patience with the other's adamant refusal to submit. Here he had returned in triumph from harrowing the underworld and the forts of Põrgu, he was a hero, he had brought treasure with him, and he had brought the maidens to please his companions. He had come home to be a king and to hold the reins of power, only to be balked at the very end by this one vexsome boy. What was the point of rule if commands were not obeyed?

The Kalevide sat stolidly in his father's oaken high chair and glowered down at the cup-bearer, who was pacing nervously back and forth between him and the hearth. The boy seemed changed. He had aged in the time since the Kalevide had seen him last. He had grown taller, but also leaner, and lines had come into his face. His cheeks had lost their ruddy shine and taken on a hollow pallor; his dark eyes were set deeper; his lips pouted. The Kalevide wondered if he knew him anymore.

On the other side of the hall, on the women's side, away from the door, the three maidens sat on the floor, sorting through their piles and piles of clothing, the silks and satins they had stolen out of the Sarvik's stores. One by one, they held garments up to the light or passed them back and forth, each considering how this or that would look on her or on the others. They had to decide what they were going to wear for their weddings and also how to divide the bundles fairly between them. Once they were married they would no longer be able to share everything, as they always had during their maiden days. Now they must agree who would own each article, each blouse, each skirt, each shift, each kerchief, each ribbon. The eldest sister and the youngest, both certain of their husbands, examined every piece with radiant delight. They fondled the fabrics, fingered the needlework, exclaimed that they just simply must have this one or that, and then declared just as surely that it was absolutely perfect for the other. The second sister had begun the play with the same spirit but as time dragged by, her attention was drawn more and more to the dispute droning across the hall. After all, it concerned her fate and fortune as much as the cup-bearer's. It was the life she would have to lead. She wanted to join the men, to tell them how she felt about the matter. Perhaps she could end the quarrel with one word. She had even tried, only to be sent abruptly back to her place by the Kalevide, who declared that he would settle this for her, she need not trouble herself or worry, he knew what was best. Thus, while her sisters grew more merry, the second maiden gradually fell silent. While the heaps of chosen clothing grew higher in front of the other two, her own was less than half as large. She hardly noticed; it was not important.

On the men's side of the house, the Sulevide sat upright on a bench with his back against the wall. In his hand was a bowl of ale, but he did not drink. He was contemplating the future and thinking of raising sons.

The Alevide ambled about the entire hall. At times he stopped by the sisters, in part to admire the exotic hand-worked stuffs they showed him, but more to stand close to his betrothed. He was constantly drawn back to her, and if he wandered away, he soon returned to her side, until finally in play she sent him away. Time enough, she said, time enough later for the two of them.

Thus dismissed, he strolled to the niche where he studied the great iron-bound book chained to the wall. Although the cup-bearer had found it some weeks earlier hidden behind the years' accumulation of trash and debris, no on was interested in it except the Alevide. He, alone, felt its summons or suspected its power. For long parts of the days he would stand in front of the Book in its niche and try to sense the mysteries it contained. The covers were locked. He could not guess what words were written on its pages, yet he felt that a deep force was seething within, a force that seemingly only he was sensitive enough to heed. Several times he had asked the elders of the village to tell him about its origin, but they knew little. The Book had come with Kalev, they said, and some believed it was vital to Kalev's house and to the fortunes of all his people. The life of Viru was in some way bound between its covers. That was all they would say. Since the Kalevide's return, the Alevide had tried to learn about its secrets from him, but was rebuffed each time.

"I don't know anything about it," the Kalevide had said when asked. "And I don't care. It's a book—nothing to me." The thing had been his father's; hence he would keep it. It had no other importance; he could not read its words.

While the others occupied the center of the hall, the Olevide lounged on a wooden couch built against the side of the oven. There, out of the way of everyone, apparently forgotten by all, he whittled on a small chip of wood. It helped to steady the turmoil in his mind. Deftly he carved a little fox-cub; with a subtle twist of the knife, he made it smile.

The only other person in the building was an old woman slowly sweeping the floor with a bundle of twigs. Once the floor was scrubbed, she would wash the benches and tables, then clean all the plates and cups for the guests who would come to celebrate the weddings and the king's return. Already messengers had been sent to the outlying hamlets; runners were dispatched to Laane and to Harju in the west to call all the people to come together in festival. In the nearby huts women were busily baking bread and cakes and boiling meats, preparing all the dainty dishes that would be needed for the feast. In the Kalevide's own bathhouse the two eldest mothers brewed ale amid seething clouds of steam. Although there was hardly time to make the beer, it must be begun. Without the rites of fermentation, one of the last of women's mysteries, there could be no living marriage, no growing, fruitful love, no bond that could be expected to be fertile. So the old ones maintained and all believed.

Heedless of the others present, the Kalevide and the cup-bearer continued their argument. The son of Kalev was overbearing, the boy rebellious. His voice grew shrill; nothing else changed.

"You're not being reasonable," the Kalevide said heavily. "Tell me once again why you will not have her."

"I have told you. I've told you and told you and told you."

"Then tell me again."

"You don't care. You don't listen. I do not want to marry her, that's all. Don't make me say any more."

"I know you have a reason. You must. Don't you like her? She's young; she's beautiful; she's quiet and gentle. What more do you want? Is something wrong with her?"

"No, she's fine."

"Is something wrong with you, then?"

"Oh, leave me alone. You don't understand."

"Tell me then, help me to understand. Is there someone else you'd rather have? Do you want one of the others?"

"It isn't that at all."

"Well, what then? You're being very childish."

"And you're being very paternal."

"I am the king."

"So?"

"Are you going to tell me?"

"I can't; please don't ask me."

"Of course you can. You must. I am asking."

"You don't . . . I don't know. . . . Why do I have to marry anyone anyway?"

"You know that's a foolish question."

"Don't you want me to stay with you? Are you trying to send me away?"

"Are you refusing the girl for my sake? Because you think I'll be lonely? But I'm doing this for you, for your happiness."

"No—I—I only want to live with you. Now, leave me alone."

"Of course you do. And you may. I've already said you both can live here."

"That isn't what I mean. You don't understand. You . . ."

"I do understand. Of course I do. I want you to be happy."

Suddenly the second sister beat her fists on the floor, crying, "Stop it, stop it, stop it!" Then, sobbing, she flung herself across the room and out the door.

Her sisters watched her go without a word. It was useless, they knew, to try to stop her, better to let her cope alone. The Olevide rose to follow her, but the Kalevide ordered him to stay where he was.

"You go after her," he ordered the cup-bearer. "Bring her back, apologize, make it right with her."

"You go. You go out and tell her you'll marry her yourself, if you think it's so important. Go on, why don't you?"

The Kalevide shook his fist angrily. "Listen to me, you cub . . ."

Outside on the porch, in the cooler air of evening, the maiden could still hear their voices quarreling. Although the words were distorted, she knew from their tone that the argument had intensified. It hurt her head to think of them inside shouting at each other, wrangling over her, while she could do nothing. Why wouldn't they ask her what to do, she cried to herself, why wouldn't they listen?

To escape the nagging sounds filtering through the walls, she fled across the courtyard and then retreated farther back among the barns and smaller outbuildings, where the evening still held a sheltered peace. Here the only noises were cattle settling in their stalls. The late lingering twilight of summertime, together with the rising moon, gave her light enough to find her way between the storerooms as she stepped in and out of the shadows. There in the quiet she allowed herself to lapse into reverie among the little houses with their carved doors and scalloped moldings under the eaves and windows. By daylight they appeared brightly painted; in this hour they were pale and more somber in many shades of grey. If she married the cup-bearer, as was decreed, one of these houses would be hers, she mused, a private place, a storehouse for her own belongings, a refuge where she could go to be alone and none could hound her. It was every maiden's dream, wasn't it? So everybody said. If she married the cup-bearer . . . No! Why didn't they ask her? If she were given a choice, she would not have him. She wanted the boy no more than he wanted her.

Suddenly without warning, a pair of snake-like arms encircled her waist and threw her to the ground. She struggled fiercely and began to scream, but her assailant clamped a horny hand across her mouth to smother her. He wedged some foul cloth between her teeth for a gag, and tied her arms with rope, deliberately twisting them. Pain shot through her shoulders. She writhed away, but he held her. Then, when she was bound and helpless, he yanked her brutally to her feet and alternately dragged and shoved her along the alley between the stables, down the path, out of the enclosure, and across the untilled meadow. Only then could she see glimpses of her captor. A sorcerer.

Her stomach rose in horror, and she choked on the gag. He rushed her mercilessly across the pasture to the place where his steed was tethered, waiting to carry them away. With dread she glanced at his hideous face, his thick, protruding teeth, his slanted eyes, his twisted, beak-like nose. She shuddered at his misshapen body, then closed her eyes, unable to bear the sight. What did he want with her? Often she stumbled on the rough ground, and at times tried to run away, but could never break the terrible grip that held her. When she fell, he dragged her with a strength she knew was more than human.

Long had the sorcerer pursued the Kalevide. With an implacable lust for revenge, he had now returned to work another woeful act on Viru and its king. The maiden herself was nothing, a token in a game. He had wanted Linda and been despised; let Linda's nation pay him with another bride. From the messages of demons, of dwarves, of Letts and outlaw men, from words hurled on the far-flung winds, he had learned that the Kalevide had broken from his enchanted sleep. He had heard of the venture into Pōrgu and of the incredible escape from the Sarvik's keep. He had needed to hear no more. On a horse conjured from a tree stump, he had ridden in haste from his lair and crossed the width of this land. He had arrived in time to greet Viru's returning king.

The sorcerer forced the maiden onto his horse's back, then mounted behind, with the skirts of his robe bunched up about his waist. She felt his pointed fingers grip her belly as he prodded the beast into a jolting trot. They began to move toward the moonrise. He was taking her to the eastern hills where he had a den in readiness.

The old woman, finished with her sweeping, put her broom aside and dragged out a heavy wooden table, which she laid with a light supper to sustain her master and his guests until the wedding feasts began on the morrow. From poles laid across the roof beams she took down loaves of bread and piled them on a wooden platter along with slabs of cheese and pieces of honeycomb. Ale was served in clay cups and horns. The Kalevide and the cup-bearer were still arguing, although neither had anything more to say and both wished they could let the quarrel die.

"Where is your sister?" Olivede asked the two maidens as everyone gathered at the table. They had all forgotten her completely. The servant continued to lay out the heavy earthen plates.

The youngest sister went to the door and called across the courtyard, but not even an echo returned. It was not like her sister to stray or stay away. With the Alevide and the Olevide close behind her, she went out to look. Soon the eldest sister and the Sulevide followed, suspecting treachery. They quickly found the maiden's kerchief where it had fallen in the struggle; from there it was easy to see the track leading across the meadow where the high grass had been trampled by the sorcerer and his captive.

The Sulevide hastily ducked back into the house to collect his crossbow and throw some provisions into a bag. The others, too afraid to tarry, set off immediately in pursuit. As soon as the Sulevide caught up with them, all five raced through the dew-laden, moonlit grasses like silver hounds. The Kalevide and the cup-bearer remained behind, seated on opposite sides of the table, engrossed in their argument and unaware of the trouble that had begun.

The makeshift horse loped tirelessly with a stiff-legged gait along the paths that went beside the gray, rolling sea, through soft salt marshes and high stiff grass. At times it crossed over higher downs and meadowlands, only to return inevitably to the desolate, storm-swept shore, until at last it turned aside and entered the maze of knolls and fells that lay by the eastern marsh of Viru. The maiden on its back sagged miserably, swaying with each uneven step, but the sorcerer held her and never once relaxed his painful grip. Throughout the journey he hissed foul endearments in her ear, but except for holding on to her so she could not fall or escape, he never touched her. If he had, she would not have resisted. She was too weary from the toils of the ride and too exhausted by fear to struggle any longer, and she was too numb even to have felt him.

They did not stop at all in the night, nor the next day, not even to rest or eat. With every hour the maiden was drawn steadily farther from the hall of Viru which once had seemed to offer perfect protection and now, in her despair, seemed so far away. In the morning the sun failed to shine; the sorcerer had summoned a heavy overcast of cloud and fog to kill its light. There was no rain, nothing to wash away the horse's tracks or to conceal the path, just gloom enough to hide the sun which the sorcerer detested so. Cold winds blew; the maiden shuddered uncontrollably with a chill which now replaced all normal feeling.

They crossed another river and so came into the wretched regions of Ingrija where only witches and outcast men were known to dwell. Once it had been a fair land, bright with woods and running streams. Then all the trees were cut; when rain fell, the rivers carried all its fertile soil into the sea. The greed of man was satisfied, and only a desert remained. In the middle of a field of stones the horse finally stopped in front of a decrepit hut of bark and sod. The sorcerer shoved the maiden inside and out of sight. He himself squatted in the doorway to await the chase he knew must come.

The five who followed raced in silence, like shadows, between the trees and across the downs. At night they ran by moonlight through a world of black and silver patterns and the awesome shapes of guardian trees and stones in the land of Taara. In the mists of daylight their path was easier; it held fewer terrors than the trail of night. Yet many fears remained. They knew too well that a sorcerer had their sister. They could only pray that when they reached her, as reach her they must, they would be strong enough and quick enough to wrest her from her torment.

They traveled as fast as they could, but never so fast on mortal legs as the sorcerer's steed had sped. The Alevide and the youngest maiden soon lagged behind the others. Having come so lately out of Põrgu, she lacked the strength to run for long and often had to walk, despite her desperate longing to help her dearest sister. The Alevide would not leave her side; he stayed with her in the hope that his closeness would be a comfort. It was a wish unspoken, but shared. The Sulevide and the Olevide outstripped the rest. They vied for the lead, both, for different reasons, determined to be the first to reach the maid. The eldest sister went between the two pairs. Although she wanted to keep pace with the Sulevide, she, too, wearied and had to walk while he went on ahead.

On the third morning they came into the region where the sorcerer was waiting. In a canyon of stone the Sulevide, leading now, startled a vulture off a corpse. Rising heavily from its corrupt feast, the dark bird climbed into the sky. Of itself the vulture was a small sign of no importance, a single, unexpected jolt in an otherwise deserted waste and silent day, but it was enough.

It was enough to warn the sorcerer that pursuit was near. As soon as he saw the creature rise, he cast a spell to conjure from the dust a flood that filled the plain around his hut. In the middle of the lake the knoll with his hovel became an island, open to view but inaccessible, secure from all invasion, a mockery to men. Once the enchantment was wrought, the sorcerer withdrew into the hut and barred the door. Forcing the maiden into a chair, he bound and gagged her again, lest she cry out to her sisters and so destroy the spell from within.

Frustrated by the lake, the Olevide was about to wade headlong into it, but the Sulevide held him back. Who could know, he said wisely, how deep the water was, or what creatures lurked beneath its waves? Agreeing reluctantly, the Olevide could only gaze with anguished longing at the silent hut which seemed to float, as though in a dream, on the water, laughing at him for being mortal, so close yet not to be approached.

When the youngest sister arrived with the Alevide, she did not even pause to catch her breath. She had brought the wishing wand with her, and with it, as before, she shaped a bridge that arched like a rainbow across the seething lake to the island. All five rushed across it together. There was no time for anything but a swift attack; they could plan no feint, they could employ no tricks.

The Sulevide kicked in the flimsy door. Close behind him, the Olevide charged inside to confront the sorcerer, who rose before them masked in his full ferocity. Undaunted, the Olevide grappled with him, the one who had stolen his beloved from him and caused her unknown grief and pain. The force of his attack carried them both over backward, and they fell across the fire that was in the middle of the single room. Shaken out of its slumber, it spewed sparks upward. Coals leaped into the straw scattered on the floor, where they began first to smolder and then to quicken into flame. While the Olevide and the sorcerer wrestled for their lives, the two women freed their sister from her bonds and led her quickly from the burning cottage.

Fire licked along the edges of the walls. Fed by brands which the Sulevide lit and flung into the corners, flames leaped up and broke through the thatching. They strutted on the rooftop like a red cock. When the blaze was burning so fiercely that no power, not even sorcery, could check its wrath, the Sulevide called his comrade to flee, and, just as the ceiling collapsed in a cascade of fire, both he and the Olevide staggered through the doorway to safety.

Behind them, the sorcerer stood surrounded by roaring flames. A wall disintegrated; he was sheathed in raging fire. Smiling once at them all, he made an evil sign with his finger. Then suddenly, as the hut crashed down around him, he vanished in a burst of thick, black smoke.

The maiden threw herself into her elder sister's arms to hide her face from those final moments of horror, but when the Olevide came safely from the fire and stepped to her side, she turned and joined his embrace. It was then he vowed that he, and no other man, would be her husband, and she, awakening in relief for being free, pledged herself as readily to him.

The six could now wander leisurely back to Viru, taking time for rest and time for the maidens and the men to learn each other's ways. Strolling along the trails, the Alevide and the youngest maid disputed playfully about the wishing rod. After the sorcerer's demise, the lake he had created had disappeared to become mere dust again, so the wand had not been needed for their return, and the Alevide, in his one act in the battle, had recovered it. The maiden thought it proper for him to keep it now, concealed in his trousers until it might be wanted. He preferred to return it to its place beneath her skirts where, he said, it rightly belonged. It was a trick, but they were five days walking back to Viru, and before the fifth day was done, she was pleased to yield to the cunning of his arguments.

27   When they returned to Viru, the atmosphere in the Kalevide's hall was far different from that which they had left. Then the air had been close and somber, with tension building and only the light-hearted remarks of the maidens to relieve the strain. Then there had been the persistent quarreling between the Kalevide and the cup-bearer, the desul-

tory wandering of the Alevide, and the Sulevide's staunchness. Now, however, they found the house brightly lit with torches and burning pine splints. Summer flowers, draped from all the beams and rafters, spilled like water over the walls. Large boards were in place; women were rushing back and forth, bringing out the plates of cakes and platters of meats to bury them. Pots were brimming with cream and honey; bowls overflowed with summer fruits and nuts. Kettles of porridge chuckled on the hearth. Fresh loaves of bread were pulled from the ovens and immediately piled, steaming, on the tables. Barrels of ale and beer were brought from their cellars and lined along the walls. Even the new-made brew, prepared in honor of the weddings, was poured foaming into sprucewood troughs; the open room was suffused with yeasty smells.

Many of the people had already gathered for the festival, and more would come. All the men and women from the nearby hamlets had arrived, bringing along their children and elders. Many appeared from the farther provinces to join the celebration which would last for days. Townsmen and villagers were there, and even the lone-men, those who dwelt by themselves in the deep forest and by streamsides, who shunned the company of others, who were not yet willing to forego their ancient ways but chose instead to live in solitude and harmony among the trees. One by one, these, too, straggled in to share a rare taste of merriment with other folk.

The three sisters, rejoicing in the end of their sorrows, darted through the bustling crowd like swallows, tasting dainty meats, sipping everybody's ale, sucking tidbits of honeycomb, and dipping fingers into sweet cream, flashing bright smiles everywhere, blowing kisses to the cup-bearer, bowing to the Kalevide, then all in a hurry gathering up their silken raiment and rushing out to the bathhouse to adorn themselves for their marriage rites.

The Kalevide, meanwhile, listened gravely as his men reported the maiden's rescue and the sorcerer's demise. Grumbling only slightly, he accepted the Olevide's claim to the second sister's hand if the cup-bearer would not have her and if he would pledge his services to the improvement of Viru. The Olevide gratefully agreed.

In the bathhouse the sisters eagerly stripped off their soiled and travel-torn garments and three times reveled in thick clouds of steam. They washed their bodies well with scented bath whisks, then, filled with the flush of fragrant heat, ran naked into the cool night air, heedless of who might see. They were still maidens; soon enough they would be wives.

Dashing into the storehouse they had claimed for their dressing room, they decked themselves in satin shifts and silken gowns, in lace and linen, with gems and precious rings, with belts and brooches of gold. In that tiny space, packed with chests and shelves and cupboards overflowing with cloth and treasure, accumulated over the years by Linda as well as what they had brought out of Pŏrgu, there was hardly room enough for all of them at once. Each was always exactly in the other's way, none could turn around. The air grew close and steamy from their hot, pink bodies scented still with birch and willow. Playfully pushing back and forth, shoving and jostling, they pulled dresses over their heads and slipped on overblouses. Their skirts were bright blue and crimson and fawn; the sleeves of their shifts were embroidered with copper and silver and stones. They tied flower-stitched garters to their knees and donned lace and linen aprons. Ribboned slippers sparkled on their feet.

Although they were all rushing madly to complete their dressing and rejoin the others, they still stopped now and then to straighten another's seams or hems, or to insist her brooch must certainly be changed, or her belt, or this or that, thus undoing all her handiwork. Yet each took it laughing, for it was meant in love. At last the two elder sisters brushed and braided their hair and bound it tightly under stiff headdresses and veils of silk in the manner of married women. The youngest let her honey-colored hair hang loose, fastened only with a bit of lace and a scarlet ribbon, since she was, she insisted with a wanton's smile, still a maid.

When, finally arrayed as brides, they approached the house, all singing ceased. Dancers paused mid-round; all faces turned to greet them. Then everyone was silent, stunned. These, thought the people, were not the scruffy maidens who had straggled home with their king. These were rather grass nymphs, perhaps the meadow-queen herself and her two handmaids. The sisters merely stood inside the door and smiled their radiant joy at everyone. When, after a moment, their husbands, the Alevide, the Sulevide, the Olevide, each stepped forward to claim his bride, the clamor surged again. The roar of songs and talk and laughter filled the air louder than before. Men buried their faces in foaming bowls of ale; women scooped thick slices of boiled pork and salmon off platters, and devoured them hungrily. Children, scrambling on the floor between their elders' feet, crammed cakes and pies into their wide-gaping mouths.

Seated on a stool next to the doorway, a tall, thin man, clad in a long gray robe and a gray woolen cloak, somewhat worn, carefully examined all who wished to enter. When the sisters stepped past, he glanced at them with a quick gray eye, then let them pass unchallenged. He knew they were not nymphs, not the meadow-queen nor any kind of spirit, merely mortal women full of joy. It was his business to know. If he noted their beauty at all, however, or thought of the happiness glowing around them, no one could ever know. He did not tell. This was a wizard—a poor, impoverished wizard, to be sure, but a wizard nonetheless. Under his breath he was chanting secret words in a whisper too low for human ears to hear. His songs kept all unwanted guests away.

He was not there to bar the race of men, but demons and dwarves and all the uncouth wights who, attracted by the sounds of feasting, were likely to creep from marsh and woodland to steal the fancy meats from unsuspecting folk. Although demons were a nuisance, unpleasant boors lacking wit, it was the ox-knee people, the dwarves, who were most ruinous. Once installed in a house, they could strip it of all provender in moments, before anyone ever knew they were there. Tales were told, and some believed, of rich kingdoms utterly devastated by such visitations, until perhaps some prince or ploughboy, usually armed with a magic hat or secret ring, came from abroad to free the land from its plague, thus to win a princess's hand. Children's tales, the wizard knew. He had no such enchanted tools, only an eye that was just quick enough to see the swarms clustered at the gates and the few squatting in the corners of the room or on the roofbeams, who had managed to slip past him or who had entered through cracks in the woodwork or other hidden passages. He also had a few words of power, not many, but enough to drive them away again.

It was lowly work for a wizard; he understood that well. None of the great ones of the north would deign to be a doorkeeper. But then too, he knew, he could not do the work they did, which was why he had not emigrated with the rest of his race in the age of long ago. He had none of the great powers they had; their songs were not his. Nor his theirs. So it was that all was fit. Here there was work for him, a job no one else would do, where he could use the small skills he had and earn a meager living doing what he liked to do.

In the courtyard dancing ruled. On the turf and gravel the people danced the dances of Harju and the Westland. There were jigs and reels. Couples turned and foursomes circled. Figures of eight danced the cross-dance, the high dance of Viru, reserved for weddings and exalted holidays. In each set, four pairs were arranged in a cross-like pattern; opposite couples advanced and fell back, forward and back, skipping as they danced, after which all went round the circle and reversed, whereupon the second pair of couples took their turns and all went round again. They danced until they were sure their legs would fail, and then they danced some more. All the while the youths and maidens sang their songs for dancing, while at times the rest, the watchers and bystanders, joined their voices to the tunes.

The din inside the hall became a chaotic racket. The walls and rafters trembled with the noise. To anyone who did not feel himself a part of the company, the talk and laughter, mingled with loud and lively songs and underscored by stamping feet, all set against the crash and clatter of plates and knives and servingware, would have seemed a vast confusion of noise, a senseless chattering inside his ears. To those engulfed by the revelry it was a joyous rout. The beer was fresh and good; it bred great singing.

From time to time the gray wizard, with the skirts of his robe and cloak flapping behind him, dashed across the length or breadth of the room, willy-nilly shoving through the throng, heedless of who or what was upset, waving his stick wildly at shadows unseen in a corner or underneath a bench or table. Quietly then, and with dignity, he would resume his seat on the stool by the door. The guests smiled as they watched him. They were bound to respect the wizard, but they could not see what he could see.

In the midst of all the tumult, the old women who were married moved between the three sisters and their husbands-to-be, forcing the maidens back to the women's half of the house, away from the men. There they closed around the brides and began to torment them by telling tales of what marriage must mean to their lives.

One after another, the crones revealed the fate awaiting a maiden who would wed: the happiness of youth and innocence would end; life would become a time of toil and hardship. Early in the morning she would have to rise to draw the water and fetch the firewood so she could prepare her husband's breakfast while he lay abed. She would have to labor late into the night with her cooking and cleaning and washing and weaving, not to mention tending cattle and toiling in the fields, while always making certain there was bathwater heated for her man at whatever hour he might want it. Even at night in bed she would know no peace. She must expect her husband to scold her, perhaps even beat her, and she must bear it patiently. If he had kinfolk, her lot was twice as hard, for she would have to serve them, too, and endure their insults and blows. When she married, she became a servant, a creature of her master's will, and if, when all else was done, she found she had a moment free, she must devote that time to her children, never to herself. She would have to have many children; it would please her husband.

From the other side of the room, meanwhile, the sons of Alev, Sulev, and Olev looked anxiously for their brides, but could not see them through the crowd. No one told them what the old wives were saying: no men knew, for it was a women's secret. The bridegrooms, too, stood some instruction, even if it contained less teaching, less warning, and more jokes and boastful ribaldry. Their comrades taught them how to treat their new wives, how to be true and understanding, how to stand as shields and protectors to their brides, how to keep them from the hardships of the world. If they found their women to be unskillful, they should be forbearing and teach them gently, at first in bed, then with speech, next by looks, then threats, and finally lashings. They were cautioned, however, that if they must use the whip, it should first be one of reeds and horsetails, next of sedges, lastly switches of birch or rods of willow, and when they had to beat their wives, they should beat them kindly.

The women told the maidens of the torments and unending trials that were inflicted by their husbands, and all the tales were true, taken from the experience of those who told. Yet even so, they were spoken in a teasing spirit because, among these people, it was a part of the marriage ritual. The women knew, again from their own experience, that there never was a bride who listened well to what was said. All were too eager to be wed.

Late at night, when everyone was weary with dancing and with the rowdy songs that went with drink, then the old ones sang. It was with them that the true enchantment of music lay. The young men had sung their hymns to hunting and the chase, the maidens their praise of fields and fertile things, even small children had piped their rambling, nonsense verses, till silenced by embarrassed parents, but when the white-haired men and women took the singer's place on the painted bench beside the hearth, then there was stillness in the hall. All left their talk and put down their pots of ale to listen with rapt attention and admiration. The elders sang true songs, songs that stirred feelings in all hearts.

Perhaps an old man would sing alone as he plucked a five-stringed kantele propped on his knee. Perhaps two men would sing together, or two women, both bent with age. Facing each other, their arms entwined, they would rock back and forth in the rhythm of their song. The chants they sang were ancient lays, remnants of the days when they, and the world, were younger.

In the hour before sunrise the Kalevide, feeling lonely and restless, rose from his throne-backed chair and stepped clumsily between the bodies of sleeping men, his people, his subjects, who lay on the floor or on benches along the walls, wherever they had chosen to collapse. More were outside, asleep on the ground; others had found shelter in the barns and byres and in the small storehouses. Some slept peacefully in the bathhouse and the maltroom, surrounded by sweet steam. It was the fifth night of the wedding, and the festival continued, as it would for many more nights, until the Kalevide's food and drink were exhausted and he had given his guests the last of his gifts.

Stepping outside, he stood for a while on the porch, breathing air which was cool for a summer's night and heavy with moisture from the sea. In the doorway sat the wizard, ever vigilant. The Kalevide nodded once to the strange gray man, but neither spoke. Then, without thinking, he turned abruptly and strode up the path toward the knoll where his father was buried. For the first time since his return as king, he wished to look at Kalev's grave.

Elsewhere husbands lay with their wives. The Alevide had led the youngest sister to his little hut at the forest's edge, where he had begun to found his community. The Sulevide had taken the eldest sister behind the walls of his fortress. The Olevide and his bride lay together in a small bower built of greenery in the open air because he had no house to offer her yet. In time, however, he would erect three cities of stone in her honor. In a closet bed in the great hall, the cup-bearer slept alone, alone because he chose to be. The Kalevide was alone because he was king.

The first faint shades of light spread from the east over Viru as he walked the meadow beyond the gate to his home. The high, uncropped grass was bent by heavy dew and wet his bootless feet. No wind blew in the dawn to stir the brooding mist. Once or twice he passed the shadowy forms of horses grazing in the field. Out of nothing they took shape as he approached and into emptiness they disappeared as he went by. With an ache he remembered the white mare, then thrust the image from his mind. She was nothing but a dream, he knew. These were merely the shaggy draught ponies brought by a few of the guests from the distant provinces in the west and turned loose to feed while their owners enjoyed the feast.

[265]

The Kalevide climbed the hill to face the cairn that marked his father's tomb. Beyond it lay only the endless prospect of the sea, gray, asleep. For a long while he stood silently, awed by the loneliness of the view. The muted atmosphere of mist and dawn filled his heart. In the dimness loomed the mound, so overgrown with thistles and briar bushes, with a few harebells and golden asters here and there to add, in daylight, a glint of color, that other eyes, unknowing, would never suspect that here lay hidden the body of a man. The Kalevide knew. This was the cairn his mother was building on the day he was born, and to him it seemed that here, as nowhere else, their three lives were joined. The father he had never known in life, never seen, never heard, known only as a heap of stone. The mother, who had laid the stone, who was also dead and lost to him. And himself.

"I am the king," he announced simply to the tomb, or to himself. "I will be king, as I was meant to be. As you wanted, Father, so it shall be. I can do it now. Be a king."

Circles closed. He had lost his mother, he had searched for her, he had wanted to search; now he could search no more and must believe he would never see her again. The sorcerer who had stolen her was dead. His brothers had gone, leaving him alone to be the king. Yet, as was foretold, other men had come, to be his friends, to manage his affairs, to look up to him as their lord. He even had a wizard in his service now. Viru flourished, the people prospered. There was peace. Nevertheless, the Kalevide knew something was missing. Everything had come together, yet a void remained, and it was in himself.

He was not satisfied merely knowing good things were true. The pretty prospect he had seen from the hill overlooking Viru on his return from Põrgu with the maidens, the bright green fields, the golden grain, the cloud-white sheep, the happy workfolk, was not enough. He was the king; he wanted more. It was a yearning he could not comprehend. It was Kalev's lust for power born again, coupled now with his own need to fulfill his inner image of his father, to be a king, to be a hero.

"I will build Viru and make it strong, for you, Father," he vowed. "I will lead your nation to the empire it deserves, the power you desired. You had dreams, I know. I've had them, too. Dreams of riches, dreams of kingdom. I will make them true."

He fell silent, overwhelmed by the immensity of his promise. When he had had Kalev's sword it had seemed so easy to lead his people to wealth and glory and to establish a lasting kingdom. Now the sword was irretrievably lost, and the illusions had faded. The Kalevide realized he had no idea what to do to fulfill the promise he made, any more than he understood what it meant to be a king.

Linda had never taught him such lore because she never knew it. Kalev had not taught him because he had died too soon. If he had only known his father in his lifetime, the Kalevide thought, he could have followed him and so become the son Kalev had desired, the king he had conceived.

"Who taught you?" he asked the tomb aloud. "If I knew, I could seek them, and they would teach me, too."

Raised in Viru as he was, the Kalevide knew only one method to solve a problem, any problem. To know the source of a thing is to master it. A smith learns the origins of his ores, a healer the birth of the sickness or wound he cures. To realize his father's dreams he must likewise discover where they came from. To understand his father he must find his father's origins.

"I will seek your birthplace," he declared.

Some said that Kalev came to Viru from the end of the world, far beyond the sea. So be it, the Kalevide resolved, he would travel where he must. He could hunt no more for Linda; that quest was done. He was free to undertake this journey, wherever it would lead. One last great voyage; it would fill the emptiness he felt. Afterwards, he could justly claim the power that was his due as his father's heir. Then he would truly be king.

In the quickening light of dawn, before the sun broke above the earth, a raven flew out of the mist and landed on the burial mound. It preened its feathers. It opened its mouth. It spoke with a woman's voice.

PART III

28   "Far away there is a lake," the Kalevide said. "It spreads without end over a flat plain where no hills or mountains rise and where no rivers run. Rushes looking like swords and lances grow around its banks. There, if a man stamps his right foot twice, the ground will open. Behind that door lies the world's end. This the raven told me; it must be true."

"It is the entranceway to Põrgu," his companions said.

"I intend to seek that sacred lake," the Kalevide said.

The others were too stunned, for a moment, to reply. The Alevide muttered again that it was the way to Põrgu, but the Kalevide did not hear.

A few days after the weddings were over, the Kalevide and his friends had gathered on the porch of his house in the quiet of the afternoon. The Kalevide himself was sprawled out, full length, in his great chair. The cup-bearer was seated on the step in front of him, while the Sulevide took a straightbacked chair at his side. The Alevide and the Olevide were perched on the railing, discussing ways to control the weevils which had lately invaded the wheat fields. The Alevide thought they should feed them and build them houses beneath cool stones. If they were kind to the weevils, the weevils would be kind to them, he said. The Olevide was for building traps. It was a desultory conversation having no end of its own, until the Sulevide said, "I say crush them with your heel," to which there was no reply.

It was in the uncomfortable silence following the Sulevide's remark that the Kalevide spoke of his plan to seek the world's end.

"I mean to find my father's origins," he said. "Somewhere where the earth and sky merge I will find his birthplace, and there I will learn his secrets."

Only the cup-bearer seemed excited by the news. Here was the adventure he needed to pull him out of his growing melancholy. The rest were merely astounded.

"How will you find this place, this lake?" asked the Alevide, the first to recover his wits. "Do you know where it is, even the direction?"

"No, not really. I've never been there, have I? But I know Kalev came from the north, so I will begin by searching there.

Somewhere beyond Soome, beyond Turja, beyond Pohja, perhaps, I must find the end of the world.''

"That is far for a man to travel," said the Olevide. "How do you plan to get there?"

"If you get there," murmured the Alevide.

"At first I thought I would ride on the wings of an eagle. I'd fly as my father flew across the great distances. But then I thought, if I rode the eagle's wing, how could all of you come with me?"

"Us!"

"Of course. All of you. How could I leave you out of this? So I think we'll go by boat. A long time ago my father and mother planted some oak trees that are full grown now. They're straight and tall. The son of Olev can fashion them into a ship for us. Can't you? You did tell me you could build ships. Kalev would be pleased to have his timbers used for this, I think.''

Before the Olevide could reply, the three sisters, who were sitting on the far side of the porch, the women's side, said they would be glad to join this venture with their men. The Kalevide glared at them. They were supposed to be busy with their spindles and wool cards, resuming the toil they thought they had left behind in the underworld. They were supposed to be gossiping about small women's things, not intruding on the conversations of men.

"No," he said. "This voyage will be filled with dangers, and the sea is no place for women."

Sharp retorts quivered on the lips of both the eldest and the youngest sister and in the heart of the second, but the Alevide interrupted.

"You may want to go," he said to his wife, "and I'd like to have you with me. But if you do go—despite our king's humphing—you'll have to go without me, because I, for one, can't leave Viru. Not now. It's the middle of my harvest, and I can't abandon it. In fact, if the rest of you have nothing else to do, instead of sailing off across the seas, stay and help out a bit. I need every pair of hands I can find in the fields. Besides, this venture is foolish. The world has no end."

The Kalevide was about to reply when the Sulevide leaned forward.

"We dare not travel later," he warned. "If we go, we must go now, and it would be better not to go at all. Must I remind again of the threat of war hanging over Viru? We have a respite now, but it will be brief. The iron knights are gathering their forces even now. When they are ready, they will strike. Not this autumn perhaps, and not this winter, but very likely this spring, and with a certainty by summer, especially if we go away and leave the country unprotected.''

"I don't know what will happen months from now," said the Olevide, "but I do know this. You can't sail now. Not this month, not next. Not if you expect me to build your ship. I can build it for you, don't worry, but it takes time. Several months at least, since this must be a very strong ship to survive the sort of journey you're planning. It takes time to fell the oaks and hew them into planking. It takes time to shape the boards and bind them together. It takes time, that's all.''

"Not oak, not wood," muttered a soft voice from the corner of the porch. The gray wizard leaned out of the shadows where he was sitting unnoticed by the others. Although, following the weddings, he had been engaged to stay in the Kalevide's service, he was generally ignored by most of those around the farm who did not understand his work. He spent his days seated on his stool, hidden in shade, constantly on guard against unseen beings. In his gray robe he blended into the shadows and thus, as a wizard, he lived, forgotten by those who could most use his meager powers.

"To the north you sail," he said. "To the north, far north, where the fiery lights battle in the skies' undying strife. Sail there, to the north, sail in a vessel of wood, of oak, a ship of tree, let the spirits of the northern lights find delight with spears of frozen flame to light your ship in fire. Sail northward, if you sail, sail in a vessel shaped of iron, in a copper ship, in a craft of tin.''

"Our ship shall be wrought of silver, then," the Kalevide declared.

"What of your enemies?" the Sulevide insisted when it was clear that he was still intent on the voyage. "Do you mean to abandon your country to them?"

Angrily the Kalevide silenced him with a sign. Such thoughts were unthinkable, and he would not hear them spoken. "As long as I am king," he swore, "I will not forsake my kingdom, not as others have forsaken me. I will defend my people until I die. But this is a journey I must take. We will leave in the spring, before the enemy has begun his march, before the Alevide is bound to his fields, after the Olevide has built our ship. And if there is danger, as you believe, I shall leave the Olevide behind to raise fortresses for Viru. Will that suit you? Once we have stout walls, stone walls, no invader will dare attack.''

"The country needs a secure defense, it is true. And fortified towns will deter attack, since the enemy will have to prepare to mount a siege. Nevertheless, it is unwise for you to leave these shores at any time next year.''

''We won't be gone for long. You'll see. And once we've made this voyage, we'll be much stronger and better able to meet the foe than if we hadn't gone. You are concerned about holding back an invasion, I know, but I'm planning more. I'm thinking of the future. When we return, we'll lead the army forth. We won't hide behind the walls; we won't wait for the knights to attack. We will march out against them. You and I, we shall drive the enemy not only from our lands but from Lati and Leedu as well. We will force them out of their citadels of stone and send them flying, until they threaten Viru no more. We will push them all the way to Saksaland if we must, but we will free our borders of their menace for all time. We will sweep the Letts and all such outlaws out of the marshes and make their land fit for men to live in. Once we have made this voyage, once we have learned the secrets that Kalev knew, we shall be invincible. No power on earth will stand between us and glory, fame, and honor. You, the son of Sulev, and I, Kalev's heir, the king of Viru, will lead armies across the world. The Olevide will follow to build roads and cities, walled cities built of stone. The Alevide will make the empire flourish. This is the reason for our voyage; this is why we sail. We shall achieve the dream, and we shall raise our sons to follow us, and throughout the western lands all peoples will sing our names.''

Nine months passed from the moment when the Kalevide first conceived his plan to the time it could be realized in the world, nine months from high summer to bright spring. For the Kalevide the time seemed interminably long. The first snows of winter had come early, and the dreary months had dragged and dragged and dragged, as if deliberately thwarting his desire to depart. It was the work of the northern sorcerers, he was sure; they were, so the Sulevide reported, at work reshaping the world's weather, forcing winter to crush the spring. What he did not realize, however, was that all that time was needed before they could begin their journey. Every moment in the ice-bound days and weeks had been filled making preparations.

One day the Olevide had disappeared with the gray wizard to seek the songs which would bind the sheath and ribwork of the ship together and make the magical craft worthy of the sea.

When they returned, months later, having learned the lore required, they sang a shining vessel far surpassing any mortal ship.

The Sulevide was too concerned with the safety of Viru's borders to think much about journeying to distant realms. He trained the men who would stay behind in the arts of combat and daily devised new designs for the defense of the different hamlets in case attack did come while he was away. He dispatched runners in every direction to gather information and to spy on any foreign activity that might spell a threat. Fot the time, it appeared, the nation was secure. The iron knights would probably remain in their castles in the Lettish lands until summer. After that, the Sulevide knew, there was no surety of safety. Moreover, word came of another enemy approaching rapidly from the east. Unable to measure the magnitude of this new threat, he could only urge the Kalevide to complete the voyage as quickly as possible. The line between peace and war would be drawn very thin before they returned.

The Alevide was fully occupied planning the spring's planting; he had no time to dream of ploughing the sea. His helpers and workmen were assigned their chores early, so each would know who was to plough and who to harrow and who to sow, who was to watch the herds and who the flocks and who the bees. He taught the elders of the farms as much as he could of the arts of growing. Such songs as he had learned he shared with them all. For the rest, for what he knew but could not teach, the little tricks that had no names, he trusted to the wisdom of the folk to see them through. They had lived long in the world and had sense enough to read the nature of the land and act accordingly. They would do well enough, he knew; they did not need him. At the very worst, they would suffer no more than if he had never come to their country.

Only the cup-bearer seemed as eager as the king to make the expedition. He took it on himself to collect the equipment, gather foodstuffs, pack clothing for the voyage, making certain everyone had everything he would need. For him the winter months passed swiftly, as he was carried away by his own private plans and dreams of great adventure.

In its time the ice unlocked the shores of Viru and opened the way for a traveler. Plans became firm, dreams became real. The Kalevide could stand at last on Kalev's knoll basking in sunlight which flashed off his golden armor like fire. He felt as though he were the reborn sun itself.

On the shore below him his silver ship lay in her cradle at the water's edge waiting to be launched. Her bright metal sides and decking, her silver mast, glittered in the slanting light of morning while foaming waves rolled gently up the shingle to wash the ground beneath her gleaming hull. He had named her *Lennuk*, *Flyer*. This was his eagle, the wing to carry him to the very limits of the earth.

The men he had chosen to accompany him were gathered on the beach, anxious to depart, a score of men all deemed brave enough not to shrink from the unknown. Most were laughing to mask their nervousness, boasting to their home-bound friends of the deeds they meant to do in the far reaches of the world, taunting those who would not, or could not, venture with them, and playing simple jokes on their comrades who would. A few, shy of the banter, stood apart. Some were still bidding farewells to their families and wives, unsure when they would see them again.

At the Sulevide's behest, the Kalevide had dressed them all in uniform iron helmets and shirts of mail. They might encounter hostile forces in foreign lands, the Sulevide had said, and the men would suffer if not protected; they should also look more like a regular company of fighting men, for that would impress the folk in any port where they might stop. As far as the men themselves were concerned, however, they knew that as soon as they boarded ship and were underway, the helms would become bailing tins or soup plates, and the iron shirts would be hidden in inaccessible corners below decks, if not cast overboard altogether. Who would wear such weight on the water, they exclaimed to each other, what if the ship overturned? The men of Viru still had much to learn of discipline.

The Sulevide himself wore his accustomed copper helm and carried his copper crossbow. Although the Kalevide had pressed him to accept new armor in honor of the voyage, he was more comfortable with the gear he knew and did not care to change. It was a general's preogative, he said.

He waited close by the ship watching the crewmen to ensure that none strayed far from their duties. He wanted them to be ready to embark the moment the signal was given. On the other side of the silver hull the Alevide stood, gazing across the sea. He was clad in silver armor and carried a silver spear in his hand.

"Why?" he had asked when, a few days earlier, the Kalevide presented him with the arms.

"It befits your rank," Kalevide replied.

When his wife had admired his appearance in the shining suit, he had accepted it, although he felt foolish in armor. Now, however, the silver sheen of shield and mail seemed to draw him to the ship, so that he felt as much a part of her as the mast or the high curving prow. He would have sailed anywhere with that ship, even to the ends of the earth.

Although it was a land-bound world he knew best, the Alevide admitted—to himself, though to no other—he was looking forward to this voyage. Ever since he had first seen the wide expanse the sea always presents, he had longed to cross it and to feel himself surrounded by nothing but its great openness, and then to go on, to discover what lay beyond such unbounded distance. He could not tell the Kalevide, nor even his wife, but the yearning for the world's end was a dream he, too, knew well. Unlike the Kalevide, however, he was not looking for the road to wealth and power; rather he longed to experience the feeling, if only for a moment, of having come to the farthest point, the final reach of land or sea, and knowing there was nothing, absolutely nothing beyond him, that he could not be encompassed by anything at all on earth.

Unencumbered by such dreams and fancies, but filled with others of his own, the cup-bearer scampered back and forth at the water's edge, aching to embark. He picked up stones from the shingle and skipped them in long ducks and drakes across the gently lapping waves of the cove, just as the Kalevide had done as a boy, then, tiring of such childish play, he scrambled up onto the deck, where a stream of workmen were storing away the last of the cargo. Bales and kegs and boxes and bags of provisions were lashed beneath the rowers' benches. Here were silken sails and linen yardage, chains of solid silver, barrels for fresh water, barrels for beer, barrels of dried and salted meat and fish, barrels filled with uncounted loaves of bread. The cup-bearer knew every keg and chest. They were his as much as anyone's, more, perhaps, because he had gathered the stores together and packed them carefully when no one else would take the responsibility. Now, crouched in the narrows of the bow, he waited hungrily to be gone, to leave this land behind, to bid farewell to Viru.

Many men and women from the village stood about in tight clumps and knots, not knowing quite what to do but waiting to wave good-bye to those who were sailing and to see their king begin his high quest. None of them really understood what the Kalevide meant to do on the voyage or why he was taking their best men away, but discussing the matter quietly amongst themselves, they decided the venture must be important and for their good. He had assured them this was so, and they believed him, else why would he leave them?

[277]

The wives of the Sulevide and the Alevide stood together, apart from the others, unable to face anyone else or even speak to each other, weeping softly to themselves. They had already bid farewell to their husbands, even as other wives bid farewell to theirs, so there was no need for them to stay on the shore, but still they could not leave, not until the ship had sailed. Their sister, the Olevide's wife, was left alone on the beach. She would be going home with her husband when the day was done. For the eldest and the youngest nothing remained anymore except to wait until their men returned, and to pray they would return.

The Kalevide turned his face toward the sky. He raised his arms and the one word, "*Lennuk*," sprang from his lips. It rolled across the strand and far over the waves to prepare the water and the spirits who dwelled there for the coming of the ship. The word rose through the air and flowed into the clouds to signal to the highest lord of all that now the vessel was to sail. The sound returned in echo from the forest behind the shore, as though the oak trees too cried farewell to the craft that could have been their sister and to the men who should have been their sons.

Spreading his arms, the Kalevide sang the song that would carry his silver ship into the waiting waves:

> Ahti, lord of seas
> and oceans, white-bearded
> lord, receive this vessel;
> Vellama, Ahti's lady,
> mistress of the waves
> and currents, take this flyer,
> embrace her, clasp her, hold her
> on your bosom; Ukko, lord
> of clouds, watch her, keep her,
> grant fair sailing, warm winds
> and weather, gentle days.

While the deep sound of his singing filled the air, the crew closed around their ship and leaned against her, all but the cup-bearer, who remained nestled in the bow. The Olevide stood on a platform, shouting instructions to his workmen manning the machines and handling the hawsers that launched the *Lennuk* down the track into the waves.

With a sudden rush the silver vessel slipped on its rollers and plunged from her safe berth on shore into the cream-white sea. It was as though in that fleet moment she was born. Given birth, she entered, innocent, into the elements of her world. A high, thin spray washed over her prow and caught the colors in the sunlight, myriad rainbows reflected off her gleaming decks, then all subsided. The startled waves grew calm again; the ocean sighed to receive its own.

With a thrill of pride the Kalevide watched his crew scrambling over the ship's low sides to take their places on the benches. He shouted once to his men, then leaped from the summit of the knoll. Half-sliding, half-running, he raced down the slope and plunged into the water to wade to his vessel. A host of villagers splashed with him through the sparkling waves to help him turn the *Lennuk*'s prow around. With a mighty shove against her stern, he launched her into the deeper water. Just as the *Lennuk* seemed about to break away, he clambered over her gunwales to take his station by the long steering oar. The people cheered. He waved to them, the blessing of their king, then turned his eyes away to gaze upon the long waiting course to come. The ship passed safely though the shoals at the mouth of the cove and entered the unending sea. To the folk on shore the *Lennuk* seemed, as she glided over the silver, sunlit water, a brilliant wing shining on the wavelets with a golden godling riding on her back, being borne away from them.

29   The first day's sailing was the pleasure the Kalevide dreamed. The *Lennuk* coasted easily westward along familiar shores, stopping now and then at the outlying fishing villages to let the people behold their king. Throughout the nation this was a day of celebration, the bright beginning of a glorious quest. The Kalevide, in his golden armor, glowed with the radiance of grandeur. Some outlanders, who had never seen him nor heard of his rule, hailed him now as the sun, bound on his western voyage to paradise. Those who were of Viru received him as Kalev's son, their champion.

All that morning and afternoon the *Lennuk* cruised the length of the sea's long arm that lay between Viru and Soome in the north. The sun smiled on the ocean and smoothed its rough waves. Gentle breezes whispered out of the south and west, carrying soft tales of pine wood and meadow grass. The silver vessel swooped between small islands. Dipping her wings, she swept around shallows where glistening water swirled in golden wavelets. White-faced seals, like water nymphs, played beneath her curving breast; bright-winged terns darted through the curling foam at her tail. Dolphins led the *Lennuk* along safe roads known to them alone.

If any of the crew had begun the voyage uncertain or afraid, they soon cast their doubts and fears aside. Like their captain, they yearned for the thrill of high adventure and the challenge of the far unknown. With a hard good will they pulled on their oars to send the silver ship flying through the water like a swan skimming homeward over the sea. Under the Sulevide's stern eye the crewmen practiced discipline, and as they learned the art of rowing to a common stroke, the strength of twenty men became a single driving power. Silver oars devoured the sunlight on the waves.

When, however, the last islands were left behind and the last glow of daylight lay on the water, the *Lennuk* folded her wings and glided gracefully under the breath of the evening wind. The silver square of silken cloth raised on the mast filled with the steady blow from the south. The men rested. Kegs were broached and toasts drunk to the success of their bold venture: fame to every man, victory for all! One of the men unwrapped his kantele. As darkness fell, he sang songs to the sea.

On opposite sides of the ship, the Alevide and the cup-bearer each looked with longing across the wide ocean. Both were dreaming of what was yet to be.

In the bow, the gray wizard was wretched. Unhappily he bent over the rail, as he was bid, to watch for hidden rocks and whales and other hazards of the sea. Since his eyes were keener than any man's, the Kalevide had compelled him to come on this voyage, even though, the wizard was certain, it would hold no joy for him. Water rushed by. The ship heeled with the wind. It swayed; it rolled with every shallow wave. The wizard moaned. He could not see. Staring into the gray depths, pretending to watch for sunken dangers, he was really fighting desperately to control the depths of his own body. There should be a charm against sea-sickness, he thought, some compelling song to sing, but in his misery he could remember no words, only groans. If only his powers were greater than they were. He knew the languages of all men and beasts and birds—another reason the Kalevide had insisted he come—but here at sea only sea gulls screamed, and in their voices there was no comfort.

At night the stars of the Great Bear rose out of the water and smiled benevolently on the silver ship far from any friendly hand. The Kalevide leaned on the steerboard and swung his vessel into the Bear's beckoning jaws. The men slept, rocked gently by the waves and lulled by the songs of water running smoothly beneath their peaceful bed. It was their last kind night.

Before morning the skies had lowered under a heavy overcast. The wind had shifted so that it poured now out of the east in ragged gusts that presaged heavier gales to come. It was sent, no doubt, by the sorcerers in Soome to fend the foreign ship off from their land. Soon it blew too strong for sailing. Once more the men rowed, but it was no longer a pleasant exercise. They rowed for their lives. For the first time, everyone on board felt how truly small and fragile their ship was when matched against the unmeasured sea. The *Lennuk* pitched and rolled like a toy on the ever-increasing waves. Straining with all his strength and weight, the Kalevide fought the tiller to hold his chosen course while the oarsmen struggled equally to maintain headway.

Then out of the gray mists a gray ship appeared. Bound on a course across their own, it sailed into the very teeth of the wind. The Alevide was the first to see it coming, like a specter on the sea, and he quickly alerted the others. Only the wizard did not gaze in awe at this mysterious vessel. It approached rapidly, crossed their path within hailing distance, then passed on without a word, without a voice or cry, without a sound. Some of the men made signs against evil, for it seemed a ship of death, a carrier of spirits. With all sails set, it glided smoothly through, or perhaps above, the churning waves. Despite the fierce opposing wind, all its canvas, all its many sails flying from three tall masts, were bellying forward, swollen as though to burst. Its taut ropes quivered. As the strange ship passed by them, the men on the *Lennuk* could see that no rowers manned the benches, no sailors stood at the lines. A single man controlled this huge craft; he steered with one light hand on the helm. Under his arm was a bagpipe, over his shoulder a knotted cloth. Thus they knew him for a wind-enchanter; the ship was carried by a conjured wind.

No sooner had the foreign trader passed out of sight, disappearing eerily into a bank of cloud, than storm struck in all its fury, leaving the *Lennuk*'s men no time to speculate on the enchantment they had seen or to ponder the powers that propelled that mysterious craft. The gale pressed the Kalevide's ship over on her side. Desperately, he wrestled with the steering oar to head her into the wind before she capsized. He had wrestled demons; he had grappled with the aurochs. He had met the Sarvik himself. This was no less a test of his strength.

The light ship leaped wildly on the waves. Like a living thing, she reared her head and fell, to rise again. The men could no longer row. They no longer tried. Heavy waves swept over the decks and over them. Anxiously, they clung to any solid thing within reach to keep from being carried away. They prayed. They prayed as they had never prayed before. With frightened voices one after another called to the powers of the air and of the sea to protect them in their peril. Their words were whipped away with the wind.

The Kalevide shouted angrily for the wizard to cast a spell to counteract the storm. If these were winds sent by sorcerers, only a wizard's lore could quiet them. Not for nothing had he brought his servant on this voyage.

The gray wizard, however, lay moaning in the forward bilge, insensible from seasickness, unable even to raise himself out of the water and filth swirling around him. If he could not call up a chant against the storm in his stomach, how could he sing to quell the tempest of the world? From time to time, between groans, he did try; he tried to speak the words heard long ago, but his tongue would not serve him, and he could only mumble, "Go, winds, depart, across nine seas, go—" The sounds barely passed through his clenched teeth. "—go to your family, now, winds. Go, depart, fly—oh-h-h—homeward now. Find your—oh-h—kindred. Blow—"

It was hopeless. He could not possibly remember the words and formulas, much less sing them as they should be sung.

The wizard knew, as few men knew, that a charm does not have to be repeated exactly to be effective, but every incantation does require deep concentration, and for the moment that was quite beyond his power. The storm would rage despite him.

For seven days and nights the high winds howled. For seven days and nights huge waves tossed the tiny boat with a wild delight. For seven days the days were like the nights; for seven nights there was no dawn. This was the true storm, the tempest trained by the sorcerers of the north and driven down upon the frail silver shell. Hidden far away in their mist-shrouded fells, the evil masters, bearded ones, wrought such force as only they could wield to ward all strangers from their shores. Only wind-enchanters and wizards could penetrate their bitter barriers. The *Lennuk* was at their mercy, and they had none.

The silver sheath of her hull groaned with every wave, her mast bent before the wind like a willow wand, but the Olevide had sung his songs of shaping well. His ship was strong enough to survive any earthly storm, and many that were not. She rose high on the towering gray mountainous seas; she did not sink. She rolled, but did not capsize. She withstood every battering and did not break. The *Lennuk* was like a silver bubble bobbing on the water.

Sometimes she ran forward before the wind, sometimes she was knocked back, sometimes she drifted sideways, wherever air or water would take her. At times she was spun in circles, tossed like a toy in the hand of the storm. The sailors no longer knew where they were or how they were headed. East or west, north or south, all directions became one. There were no landmarks, no shores, no ports, no beacons to give them their bearing, no stars in the sky, no sun. All anyone could see were the countless cliffs of water on every side, and the black cover of clouds overhead matched by the blackness of the sea.

For seven days and nights the Kalevide and the Sulevide alternated shifts at the steering oar, although their course no longer mattered. They fought to keep the *Lennuk*'s bow turned into the wind. They fought for the sake of fighting, so they would not surrender to the storm's fury. Only the Alevide felt the glorious thrill wrapped within the gale. Sitting on a forward thwart, he leaned into the wind as though to drink all its power, all its violence, into him. Wet hair streamed back from his face; water poured down his cheeks. He wanted to cry aloud with a fantastic, terrible joy.

Early on the eighth day the winds suddenly died. The sky burst abruptly into blue. Soft white clouds took the place of the wrathful stripes of iron gray that had whipped the sea so unmercifully. The air itself held a golden hue and a calm peace like a note in a divine song. The wild, rising waves subsided. The ocean was restrained by a commanding hand. The Lord of Waters ruled.

Though weary and battered by the storm, the *Lennuk*'s crew hailed the new day like children reborn, carousing in song, basking in sunlight, laughing unrestrained. Some sighed for safety restored; others cherished the chance to rest, released from terror and toil. It was a bright morning. A new land loomed nearby.

No one recognized the shore that rose before them. No one had ever seen such a sea, either, and as they studied them, they lost their first fresh enthusiasm, for they had found a forbidding realm. The sea was lighter than the seas at home, as if it flowed with liquid ice and stone instead of water. It was cooler, and less friendly. Its paleness drew the warmth and cheer out of the day. It bleached the sky. Ominous cliffs loomed over the uncanny sea, bleak and barren walls to bar them access to the land. There were no harbors, no soft beaches, only the hungry teeth of jagged reefs. Nothing in Viru had ever seemed so hard or so cold. They had come through the curtains of storm to emerge, the men feared, in an unknown world, a world too harsh, too stark, too unkind for men.

For several days the *Lennuk* coasted along the shoreline, dwarfed by the dark towers of stone, seeking a safe haven. She was like a white bird paddling below a mountain searching for a home. Her crew learned again the hard labor of rowing. Once more they knew weariness. Clouds closed over them. The pale blue sky faded into a vast sheet of unbroken white. Although no new storms threatened, the sky, lacking color, lacked joy as well. The Alevide began to ration the few remaining stores. Much of the water and foodstuffs below decks had been fouled by seawater. It must be replaced soon, or all would starve. Yet days passed into days, and no landing site appeared. The Kalevide steered his ship. The Sulevide maintained the count for the oarsmen. Their labor was monotonous, like the sky, like the days. In the bow the cup-bearer gazed at the unkind shores. He alone still looked for the promise of the new land; he alone looked fondly at the high cliffs, for he still hoped to find that which he, and he alone, was seeking. The others merely rowed.

Eventually the discovered a narrow inlet with a small shelf of gravel where they might beach their ship for repairs. Entry was risky. The cove was guarded by repeated lines of rocks like the jaws of an angry fish; waves broke relentlessly over the shoals and against the cliffs. Nevertheless, they were forced to try a landing. The men were exhausted; they could not go on. Their water was gone and their food nearly spent. Here a thin, trickling stream offered at least the chance of fresh drink. The flesh of seagulls could be meat.

The crewmen were so desperate to reach firm ground they would have leaped into the sea and swum to shore, leaving the *Lennuk* to find her fate alone on the open water, if the Sulevide's discipline had not held. They kept to their benches. Only the Kalevide would not wait. He jumped overboard and waded ashore, carrying a cable with which to pull his precious vessel through the reefs. On the beach his men staggered one by one across the shingle to collapse from relief and fatigue. The *Lennuk*, freed of their weight, danced lightly on the milky water.

"What forsaken place is this?" the Sulevide asked.

He was uneasy not knowing where he was and hence what enemies lurked nearby. In this land all his skills in determining direction and location were useless. The sky was too overcast and featureless to permit reading. The stars had all been covered by night; by day the clouds remained to hide the sun. If anyone could have said where they were, it was the gray wizard, and he was still too sick to open his eyes.

The Kalevide shrugged. Unless it was the world's end, it did not matter much where they were.

The Alevide merely stood at the water's edge and stared, fascinated, at the vast distance they had crossed. He saw a great mystery in the invisible space to the horizon. The cup-bearer scampered down the beach alone.

Lines of black-winged gulls streamed from the cliff and swept over their heads.

"Lapu," "Lapu," "Lapu," they screamed, one after another. A wretched, desolate cry, it told the name, no more, of that harsh impoverished realm.

While the Sulevide took charge of the crew and set them to reconditioning the ship and the Alevide remained immobile, enraptured by the sea, the Kalevide walked the length of the cove to scout the nature of the land they had discovered. He was looking for signs of the end of the world. Even if this were not it, he thought he might at least find clues to its whereabouts. Across the inlet the cup-bearer was already perched halfway up a cliff and seemed to be climbing higher. What was he doing, the Kalevide wondered, as he, too, began to climb, scrambling over the rocks along the tiny stream. Probably gathering birds' eggs, he decided. A useful thing. Helpful. He was a good boy. The Kalevide waved to him once and then forgot him; his own goal was more important, he thought. The cup-bearer did not wave back.

Even though the stream's water was pure, nothing, not even moss, grew along it. The ground looked as though it had been blighted by some dreadful curse, cast forever fruitless, either in punishment for some unknown sin or as a guard to discourage all who might be cast onto those shores from penetrating farther. Such desolation would dishearten any who thought to explore. Here the soil was gray and lifeless. The stones bore crusts of lichen and a constant coating of bird droppings. A few tufts of dry grass struggled to survive in the cracks of the cliff, otherwise, all was bleak and barren. It was no world for men to seek.

When he emerged from the cleft cut by the streamlet, the Kalevide found himself on a flat, treeless plain extending into vague distance far away from the sea. Here strong breezes blew, winds born far off in the north and allowed to grow unhindered by any obstruction. No hills blocked them; not even a tree stood

[285]

in their way. Gusts and whirlwinds twisted the Kalevide's hair and tugged at his cloak. They blew cold. His eyes watered. In the distance a shadow lay between earth and sky. It could have been a cloud, or a line of stunted hills. To his blurred vision it looked like the wall he expected would exist at the world's end.

For hours the Kalevide marched toward this shadow, following the stream which was his only landmark on the barren plateau. The land seemed uninhabited by all except the harsh-blowing winds; no human would willingly dwell in such a lifeless waste where the only songs were the howlings of gales.

Nevertheless, he discovered a place where people lived. It was only a small hut alone on the plain beside the same slender stream, a far cry from the great city he hoped to find in the land of his father's origins. In front of the cottage grew a narrow plot of grass, a bright green jewel in the desert. In front of the door a young dark-haired maiden was spinning wool with a spindle. The yarn was to be woven into a blanket for her father. Silently, the Kalevide crept up behind her. She was singing a simple song about a milkmaid who once, while walking on the moor, had found a cock and a hen. The cock escaped, but the maid captured the hen and took it to her home where it grew to be a beautiful princess. Many lovers came to woo her; among them were the sun and the moon and "the Kalevide!" The Kalevide shouted lustily, leaping suddenly in front her.

The maiden screamed, dropped her spinning gear, and fled into the hut before he could touch her. Immediately her father appeared in the doorway to see what had frightened his child. In his country, so far from other men, dangers were rare.

"Is this the way to the world's end?" the Kalevide asked.

The man glared at him with a mixture of amazement, repugnance, and rage at having his solitude disturbed. He did not move from the doorway.

"Is this the way to the world's end?" the Kalevide repeated a little louder, thinking the man might be deaf. The brown eyes of the maiden peered at him through the hut's round window.

Now the man stepped toward the Kalevide. He was wearing the simple robe and peaked hat of a wind-enchanter. Around his neck was draped a long, rolled cloth, like a blanket, which was knotted many times. Each knot bound a wind that he had captured, the more knots he untied, the stronger blew the breezes and gales at his command. For a price he would sell a wind; that was his trade, after all, and that was his nature. He would earn a profit, but he preferred to live and work in secret.

"Is this the way to the world's end?"

The maiden barred the door behind her father. No one would ever enter the hut without his leave.

"It is a fool's question," the wind-enchanter said at last. "The earth and sea have no end. Those who seek it find only death. That is their end. That is the end of their world. They die on the Island of Fire, if not before."

The Kalevide had never heard of the Island of Fire, and did not care if he did unless the end of world were there.

"I have been told of a lake," he said, describing it as the raven had. "Once I find that place, then I have found my goal."

"That is only the road to Põrgu," the man said coldly.

30   "Only the road to Põrgu,"
Varrak, the wind-enchanter, repeated ominously. "The road to death. Death is the end you seek. Death is the world's only end."

"That cannot be," protested the Kalevide. "It must not be, not for me. I must find my father's origins, the country of his birth. Kalev came from somewhere beyond the world, and that is where I'm going."

"He came from Põrgu; he came from death. Go home, Kalev's son. Go home while still you can, while still you live. Go home, young man, to your own birthplace. Seek the origins of yourself. Already you have come too far. Go home. If you are lost, I shall guide you away from here. This much I will do for you, I will guide you home."

"I don't need anyone to show me the way home, and I'm not turning back anyhow. Not on your word. If my road leads through Põrgu, as you say, well, then that's the way I'll go. I'm not afraid. And nothing you can say will stop me."

The Kalevide took a step, intending to continue northward across the land toward the distance far away whether or not this old man would help him.

"Go no farther in my land," the wind-enchanter said. "Go no farther. If you seek the world's end, then seek by sea. Only by sea will you pass the terrors on the way."

The Kalevide turned back. "I thought you might help," he said. "If you'll guide me the rest of the way, I'll pay you well. Pilot my ship and keep us free of storms, and I'll give you anything you ask. Take me to the gates at the end of the world,

[287]

that's all. If you don't want to go any farther, that's all right, but guide me that far, please.''

"You will pay, foolish son of Kalev? What will you pay to pursue your folly?''

"Whatever is right. I have wealth enough.''

Varrak considered him darkly. His black eyes studied the young king's open face, but saw no guile. The offer was genuine. The Kalevide had innocently chosen to trust him, and no wind-enchanter will pass a chance to earn a profit. In his own mind Varrak called up memories out of the Kalevide's past, memories long forgotten but never lost, images the boy had seen and put aside, patterns he had received that were first laid in place by his father. To someone of the wind-enchanter's race no thought in time, no wish, no vision seen or dreamed was ever lost, or ever hidden. All were captured in the air and carried on the currents of the wind. To one who listened to the voices trapped within the smallest eddying breezes, no word, no deed of man, however far, however long ago, could be concealed. Varrak was such a one, and he was one who remembered all that he had ever learned.

"I will pilot you and sell to you my little winds,'' he said at last. "I will guide you and steer you well. To return you to your home, I would do as a gift to you. To take you beyond my land, I will have my price. I require that which now is chained to the west wall of your house. No more than that, but that I will have.''

The Kalevide tried to remember which of his treasure chests he had left where, but memory fled. It did not matter.

"Done,'' he said gladly, seizing the other's hand to seal the pledge. Henceforth, he was convinced, the journey would go well.

Varrak stepped briefly into his hut and closed the door in the Kalevide's face, for there were secrets there that no man must see. Inside, he prepared the sacred bagpipes used to charm the winds and collected the other instruments of his art. While he was away, his daughter, would nurse his tiny, infant breezes that were still too young and tender to be allowed to feed and grow on the vast, unbroken plateau, or to play alone on the open plain or the farther hills. Despite her youth, she was a capable shepherdess who had often helped him in the past. The wind-enchanter felt little apprehension in leaving her alone, since no one was likely to come to that remote corner of the country during his absence, but he did leave her a heavy drum with which to summon the great gales to her aid in case of danger. Thus she was protected well.

Coming out of the hut again, Varrak pulled his cap well down over his ears and wrapped an old ragged cloak around his body and his gear.

"Where we are going," he explained to the Kalevide, "where we are bound, the winds are cold and winter lives the year around."

Together they retraced the Kalevide's steps across the wind-blown moor. Neither spoke. The wind-enchanter blew light airs through his bagpipes and small breezes came and frolicked around him. In and out between his legs they played, round and round them both, raising whirlwinds of dust. Varrak spoke to them fondly, calling each by name. The Kalevide was awed and somewhat ill at ease in the presence of this power. To him the bagpipes' sounds were raucous and disturbing, the winds troublesome, but he was pleased and grateful to have the enchanter with him and bore his discomfort in silence. If there were small winds to suffer now, at least there would be no more storms once they were on the sea.

Night fell before they reached the inlet where the ship was resting. When they came finally out of the blind passage of the cleft which split the cliff wall, the silver vision of the *Lennuk* appeared like a specter before them. She seemed poised on the water as though willing herself to fly. Beyond the shelter of the harbor, heavy breakers rolled thunderously against the cliffs in their unending war with stone. Their booming sound was the only sound on the shore. Even the sea birds had fallen silent in the night. Smaller waves, the children of the ocean's swell, played around the ship's gleaming hull with curling foam. She shimmered like the pale and ghostly spirit of a wondrous swan illuminated by a faint white light captured from the surf itself.

Shadows of men rose silently from the shingle and became alive as the Kalevide and Varrak crossed the narrow beach. The crew had been asleep, like seals sprawled on the shore, but now they clustered around their king to hear what he had found in the desolate land. Was this the place, they asked, had they truly come to the world's end? In every man's heart was the question: Was the voyage done?

"There is far to go," the Kalevide told them as he presented the wind-enchanter. Varrak would be their guide, he said, and they would follow his instructions as faithfully as they would follow his own. At once the enchanter commanded all to board the waiting ship and make her ready to sail.

The Alevide could not understand why it was necessary to leave in such a hurry. How could anyone enjoy a journey if he was always rushing? The Sulevide was uneasy about their pilot.

"No one knows him," he said to the Kalevide. "He may be in league with our enemies. You cannot trust him."

"I met his price," the Kalevide explained.

"He is a wind-enchanter; the men will not care to sail with him."

"It's all right. It isn't sorcery." For the Kalevide that was enough.

They had taken their places on board the eager ship and were about to sail when the Kalevide suddenly remembered the boy.

"Wait! Where is the cup-bearer?" he cried.

No one else could say. The Sulevide reported that he had last seen him climbing on the cliffs, but that was much earlier in the day.

"About the time you went inland," he said. "I saw him then about halfway up one wall. But the men and I were too busy with the ship to mind the boy. He should not have wandered off alone."

"Could he have fallen? Maybe he's hurt."

"We would have heard him cry."

"I was studying the sea," the Alevide replied when asked. "I saw nothing but the waves. But don't worry, he can take care of himself. He's a tricky lad."

None of the others knew more. Anxiously the Kalevide stood by the mast and shouted for the boy. There was no answer but an echo off the rocks. Unconcerned, Varrak continued his preparations for their departure. The last lines binding the ship to shore were cast off; he began to play a tripping air on his bagpipes. The Kalevide called again and again, and still there was no reply, but just as a pleasant zephyr pushed the *Lennuk* into the surf, the cup-bearer suddenly appeared at the water's edge. Plunging into the waves, he caught the oar held out to him by the Sulevide.

"Thanks," he said breathlessly when he was finally safe on board. "Why are you sailing? I thought you wouldn't leave before morning."

The Sulevide nodded toward the wind-enchanter, who stood sternly on the after deck deep in concentration, guiding the vessel through the shoals.

"Where were you?" demanded the Kalevide. He seized the boy's shoulder and shook him till his teeth rattled.

The cup-bearer ducked away. "Oh, just looking around," he said, starting toward the bow.

"Look at me! Don't you ever go off like that again."

The boy shrugged. "You were going to leave me, weren't you?" he said bitterly, cruelly, then sat down beside the Sulevide. "A dreadful place, this. Nowhere I would want to live." The war-master merely nodded.

Gathering speed, the silver *Lennuk* glided away from the harbor, skimming over water as smooth as a polished sheet of stone, while rough and broken waves churned on either side of her. Outside the inlet the swells were even more imposing, yet the small ship slid along her track between them entirely undisturbed. The crewmen had nothing to do but lean back on their benches, idly watch the seas pass by, and dream. Standing alone at the helm, the wind-enchanter guided the craft on her course with only the lightest touch on the tiller. It was easier to steer with his winds. Whistling notes whined through his bagpipes, singing the tunes that told the breezes how to blow. The steering oar was needed only when, in its exuberance, a playful gust or wanton puff pressed too hard on one side of the sail and pushed the ship from her true line between the waves. At first Varrak loosened only the first of the many knots in his cloth to release no more than a pleasant breath of air while the *Lennuk* passed through the shoals at the mouth of the inlet. Later, beyond the shelter of the overhanging cliffs on shore, he untied more and stronger winds and let them blow freely. He turned the vessel's silver prow northward; the ship flew across the water.

For the first days Varrak wrapped the *Lennuk* in clouds of fog to conceal her from the eyes of sea-borne raiders, whose swift, low-slung dragon craft were known to roam the northern seas. Where the Kalevide was bound, however, no others went, and soon the risk of pirates was left far behind. When he released the spell of mists at last, the uncovered sky appeared strangely pale. The air was chill. All around them the wide reach of the sea was deserted. Here not even dolphins played. The waters ahead ran forever smooth. The men were lulled by the very peacefulness of their voyage. The perils of the past seemed far away.

Suddenly a whirlpool yawned in front of them like an open mouth. It appeared so suddenly, where no danger should have been and where none had been foreseen, that even Varrak was taken off guard. That hungry vortex spun too close for him to steer the flying vessel free of its voracious draw. The *Lennuk* was torn out of his control, or the power of any man, and sucked

[291]

into the maelstrom's all-devouring pit. At one moment she had been upright, the next her bow tipped and she plunged into the churning stream.

The helm was useless. Varrak let go of it and let the *Lennuk* follow any course she could, unhelped and unhindered by any master. His winds spilled out of the sail and flew to freedom in the placid sky. It was a pleasant day, clear and calm. The sun beamed seductively. Everywhere else on the ocean the water was smooth and serene. In that one place, however, the ship was tossed more violently than she had been in the worst of the earlier storm. Yet, she neither sank nor capsized. She was light enough to float on the whirling currents, and so she sailed, revolving crazily, ever around in unnatural circles without end.

The Kalevide lurched aft from his position by the mast to confront the wind-enchanter.

"Do something!" he shouted.

"What would you have me do?" Varrak replied coldly.

"Make a wind, untie your knots, blow your bagpipes, do whatever it is you do, but do something! Get us out of here!"

"My powers are with the winds, and my winds have fled. Water traps us, not air. I have no steerage; how then shall I guide a wind when in every direction we spin?"

Shoving him aside, the Kalevide charged back to the bows where the gray wizard was cowering in the coil of rope he had long since claimed for his own small place of refuge.

"You, wizard, get us out of here. You have spells, cast a spell to control these waves. Sing a song to charm whatever spirit in the water has seized us."

"I?" groaned the wizard. "I charm this spirit? My business is with dwarves, imps, little folk. I never said I knew anything of greater powers." Then he dived back into his burrow, clutching his belly in fear and rising nausea.

Hastily, the Kalevide called his other comrades amidships for counsel. The sail, empty and useless, flapped wildly aloft, and no one dared draw it down while the ship reeled so. It thundered over their heads, almost an omen of disaster. Water spilled over the ship's sides.

The Alevide, striving to understand the nature of the phenomenon that had caught them, gazed deeply into the mill of green water. Soon he became too distracted by the depths of the mystery to be concerned about the peril it contained. He could not listen to the Kalevide's ranting. When a wave washed over his knees from the gunwales, he said absently, "We should bail out the water." It was the best advice he could suggest.

The cup-bearer shot him a look of complete disdain. The Kalevide kept shouting, "What should we do? What can we do?" He too caught a glance of scorn.

"The wind-enchanter promised to guide us," said the Sulevide. "He said he would deliver us through dangers. Compel him to keep his word."

"I promised that there would be perils on this voyage," said Varrak, creeping forward to join the council. "Here you see the first of them. Perhaps it is the least. Perhaps it is the last. I promised you trials. I did not promise to bring you through them all, such a pledge would be foolish. No man can be certain of so much."

"You said you would use all your skills," the Kalevide replied angrily. "But you haven't done anything yet. I'm still waiting to see you do what you said. Or do you intend to let us drown? You'll drown too."

"A wind-enchanter will never drown. Not while he has skill and wit and a little wind left in his bag. It may be that my winds cannot save this vessel now, yet there is always more to do. There are tricks that any man may try. If they should work, you shall be saved. If not, then you shall find your journey's end. And is that not what you seek?"

He left them abruptly, before anyone could reply. From the rubble floating loose in the boat, Varrak caught a small barrel once filled with water but now empty and buoyant. He wrapped it in a scarlet cloth and tied crimson ribbons to its sides, then a line attached to one end, flung it overboard, letting the cask float freely on the madly swirling water.

Soon the violence of the whirlpool increased; the ship leaned ever more dangerously. Gear that was not well lashed broke loose and spilled into the sea to feed the vortex. The men cried aloud in panic, certain they had come to the moment of their death. Suspecting treachery, the Sulevide crept up on the wind-enchanter and seized him from behind.

"What evil have you done?" he cried as he began to throttle his victim. "What demon have you summoned with that offering?"

His grip was firm. He knew that as long as he could hold on and keep Varrak from escaping on some beckoned wind, Varrak would let no terror strike the ship, no matter what it was that came, lest he, too, be destroyed by the unnamed fiend. The wind-enchanter, small in his grasp, did not struggle; he could not reply. He merely watched the shadow rushing to the surface from the ocean's greatest depths.

Out of the sea it climbed, high into the air, towering over the frail, mortal ship. The sky grew dark, the sun obscured. Men screamed. It was no demon, however, no dread spirit of the deep abyss. Only a whale. For a moment it stood poised on its great tail flukes, the red-coated bait clamped firmly in its jaws. From its blow-hole spun the two-fold spiraling waterspout that had caused the whirlpool.

The men gazed in awe at the whale's vast bulk and at the scars and barnacles marring its dark hide. Free-flowing winds seized the crimson streamers and blew them back from its monstrous head like veils. At the pinnacle of its leap, the leviathan turned and fell, belly flat onto the sea. One last wave exploded against the *Lennuk*'s sides, and then the danger was past. Having belayed the line, the wind-enchanter now let the giant fish tow them clear of the water that was still churning behind them, although the waves were already subsiding and soon would be still. The vortex collapsed; water washed away the last traces of the whirl-pool. Varrak released the rope, and the great whale, dweller of the deeps, as old as the ocean itself, swam away across the sea, tossing its bright, beribboned plaything on the waves.

With calm restored, the wind-enchanter shook out his bag-pipes and prepared to call his winds back to him. For a while there was a waiting silence as everyone else watched in wonder, in amusement, in secret dread. The leather belly of the pipes filled with air, then a dreadful squall burst from the drones such as no man had heard before. The pain of the noise forced them to clamp their hands over their ears or hide their heads in barrels, but to the winds it was sweet music, and it needed to be loud if it was to summon back the wide roving gusts and gales that had strayed far from the ship. One by one the errant breezes returned and let themselves be bound again within the wind-enchanter's cloth. Once caught, they were docile enough. Varrak left just enough free and dancing to his music to refill the sail and push the ship once again on its peaceful course. The sharpest-eyed among the men could just barely see, far away to westward, the vague shape of the whale rolling happily with the waves. To most, however, it was merely a darkness on the water which might have been an island or the shadow of a cloud.

When the Kalevide joined his pilot by the helm to thank him, Varrak did not respond. He merely raised one arm and pointed toward the distant north, where they were headed. Dark plumes of smoke could just be seen coiling above the horizon. An ominous pall hovered over the edge between sea and sky.

31 Jagged mountain peaks jutted out of a muddy sea to thrust angry faces at the sky. Columns of fire spewed out of their broken tops, spreading evil clouds of red-brown smoke in all directions, clouds reflecting the color of the flames seething within the mountains' raging cauldrons. The entire sky seemed ablaze with a mad, tormented fire. Poisonous fumes enveloped the *Lennuk*'s decks. The wind-enchanter draped a cover of fresher breezes over the ship, yet even so the reeking vapors penetrated his canopy, choking the men, burning their eyes and throats with their sulfurous stench. The sun at its height was dimmed behind that fearful pall, until it seemed no more than a baleful orange disc, a sad object devoid of warmth and life. Darkness would have been preferable to that smothered light. Ashes rained over the water; they dyed the ocean red.

The men of the *Lennuk* were chilled with the wind of deep foreboding, yet Varrak steered them closer to the island. Through the blurring haze they could see the bones of ships cast upon the rocks and abandoned in despair. These were the vessels which had brought wanderers through the ages on the quest for the world's end. This was the end they found. Broken masts and naked ribwork strewed the red cinder shore. They looked like the corpses of beasts, carnage left in epochs long ago, as though the last wars of the world had raged on these beaches and none had survived. All the ruins were charred, crusted with black charcoal that caked the planks and spars like the terrible scars of plague. A few still smoldered; most were cold. The scorched remains of sails still clung to some of the masts, but long ago they had fallen into rags, useless scraps of cloth that could never hold a wind again. These were no more ships for sailing men, only hulks to mock the dead.

Bombs of fire fell on the sand, molten stones cast from the mountain tops, exploding when they struck. If they touched wood, they lit small fires which blazed a while, then died, to be relit another time, as though the island knew it must conserve its dwindling fuel. Here there were no living trees; nothing dared grow amid such bombardment. Only the ships' aged timbers burned, and these were becoming ever fewer. It had been long since anyone had landed, long since anyone had been drawn to this island by the search for the world's end.

Fiery missiles sought the *Lennuk*, hungry vultures of fire to feed on the swan's young flesh, only to fall into the sea and die in steam. Whenever the men heard the loud roar-whistling screams in the air, they dived under their benches in fear, but Varrak, knowing these shores and their ruin, held the ship far enough from the land to keep her free of danger.

"This is the Island of Fire," he said grimly to the Kalevide who alone remained unshaken. "This is the land whereof I spoke, where those who seek the world's end complete their journeys."

"Put me ashore," the Kalevide said eagerly, too excited by the possibility of the end of his journey to question the wind-enchanter's words. Like all heroes bent on the quest for the world's end, he did not notice the desolation of the land or the rubble littering the beach. To him the noise, smoke and fire were no worse than what he had experienced in the foundries of the smiths. Such a clime could have borne his father. That was all he cared about.

"You are a fool bound on a fool's quest," Varrak said.

"Put me ashore," the Kalevide repeated.

"You will die here."

Before the Kalevide could reply, the Sulevide reiterated the warning. "You must not go. The risk is too great. You may die, and too many depend on you now to jeopardize yourself unnecessarily. You are the king."

"I thought you said a king should lead his men. He should go first when there is danger."

"In battle, yes. The men expect that; it is the king's duty in a war. This is different."

"But what if the world's end is here! I have to find it. And even if it isn't, I still want to know what lies beyond those mountains. We can't come this far without discovering all we can. I want to explore the island."

"Let another go first. I will go myself. I am experienced in scouting and exploration, and the risk will be less for me. So will the loss if I do not return. Set me ashore," he said sharply to the pilot.

Varrak did not care what others did. He would not step on shore himself, for he knew too well the perils there, but if anyone else wanted to brave the fury of the fire, he would not prevent him. Each man must be his own fool.

"Be careful," the Kalevide said reluctantly, wishing he were going, wanting the glory.

"I will," said the Sulevide, readying his crossbow and preparing to disembark. He knew there would be no fame from this, only a brief, dirty battle. "Wait two hours," he said. "If I have not returned by then, go on without me, for I will have fallen."

Varrak ran the ship into a cove sheltered by three small hills. Even these were filled with violence. Flames shot into the sky from the first; the second belched reeking smokes. From pits within the third white jets of steam and boiling water spewed. Seething mud and lava flowed down their slopes to fill the valley where the three hills met.

As soon as the *Lennuk*'s silver keel scraped the rough-edged gravel, the Sulevide vaulted over the side and ran swiftly across the beach. Shots of burning rock streaked around him, but he dodged, running in zig-zags over the strip of exposed land toward cover. He ran doubled over to present a smaller target and now and then ducked under or behind a blackened timber when the fire came too close. In his hand he clutched his copper crossbow, although there was nothing mortal he could shoot. Those on board the ship watched him in horror. One missile exploded at his feet in a blinding flash of fire.

"He's down," cried the Kalevide.

The Sulevide rose again and scrambled across the burning crater, running fast toward an area where a wall of long-hardened lava offered some slight cover. Once he glanced back over his shoulder to see the ship begin to pull away, but he was too pressed to look further. His own survival required his complete attention. No retreat remained.

Aroused by the presence of a man on the island, the torrent of fire increased in fury. Hastily, Varrak backed the *Lennuk* away from shore. His winds were troubled, skittish, difficult to control. The ship slewed in the boiling water. Then, just as the boat began to move freely, the cup-bearer sprang over the side.

"Wait!" he cried to the Sulevide.

"Come back here! You!" shouted the Kalevide.

It was too late.

"Turn around," he cried urgently to the wind-enchanter. "Turn around, go back!"

The ship was under way, however, and Varrak would not turn again into the teeth of destruction. He would wait the designated time well out of range of the mountains' wrath. Then he would turn the ship away and sail on. So it must be. The last look the Kalevide had of the boy was of him scrambling out of the water and crossing the pock-marked beach, dodging and zigzagging just as the Sulevide had done.

The son of Sulev, unaware that the cup-bearer was behind

him, had already worked his way inland amid the wreck and ruin of what had once been land. Here the dangers were less intense, for most of the shot fell on the shores themselves in the island's effort to ward off invasion, but many red-hot stones fell around him, nonetheless, compelling him to keep constantly alert, listening to the stinging sounds of fire seeking him. More than once his copper helmet saved him from swift death. Geysers opened suddenly to shoot without warning, as though he had tripped unseen triggers buried in the quaking ground, but he was too wary, too experienced, to be taken by such simple traps, or by the fissures and crevices concealed under deceptive coverings of ash and dust.

He went slowly, destined for the highest mountain peak, which he deemed to be the chief of the island's hostile forces. The Sulevide crossed the wide fields of ashes lying as smooth and white as snow upon the ground's dark underarmor of lava. He walked amid feather-plumes of steam, reminders of the heat hidden beneath that crust. To reach the distant mountain he climbed a long ravine walled with black and polished glass, revealed when, long ago, some violent wrench of the earth had sheared the gray stone shell that once had covered its face. The rest of the ground was a rubble of blasted, burned-out rock. All the living matter that was earth had been devoured in the deep furnaces of a fire which left only the husks of cinder remains disgorged and hurled chaotically over the mountainsides.

The wind-enchanter's report, that the land was utterly dead, was not true, however; not quite. Now and then the Sulevide walked on tufts of grass that somehow managed to survive the fires on the middle slopes, and once he passed a stunted spruce tree which had found a lonely foothold in the soilless earth, where it lived, a brilliant spot of green surrounded by the endless fields of gray and brown and rust that were the lava's hues. One tree in all the waste, yet perhaps it was a sign that hope might come and claim that ruined country.

On the lip of the high volcano the Sulevide gazed into a pit of molten rock stirred by rumbling deep within the entrails of the earth. The heat of it singed his hair and eyebrows and scorched his coat; too soon he was forced to retreat. Here there was no life. Beyond this peak there were only countless others, each one as desolate. Further exploration of the island would be fruitless.

When, at the end of the appointed time, the Sulevide signaled from the shore, the *Lennuk* swooped like a bird to take him off the island and whisk him out to sea again. As soon as he was safely on board, before he could recount what he had seen, the Kalevide asked about the cup-bearer.

"The boy?"

"Where is he?"

"Why? Did he go off again?"

"Right after you left. He said he was going with you."

"The scamp. I never saw him."

"We'll have to go back."

"It is pointless. He must have gotten caught in the fire. He could not survive there for long."

"We'll have to see. We can't leave him."

A white bird lit on the *Lennuk*'s curving, silver peak. It called three times before flying on again, bound on its own voyage beyond the world.

The gray wizard, who professed to know the tongues of birds, crawled clumsily aft to find the Kalevide.

"The white one says the boy has found the country that lies behind the mountains of snow," he said. "She says he is with the nymphs and will return to us no more. The ship should sail on. These are the words the white bird says."

Varrak, the wind-enchanter, nodded in confirmation. Aghast, the Kalevide turned to the Alevide.

"He was your friend," he cried desperately.

"The boy will be happy where he is. He's come far to find his haven; we should leave him there."

"Be we can't abandon him. We have to do something."

"Listen to the birds; the words they speak are wise enough if one will only heed them."

Long ago, Linda had said much the same. The Kalevide bowed to their advice. Disconsolately he signaled to the pilot to steer away from the wretched, burning island.

"Thus men find the ends of their quests," Varrak said, but the Kalevide would not listen to him. He buried his face in his arms and ached for his friend.

They sailed farther north, along seaways no longer familiar to the wind-enchanter. Never before had he ventured so far; never before had he been compelled to guide men beyond the Island of Fire, for none before, of those few who managed to escape the wrath of the flames, had dared to continue his journey; all had begged him to take them home again. Thus, when the crew pressed him with questions about the course ahead, he could not answer. He could not say if there were more dangers to be faced, or if the rest of the voyage would be peaceful. Perhaps the island was the worst that man could suffer, or perhaps it was merely a shadow of what lay ahead. No one knew. Of the world beyond the land of fire, no true tales were told by men. Varrak could only stand patiently beside the helm and urge the vessel forward cautiously, feeling his way across the unknown leagues of sea, and wait, as the others waited, in thoughtful silence for what would come.

The light of the sun grew dimmer as they ventured north. It seemed to shine through layers of ice high in the air. No longer rolling high above the horizon, it rose late and low and then retired, after a few hours only, behind the world's rim. The *Lennuk* sailed, for the most part, in darkness now, or in the long twilights of dawn and dusk. When the brief daylight came, even the sea was hidden, wrapped in a mantle of mist and frost. Everything was obscured. The towering mass of land looming out of the ocean to the east was barely visible.

Whether this was a giant island or a peninsula of a greater land, none could say for certain. Although the seas clearly swept beyond its headlands, past which they were sailing, its shores spread eastward much farther than anyone could see, to disappear in the distance in the haze of fog and cloud. Unlike the angry land they had left, this was calm and cold. Deep fjords and bays cut the shoreline and presented countless harbors. There was even a belt of green thriving along the water's edge; forests and fields invited landing. Beyond these meadows and woods, steep mountains of ice rose massively into the sky. Glaciers stretched down their narrow valleys to touch the sea at the head of every fjord. They looked like the blue and white frozen fingers of a gigantic creature come to cover the earth. Above the high peaks and in the upper passes, white walls of a greater ice appeared, the brow of the beast itself, lurking behind the mountains and gathering its strength to strike, to strike, or to creep, with the imponderable slowness of ages.

"Will you land?" Varrak asked the Kalevide. "Or will you sail on?"

"Is the world's end here, do you think?"

"I do not know what is here. These shores are strange to me. The sea extends beyond this land. You have not yet reached the end of your sailing if you wish to go on. Do not think to find the world's end here. Or elsewhere."

"What do you think?" he asked the Alevide and the Sulevide together. The gray wizard crouched near them, chanting charms to end the voyage there and then.

"The men could use a rest," said the Alevide. "Except for

[300]

our brave champion here, no one has had a chance to be ashore for a long time."

The Sulevide did not hear his sarcasm. "That was hardly relaxation," he said. "The land here looks safe enough—although one can never be certain."

The wind-enchanter steered the ship around a dark green island and into a bay of white-blue milky water which offered a well protected anchorage. Here the mountains were somewhat farther inland than elsewhere, so there was more room to explore. Joyfully the crew disembarked, grateful to have firm ground under their feet once more. Not since the hard shores of Lapu had they trod on solid earth. Led by the gray wizard, they scampered like goats along the beach and rolled like kids in sand that was alive with nuggets of gold and silver and copper. It seemed a virgin country, unspoiled ever by the touch of men.

"Look! Everywhere!" they cried to their king, showering fistfuls of gemstones into his hands. They begged to be allowed to go inland to see what other marvels they could find. They were so carefree and eager, the Kalevide gave them leave, though he would remain behind with the ship. He was still brooding over the cup-bearer's defection. Although he must still pursue his quest, as though his life depended on it, all the joy had gone out of the adventure. It hurt him deeply to have left his friend behind, even if it was the boy's own choosing. The cup-bearer's departure cast a dark shadow of doubt over the entire voyage. He felt as though his fortunes had begun to wane. If he did not find the world's end, the Kalevide did not think he could return to Viru.

The Alevide and the Sulevide were about to join the party ashore when they were called back.

"Are you going to leave me too?" the Kalevide complained.

So they stayed behind and kept their king company while the others explored. In the pale light of afternoon the Kalevide and the Sulevide lay down on the *Lennuk*'s silver decks to sleep, leaving the Alevide on watch alone.

Not quite alone. Varrak, too, remained on board, seated by the steerboard, wrapped in his ragged woolen blanket, savoring the icy winds that blew through the mountains' frozen rifts and down the glacial slopes.

Under the leadership of the gray wizard, the rest of the company wandered inland on a long, meandering course, winding between tree-like stalks of plants. Here there were no trees, but the plants and herbs grew taller than the pines any had known at home. They formed a forest thicker than any firs. The men traveled like mice through the meadow grasses. Not being mice, however, and not being accustomed to traveling through blades of grass, they quickly became disoriented. All landmarks of a kind they could understand were hidden by the thickness of the growth, and the signs small animals use to distinguish one path from another were unknown to them. They crossed and recrossed their one trail countless times without recognizing it. They were lost.

The gray wizard, insisting that only he had wisdom enough to guide them safely back to the ship, took them farther and farther from the shore. Disturbed by their scampering, a bird burst suddenly from its nest and hovered over them. The men cowered in fear. Its wings filled the sky; its talons looked like tree trunks, its beak a cavern, but the thrush fed only on gold and silver and copper ore, and was not interested in men. It flapped away to find another meadow where it could feed in peace. The sailors fled in panic.

Forsaking all hope of returning to the safety of the ship, they simply ran, filled with fears of things they did not understand, afraid of beasts so much larger than they were. Soon night enclosed them. In spite of the chill and damp and the uncertainty of their plight, they chose to rest where they were, in the shelter of a foreign-looking bush, rather than go on into darkness. Morning often brings bright counsel, said the wizard confidently, never for a moment doubting that when daylight came he could find the proper path again. A wizard must have a few skills missing in other men. The rest of the crew were too much awed by his reputed powers, small though they might be, to argue.

Instead of cheer, however, the first faint light of dawn brought more terror. They were captured. Before they woke, before they could flee, before they could fight, they were discovered and imprisoned by a child of the race of the land.

She had risen early that morning, earlier even than her father, and had gone into the meadow to play. There, squatting on the ground to peer at dew-drops caught in the cups of wide gray-green leaves, she had inquisitively turned over the leaf that had been the men's hiding place. Not knowing what such tiny creatures could be, she scooped them up, wrapped them in her apron and carried them home to show her father. He could tell her; he knew everything. The men awoke in the clutch of a child, trapped in heavy folds of cloth, violently shaken by the bounce of her toddling run.

"Papa, look," she cried. "Look what I found, look, Papa!"

In wonderful delight she unfolded her catch, spilling them onto the ground by the giant's feet. "What are they, Papa? I found them in the cabbage, sleeping like fleas, sleeping in the cabbage leaf, all stiff with dew drops. What are they, Papa? Can I have them? Can I keep them, please? To play with, Papa, please?"

Seated on a great stone chair in front of the doorway to his cottage, red-bearded Eirik looked up from the stone hammer he was mending for the morning's toil. To the men on the ground he seemed a mountain come alive. Gently he put his mallet aside and prodded one of the small beings with his finger. The man screamed. To the giant it sounded like a squeak. The gray wizard rolled aside to avoid the battering ram of the finger and sat up. He felt himself a dwarf beside this monstrous creature.

"What are they, Papa?" the child pleaded insistently.

"I do not know, Daughter. We will have to see."

Then, in the age-old fashion of all ancient races, the giant plied the wizard with riddles to probe the depths of his wisdom.

"What is it?" he asked, "that walks upon the grass, strides along the fence-pole, and treads the sides of reeds?" His voice boomed as though out of a world-deep cavern.

Of all the men the gray wizard alone breathed easily, relieved that the riddle did not match the giant's weight. He must, he knew, give a good account of himself, and do it quickly, for he could not hope to withstand a long bout of questioning. Though he was a wizard, the roots of his learning were not nearly as old as the other's. He could not begin to contend with him in deep lore.

"The bee!" he shouted at the top of his voice. Eirik smiled broadly; his teeth were shaped of stone.

"What is it," he asked again, "that drinks from brooks and wells and sips as well from the stones on the banks?"

"The rainbow!" cried the wizard, afraid his voice would crack.

"What is it that hisses through the meadow grass and rushes above the blue-tipped forest?"

"The rain!"

Satisfied with the answers he heard, Eirik turned to his daughter, saying, "These creatures, though small, have some sense and understanding. They have feelings, sweetheart, so they're not for you to play with. You should carry them back to where you found them and put them back in their nest. And darling," he added as she scooped the men back into the folds of her apron, "carry them very carefully. Do not let any of them get hurt, for they are delicate little creatures."

[303]

The child nodded deeply and, with the men cupped preciously in her infant hands, tip-toed across the pasture, taking tiny, precise steps lest she stumble with her treasures. At exactly the place where she had found them, she knelt deliberately and was about to set them on the ground, taking the utmost care, just as her father told her, when the gray wizard began to sing to her. It was not one of the songs he sang best—a charm meant for dwarves would have been absurd—but he hoped it would serve to win her to him.

Delighted, the giant's daughter raised her hands to her ear to listen to his singing. At the top of his voice he bellowed how nice it would be, how pleasant it would be, how lovely it would be, how happy it would be, how much fun it would be, if she would carry them to the shore and to the ship and help them out to sea, but how cruel it would be, how careless it would be, how cold it would be, how wet it would be, to leave them in the smelly cabbage plant where only slimy slugs and snails would like to be. It was improvisational nonsense, of course, but his delicate, thin voice charmed her, and she agreed. With a bound she dropped them all into her apron pocket and skipped merrily across the meadow to the nearby cove. The men bounced crazily in the soft folds of wool, but after riding on the open ocean for so long, after surviving the whirlpool and the storm, it seemed no more than mad amusement.

On board the resting *Lennuk*, the Kalevide woke with the sky growing darker as though obscured by a vast, threatening cloud. In the shadow a chill wind swept across the decks. Eagerly, Varrak, the wind-enchanter, scooped it into his cloth. Leaning over the pretty silver toy, the giant's daughter shook the men out of her pocket. They rained like mice all over the boat, on the benches, in the bilges, from bow to stern, but none were hurt. Then, as the gray wizard and the Kalevide both shouted their thanks, she pushed the ship off the shore and far out to sea. As they sailed swiftly away, the child stood ankle-deep in the bay and blew them kisses of farewell.

32   In the farthest north the sun could no longer rise. The *Lennuk* had sailed beyond the line where its light would shine. She sailed beyond the limits of the moon and on, through deep gray waters colored only with endless shades of twilight and dark. Cold consumed the crew. They no longer

spoke to one another; sound itself seemed frozen in the air. Silence grew like crystal. The men sat huddled on their benches, each one drawing inward into himself in an effort to conserve the last spark his life contained to sustain himself on its faint warmth alone. Their eyes grew dark and hollow; they stared sightlessly at nothing. Their cheeks were sunken, the skin on their faces brittle from the cold. Every breath was pain. Varrak, the wind-enchanter, steered the ice-encrusted ship unwaveringly, guiding her ever northward, but he, too, was nearing the limits of his endurance.

In the strange half-shadowed light they glided soundlessly past looming shapes of icebergs destined southward, where they would melt and die unobserved. Some, as large as islands, towered over the tiny, fragile vessel. Within their ice-bound peaks were caves where cold winds crouched and whined and cried to be released. Other icebergs were small, shaped like bodies afloat on the sea, the forms of men and beasts grotesquely molded and twisted by the lapping tongues of water, washed, and then set adrift to pass slowly away to be forgotten. They rolled like corpses on the waves of the *Lennuk*'s wake.

Overhead the burning northern lights brought the night alive. The spirits of the farthest sky entered their eternal dance, their march of endless strife. Back and forth across the plains of heaven they surged in undulating currents. Around the night's dark field they weaved and feinted, shook their silver spears and flourished golden shields, strutting in mimicry of the wrath of men. Waves of light swept across the far-arched sky. Shafts of glowing fire shot into the sea. The water was set afire. A bright silver radiance touched the icebergs and touched the *Lennuk*'s polished decks. The gleaming metal, though quivering with the light, could not burn. Sheaths of ice on the yardlines, the glaze of frost on the sail, shimmered with the pulsing fire of the sky's deep mystery. The crewmen wept with fear. The Kalevide rejoiced. He longed to join the spirits in their brave dance, to march across the world ablaze with gold and silver fire. His armor glowed with the reflection of the flames.

The aurora rained light enough for them to navigate the ice floes. Slowly in the silver night the ship advanced while all around her grew slow and heavy. Even the ocean seemed to gell. Only the sky was alive.

The sea narrowed; it folded in upon itself, enclosed within a wide, flat reach of land, the outermost shelf of earth. The ocean ended. The *Lennuk* sailed as far as a ship could sail, her keel scraped on gravel, she rested. A tribe of people, half-man, half-dog, stood on the shore, enshrouded in fog. They had long, pointed faces and sharp teeth; their clothes were skin and fur, though they were naked below the waist. Long, bushy dog's tails drooped between their legs. When the Kalevide disembarked, however, they disappeared into the gray glaze of mist. He stood on the shore alone.

A vast, half-frozen desert extended as far as a man could see, and farther than he could walk. Leaving the others with the ship to guard her against unknown threats, the Kalevide, the Alevide, and the Sulevide entered that bleak, frost-tinged land. Beyond the shore lay endless swamps and marshes and unnumbered small lakelets. Under the vague, uncertain twilight cast by the wavering curtains of the northern lights, it was an eerie, unreal world. Shrubs that were less than trees seemed shaped out of shadows. Mounds that were less than hills seemed barrows raised to bury corpses. Pools that were less than lakes looked like black and depthless pits designed to trap the foolish and unwary. Here no living creatures dwelled. Wandering herds of deer did not venture so far north. The soaring white hawks of fable shunned the barren plains where no hares or foxes ran. For this they had traveled so far and endured so much, to discover a wasted land that went on and on and on into distant realms of emptiness.

The three marched ever inland. Their destination, the Kalevide insisted, was nothing less than the meeting place of earth and sky, but when the greater dark that was true nighttime came, it hid the line where the two joined. They could no longer see the way ahead or know how far they had to go.

A column of flame flared in front of them from an unknown fire. Towering to the sky, almost a beacon, a pillar of light to mark the night, it was the only thing visible anywhere. The Sulevide drew back, reminded of the dangers of the Island of Fire and always hesitant to approach where enemies might hide. The Alevide, however, walked blithely forward, heedless of the sinks and pitfalls hidden in the dark, because he was curious to discover what lived in that forsaken land. The Kalevide went with him, hoping to hear news of the world's end.

A bonfire was blazing under a great iron pot. An old woman jabbed at the coals with a stick, releasing clouds of sparks streaming skyward, carried on the wind of their own creation. She was small and dark, a creature of bone and age, wrapped in a cloak of feathers for warmth. Her face was pinched and nearly black from the cold, but the circles of her eyes glowed with the color of the fire.

"What are you cooking, little mother?" asked the Alevide when he was close. She did not reply but only stared at him and poked the embers relentlessly with her stick. He peered into the pot himself.

"Cabbages!" he exclaimed with joy. "Cabbages! Oh, mother, bless you. Cabbages. I expected something awful." He laughed. "Fishheads, or worse. Tripes perhaps. Oh, little mother, we are hungry travelers. Won't you find it in your heart to feed us, oh, please." Still she did not answer; she did not turn her eyes or cease stirring the coals.

Silently, the Sulevide stepped out of the darkness beyond the firelight. His crossbow was raised, but she never glanced at him. Her eyes were fixed on the Alevide, who checked the Sulevide with a sign.

"Here, little mother," he said, "take a rest. Aren't you tired? You must be weary of that long stirring. Rest a while, while we watch your pot. Leave it to us to keep it safe. See, my friend is armed; we'll keep all dangers at bay, don't you worry, little mother. When the soup is done, then you may decide to feed us, if you wish. There is no hurry. Rest yourself, and do not worry."

Stiffly, like a bird, she rose to her feet and put the stick in his hand. Pointing with a withered claw, she showed him where firewood was stored, then hobbled away into the shadows beyond the light.

"Tricky, tricky. You've got to be tricky," hummed the Alevide to himself as he smelled the soup. To the others he said, "Sit yourselves down, my friends, we'll soon see what we will see." He dipped his finger into the broth and licked it for a taste while doing a little dance. "O, cabbages, cabbages."

Just then the crone tottered back and shook her bony finger in his face.

"You watch out, you," she croaked. "Watch out for strange little boy, who will come, who will take my soup, you don't watch out. Do not let him, do not let him leave me nothing, nothing in pot for me, you!!"

"Oh, little mother, do not worry, do not fret. We will watch your supper well, as well as if it were our own."

She nodded sharply and crept away again into the bushes, where she slept in a wolf's den. Throughout their exchange the Kalevide had said nothing. He simply stared at the strange, haggard woman.

Since he had been given charge of the kettle and stick, the Alevide insisted he take the first watch while the other two rested. And if he had to sip the soup now and then, why, he said to himself, it was only to see that it was seasoned properly. Both the Kalevide and the Sulevide were soon asleep and snoring. In the comfort of the fire the Alevide, too, nodded, wrapped in the deep stillness that filled the unbounded world. Nothing disturbed the darkness. No stars shined over that land. They had come beyond the northern lights. Beyond that small island of fire the night was complete.

The glow of the embers entranced the Alevide's eyes, and he was drawn into dreams shaped from patterns in the coals. In his mind memories, mixed reflections from days long past in his homeland far away in the forests of the eastern world, mingled with images of Viru, now his home. In the mysterious manner of dreams, impossible combinations of impressions, happy boyhood moments in the forest, a farm in Viru growing green in springtime, delights with the woman who was his wife, melted together and became one. The calm that comes with silence lay upon him. A log settled on the embers. The Alevide noticed the shift in images, then slid into another untroubled reverie.

A tiny creature crept stealthily from the grass into the circle of soft light. No taller than an ox's knee, less indeed than three spans high, it approached the kettle timidly. Small, curving horns jutted just behind its ears; a little goat's beard decorated its pointed chin. On a collar around its neck tinkled a golden bell.

"May I taste your soup, great sir?" it begged humbly, bowing low at the waist to the Alevide.

Its appearance so well suited his mood that the Alevide drew the strange being forward. "Do not drown yourself, little one," he said gently.

"I need no spoon," cried the dwarf as, with a bound, it leaped to the cauldron's rim. At once it exploded toward the sky, growing as tall as a pine tree, towering to the clouds, rising to the height of seventy fathoms, then vanishing silently like a mist.

Only a smell of charring lingered in the air. With a start the Alevide realized the kettle was empty and the bottom burning. With a weary sigh, he refilled the pot with water from a nearby pool and added some fresh cabbages, which he found stored beneath a stone. The soup would take a little longer than expected, that was all. Quietly he woke the Sulevide and told him to take his turn on watch. Lying down beside the Kalevide, he decided not to tell the others what had happened. What was done was done, there was no need to boast of it.

[308]

The son of Sulev sat stiffly through his vigil, his crossbow primed and ready on his knee, his eyes constantly scanning the perimeter of firelight. Although alert to any danger that might break through the looming wall of darkness lying at the end of the world, he was not at all prepared for so small a thing as the dwarf that reappeared. It seemed so small and fragile and free of harm. He was no more suspicious than the Alevide had been, and he fared no better.

When the Kalevide's turn came to watch the twice-refilled kettle, neither of his companions told him what to expect, and, if they had, he would not have heeded them. Left alone, he brooded through the long hours of night, worrying about his quest. It had not turned out as he had dreamed. The cup-bearer had deserted him. The violence of the Island of Fire had shocked him as the majestic grandeur of the Land of Giants had humbled him. Worse, the end of his search, the world's end, seemed no nearer, and he did not know how to bring it nearer. Somehow, somewhere, the adventure had gone wrong and he with it. Because he could not understand how or why, he believed the reason was within himself. The journey was a failure because he was. He had undertaken to fill an emptiness in his heart; instead he had found an empty world. He felt no triumph, no glory, no sense of accomplishment, only an increasing apprehension. So when the small creature came again and bowed before him as it had bowed to the others, he did not smile as they had or invite it to come closer. Neither did he turn it away, however.

"May I taste your soup, great lord?" the dwarf begged for a third time.

"If you give me your bell," said the Kalevide without thinking.

Again the creature bowed, nearly touching its forelock to the ground. Then it detached the tinkling bell from its neck. The thing meant nothing, a small charm, a toy, no more. As soon as he received it, the Kalevide suddenly felt disgusted with everything, the dwarf, the soup, the quest, himself. He gave the dwarf a fillip on the forehead that sent it tumbling over backwards. There was a crash of thunder, and the beast sank away into the earth whence it had come. The only trace that remained was a wisp of blue smoke which soon floated out of view, that and the golden bell in the Kalevide's hand.

The noise woke the two sleeping men and summoned the old woman from her nest. While they all supped on warm cabbages, the Kalevide told them what had happened. He told it straight forwardly, without imagination or embroidery, without boasting.

The Alevide and the Sulevide both kept their own secrets while the old woman sucked her soup noisily and said nothing. In the deep blackness of the night beyond the ring of firelight the daughters of the meadow-queen danced and sported in the grasses.

When the meal was finished and the pot rubbed clean, the crone dragged herself away once more. The Sulevide resumed his broken sleep beside the fire. The Alevide was also about to retire when the Kalevide called him back to stay a while with him. Both were quiet. They stared into the red-white world of the fire and mused in their separate thoughts. When he did speak, the Kalevide's words were somber.

"If anything happens to me," he said, "I want you to return to Viru. You and the Sulevide. Varrak will show you the way; he will want to be paid. Pay him. —I want you to go home to your wives and not worry about me. Do whatever you have to do to help the country. Protect it, the Sulevide will know how, and make it grow, that is for you to do. Do not worry about me, but remember me, and tell the others. Go home to your wives, have sons. Maybe they can do what I could not."

"What are you talking about?" the Alevide said lightly. He could not read his comrade's mood and did not know how to respond, but he wanted to console him. "What could happen to you?"

"I don't know. Maybe nothing. But I have a feeling—I don't know—something isn't right." He could not shake the gloom that spread over him.

"It's all too dark. I think we went wrong—I went wrong—somewhere. We haven't found the world's end, have we? Maybe we never will. Maybe we'll go on looking forever. Maybe there is no such place, and maybe we'll never know. What will we do then?"

"What do you want to do?"

"I don't know. That's just it, I don't know. I can't go on searching forever, and yet I can't go home without finding it."

"Does it matter so much?"

"Yes."

"Why?"

"I have to find my father's origins."

"Yes, but why?"

"To find myself."

The Kalevide clenched his fist. He was still holding the dwarf's little golden bell. It made him feel foolish, and he was about to toss it away when the Alevide stopped him.

"Keep it," he said, without knowing why.

[310]

The Kalevide shrugged; it was all the same to him.

"Maybe I should go on alone," he said after a while. "I have to keep looking. Kalev must have come from somewhere. The quest can't be as vain as everybody says it is, even you. But if I have to go on, and on, and on, all my life perhaps, you should return to Viru. Take the others home, and take care of my people. You are my steward, rule them in my stead. Go home to your wife. I want you to." He wanted to weep but would not let himself. He felt very much alone.

"Look," the Alevide said cheerily, "tomorrow will be a brighter day. We'll go back to the ship, then we'll sail around some more, look somewhere else. Pretty soon we can all go home together. Home, to Viru. Think of it! The land will be very beautiful now."

"I wish the cup-bearer had not left me."

33   The morning was no brighter than the day before. A sunless light suffused the air, feigning a daybreak that was no more than a deep pall of gray which scarcely overcame the dark. Heavy clouds pressing down from the sky joined with fog rising off the cold ground, so the Kalevide could not see where earth and air divided. A dread murk surrounded him; the world itself was imbued with the emptiness he felt inside. The plains were flat and barren, wasted, deserted, devoid of life. And so was he.

A wide sheet of dirty water lay before him where the dwarf had disappeared. Beyond the lake there was nothing; no hills, no mountains, no rivers, no streams, only the single thick haze of mist and cloud that replaced space itself. Around the edge of the water reeds and rushes shaped like lances grew; their feathered tassels drooped like pennants on a windless day.

Slowly the Kalevide realized that he stood at the very place the raven had described to him on Kalev's knoll. Having reached it unwary, he could scarcely comprehend what he had found. The lake was far different from what he had imagined. Instead of being bright and blue with sunlight sparkling on rippling wavelets, the fitting vision for a finished quest, it was drab and bleak, but the raven had never promised there would be light.

The Alevide and the Sulevide were still asleep, rolled tightly in their cloaks for warmth, oblivious of his discovery. Without disturbing them, the Kalevide walked to the water's edge. If this was indeed the threshold to the world's end, then let it take him now. Let the gates swing open, let him enter. Let him finally and completely lay aside his doubts. Standing in the mud amongst the reeds, he stamped his right foot twice, as the raven had directed. Let this be the place, he prayed to the powers that guarded him. Let it be. Without a sound, the secret doors slid open, revealing the passage that would lead him beyond the earth and into another world.

Clouds of smoke and steam rolled darkly within the mouth of the gaping tunnel. Feeling the pull of the outer air, they billowed forth enveloping the Kalevide. The fumes seared his throat, when he thought to breathe. They burned his eyes, blinding him so that he staggered back in pain and fear. In a moment the doors would close, never to be reopened. Yet before he had withdrawn a pace, a voice halted him. It was the voice of a woman. It sounded like the raven that had spoken to him on Kalev's knoll and lured him hither. Now it rose from the bushes where that hag-like witch of the kettle had hidden herself to sleep.

"Sound the bell," she said.

The Kalevide's hand was still holding the tiny, golden bell which he had taken from the dwarf. Feeling foolish, he rang it gently. Its note was high and clear; like a drop of dew passing through the gloom and blinding clouds. Instantly all the smoke disappeared, the spell dissolved. A long, slow-sloping downward path lay open to the Kalevide, and uncertainly he took it.

Stepping into the inviting passage away from the upper earth, he entered the underworld's strange domain. Darkness grew around him and closed the way behind. He could not return. If he had reversed his steps, he would have found no opening behind him, no gateway, no door, only a long road without an end. Such was the path he had undertaken. Beyond the world's end there is no stepping back. Nor did the Kalevide have any intention of turning around. However strange and unearthly the way ahead might be, he meant to go on, to seek the secrets which had been Kalev's and which were, as a result, now a part of him.

The dark that embraced him was impenetrable and boundless, dense enough to touch. With no light to guide him and nothing on hand for a torch, he could only grope along very slowly, holding his arms before him like a blind man, feeling the edge of the wall to lead him. His only comfort was that here there was room enough to stand and walk. This passage was not so tight as the tunnel he had taken through the mountain to the Sarvik's back door. Here the road was wide and open, but for the ponderous darkness.

"Sound the bell," said a small voice near his foot.

He had been concentrating so much on his blindness that he had not thought to listen for sounds inside the cavern. Suddenly the scampering of tiny feet close at hand filled his ears, and he realized with a shudder that he was not alone. Others walked the passage with him, other beings that were not men. Tentatively, because he knew no better thing to do, he rang the tiny bell and heard again its gentle note. At once a soft gray light grew up around him, dim, but bright enough to show the way. It spread forward and behind, far enough to reveal his next few steps and the steps where he had just been, before fading away into the absorbing dark. The light cast vague shadows on the floor and ceiling and walls of the tunnel but lit nothing clearly. Nevertheless, it gave an opening in the world of darkness; for that the Kalevide was grateful. He looked around for his companion to thank him, but no one was there, only a small mouse darting up the path ahead and disappearing into the dark beyond his rim of light.

Now the Kalevide walked faster, with a full stride, since there was nothing in the tunnel to detain or distract him. It was a long, unending path that neither turned nor divided, but always went straight ahead, always sloping slightly downward. His mind became as blank as the corridor's bare walls; he scarcely noticed the way ahead, for there was nothing ahead to notice. Unwittingly, he walked through cobweb that was nearly invisible in the pale, gray light of the dingy passage. With distaste, he stopped and brushed the clinging threads off his arms and out of his hair. In a little while he ran into another. The farther he went, the more there were, and they were impossible to avoid, as they were strung across the width of the tunnel. For a while he tried to sweep them down, swinging his arms like brooms, but the webs became heavier and soon clung in sheets to his skin.

As he stumbled, the nets and snares fell over him more and more frequently. With every step they multiplied and wrapped themselves around his body until he realized with horror that he was being encased. Webs heavy with dust caught in his hair and lay over his face. They got into his mouth and choked him. He could not breathe; he could not scream. The sticky filaments rained down on him. Fibers wound around his arms to bind them, twined around his legs, trapped him. When he tried to stoop to pull them off, wide sheets draped over his back and enveloped him. They multiplied far faster than he could remove

[313]

them. Soon his strength began to fail. He fell to the floor, writhing in agony among the coils and folds of the unearthly threads and fabrics, and with every twist and turn of his body, he fastened himself more tightly into the trap. He was smothering in the dirty sheath of webbing.

A toad crouching on the smooth stone floor watched his struggle. Perhaps it was waiting for the beast, whatever it was, which had cast these snares and would surely come soon to claim its catch. Perhaps it merely gazed, amused, at a mortal's anguish. Slowly the toad's heavy eyelids closed and opened. It spread its thin-lipped mouth to smile.

"Sound the bell," it said.

The Kalevide groaned. He could barely move his hand, which still clutched the golden bell. It was just able to ring through the muffling folds of cloth. Yet only one note was needed. Spun of the stuff of spells and fears, the cobwebs dissolved. The Kalevide scrambled to his feet and ran in a panic from that place. He did not stop until he reached a narrow rivulet running across the floor of the tunnel. Then he threw himself down to sip its cold, tasteless water while he fought to still his throbbing heart. For a moment he caught his breath, but he did not dare linger there for long, lest the creature of the webs pursue its prey.

The streamlet looked no different from the many others that seeped out of the walls and trickled across the stone pathway. It was scarcely two spans wide; he could bridge it easily with his hands, but every time he tried to step over it his foot sank in the mud in midstream. Again and again he stretched his leg across the tiny trickle of water, only to find himself mired more and more, and then when he stepped back everything was normal: the ground was firm, the stream a gentle rill. Nevertheless, for all his efforts he could not reach the opposite shore. Dismally, he stared at the mocking water. He wanted to weep.

"I have waded the lakes of Viru," he moaned aloud. "I crossed Lake Peipus in a storm with a load of timber, and it slowed me less than this damned little stream."

In a rage he kicked at the cave's rock floor, then tried once more to step across. Again his foot was caught in the mud midway. Refusing to be balked any more, he attempted to force his way across. The more he struggled, however, the more firmly he was held. He sank deeper into the thick, cold slime until it gripped him above the knees and thighs and seemed to grope for his loins. Now he could not even retreat, much less go forward. The mud was swallowing him. There was nothing to hold onto, nothing with which to pull himself out, nothing to push against. There was no bottom to prevent his sinking forever. There was nothing he could strike in anger. Then, feeling his defeat, he ceased to fight.

"Sound the bell," said a small, red-shelled crayfish peering at him from the side of the stream.

As soon as he did so, the brook vanished. The mud and muck, the slime, the water disappeared and left him standing free on the firm, hard floor. It was as though the mire had never been. His boots and legs were dry. Only his mind in memory retained the marks of sinking into mud that had no end. His skin crawled as if still feeling the ooze.

Now the Kalevide proceeded through the tunnel with less pride than he had ever felt. He was no longer so bold in his adventure, bound in quest for honor's end. The traps that were assailing him were no fit perils for a hero to overcome. There was no glory to be sung of mud and mire. No honor in a spider's web. No fame in darkness.

Deep within the cavern all sense of space and time dissolved. Distance was a mystery, direction a riddle. Duration had no meaning for a man. Nothing marked the passing of minutes or hours, nights or days. No sun or moon or stars ever ventured into that dark abyss to count the cycles of years. The Kalevide could not tell how long he endured the dangers of the tunnel. It might have been for hours or days or months, or it might have been forever in the deep land beneath the world of night and day.

A mosquito bit him behind the ear; not much of a distraction after the nightmares he had already survived, an annoyance rather, which he merely brushed aside without thinking or chanting its name. Another mosquito came out of its hiding place in the cracks in the walls, and another. Swarms buzzed around his face and whined insanely in his ears. He slapped at them, but there were too many. For every one he killed, more landed on his neck and arms. They bit his lips and the soft place beside his nose. They crawled beneath his shirt and trousers. They stung his genitals.

Frantic, the Kalevide tried to escape by running. He fled down the passageway like a maddened bull. The mosquitoes followed in a screaming black cloud. The covered his face, walking on his eyes, stinging the lids so they swelled and he could not see. They crawled into his mouth and bit the inside of his cheeks and his gums and his tongue. They found the inner passages of his nose. He could not breathe. When he opened his mouth to gasp, he inhaled a small swarm and choked. Songs are sung and tales told of a northern folk, kin, no doubt, to wizards, who could live

[315]

among such insects and who would blithely suck them in to eat. For the Kalevide, however, it was agony.

"Sound the bell," said a small black cricket beneath a chip of stone.

Somehow the words penetrated his frenzy. He stopped running. Through his flight he had held the little bell clutched fiercely in his fist, locked in silence. Now he let it ring with a will. At its first note the swarms of mosquitoes vanished as if carried away by a fresh breeze on a mountaintop. As the mosquitoes disappeared so did their bites. The Kalevide's skin was unmarked. All the welts, all the swelling, all the pain and itch were gone. Only his memory still writhed.

Sinking wearily down onto a slab of stone to catch his breath, the Kalevide thought at last to tie the golden bell to his wrist, with a bit of thread unraveled from his shirt, so it could ring out loud with every step and ward away any new dangers before they appeared.

For a moment he thought something was watching him, that there were eyes in the black faces of the shadows. Out of the corner of his eye he detected motion, the merest change in the patterns on the walls where there should have been no change, but when he went to investigate, he found nothing there that could move. Returning to his seat, he tried to convince himself it had been a trick of the light, or of the mind. Nevertheless, the more he stared at the wall, seeing eyes without seeing them, the more certain he became that something had come into the cavern, something conscious, something malicious, whose presence he could sense. What it was and how it was there were mysteries. It had come out of the nether space between light and dark and belonged to neither, and it made him afraid.

An unbearable roar rose up from the deep world below. The Kalevide covered his ears to shut out the awful sound, which had no meaning or sense and only added to his fear. For a long while he sat huddled thus, with his hands over his ears and his knees drawn up under his chin, staring stupidly at the floor, seeing nothing because there was nothing to see. One arm drooped down. He let it swing slowly back and forth, back and forth, sounding the bell to drive away evil spirits. Although it was soothing to his ears, it did nothing to dispel his inner dread.

Once he was convinced he saw the being itself, or one of them, standing in full view in front of him at the very edge of his circle of light. It was a dark, squat creature, shaped vaguely like a man, but not a man, with a black, shining face and white, slanted eyes. For a while the Kalevide stared directly at the thing without realizing what he saw and thinking only of the shadows. Then suddenly, without reason, the image took shape out of the darkness, and he beheld the demon standing in front of him with his hands on his hips.

In his mind he rushed it—leaped off his stone bench, charged across the corridor, caught it by the throat and throttled it—but he never moved at all. He stared at the blank wall and swung his arm to ring the bell, while the vision of his fear faded into the shadows. Dumbly the Kalevide wondered if any of it was real, or were all his terrors born inside himself.

Eventually he roused himself; he could not stay forever in the heart of that tunnel that was heartless. Letting the dwarf's bright bell sound freely, to ward off any further traps or snares or pitfalls or beasts, he went on once more, shuffling wearily, burdened by hopeless dreads and fears that no spirit's charm could ever dissolve.

Far away within the bowels of the underearth, hordes of demons, the fiends who dwelt within the deep abyss, convened to decide how to meet the man who intruded without reason into their land. Hearing the thunder of his bootheels and feeling the rumble of attack through the stone they had dispatched sentinels to watch the tunnels and dark passageways, and ordered spies to scout the invader whose tread was heavy enough to shake the foundations of their empire. Darting silently through the maze-like shafts and galleries cut in the body of the earth in ages past, they had slipped and flitted over the stone like the shadows they were, beings without form or substance, watchers, eyes only, dark wardens of the dead.

Sent forth merely to measure the enemy, the scouts had soon returned to report the presence of the living man who walked within their domain. Their leaders listened to each report with increasing consternation. The deeds of the Kalevide in the Sarvik's private hall were still too well remembered for anyone to rejoice in a second coming. Some of the demons were eager to attack at once to avenge the outrage this man had done. While the sounds of their wild battle chanting rushed through the caverns of the world and sent fear into the minds of simple men, somewhere in a dark hole deep within the earth the Kalevide heard the same demented cries and pressed his hands against his ears to shield them from the pain.

Others in the demon brood, older, wiser perhaps, urged restraint. Let them bar the passages, they said, to prevent this man from penetrating farther, and all would be safe. They could easily seal the remaining tunnels that led to their realm; once behind closed walls they would be secure enough. Better to retreat in safety, they argued, than to be defeated like the Sarvik. To this counsel the younger ones screamed derision. What would the other companies and commands, manning the other gates, say to hear to such caution and cowardice, they cried. What insults would they have to endure if they hid from this single man? Cheering loudly for victory and vengeance, they prepared to attack immediately regardless of risk. Pride and honor required them to fight.

Before they could rush off, however, their captain called them back. They must wait, he commanded, while he himself assessed the enemy. One man, he allowed, did not seem such a great threat, but this was the strongest among men.

Thus the captain studied the Kalevide. For a long while he stayed at the edge of shadow without moving. He had advanced through darkness, and he remained in darkness. He became the dark itself. In his being he was nothing more than a blackness which he animated and, as he chose, shaped into the shadow of a man. Standing in the center of the tunnel just beyond the line of the Kalevide's dim light, he watched the man he had come to see. To the demon's surprise, the Kalevide was merely playing with a child's toy, a tiny, golden bell, letting it swing idly back and forth at the end of his long, limp arm. Although the man looked beaten, his face washed with worry and care, it was the foolishness of the bell that resolved the demon's doubt. Little here was worthy of his troop's concern; let them fight who would. Let them drive this mortal from the lands where he did not belong, if that was what they wanted. It would do no harm, and could be good training for his troops. So the captain slipped away to summon his command. Letting his shape dissolve, he disappeared into the unformed dark. He had no form outside the Kalevide's mind.

Ringing his bell, mumbling songs of counter-spell for courage, the Kalevide trudged through the long cavern beneath the world. No more unseen entrapments hindered him, but, soon another light began to grow in the tunnel. Deeper and redder than the glow he carried, like the color of blood, it cast writhing shadows upon smoke-smeared stone. A river of pitch, spanned by an iron bridge, flowed through the abyss. Flames flickered on its surface and gushed thick black clouds of smoke which filled the passageway. Mustered about the bridge were the captain's troops.

The demons were deployed in four detachments, one on the

bridge itself, one spread along the nearer bank of the river. The third was stationed to hold the rear while the fourth marched in front of them all. Strutting back and forth between the companies, the captain shouted obscene insults at his men to incite them to the frenzy in which they fought their best. Now he was clearly visible. In the bloody, writhing light he looked like a short, misshapen man, round with fat, wet with oil, the color of a raven's wing. By shaping himself to be the very opposite of this tall, gold-haired mortal, he set himself to be a mirror for his fear. Let the Kalevide fear him with all the dread and terror in his being until his very spirit should melt.

The Kalevide did not wait for them to strike.

"Frogs!" he shouted, charging into the horde, his arm swinging, the bell ringing.

The forward company immediately fell away to either side, leaving him a clear avenue to the bridge. There he was met by a shower of arrows from the archers on all sides, but their feeble darts merely rattled off his golden armor. The nearer fiends immediately closed around him. They struck at him with battle axes and spears; he had no weapons but himself and his two strong hands.

Like a wall, the Kalevide stood against them all. The bell was ineffective, but his fist was not. When one hapless youth ventured too close, he wrenched his spear away with one hand while he broke the child's jaw with the other. Then, using the boy as a shield, he pushed through the melee easily. For all their eagerness and bravado, the demons fought him foolishly and ineffectively. They rushed forward, jabbed half-heartedly with their spears or swung blindly with their axes, as often as not hitting one of their comrades, then fell away in panic lest they themselves be struck. The young warrior's body took the brunt of their blows, but no one seemed to mind. They would kill their friends as willingly as their foes.

Driving through them, the Kalevide kept chanting at the top of his lungs, "Frogs, frogs, frogs, frogs."

The middle guard fell back. Fresh hosts appeared. They crawled from the burning river itself until the bank was covered with reptiles created out of tar and ablaze with its fire inside them. Their battle cries screamed hideously in the air and inspired them all to madness, but as warriors they were utterly inept. The Kalevide pushed through their pack unscathed. Since he was caught up in the desperate need to defend himself, he was not troubled, as he was supposed to be, by the terror seething all around him. There was no time to think of what was happening.

Although he fought as blindly as the enemy, he fought with deadly effect. Foe after foe fell to his stolen spear.

In despair, the captain called his troops to retreat. Even if he summoned his last platoons, held in reserve, he could not conquer this wild man. It was better to preserve his few remaining forces for another, more auspicious battle than to sacrifice them all for nothing. As his men gave way before the Kalevide's onslaught, he herded them across the iron bridge and down the road to the fortress, where they would try to throw up barricades to protect the inner lands. If he had known that one person could fight so ferociously, he would never have ventured into battle against him. He would have stayed behind stout walls from the start. Too many ruses were available to have risked defeat by this mortal who fought so differently from all the others who came into this quarter of the realm. His demon's methods were not meant to fight the living. Now the captain could only hope that enough of his troop survived to hold the ramparts and keep this menace from entering the forbidden kingdom.

The Kalevide chased the retreating demons over the bridge, but when that was won, he halted and let the enemy flee. His position was secure enough that he need not fear retaliation or counterattack. The enemy was routed, on the run, like frightened rabbits scampering over black, burnt-out fields. They would not return. Weary, the Kalevide slid to the roadway to rest. Once more, he told himself, he had prevailed in battle, once more he had vanquished an unholy foe, but there was no sweetness in this victory. He felt no pride in his success.

On every side lay the black and bloated bodies of the slaughtered enemy. Already they stank of decay and were melting into putrid, oil-like pools. With disgust he dropped a few of them into the fiery river below to burn and add their flesh to its molten pitch. He could not bear to touch the rest. Crossing the iron bridge, the Kalevide let his boots drag on the heavy metal plate. Their sound announced his coming to all who cared to hear.

Ahead a fortress shaped of stone loomed like a mountain within the hollow inside the earth. Standing in front of its mighty gates, the king of Viru seemed a tiny creature indeed at the door to the domain most dreaded by men. He hammered on the portal, demanding entrance, but no one answered. Above him, in the heights of stone, grotesque faces leered down. They were only graven on the walls and carved from stone, however. The high battlements were deserted. No wardens marched on the balustrades; no sentries stood on the parapets.

The Kalevide pounded on the gates again. Three strong blows broke them from their hinges to open the way to him. His fist battered down the grillwork, meant for an inner door to bar unwanted visitors, then ripped aside the chains used to operate the heavy sliding gates. Inside the walls, the vast square was also deserted. Seven roads separated here. Far away they would meet the seven rivers that flowed around the islands of the dead, but the son of Kalev was not yet destined to follow any of these paths. Straight across the courtyard he marched, past empty booths and trading stalls, past wagons and carts which merchants had abandoned when they heard of his coming. When no one came against him, he overturned as many of these as he could, then trod through all their goods and wares, smashing everything blindly, without regard for worth or wealth. Still no one challenged him. Now and then he imagined he saw the fleeting shadows of fleeing demons darting down the aisles and through the vaults and arches along the balconies and upper tiers of the walls, but they were no more than glimpses which he heeded not at all. It seemed to him as though the entire castle had surrendered to him without a struggle, and all its folk had run.

On the far side of the yard he found a small inner door. Without even knocking or trying its latch, he smashed it down with one sharp kick. Door, doorposts, bolts, and bars fell crashing to the floor. Inside he discovered a compact chamber fashioned like the anteroom of a greater hall. It was lined with thick crimson drapery and carpets. Lamps of oil, burning in their recesses, filled the small room with a warm yellow light that enriched the deep color of the tapestries. The Kalevide noticed none of the beauty of the chamber, however. Seated on a low three-legged stool was a woman spinning linen thread with distaff and spindle. She was small, dwarfed by the high-hanging textiles; her face was dark, with wide-set eyes; her hair was brown. She wore a simple dress of brown woolen stuff. As he stormed into the room, the woman looked up at him. She was the perfect image of Linda, the Kalevide's mother.

"I thought you were dead," he cried in anguish, throwing himself down on his knees before her. "I thought you were dead."

34 "I thought you were dead," he cried over and over again. "You were dead, but you are alive." His words were muffled in the folds of her robe. The Kalevide knelt with his face buried in his mother's lap. Linda wanted to embrace him, to throw her arms around his neck and clasp him close to her breast as she had done long before in another world, but her arms could not reach around him, not when he was kneeling. So she merely brushed his hair with her fingertips, running her hands through the thick, tangled locks. His hair was as golden as she remembered, the color of spring sunlight, and as unruly. Fondly she folded it back and caressed his head. The Kalevide sighed. The golden helmet slipped from his fingers onto the carpet.

"I thought you were dead," he said again. "I looked everywhere for you—all the lands I knew. I even went under the earth for you. I hunted and hunted, but I couldn't find you anywhere. And then I couldn't look anymore. I gave up hope. I thought you were dead and I would never see you again."

Linda listened to her son's words; she drank them in like milk. They flowed through her, and yet she did not answer. Although she knew the pain and love that brought them to his lips, she did not speak to console him. She caressed him without a sound. The Kalevide closed his eyes; he even turned his face away. Her touch was soothing, yet he could not look at her. He was too much afraid she would vanish before his eyes. He feared she might become a vision of his own imagining, a creature born of the delusions spawned by his journey's trials and his own desires. So long as he only touched her and did not look, so long as he could hold his arms around her broad hips and feel her thighs beneath his cheek, then she was most real, then she was his mother truly, the one to give him comfort.

Tenderly, Linda raised his face between her hands to see his eyes. He looked at her then, staring with a mixture of fear and joy and anguish. He rejoiced to have found her again so unexpectedly, but grieved to think how he had forgotten her and quit his search unfinished. To see her now brought back all the pains and sorrows he had felt in his short life. He could no longer speak; the feelings in his breast were too deep. He wept. Tears drew scars through the dust on his cheeks. He wanted to turn away again and hide his face, but she would not let him go.

Without a word she gazed at him. His eyes surprised, even shocked, her, for they were darker than she recalled and set deeper in his face. The shadows born of brooding, outlined now by the tracks of tears, ringed them like a mask. Lines of frowning were etched into his brow which should have been smooth and smiling. His lips were drawn tight; they trembled as he looked at her.

In her heart Linda had lost the count of time, she knew only that it had been long since she had seen her son or felt him in her hands. When they had parted, he had been broad-faced and smiling, unsure of himself but eager. He had set out with his brothers to hunt in the forest, leaving her alone in the house. Then the sorcerer had come and taken her, and everything had changed. She had escaped and her body had been enstoned. Her sons had returned to find her gone and the house empty. He had been a boy then. Now she wondered what he was. She could not believe he was yet a man.

Silently she caressed him. Viru was so far away. The hall she had known there would not see her again. The meadows filled with wildflowers, the woods which she had loved, would never hear her songs. Already they had nearly forgotten her; their small inhabitants had other loves. The birds, her special friends, had flown away. Even in her own mind Viru had become a dream no longer real, a part of another world that was no longer hers. The memory of her life there was as unreal to Linda as her dwelling in this fortress in the world beyond the ends of the earth would seem to anyone still entrenched in mortal lands and lives.

Linda never questioned how her son had broken through the barriers that separate the worlds or why he had left the living world behind to embark on the dread journey which no mortal man should make. She never asked him of his quest or inquired about his life. She spoke not at all. Words were denied her in the underworld. Nor did the questions come into her mind, to hover unspoken while she held him. Linda was never one to seek for causes—not in her life, not in her afterlife. It was enough to her that she felt his suffering.

There were two bowls on either side of her, each filled with an amber liquid. One held the water of strength, the other the water of weakness. Still without speaking, Linda pressed the Kalevide away from her and offered him the cup on the stand to her right. Raising the cup in toast to her, he drained it to the dregs. This, he thought, was the signal of the end of his quest. He had set out to seek his father's origins and had found instead the mother whom he loved but had forgotten and given up to death. All he had to do now, to redeem himself, was rescue her. He had strength enough, he was sure. They would return to Viru gloriously together. The triumph he had sought in his quest would flow from Linda, the mother of his people.

The liquor pulsed in his body and rapidly restored his vigor. Its power rose out of his stomach and surged through his limbs. His spirits revived. Once again he stood tall and strong. The confusion of grief and joy he had felt a moment ago on seeing his mother after the horror of his passage through the tunnel had nearly strangled him. Now he rose in exultation, mighty and rejoicing. The fire of strength reborn burned in his arms and legs. Without realizing what he was doing, he wrenched a huge stone slab from the floor and hurled it through the small door set in the wall behind them. The little room had suddenly seemed too much like a prison cell.

The Kalevide leaped through the shattered doorway to confront the guards he knew must be stationed there. His cries rang off walls hewn of stone in another, larger, chamber behind the door. Charging in, he found, however, not a garrison but only one old woman busy with her spindle. Despite the crash of the stone, despite his bellow, she scarcely looked up at him. A brief glance, then she returned to her spinning, though now a slight smile curled at the corners of her mouth. She had the face of a dog.

Unable to check his rush, the Kalevide careered across the room and crashed against the far wall. The force of the liquor still swelled within his body. He could not control it; he needed to release the power it produced. In one swift motion he seized a heavy stone table and swung it over his head. He whirled, prepared to fling it at anyone attacking him from behind. There was no one. The woman was alone. She was absolutely defenseless, and yet completely heedless of his assault. He felt suddenly exposed and very foolish.

"The bell you have," whined the old woman, "it is my son's bell. Please, you will give it to me to keep for him."

The table thudded to the floor. The Kalevide was dumbfounded. The dwarf's small golden bell was still tied to his wrist, forgotten. Angrily he ripped off its bindings and thrust it into his pocket.

"If it's your son's, I'll give it to him myself," he said sharply. "I have words to speak to him, for he left too quickly the last time I saw him. And if your son isn't here, I'll give the bell to your master to hold for him, but I won't give it to you.''

"Yes, yes, give it to my son, give it to the master. Give it to anyone but the poor old woman who is harmless and alone and only asks for a little comfort and courtesy for her last days. But my son is not here, and the master is not here. My son is the master here, the master is my son, but neither one is here.''

"When will he be back then?''

"In two days' time or three, we shall see. He left yesterday and left his mother alone with no one, just like a son, just like a son.''

"Well, I'm going then, and I'm taking the bell with me. Maybe I'll bring it back another time.''

"Oh, no, you need not go, not so soon. You are safe here until my son returns, if he returns. Stay a while to cheer a tired old woman. You shall be my guest. Sit beside me here, young man, and I shall give you beer. Will you have some? Drink this cup and tell me all your hero's tales. You shall see you can trust this lonely woman who has nothing now but age.''

The Kalevide was confused. This was not what he had expected. The old woman was offering him one of the cups from the stand beside her just as Linda had done. Could he trust her? What was in the cup, the water of strength or of weakness? He looked back to Linda for advice but she had turned away to take up her spinning again. Was she ensorcelled, he wondered, and would that happen to him? The old woman sat very still while he paced nervously back and forth trying to understand what was happening.

Several other doors led from the room to other passages and hallways. In his agitation he opened them all, but no one was hiding behind any. No one listened; no one spied on him. No one cared that he was there, except the old woman. Then he came to the secret door nearly invisible in its hidden recess in the wall. This was the only door that was locked.

"What is this?" he asked. "What are you hiding in here?''

"It is nothing,'' the crone replied. Already she, too, had begun to ignore him. Although she still held the cup in her withered hand, she did not move at all. She did not look at him when she spoke.

"Someone is there. I can hear voices behind this door. Who is it?''

"There is no one. No one is there. I am a poor woman, alone and old. No one comes to see me, no one cares to call.''

The Kalevide rattled the door on its hinges, but it was securely

[325]

locked. While he was looking for something with which to break it down, suddenly a tremendous noise filled the stone chamber. The locked door sprang open by itself. A horde of screaming, black, masked warriors leaped into the room.

Like the demons beside the bridge, they were small and thin, with bodies shaped like sticks but lithe enough to bend and writhe around the Kalevide. Insubstantial as shadows, yet they howled in high, shrill rage. Wildly, he fought them off with his fists. The water of strength still coursed in his veins; his arms pounded with its force. With every blow he struck a fiend, and every one he struck disappeared, as though having done its duty once it was allowed to withdraw, to dissolve and vanish in the air, to live again in the shadows far away deeper in the abyss beneath the mortal earth.

The demons themselves never harmed the Kalevide. In this land of death they could not kill. They had no weapons except their fear and that had no power over him anymore. Even as they attacked, the result was foreknown; the effort was merely the last spasmodic twitch of a reptile already dead.

In a short time the Kalevide had cleared the room. Except for the old woman who was still sitting with the cup of ale in her right hand, only one other remained, the captain of the guard, who squatted on the floor like a fat, bloated, black frog, staring at him with round, unblinking eyes. Roaring for vengeance, the Kalevide rushed at him. He needed something substantial he could grasp and crush, something he could rend with his hands, something he could kill. Here were all the frights and fears that had been raised in his mind. He needed to seize the fiend's throat and throttle it forever. When he reached it, however, this demon, too, disappeared. It dwindled in size and sank into the floor, and no trace of it remained to mark where it had been. The whisper of the old woman's wheeze, which might have been a laugh or a sigh, sounded in the hanging silence as though to mock him.

The Kalevide would have struck her, but then he sensed that one more person was still inside the closet out of sight. Once more he felt the tingle of being watched by something in the dark. Concentrating with all his might, he could just discern the glow of two faint eyes beginning to shine. The fire in them grew. The eyes were sharp and slanted. They gleamed. A mouth grinned at him like a cat's. Fangs opened. The creature hissed.

The Kalevide stepped back. This was not like the other demons. This was solid; it was real. It was coiled to spring.

"Yes-s-s" it hissed again, drawing out the sound to savor it.

"Yes-s-s-s, you shall see me, small one, so—" This was the voice of the Sarvik.

The Kalevide gasped. Suddenly he realized where he was and who was against him. For the first time he understood the quest the raven had offered him and where it had led. Desperately glancing around the room, he saw it was the same stone chamber where he had met the three maidens on his first visit to Põrgu. He had been too filled with the sight of Linda and too distracted by the old woman to notice it before. If this was Põrgu—the thought raked through him—what was his mother doing here? What did it mean? He whirled around to look for her, but she was still sitting on her stool in the antechamber, calmly spinning thread, oblivious of him.

The Sarvik laughed. "Welcome, little brother," he said amiably. The look of astonishment and dismay on the Kalevide's face at this moment was well worth the disturbance he had caused among his demons. "Welcome to my house once more. I have been waiting for you for a long time, but I knew you would come to me one day. After all, you promised."

The Kalevide was too stunned to speak. He edged away as the Sarvik emerged from the closet and slowly took shape out of the shadows.

"Yes, you have kept your promise. Of course you have. Your word is good, is it not? You are a true man. So, little man," the words turned icy, "if you are true, you mean to restore to me what you stole before. Yes? That is why you are here, is it not? You have brought back what is mine."

Still dumbfounded, the Kalevide only shook his head and looked at the Sarvik blankly.

"You have brought it all back to me? Of course you have. I recognize the armor you wear. But where is the rest? You stole so much gold and silver, have you forgotten to bring it? Were you in such a hurry to come back to me? Foolish boy, now you will have to go home again to get it. Shall I let you go, do you think? Where are my maidens? I do not see them. Did you forget to bring them, too? Foolish boy, I miss my maidens. They were nice to me. Have they been nice to you? They used to scrub my back with bathwhisks; do you like that, too? Where are they? Why did you take my maids away?"

"I freed them, is what I did," the Kalevide said for his honor, able to speak at last. "I didn't steal them; I set them free. They were your prisoners, your thralls. Well, I took them home and gave them husbands."

"Do not pretend with me. I am the Sarvik, remember. I know

what you have done. I know you are a thief. I know what you stole. Where is my wishing hat? Where is my rod? You carried them away; did you bring them back to me?''

Now the Kalevide could laugh himself. ''Those things I never took. True, I may have borrowed some of your gold and silver. I won't deny it. You had so much, you couldn't miss the little I took, and anyway it was gold you stole yourself from the barrows of the dead on earth. I returned it to the world of men, where it belongs, that's all. The maidens went with me willingly. But the hat and the rod I never took from here.''

''Oh? They are still here perhaps? They are still in my cupboard? You see them there, do you?''

''Maybe some brown-eyed maiden borrowed them, but not me. I don't play with sorcerer's toys. I meet my enemies fairly, as a man. You know that. You felt my strength when we wrestled, but you ran away, like a coward. Like all your demons. You all run away. You are a coward, and I have no more to say to you. I'm going out of here, and I'm taking my mother with me, and if you try to stop us, you'll see what a man's strength really is.''

The Sarvik did not reply for a moment. Instead he strolled to the center of the room. Much smaller than the Kalevide, he looked like an old man, older and more tired than on their first encounter. His hair was whiter and his face more pale. The Kalevide would have laughed to see him if he had not known from experience what strength was concealed in the small, evil man. Despite his proud boasting, he felt the same fear all men feel when they face the source of their dread.

''So, you will show me strength?'' the Sarvik said. ''You wish to wrestle some more, yes? You are a foolish, foolish boy. I do not know how you escaped me before, but this I know: no man leaves Põrgu twice.''

Crossing to the old woman, his mother, he took the cup she still held in her hand. She had not moved at all since the host of demons had burst into her room; her part in the pattern was already played. The Sarvik, thinking the cup was meant for him and contained the water of strength, drained it quickly, then waved toward the second bowl still on the stand.

''Will you have some beer?'' he said generously. ''It is good. My mother brews it herself.''

The Kalevide shook his head. One thing he knew, he could not trust this man, and the draught he had drunk from Linda was enough for him. In the same moment the Sarvik pounced.

The sudden push was hard, hard enough to drive him back-

wards over the stone couch where the old woman sat. The
Kalevide landed with the Sarvik astride him. Dazed, he shook
his head and tried to rise, but the Sarvik had him by the throat
and was trying to beat his unprotected head against the stone leg
of a table. The Kalevide groped behind him and managed to pull
the heavy stand down on top of his enemy. It had no effect. He
tried pummelling his back and ribs, yet that, too, was in vain.
Gripping the Sarvik's hair, he was barely able to pull that evil
head backward and away from him. The Sarvik snarled and
showed his hidden fangs; venomous saliva dripped from his lips.
The Kalevide worked one knee into the other's groin, and then
his free hand, and with a desperate shove finally threw him off.
Both sprang up as one. Now they grappled. With his longer
reach, the Kalevide could catch the Sarvik's leg and throw him
to the floor. The latter, however, despite his age, was far more
agile, and he was incredibly swift. Each time they fell, he would
turn and twist away to emerge on top. Although the Kalevide's
armor helped protect his body from the worst attack, his face and
head and lower limbs were still exposed. The Sarvik sank his
teeth into his bare neck.

For a long while they rolled back and forth. First one would
be on top, and then the other. The Kalevide caught the Sarvik in
a hold with one arm around his throat and the other around his
thigh; he strained to bend him back, hoping to break his neck,
but even as he pulled the old man's body, it seemed built without
a bone, a being shaped of pliant sinew alone. The Sarvik himself
fought without control or constraint. When he broke the Kalevide's
hold and caught his own, he bit, he scratched, he gouged, he
tried to tear the young man's member off. Their combat lasted, if
time could tell within the depths of Põrgu where time had no
measure, for seven days and seven nights.

Once more the Kalevide fell flat on his stomach with his
enemy on his back, groping between his legs, trying to tear them
apart. Pain ripped through his middle, but he wrenched his
shoulders around, reached the Sarvik's exposed foot, and twisted
it until the other was forced to let go and spin away. The Kalevide
lurched to catch him by the waist but the Sarvik was too quick;
he scrambled away. Slowly the Kalevide lumbered to his feet.
Both men were gasping for breath; both had begun to weaken.
Anxiously, the Kalevide looked around the room in fear that the
demons had returned. There was no one. The Sarvik's legions
had deserted him, so that he fought alone against the man of
earth. The old woman was still there, motionless on the couch,
staring at the wall; her role was done and soon she would be free

to go. Linda remained in the alcove. She had turned around to watch the battle from her doorway, but she could not move to help her son.

The Sarvik aimed a swift kick at the Kalevide's belly. The Kalevide barely dodged aside, caught the foot and shoved back, throwing the Sarvik over backwards. He dropped with both knees onto his chest. A gasp of wind exploded from the old man's lungs, but he did not cry out. With claws unsheathed he raked the Kalevide's face. Blood streamed around his eyes. Nearly blinded, the Kalevide strove to choke this man who hurt him so. The pain was searing. Without the strength from the enchanted liquor he could never have endured it. In his mind he kept screaming over and over again, "I can defeat him, I can defeat him, I can defeat him."

As the Sarvik kept digging for his eyes, the Kalevide released his throat and began madly pounding the face in front of him. He had ceased to think; he fought more like an animal, depending only on whatever strength was left in his body.

When the Sarvik wiggled out from under him, and both slowly rose again, they locked their arms together, and for a long while merely hung in that position, just as they had during their first wrestle. Then the Kalevide dropped to his knees and brought the other down with him. They rolled over and each caught the other in a hold which neither one could break. Their arms and legs were so intertwined that the two seemed to have grown together and become one single, tangled entity. The old woman, the Sarvik's mother, rose from her place and walked softly out of the hall. Linda watched from the alcove. Bits and pieces of stone furniture littered the room; jagged fragments gouged both men's backs as they writhed on the floor. Though neither spoke a word, they released their holds simultaneously and with a single will stood again.

It was painful now for them to struggle to their feet. Although the Sarvik still leered, his look had lost its earlier intensity. He was too tired to spend his strength in a glare. The Kalevide, too, was exhausted. His shoulders ached, his arms were heavy, his legs wooden. Not since he had chased the white mare had he felt so weak. Blood was clotted around his eyes and under his nose. His hair, matted with sweat and dirt and more blood, fell over his eyes. Vainly, he tried to brush it away so he could focus on his foe. For a moment his eye fell on Linda. He tried to smile but was too weary.

Looking back from the anteroom, the shade of Linda signaled for victory. She swung her distaff by its ribbons ten times around her head then dashed it to the ground, shattering its delicately carved wood. The Kalevide understood the hint well enough, but he could only shake his head, muttering, "I'm too tired." Yet when the Sarvik feinted and lashed out with another blow, he ducked under his arm and came up clutching him by the garters. Summoning the last reserves of his strength the Kalevide hoisted his enemy over his head, swung him ten times around, then dropped him heavily to the floor. Again he fell across the old man's body and, before the Sarvik could recover his lost breath, pressed his knee hard against his chest. This time he locked the Sarvik's left arm beneath his shin while pinning the right down with his other knee. Then, both hands free, the Kalevide began to strangle him. The Sarvik kicked and writhed; he struggled to hook his feet around the other's back or neck, but now he lacked the power to escape.

The Kalevide pressed his thumbs into the slender windpipe and squeezed as hard as he could. He was determined to end, once and for all, the life of this menace to all mankind. "I must, I must, I must," he cried inwardly. He knew he had to destroy the Sarvik completely if he was to survive at all. The old man twisted one more time, then his body relaxed and fell limp. He no longer breathed, but still the Kalevide continued to throttle him. "Die! Die!" he cursed through clenched teeth, but he could not drive the last of the Sarvik's life out of him. This was not a being to be killed.

At last, exhausted beyond endurance, he ceased trying. He let go of the throat and leaned back on his haunches while he fought to recover his own breath. Although the soft, defeated body of the Sarvik beneath him seemed lifeless, the Kalevide was certain it was not. Its veins still flowed with blood. It's eyes, when pried open, still glistened with hatred. "Die!" he demanded once more in vain.

When he had recovered a little of his own strength, the Kalevide dragged the Sarvik from the chamber of stone, through the long gallery to the hall of iron, where he chained him to the wall just as the Sarvik had so often chained men of earth to torture them from time untold. One chain bound his arms, another his legs. A third was wrapped around his neck. While the Kalevide was binding a fourth chain around his body, the Sarvik regained consciousness. Still very weak, he could not speak. Only a deathly rattle came through his throat. The Sarvik spat. The spittle burned where it struck the Kalevide's face, but he said nothing. He merely wound the long iron chain around the old man's twisted body, back and forth, across his chest many times, around his hips and loins, between his legs, until the Sarvik could no longer move at all. Then he locked the fetters together with iron padlocks that had no keys.

"I shall escape," the Sarvik hissed. "I shall escape. You shall see. You cannot keep me here. This is my realm; here I am lord. I shall get free. I shall come for you then. Be certain I shall come. You cannot kill me; you cannot keep me. You shall see."

The Kalevide left him mouthing foul words and walked back to the room of stone. No one disturbed him. When he returned to the iron chamber, he was pushing the huge stone slab which had been the table until they broke it in their fight. Now he tipped it on end to lean heavily against the Sarvik's chest and face. This too he wrapped with heavy iron chains, praying they would hold.

Once more he walked through the corridor of stone. Behind him the Sarvik's muffled voice continued to cry.

"You cannot escape me. You cannot ever escape me. No man can. No man escapes the hand of Põrgu. I shall come for you. You shall see. You will long to die, but you will not die. You shall never die until I have come and done with you. You shall live forever, until I am released. Then you shall suffer. You and all your people. You cannot keep me from them. All shall suffer for what you have done."

Vain curses. The Kalevide did not listen. He was too tired to care. The other room was empty now. The old woman had gone to join the forces of the deeper underground beyond Põrgu; she had her baking to do, and there was always ale to brew. Linda, too, had left. The Kalevide's heart sank. He had overcome his enemy and the way was clear for escape, and once more he was alone. It had all been for nothing. He was too exhausted, however, to feel much grief.

In one corner of the room one stone basin was unbroken. With a rag torn from his shirt he slowly cleansed the blood from his face and washed the other traces of the battle off his body, then he dragged himself back to the room of iron. The Sarvik, firmly fastened to the wall, was frothing venomous words, but on hearing the Kalevide's footsteps in the gallery, he changed his tone to a miserable whine.

"You will release me now, please?" he begged. "You will set me free? I promise I will not hurt you. You are only playing, I know. You have had your fun, but now you will let me go, yes? I shall be your friend forever."

The Kalevide passed him without a glance and pushed through

to the gallery of iron beyond the torture room. His feet rang on the metal plate, but his ears were closed to the strident howls of iron as well as to the Sarvik's mournful pleas. Walking through the room of copper, the maids' room where women had long been tormented and on through the chamber of silver, he did not stop until he reached the inner room of gold.

There he dragged heavy chests of treasure to the center of the floor, and began digging through them in search of the most valuable pieces. Countless baubles gleamed in his hands, endless chains of the most delicately wrought gold, rings, brooches, necklaces, belts, collars, torques, intricately decorated plates and gilded goblets, ornamental knives, and artful keys. Impatient with having to choose just this one or that, the Kalevide finally tore the gold-brocaded tapestry down from the wall and spread it on the floor. In a rush he emptied all the chests and boxes onto the cloth to make one giant bundle. Golden trinkets spilled everywhere.

A small gray mouse, squatting on the lid of an unused chest, spoke softly to him. "Take no more than you can carry," was all it said before it scampered away, disappearing into the wall behind the box. The Kalevide shrugged. Shoveling the treasure to one side, he tore the tapestry into four pieces, poured the gold back onto them, and tied them up into four separate sacks. With two slung over each shoulder, he made his way back through the castle's fearful passages for the last time forever.

In the iron room the Sarvik had stopped cursing and no longer begged. Now he merely moaned. He strained at his bonds and shook the chains, but he could barely move. The iron bit his flesh; the stone pressed heavily against his face. The locks on the chains were secure and could not be broken. Neither crowbar nor incantation would set him free. The Kalevide went by without a word.

Once more he looked for his mother in the alcove where she had been, and in the other halls leading out of the room of stone, but he found no trace of her anywhere. Perhaps she had never been there at all; perhaps it had been a dream, for how could she belong in the keep of Põrgu? Behind one makeshift door he discovered the passage through which he had entered the underworld the year before.

Pushing the treasure sacks in front of him, the Kalevide slowly ascended to Viru. The cavern was pitch dark. He could only feel his way forward as he crawled through the tunnel's tortuous twists and turnings. Again he felt that dislocation of time that all travelers experience when they penetrate the underearth. He lost his sense of place and direction. In the dark and narrow passageway up and down, left and right, forward and back, all became one. The entire weight of the world seemed to be pressing down on him. Once, in this, tunnel he had felt as though he were dying. Now he wished he had. It was far more difficult to return than it was to enter this cave. The moan of the Sarvik's voice followed him through the darkness.

35

He came to in a room of stone. Gray walls formed a hard corner where he lay; a gray stone ceiling seemed to close down upon him. The Kalevide groaned. He had failed; he had been recaptured. Now he was a prisoner in Põrgu and there could be no salvation. The Sarvik was free.

"I think he's awake," a voice said.

His eyes flicked open again. He expected to see a demon leering at him. Instead there were only the gray stone walls.

"Welcome home," said the Alevide, coming around to stand in front of him. His wife joined him.

"Welcome home," she said.

The Kalevide swung his head back and forth; he was confused.

"Where am I?" he muttered, afraid this was another taunting scene out of Põrgu, like the image of his mother.

"In your room," said the Alevide. "In your hall."

"I don't understand."

"No, of course, how could you? There've been many changes since you last saw your home. While we were off on our journey north, the Olevide built you a city out of stone. Don't ask me how, I don't understand such things. Perhaps the songs he and the gray wizard learned to fashion the ship helped him. It's a full city with stone walls and battlements and parapets and tall buildings and a market square, even stone piers in the harbor for merchant ships. You'll be very pleased when you see it; it's the city you dreamed of."

"How did I get here?"

"You don't remember, do you?"

"No."

"You walked. You were asleep, but you walked. We found you, my wife and I, at the mouth of the cave that comes out of the underearth. You weren't very coherent, and you could hardly stand. We would have carried you, but, frankly, you're much too large. And you insisted on walking. You also insisted on carrying those sacks of gold yourself, except for one which I carried. It was heavy enough. It was my wife's idea to look for you there," he added. "She knew where you would be."

The Kalevide looked at her gratefully, but could not say anything. He should have been happy, to have survived, to have saved the gold, to have his city, but instead he was only tired. His battle with the Sarvik had sapped his strength, and he felt now as though he might never get it back again.

"You collapsed when we reached this room," the Alevide's wife said. "We removed your armor."

"How long have I been asleep?"

"Three days."

"As long as that. How long have I been away?"

"Three weeks," said the Alevide.

"I didn't know. Underground, in Põrgu, there's no way to count time. It doesn't mean anything there. What happened?"

"That's for you to tell. We heard sounds of fighting in the distance, faint rumblings and groanings, as though there were a battle raging in the very roots of the earth, a battle for the world. What was it?"

The Kalevide shook his head. He was not ready to talk about it yet. "Tell me first about your return from the north."

"Well, as to that," said the Alevide, settling back on a stool carved of stone, "as to that, there's very little to tell. We woke up that morning and found you gone. The Sulevide thought you'd wandered out into the barrens and gotten lost. I said an eagle had come and carried you into the sky. In either case, you were gone, and there was nothing for us to do but return to the ship and head for home as you told me to."

"Didn't you see the gateway? The raven's lake? The end of the world?"

"No, the world has no end, nor was there any lake, only that wide, unbroken wilderness. Even the old woman was gone, taking her kettle and cabbages with her. So we hiked back to the *Lennuk*, and the wind-enchanter brought us back to Viru. The voyage was without incident. Varrak kept us wrapped in a mist so the men would not see the Land of Giants or the Island of Fire, and so no one would see us. The closest we came to a calamity was when we sailed into the harbor here. None of us recognized the city, of course, and the Sulevide thought Varrak had betrayed us, delivered us to some foreign land where we would be sold for slaves. He would have shot the wind-enchanter,

I think, but then we recognized the people on shore and heard them calling us in the name of Taara, so we knew we had come home."

"It was a good homecoming," said his wife.

"It was that."

"Where is the Sulevide?"

"Oh, you know him. He's worried about the war again. He's out on the battlements somewhere, training his guard for this or that. He says this time the threat is real. Maybe it is, I don't know, it's hard to believe, but people are pouring in from all over. Maybe it's just the lure of the city, because it's so new and they think there are opportunities here, I don't know."

"And the Olevide?"

"He's with his builders. They're still putting up houses for the newcomers. He's working on plans for more cities too, at least three, he says, with highways to connect them."

The Kalevide hardly heard although this was the fulfillment of his dream.

"No one knew when you'd wake," said the Alevide's wife, sensing his disappointment. "Otherwise they'd all be here. But you'll see them all later, the Olevide, the Sulevide, my sisters."

"What of the gray wizard?"

"He is gone," said the Alevide.

"Gone?"

"He never came back from the north. When the Sulevide and I reached the ship, he was already gone. Apparently, he just walked away into the wilderness to seek the solitude of the untouched, empty country. It is the way of wizards. I think I understand."

"Gone. The gray wizard. First the cup-bearer left me, and now the gray wizard. Will all my friends desert me? Will you?"

The Alevide smiled. "No," he said lightly. "No, I will stay by you, and the Sulevide, and the Olevide. We will serve you while you rule in Viru."

"Don't leave me."

"Well, I must, right now," said the Alevide, rising. "For a little while. If I'm to serve you, I must begin. I'm your steward, so it's up to me to organize the feast for you. We thought it right for the people to greet their king, now that he's returned. And chances are, you're hungry," he added with a smile. "I'm to kill the ox, which it seems no one else is able to do, and the master singer has promised to sing the ballad of the blue bird, the Siuru. It's a rare privilege for us."

The Kalevide tried to smile in return, but he was still too tired

[336]

to feel the pleasure he should have. He held up his hand as the Alevide turned to go.

"Not yet. Before you leave, I want to tell you what happened there, in Pŏrgu. I want to tell it once, before I have to face all the people."

The Alevide sat down again. His wife stood beside him. The Kalevide described very briefly his adventures in the underworld, the torments and snares of the tunnel, his meeting his mother, the wrestling match and victory over the Sarvik, his taking the treasure. He told it simply, without boasting or embellishment. Although he wanted to sound proud and bold, he could not keep the weariness out of his voice. Something in his spirit had been broken in that battle, and it would never completely mend.

"You have done a very great thing," the Alevide said as he rose again to leave.

When he was gone, the Kalevide stood and paced nervously around the room, the king's chamber. He was ill at ease being alone with the woman.

"I'm not sure I like all this stone," he muttered.

"It's new yet, and rough. Someday we'll put tapestries on the walls."

"It's still stone, and cold."

"I know." She, too, had seen the Sarvik's room.

"Is it all like this? The whole city?"

"Yes. That's why the Alevide and I have kept our small hut at the edge of the wood. We go there as often as we can, just to get away from the walls."

"My father's hall was built of wood."

"It still is. The Olevide saved it, for a monument, to Kalev, to you. That's where the feast will be. It's the last wooden structure in the city."

"I'm glad." It was important to have something of his past preserved.

There was little left to say. The Kalevide put his hand in his pocket and drew out the small golden bell, now merely a bell.

"Here," he said, "this is for you."

"Thank you," she said. "I'm sorry about your mother."

He shrugged. "She died a long time ago."

Torches were burning brightly in Kalev's hall. Tables were laden with all the makings of a banquet, plates piled high with meats, platters covered with pork and salmon, pitchers brimming with ale, bowls with milk. People thronged the room, crowding

[337]

the benches and boards on both sides, carrying on loud conversations, singing, stamping their feet on the floor out of sheer exuberance.

They paused, however, when the Kalevide entered, led by the Alevide's wife. For a moment there was a waiting silence, then they cheered. They pushed around him, to greet their king, to be close to him, to touch him perhaps for luck or catch his eye. The Kalevide recognized most of the faces around him. They were the people of the hamlet who had worked for his father; now they dwelt in the city and labored for him. He tried to smile. The Olevide pushed through the crowd to boast of his buildings. Had he seen the walls, he asked, had he seen the towers? all the city needed, he said, was a name. Did he want to hear his plans for the other cities in the other parts of the country?

The Kalevide shook his head. It was too confusing; there was too much noise. The Sulevide's wife and the Olevide's came forward and draped garlands around his neck, then led him to the dais where the high seat was and where the Alevide was waiting. The Kalevide stood awkwardly, gazing at his friends and the faces of the people gathered before him.

"You should say something to them," the Alevide whispered.

The Kalevide looked down. They had all come to honor him; he wanted to offer them something in return. He wanted to tell them of the Sarvik's defeat, so they would have hope. There was nothing left for them to fear, he wanted to say. Dwarves and demons would no longer walk the earth, sorcerers would lose their power. The night would be free of terror. This was his gift to them, but he could not find the words.

Instead he said, "The name of this city shall be Lindanisa."

It was enough. Lindanisa, Linda's Bosom. The city had a name. Without that it could not live; with it its future was determined. So they all believed. The people cheered again. The hubbub of voices rolled in the air. Everyone attacked the plates and platters devouring delicacies, filling their bellies with rich cream cakes and honey. Ale flowed, mead flowed. The wealth of Viru appeared on the table, and disappeared. They danced. They sang.

When the Kalevide's turn came, he, too, took his place on the singer's bench. Despite his fatigue, he sang an old song telling the tale of a prince who went to the shore one day and found three maidens weeping between two trees growing out of the sea, the apple tree of fortune and the oak of wisdom. The maidens told him that his little brother had fallen into the water. When he waded out to look for him, however, he found only a naked sword lying on the bottom, surrounded by water herbs. Just as he reached for it, his sister called to him from the shore that his house was besieged, his father and mother, his brothers and sisters, were all dead. The prince abandoned his brother and the sword and ran home, only to find them all alive and well. His father was smoking his pipe, his mother was spinning wool, and his little brother was playing tipcat on the floor.

It had always been one of the Kalevide's favorite songs. He liked how it built its drama but ended on a happy note; it revealed the deceit so often found in water nymphs. Nevertheless, when he sang it this time, he sang it with a sadder air, in a minor mode, and he did not know why.

Only the Alevide noticed the melancholy which crept into his friend's voice. Before that mood could spread, and before the Kalevide could start to brood, he quickly took the next turn singing and sang a silly song about four coy maidens. The Olevide followed with another about two lovers. Drinking and mirth took over and filled the hearts of everyone. Great cups and beakers filled with beer went round and round among the men; more were passed among the women. Trays of roasted meat and salted fish were cleared, and many more of cakes and cheese. The Alevide and his wife shared tidbits. The Olevide and his wife put their heads together in private conversation. In all the carouse and chaos, the Kalevide watched them with a warm glow of pleasure. It was gratifying to see a man and woman, husband and wife, loving, together. For this he had endured much. He wished only that the Sulevide were there to share their happiness, and not out with the guard.

"Perhaps you should seek someone for yourself," the eldest sister, the Sulevide's wife, said to the Kalevide. She might have been his sister herself.

He shook his head. "Not yet."

"Seek a bride in Kungla; there are many handsome maidens among the trader people, I hear, and you are wealthy enough now."

"Maybe I will. I don't know. There is still much to do."

"What about your vow?" teased the youngest sister, the Alevide's wife, who was eavesdropping. "Didn't you swear never to wed? Or did you find your sword again?" she added with a laugh, pointing to the empty scabbard mounted on the wall across the room.

"Shush. Do not listen to this child," said the eldest sister.

"Who's a child?"

"I will think about it," said the Kalevide. "When I see how the country prospers."

"Let me tell you about the city," said the Olevide eagerly.

In such fellowship it was easy for the Kalevide to put off his weariness. For a while he felt restored by the people's joy.

Much later, when the hour of the night was dark, an expectant stillness came over the company. The oldest singer, chief amongst the bards, a man clad all in white, white linen smock, white linen trousers, long white hair and beard, had quietly moved to the painted throne of song. He was not like the other men they knew, who sang songs to tell tales of glory or loss, love, or sorrow, songs emerging out of their own inner, mortal longings. He was one of the old ones, who still could hear the voice of Vanamuine, lord of song, singing on earth, who would listen and understand the music in the rustling of tree limbs and the rippling of streams over stones and the whispering of gentle winds, and who could meld this music into song. He was one of the last.

The old one braced his five-stringed kantele on his knee and touched a few tentative notes. Then he paused, as though listening, listening to a song sent to him alone from far away on the drifting wind. When he touched his harp again, melodies flowed from the strings. Deep notes reached into his listeners' hearts, lighter tones played on their fancies. He sang, and his song spread beyond the ears of the men and women gathered in the hall. It rose and floated out across the city and farther yet, across the fields and far beyond the meadows and the woods. It is said that beasts and birds paused in the wild to listen to the old one's song. For a moment a deep sense of peace and understanding rested over the land of Viru. The ancient bard sang the song of Siuru, the sacred blue bird:

> Siuru, bird, child of Taara,
> Siuru, bird, azure-winged,
> Ukko's daughter, blue one,
> Siuru, bird, with wind-like wings
> soaring on the winds of distance,
> hovered on her silken pinions
> over woods of golden pines,
> over woods of crimson apples,
> over silver birches, over larches.
>
> Siuru, bird, child of Taara,
> Siuru, bird, sky-blue-winged,
> Ukko's daughter, blue one,
> Siuru, bird, . . .

A braying squall broke over the magic of the singer's voice. No one interrupted the master bard; no one interrupted the song of the Siuru, which most would hear only this once in their lives, but this time the music was shattered. The song was destroyed; it could never be recovered. The singer slipped away from the bench and quietly disappeared.

Varrak, the wind-enchanter, clad in his tattered old blanket, stood in the middle of the floor with his bagpipes under his arm. He loosed another blast. Discordant drones, raucous chords ripped the peaceful calm in the air.

"What do you want here?" the Alevide shouted over the skirling noise.

The wind-enchanter ignored him. Lowering his pipes, he addressed the Kalevide.

"The blessings of Ukko, High One, be with you, lord," he prayed. "Reap fortune from the sky. I have come for what was promised me."

The Kalevide looked at him quizzically. He could remember their first meeting in the bleak land of Lapu, but not what they had said. He glanced doubtfully at the treasure sacks stacked in the corner against the far wall.

"I want what is mine," Varrak breathed. "I have waited long enough in this vile land; now I shall take my due. I sailed you where you wished to sail, I steered you where you would wend. Tonight I sail where I will, and I will take with me my price, my prize. You promised me what was on the west wall of your house, and I will have it. I will have it now."

Everyone looked around the hall to see what the enchanter claimed. Numberless bundles of dried herbs and roots were hung on pegs along the walls. Skeins of spun and dyed yarn were draped over hooks. Even loaves of bread were strung on poles across the beams. Under the benches there were chests and boxes, but none seemed of much account. The Kalevide's eye fell on the empty scabbard for his father's sword. It was his most prized possession.

"You want that?" he asked.

"I want the Book!"

The Alevide gasped. The Kalevide turned to the niche in the darkest corner of the west wall. The Book had been kept there for all the years he could remember, so long that he had completely forgotten about it until now. Over the years, household clutter and debris had collected in the niche, concealing the Book. Only Varrak knew where it was, and the Alevide.

"This is what you want?" the Kalevide said, pushing aside

the sacks of gold which had been left in front of the alcove. "This book?" It meant nothing to him. The Book had been his father's, so he supposed it was precious, but except for that he cared very little about it. He had never tried to read its words or even to open its iron covers, thrice bound with iron chains.

"This Book I will have," Varrak rasped.

"Take it then, with my thanks for your service."

"No!" cried the Alevide. He was suddenly afraid. "Do you know what this is? This Book is said to contain all the wisdom needed for your land, for all lands. Here are words written by wizards, the high wizards, in the age before this age, before they abandoned Viru to seek their sanctuaries in the north, before they fled from men. They took the Book with them, but Kalev discovered where it was—somehow, I don't know how—and somehow he brought it back because it belonged here in Viru. It is the secret of his fortune, and your fortune, and ours, and Viru's. It is the lore and record of the world."

"I can't read it."

"Neither can I, neither could your father. But its power works on us anyway. Can't you feel it, can't you sense the magic here? Just having the Book in Viru protects us. You want strength? Here is strength. You want treasure? This is treasure. Someday, perhaps, we'll learn to read the wisdom here. One of us might find the key, or one of our children, or one of theirs. Who knows? And who knows what secret forces might be unlocked then, what wonders we might do? And you're going to give it away?"

The Kalevide shrugged. He was too tired to argue. "I promised. I told the wind-enchanter that if he sailed us to the world's end, I would give him what he wanted. He kept his word to me, I mean to keep mine to him."

"But the world has no end."

"It has."

"You didn't know what you were offering; it was a blind promise."

"It doesn't matter. I promised. Remember your own proverb: 'By the horns the ox we wrestle; by his word the man is bound.' Well, I've wrestled the moor ox; now I will keep my word."

"That's only a proverb, words for children. They don't mean anything."

"They mean something to me."

"Think of a trick. Give him the scabbard, give him the herbs. They are on the west wall."

"I will keep my promise!"

"The price is too high."

"Say no more! Varrak will have the Book. I've never held with sorcery; I don't need wizards' work either. Where are the keys? Unlock the chains."

There were no keys. They had been lost long ago. Varrak, who knew all secrets, knew this too, but he would not relent. Nor could the chains be broken. For years the iron had absorbed the strength and power of the Book; it had drunk thirstily of the incantations, names, and origins inscribed on the ancient pages and pressed between its plates. That strength, which was likewise the strength of Viru, now saturated the chains and made them indomitable. This too Varrak knew well.

"Break down the wall," the Kalevide commanded when it was clear that nothing else would release the Book.

For the Olevide, the engineer, the challenge of removing a portion of a standing wall from a house more than outweighed any dismay he might have felt at losing the Book. With his men wielding crowbars, saws, and axes, he extricated that entire section of wall from the western side of the hall, shoring up the roof temporarily with timbers. In the morning perhaps he could repair the gap with a proper facing of stone. For the moment a great hole gaped onto the courtyard.

The Alevide was too distraught to watch destruction done. He returned to his seat and, with his wife and her sisters beside him, drank deeply from his bowl of ale, a bitter toast to the future that was lost, a salute to the victory of defeat. He feared for Viru; its greatest hope was being carried away, and with it everything seemed to be coming apart. All he knew of life was changing.

"You're selling our freedom," he shouted over the noise of hammers. "You're giving away our salvation."

"It's only a book," replied the Kalevide.

The wall with the Book attached was hitched to a team of oxen to be dragged like a sledge to the harbor. Varrak would take the silver *Lennuk* too, and no one would oppose him now.

As the oxen lumbered away, the wind-enchanter turned briefly to release another noisy squall from his bagpipes.

"Now the house of Kalev is open to the wind," he proclaimed. "Feel the wind. Feel the wind. All the kingdom shall bend before the coming wind."

The Alevide drank so he would not hear. Already he could feel the cold night air pouring into the hall. He shivered. The hole in the wall yawned awfully, a black square which let the night and the cold and the darkness come in where it should have been light.

The Kalevide sat down beside him.

"Drink some more," he said.

"You are a fool."

"It's only a book."

36   The Sulevide stepped into the banquet hall through the opening in the wall. The Kalevide rose eagerly to greet him then sat back down again, repelled by the look of the people with him. There were six adults, four men and two women, and uncounted children hiding behind their parents' legs. All were clad in filthy rags, and some were wounded. Even in the dim light of the torches the Kalevide could see fresh blood seeping through a soiled bandage around one woman's side. Yet it was their faces that disturbed him most. They were utterly without expression; feeling had long since been burned away by fear, by fire, by fatigue.

The Sulevide strode forward, his crossbow cradled in his arms.

"My men captured these people sneaking into the city under cover of darkness," he said. "They have a message for you. You must hear them now."

Very reluctantly, the refugees shuffled forward. They had not meant to disrupt the feast. All they wanted, when they sought the city, was a place of shelter, any small hovel out of the cold where they could be safe, where they could sleep. They did not want to disturb the king. Ill at ease, out of place, the men held back; they scuffed their feet and looked at the floor, each one wishing someone else would speak. The women and children hid behind them. Only their haggard faces could be seen peering around their husbands' and fathers' shoulders. The Kalevide stared at them balefully from his throne. Finally the eldest stepped forward to speak; he was one of the wounded.

"Sire. Master. Young sir. We are farmer-folk. We have a farm. A little farm. We never grow very much." He glanced around nervously at the others for confirmation. They nodded. "A small farm. We do not need much. Not far from here. Half a day. We were attacked. This morning. At sunrise. By a band of demon Letts. They howled at us. Two knights were with them. Two black knights. On black horses. I never saw such horses. We tried to fight. My sons and I. Our wives. We tried to fight.

We were told to try. There were messengers. From the city. Two days ago. They told us we must fight. Not flee. We tried. But, lord, master, young sir, we are not fighters. We are farmers. What could we do? There were too many. Our axes could not fight the iron armor of the knights. They had great swords. We could not fight them. We fled. All of us. They burned our house. That is all.'' He stepped back quickly, to be embraced by his family.

''You see how it is,'' said the Sulevide while the refugees slowly worked their way back through the crowd that had gathered close to hear their story. ''You see what it means. The war is upon us. We must prepare to march at once.''

The Kalevide said nothing. He was still gazing at the women and children as they drew away from him. He had never seen such misery written on anyone. Not even in Põrgu, where everything was a nightmare, had he seen such suffering, for this was real.

''Take care of them,'' he said softly to an elder standing near. ''Find them a place to stay. Make them comfortable. And give them something to eat.''

When that was done, he was free to greet the Sulevide. The Kalevide called him to sit beside him, to relax for a moment, to drink a bowl of ale while he told his news.

''There is no time for that,'' the Sulevide insisted. ''That is my news. You heard them. The war is less than half a day away. You have seen its work. Those are not the only refugees; they are merely the latest. Others have been coming into the city from every side for days, and they all tell the same tale. Not only are the Letts upon us, but some speak of the evil Vends from the south. And with every party march the iron knights who are our true enemy. On the eastern borders the Riders of the Golden Khan have come. The son of Alev can tell you of them, if he is not too afraid to speak. You wish to hear the news? The war has come, as I said it would. It is upon us on every side, that is the news. Now we must march before the enemy is at our gates. There is no time any more for delay. There is no time to drink your drink.''

''Surely we have a little while,'' said the Alevide. ''We have the walls to protect us, and the gates. The stones will give us time.''

''To what purpose?''

''To think of something to escape this insane war. If we are truly attacked as you say, and it seems we are, I'm sorry to say, then we must devise some trick to turn it aside.''

[345]

"A trick?" The Sulevide's voice rippled with scorn.

"Perhaps we can persuade the iron knights and the Riders of the Khan to destroy each other while we sit safely in the city."

"We would be crushed between them."

"What else can we do? You heard those people. They're farmers, not warriors. So are most of our people. They don't know how to fight; they don't want to fight. How can you expect them to face armed men? You have a few trained fighters; can they stand against the knights? Bar the gates; we're safe behind the walls. Even if we can't find a fit alternative to the war, perhaps it will pass us by. The walls will protect us, won't they? The knights don't have horses that can fly, do they?"

"The walls will hold against any force," the Olevide said confidently.

"Yes, you will be safe in the city behind stone, as you will be safe in your tomb. Is that what you want, to be so safe? Do you want to hide behind stone shields until you die? For you would die soon enough. Do you know the meaning of the word siege? The enemy will control the land around us. They will hold our fields. Nothing will come in. How will you feed our people? How will you feed the refugees who have come to us? You are the steward. How long can we last without fresh supplies? A week? A month? If we had full storehouses, we might consider standing a siege, although it is a coward's course and there is no hope in it when there is no chance of reinforcements coming, but there are no storehouses. You may not have been able to walk the city yet, my lord," he said to the Kalevide. "When you do, you will see no granaries. Where are the granaries?" He pointed accusingly at the Olevide who was responsible for all building.

"There will be granaries when there is grain to fill them," the son of Olev replied calmly.

"And where is the grain?"

The Alevide grinned, although it was a thin smile. "Come now, even you can't expect corn before harvest. Shall I pull it from the earth unripe? And who will help me? All my workfolk have been levied for your guard or for the Olevide's building. And you wonder why there is no grain?"

"And you wonder why we must march! We will be trapped if we stay behind these walls, and then we will surely be overcome. It is a good city," he said to the Olevide, "but it was not designed with war in mind."

Before the Olevide could answer, the Kalevide raised his hand for silence. "Is there any food?" he asked his steward.

"A little. It's difficult to say how much. Every family will have some stores, and the herdsmen have brought their beasts into their houses.''

"Enough to keep part of the people? The children and women and old ones?''

"A while.''

"Then we will fight,'' the Kalevide said, slowly, reluctantly. "In the morning I will lead our men to battle. The rest, who cannot fight, will be safe here behind the walls. I do not want the war to take the helpless ones.''

"We are not helpless. We can fight,'' the three sisters exclaimed. "This is our land, too.''

"No, I do not want you on the field.''

"Do not wait for morning,'' the Sulevide urged. "Every moment counts. We must march at once.''

"Morning is time enough,'' the Kalevide said simply.

The Alevide shook his head with sadness.

While his people went to their homes to prepare for the morrow, the Kalevide sought his father's tomb for the last time. The path he used to take across the untilled fields no longer existed. It had been replaced by rows of stone-faced houses. To reach the knoll it was now necessary to walk down a wide avenue to the market square, then turn at the corner onto another roadway paved with stone. The square was deserted; only shadows looked out of the empty merchants' booths. Faint whispers haunted the alleyways, but they were only mice and leaves scurrying over the cobblestones. The night was very dark, the sky deeply overcast. Clouds covered all the stars. A strong, cold wind, heavy with moisture, blew across the city from the sea.

In that late hour the folk of Viru, like the city, should have been sleeping peacefully, but this night lights blazed in the houses, and voices came through the open doorways and windows. Words floated like wraiths upon the night, and mingled with the hollow echo of the Kalevide's lone bootheels striking the pavement. The people were awake; they knew well what trouble was coming, and they were making themselves ready. It takes no time for a rumor to spread across a city. Already the men in the houses knew they were bound for war and the women knew they were to be left behind. They packed a little bread, some cheese, the last dried fish, into packs and pouches to keep their men marching on the battle-trail, scant rations for a warrior, but all there was to spare. Weapons were assembled. Men sang songs for going into combat; women mourned.

On the city walls sentries challenged bands of refugees begging entrance and protection. The gates opened and closed with a ceaseless crash and clatter of chains to admit those in need. Once inside, all women, children and aged men were directed by the warders to centers hastily set up to receive them. There they would be given soup and shelter, a place to sleep. The men, if not infirm, were separated from their families at once and compelled to enroll in the guard. If they had no weapons, they were given arms. If they had no training, they were taught to hold a spear. If they had no skill, they were encouraged to be brave. Most of the fugitives came into the city after being driven from their homes. They had watched their houses burned, their livestock slaughtered. Many had seen their friends and dearest kindred killed. Distraught and desperate, they had fled to the city, bringing nothing with them but their lives, and now they were being asked to sacrifice even those. Husbands were torn away from wives, sons from parents, fathers from young children, brothers from sisters. Everywhere sad wailing rose over the city. It touched the clouds overhead.

Slowly, sadly, the Kalevide climbed the hill to his father's grave. Here the city had not come. The Olevide had kept the knoll as it had been, wild and overgrown, to be a park, a monument, a shrine, for none would molest a place where the dead were buried and where their presence dwelled. The cairn loomed as it always had, a heap of large gray stones covered with growing herbs and flowers. The golden starflowers and blue harebells which Linda had planted over Kalev's body were still living, although they were hidden now in the overwhelming mass of unkempt vines and briars. Here and there slender saplings grew. The Kalevide stood silently beside the tomb and waited for it to speak. He wanted, needed, encouragement and counsel from his father on the eve of Viru's great moment.

The cold wind rattled the leaves on the trees and brambles. From far away came the sounds of the sea, low and moaning. A sea gull cried. He waited. In the darkness he listened for the voice to come out of the grave. He could not speak; he did not want to speak. He no longer felt that he could pour words out of his heart into his father's ears. He had grown beyond that now, but he longed for Kalev's answer nonetheless. He yearned to be told that all was well, that the day would bring good fortune, the war would be won, glory gained. The dead alone of men know the future that will come. He ached to hear his father's voice which he had never heard, but in the night he knew he would not. The only words that came to him were from the wind and

sea, and they only sighed. It began to rain; the sky shed tears for
Viru.

Disappointed and tired, the Kalevide returned to his home.
Once it had been Kalev's, now it was entirely his. It was empty,
dark, deserted. For a little while he lingered by the gate beneath
the fragments of the ancient skull, posted long ago by his father.
It leered at him through the gloom. He shivered and went in. It
was the hour of thin light before morning.

Inside he found only the remains of the hastily abandoned
feast. Everyone else was gone; the time of war had begun.
Husbands went to be with their wives, to spend one last night in
love together before they would have to separate, perhaps forever. Men without wives sought women where they could, and
found them, so they could carry into battle memories of a
happier struggle. Some simply went off to be alone. For everyone it was a quiet time, a time when each one had to decide
within himself what he meant to do when thrust into the nightmare of the war.

In the last remaining hour of night the Kalevide dug a deep pit
in the earth in which he buried all his gold and treasure.

"Take this, Taara," he prayed. "Hold it well for me, Mother
of Taara, Earth. Protect it. Yield it to no one unless he be the
son of an untouched woman, unless he come Midsummer's Eve,
unless he offer you the blood of three black beasts unblemished
by any white, first a black cock with curled comb, second, a
black dog or cat, third, a mole."

His voice was resonant, drawing power from the earth, but he
wanted to weep. Turning the soil back over the treasure sacks,
he whispered more spells to the powers he trusted so they would
guard the wealth of Viru, so something would survive the war. It
is said that the one who may unearth that gold has not yet been
born.

As the pre-dawn light swelled over the land, the rain stopped
falling. Nevertheless, the day would remain gray with a sad,
brooding weight of cloud hanging over it. The Kalevide armed
himself in his golden armor, his gloves and greaves of gold, his
golden breastplate, his golden helm. From the wall of his house
he took down the golden shield, stolen from the underworld,
etched long ago with rays to represent the sun. Now was the time
for him to bear the sword he had lost in the brook. Now in truth
and not in fantasy he was going to lead Viru's army against the
enemy. It was right that he carry his father's sword, the emblem
of his kingdom. With it in hand, victory was assured. Without
it? The Kalevide shrugged. The sword was lost. In its stead he

bore an old spear that had been Kalev's. He had fought well with other weapons before, and the strength of his arms remained.

At dawn trumpets sounded, the summons of all men to arms. From each tower they were blown; their high, shrill notes screamed across the city. In every house and cottage men rose hastily to secure their weapons and supplies. They shouldered spears or slung crossbows across their backs. A few had swords; some carried only their accustomed tools, the axes and scythes of everyday. Their wives and women clung to them and wept as they went through the doors. Children, not understanding all the haste and clamor, began to cry. Outside, the streets filled with people surging toward the gate as families tried to follow their men to war.

"When will you come back?" the women cried.

"I don't know," replied the men. "The king knows."

From a watchtower a warden's voice rose in a battle hymn:

> O, Ukko, high-lord, Taara,
> Golden-king, ancient sky-
> father, cover me with furs
> of fire while I wade deep
> in war, a shirt of flame;
> raise wide walls, high walls
> of stone, where I strive
> in battle, a shield of stone
> to keep my head from harm,
> my neck unbroken, my hair
> unturned by heavy iron,
> untouched by hostile swords.

From a second tower another watchman answered:

> Smith, come, Ilmarine,
> hammer-wielder, from under stone,
> iron-master, smith, forge
> iron swords, sharp pikes, sheaves
> of spears, arrows. I march
> to battlefields, slaughter-
> plains, fields of blood.

And from a third:

Earth, arise, awake
Dry-land, old-mother,
shelter me with living
stone from underearth.
Let boulders grow, shields
to hide me, hills. Put holes
in their centers, snakes coiled
around the holes, shelter
I may fight behind, safe
in war, lest evil hurt befall
my head, or one hair fall.

At the gate the families were separated. The women, wailing
and lamenting, and the others not permitted on the battlefield
were turned back by guards who kept them closed behind the
wall. The men were ushered through the narrow archway out of
the city. With their heads up and faces set, they marched bravely
forth to confront the war. The gates swung closed behind them.
The city they had left was given up to grief and mourning.

Three great companies set out across the plain to the forest
where the forces of Viru mustered. In the vanguard marched the
Sulevide's trained warriors, all alert and ready, eager even, to
encounter battle. They were uniformly clad in leather shirts, and
armed with crossbows, spears and knives. Behind them, in
looser order, came the craftsmen and builders led by the Olevide;
they were followed by the farmers and husbandmen with the
Alevide at their head. For most of these men the thought of war
was new and poorly understood. Skirmishes and battles, wounds
and death, that was the stuff of songs and stories, not something
to be lived. Yet now they were immersed in their own tales,
marching into an unknown future, to find glory and become the
heroes of legend or to succumb to the tide of blood.

They pitched their camp in the sacred grove dedicated to
Taara. There, despite all sacrilege, they settled down to wait for
whatever was to happen to them. The oaks of that most holy
glade, ancient trees untouched ever by a woodsman's axe, still
wore scraps of cloth and ribbon left from past days of worship.
Birds perched on their branches. They sang to the men, telling
them to sharpen their swords and spears.

The Kalevide, bright in his golden armor, stood on the brow
of the hill watching his troops march to his call. The Sulevide
stood beside him. As soon as he had seen that his men were fed
and comfortable, the Alevide joined them. He was unarmed.

"You would look braver if you had worn your armor," the

Sulevide observed. "Do you intend to fight the war looking like a farmer?"

The Alevide shrugged his shoulders. Perhaps he would not fight at all. He had tried on his suit of silver mail, his gift for the journey to the world's end, but it had felt uncomfortable and wrong for him. The sword did not fit at his side, the spear was an unnatural tool for his hand. So he had left it all behind, merely throwing an old sheepskn cloak over his shoulder, to come clad as he preferred to be.

He had almost not come at all. For a while he and his wife had considered going away while there was still a moment of peace. Perhaps they could have found a quiet place to escape the strife. In the end, however, he realized that, whatever happened, he must stay beside the Kalevide who needed him. Perhaps he did not look like a warrior; perhaps he would not fight. He had come, that was enough.

The Kalevide put his own golden, sun-like shield into the Alevide's hands. "You shall bear my shield," he said. The Alevide accepted that burden.

More horns sounded. Their high notes rang above the treetops, a shrill summons echoing over the forest, carried beyond the hills and lakes. Small animals and gentle beasts, frightened by the persistent call, scurried away through the underbrush, driven by a fear like the terror of wildfire. Peaceful, sleeping birds left their nests; throughout the forest flocks flew southward to escape the noise that overwhelmed all birdsong. It signaled battles to come, and there was no relief from its keening cry. On a hilltop a ranger heard the note coming from afar and raised his own horn to his lips to sound the warning, to send it onward across the land.

Messengers and runners went through every district and region in Viru, seeking the remote hamlets and isolated farmsteads, to alert the people to the war and to summon every man to fight.

Some, especially the older people, or people who still lived according to the older ways, who had not yet accepted the new customs brought to Viru by Kalev and by his son and by others, who had not yet ventured to the city but still clung to the life of the forest, some of these left their homes when they heard of the war and drifted away into the deep wood where they would fend for themselves and live, despite all others. They would live, for a while, but with time they would disappear. Other peoples would come into their land and hound them even from their hidden homes. Rumors would be spread of secret folk dwelling in the forest, and they would be hunted. Legends would grow, and they would be feared. They would hide; they would become shadows in the trees. Their numbers would decline, and they would be lost while the world around them changed, and then they would be forgotten. So it always was.

Most of the countrymen, though, answered the summons when it came. The men stepped forward boldly, despite the anguished pleas of those who loved them, and joined the ranks assembled among the oaks of Taara, where they waited for the war. Everyone waited. Some spent their time in camp attending to equipment, polishing leather, honing blades, dressing arrows. Others wrestled for sport, or engaged in mock duels to try their weapons and skill. Some could laugh; more were grim. Occasionally a man would sing, his voice sad and soft. Another would tell a story. Most merely sat. They spoke a few words, perhaps, but rarely to the point. They smoked their pipes. Nothing changed.

For five days they wandered in from the farther reaches of the country, entering the glade in ones and twos, occasionally in larger bands. Then, after the fifth night, they ceased to come.

"Where is the enemy?" asked the Alevide. He and the Sulevide sat, like the rest of the army, beside a small fire, waiting for something to happen. The world around them was very still, poised on the balance point between time past and time to come. The war seemed very far away. "I thought the knights were at our gates. Attack was imminent, you said. Days ago."

"It was. If we had not marched when we did, we would have been attacked." The Sulevide was sharpening his sword, as he did every night.

"Then where are they now? What are they doing?"

"They are near. An army rarely marches straight into battle. First they will scour the countryside, collecting all the food and supplies they can from the outlying farms. They will consolidate their position. They will bring up their reserves. They will survey the land so they can be sure of their retreat if that is necessary. They will send spies to measure our strength. They will plan for every possibility. These knights are masters of their art, have no doubt. They will leave nothing to chance."

"Then why, in the name of Taara, are we just sitting here? Shouldn't we attack them now, before they're ready, before they control half our land? Why don't we engage this war if that's what we're here for, or else go home and be done with it?"

"We must wait. Sometimes it is necessary to sacrifice much of a nation in order to save the rest."

"You don't mean that? You'll let them have Laane and Harju

and Jarva and half our forests? You'll let them kill, rape and burn where they will, while we sit on this hill?''

''I do mean it. We must wait. It is the price we pay to choose the battlefield. We must meet the enemy here, on this plain, if we are to have any chance of victory. Anywhere else, our men would become too scattered. They would be cut down one by one. Here, under the eyes of their city, they will stand together and support one another. Here they might hope to defeat the Letts and the knights both, after which we will be able to march out to meet the rest of our enemies, the Vends, your Riders of the Khan, drive them out and reclaim our land.''

The Kalevide came over, sat down heavily beside them, but said nothing. He merely stared moodily at the fire, summoning to himself the strength he would need to defend his people. For this he was king.

''What will happen when they come?'' asked the Alevide.

''I do not know. We will have the fight of our lives, I think. If it were only the Letts, or even the Vends, I would not worry. They are savages, and we should be able to defeat them easily. It is the knights I fear. The iron knights.''

''And the Riders of the Golden Khan.''

''Yes, and them.''

''Can we overcome them?''

''I do not know. I think so, here, on this field, if we fight as we ought. This is how it is with war, either all are killed or some will live. What more do you want?''

''I do not intend to die in battle,'' answered the Alevide.

The Sulevide smiled. ''A good trick, if you can be sure of it.''

''Neither do I,'' the Kalevide said softly.

For two days more the men of Viru waited. Then the war began.

37   The enemy came, unopposed, across the open plain. A horde of wild men, all of them naked, all of them tall and lean, fair of skin, fair of hair. They ran; their bare feet whipped through long, dry meadow grass. Their bodies were smeared with yellow ocher mud and dung to proclaim the marshes and mire-pits where they were spawned. They raced unchecked across the fields, men who had the blood of demons in their veins. For weapons they carried clubs and pointed sticks

of wood, but when they fought they would as readily use their teeth and claws to tear into their foes. They came howling savage curses in an unknown tongue.

Behind them rode a score of knights, each one mounted on a great stallion draped in black-dyed cloth. Each horse's face was sheathed in a mask of iron plate; large, flared, cup-like guards hid their eyes behind black, vacant holes. The chargers came at a slow walk, the heavy, overwhelming stride of war, each horse stepping in unison with the rest. Together their hooves drummed the awful march of death, the hard, inexorable tread that would allow no human impediment. Slow or fast, the beat of their hooves struck terror through the earth. The plain trembled beneath their awesome weight.

The knights were cased in iron armor, hauberks wrought of double mail beneath long surcoats of black silk. Their heads were covered by iron helmets. Thick plates protected their cheeks and curved around to shield their mouths; nose guards pointed down like daggers between their eyes. These helms needed no visor or beaver, but they, too, were masks concealing each knight behind a face of iron. If these were men, they were anonymous; if they were fiends from the underworld, they could not have been more horrible. These were the lords of war. The helm of one, the leader and master of them all, swept up into the high-curving wings of a hawk, it was carved with battle signs. The rest wore plainer masks; all were ominous. All bore the black guise of death.

The knights' shields were long and tapered, painted white with a black cross-like sword emblazoned on the virgin field, the symbol of the order of their knighthood and the power they served. Their lances were shaped of ebony; their swords were iron, broad, heavy, double-edged. An iron mace, axe, or morningstar hung from each knight's saddle horn.

The savage chanting of the Letts was audible across the plain, and grew louder as they approached. The knights marched silently, forever grimly. Only the dreadful footsteps of their warhorses echoed in the ground. A score of iron-shod hooves struck the earth as one, and then again, and then again, a slow, throbbing pound. It was the beating of a world-wide drum. The dry sod shook. The shock spread across the field as far as the hilltop where Viru's men waited in stunned anticipation.

"Oh, Taara," breathed the Alevide. The Sulevide laughed, a harsh, desperate laugh born out of the tension and excitement of a battle about to begin. They were standing with the Kalevide, gazing down on the spectacle of the enemy, their men arrayed behind them. The way to the city lay open and vulnerable, yet the invaders came straight toward the hill as though deliberately seeking an engagement.

Through a cloud, the Kalevide beheld the coming tide. A haze of confusion came over his mind; he saw them marching through time. The plain, to him, appeared filled with unnumbered troops; as far as the eye could penetrate, and far beyond, the field was covered with vast multitudes of tramping men, all faceless, all nameless, all clad in the drab garb of the war. The black horses of the knights became insane machines of iron, iron boxes belching black clouds of smoke, boxes containing men inside their bodies. They growled, they rumbled as they rolled across the battle-plain; they cast death from a distance, and then drove on. Black eagles, soaring through the gray clouds overhead, filled the sky; their shadows, darkening the fields below, spread fear everywhere. Black birds of iron with golden-haired men mounted on their backs, they stooped; their riders fired arrows into the breasts of men. Far away, too far to be seen but in the vision seen, great iron-sided ships, black ships, lined Viru's shores, ships that would have dwarfed the *Lennuk* or any ship known to men. They disgorged countless more companies of faceless warriors and more snarling machines. The fields of war crawled with the black insects of death.

Through the mists of madness the Kalevide perceived the dread being that was the war, the blind entity which moved behind the Letts, behind the knights, behind the force that was, indeed, marching toward him. He beheld inside himself the horror of all the struggles that would come upon his land. Waves of invaders would come in endless streams. They would come, bearing war, bringing strife, unimpeded through the long unwinding of time. The Kalevide's anger rose up in him and overflowed. The word "Viru!" burst out of him as a scream as he charged from the hill, alone, to attack his most hated foes.

Forgetting his shield-bearer, forgetting the men arrayed behind him, he rushed the Lettish horde. His legs took the slope with long reaching strides. His face became distorted by his rage; his lips drew back from his teeth as he cried aloud his terrible challenge to the enemy. His eyes seemed to swell and then explode inside his head. Racing onto the plain, the Kalevide grasped his spear near the point and whirled it around his head so that it roared like a demon in the air. Startled by the suddenness of his charge, all along the line Viru's men shouted a high-pitched, trembling cry, and then they followed their king.

The Sulevide cursed. In that one moment they lost the advantage of the hill. If they had waited, the enemy would have come to them. They would have had to, for if they had gone around to attack the city first, they would have risked being cut off from behind, but then they would have had to fight uphill. The horses would have stalled, perhaps foundered. The knights would have been forced to dismount or retreat. Once off their horses, they would have been vulnerable. Their armor would have slowed them. They would have been cumbrous and clumsy, ineffective in fighting. On foot they might have been defeated. Now that chance was past, destroyed. Already the men of Viru were swarming onto the field far away from the slope, moving among the savages in a vast melee. The Sulevide's bowmen were helpless; they had not fired a shot, and now they could not. If only the others had waited long enough for the enemy to come within range, the archers could have killed half the Letts from afar without any risk to anyone else. If they fired now, friend and foe alike would fall.

The Kalevide struck the center of the horde. The men who followed behind him moved around to the north to stand between the invader and their city. The Sulevide had no alternative but to lead his own warriors along the southern flank to hold that ground beside the forest, thereby blocking the enemy's sole road of retreat and escape. The Letts were nearly surrounded, and in the fighting that ensued they were very nearly overcome.

On every hand the savages were slaughtered. Although they were taller and had a longer reach than the men of Viru, they were less well equipped, and they fought much more wildly, making crazy swings with their clubs and jabbing aimlessly with their sticks. The small, round shields of the Viru men helped protect them; so did the leather coats and helms most wore. The Kalevide's troops fought earnestly, without great skill but with a true sense of need and valor. They were fighting for their homes. Many had been driven from their farms and had seen their holdings burned; they fought now for revenge. Others knew keenly that they were defending their land to save it from future fire and tyranny. They were fighting for the folk they loved, and that spirit served them now in the time of battle.

Although most of the men in Viru's army had never before slain men, they had often hunted and killed both bear and deer, and now they found this not very different. True, men were more dangerous than deer, but they were slower, and if they were quicker than bear, they were also softer. Spear points passed easily between their ribs; blood spurted; they died.

Many were surprised that these Letts could be killed. They had believed them to be demons, and not living men of earth at all, but their blood ran, their lives were real, and they could be destroyed. Like their king, the men soon lost themselves in the mindless rush and tumble of the battle. It became a sport, like hunting and the chase. They struck down one enemy, then turned to take another's life.

Nevertheless, Viru's men died, too. They died by the score. The Letts' sticks and staves could not pierce their shields and leather shirts, perhaps, but the heavy clubs, which they wielded two-handed, could shatter shield and skull alike, and the savagery of the Letts gave them even greater power. They fought as madmen, wildly, blindly, without caring at all what happened to themselves, utterly immersed in the swirling chaos of combat. Weaponless, they grappled with the men defending Viru. Often they fought in threes and fours against a single man. They disarmed him; they held him; they ripped his body with their naked hands. They flayed his skin; they tore off his limbs and members; they clawed his throat. They drank his blood.

The Kalevide raced everywhere, back and forth, around the battlefield, shouting to his men, encouraging them to fight their common foe with extra vigor: guard their homes; save their land. With his own courage he inspired them to bravery greater than they had ever known or even owned before. His example became their beacon. He wielded his spear as a staff, swinging it in a wide arc before him, sweeping down the enemy. One after another they fell. He struck the naked Letts and knocked them off their feet; while they groveled on the ground, he reversed his spear and thrust it through their bellies. The plain ran red with the blood and entrails of men. He planted his foot on their necks and wrenched the spear-head free, whirled and drove down others. Always on his lips were the wild cries of victory for Viru. Words without meaning forced themselves from his mouth and screamed across the field. The enemy was surrounded; they could not escape. He cut them down as a reaper mows his corn. Many tried to stand against him; they gathered in a single force to beat him to the earth, but with a joyous shout he burst through their pack and dealt his strokes with unbounded fury. His battle garb was smeared with gore; streaks of blood painted his face with the savage colors of vengeance. Later, when time allowed, he began to take the heads of Letts.

The wild men screamed loudly in their uncouth language. The men of Viru sang the lore-songs of their fathers, songs that raised their courage and gave them strength to continue in the slaughter. Throughout the battle of the plain, however, in all the

[358]

grim hours of combat, not once did the iron knights raise their voices to the war.

The riders of the black horses maintained a deathly silence that was more menacing than all the battle chants of unmounted men. The only sounds which spoke their purpose were the thud of hooves and the ringing of iron mail, the clang of armor and the dread whisper of a sword slicing through the air to bite flesh and bone. At a gallop they wheeled their high stallions in a circle in the midst of the melee. After the first onslaught, the Letts had fallen back, surrounding their masters; now the knights towered over the heads and bodies of both their allies and their foes. Freely they struck with broadsword, axe, and mace; they impaled unprotected men with their long black lances. Their horses trampled the bodies of those struggling in the dust; they crushed anyone who fell in their way. The knights cared little if it was Lett or Viru-man who died. They were the masters of the war; death was theirs to deliver.

The Sulevide's bowmen fired their bolts at these black riders, but it was a vain effort. Arrows bounced ineffectively off the iron armor. No part of the knights' bodies was exposed; their mail was so finely wrought, links within links within links, that not even the sharp-pointed tips of the crossbow bolts could penetrate deeply enough to touch living flesh. On their hands they wore iron gloves; on their legs, iron boots. Only if an arrow could find the opening in their helmets where their eyes should have been could it have inflicted mortal pain, but no man of earth could aim so well. The knights were invincible in their iron.

At first those who were fighting close tried to attack the riders with their spears, but once again the armor warded off all strokes, and the knights were too deft with their shields, and defter still with their blades, to allow intimate attack. If a man persisted and tried to pull one of them from his saddle, he was too exposed to the flash of a broadsword or the sweep of an axe to live to succeed. Some thought to destroy their mounts by striking underneath, but beneath their black satin bards, the horses, too, wore iron mail and were impervious to any eager thrust. Soon Viru's men learned that if they wished to survive, they must avoid engaging with the knights, and when they saw one near, they fled.

They were not craven; they readily reentered the fray against the naked Letts, who were easier to fight, and whom they could kill. Yet though they ran from the knights, many were ridden down. They succumbed. Their heads were cloven by the swipe of broadswords, their limbs were severed from their bodies. Those who did not die at once fell to lie untended while their blood fed the thirsty earth. The scream of the dying rose above the war cries and battle songs and above the swearing and cursing of the men still locked in mortal strife.

The Sulevide fought with deliberate skill. He turned all his lifelong training and desire to deadly use, for he had found at last the field for which he had lived his years. When his crossbow bolts were gone, he stole a sword from the hand of a fallen comrade. Hacking his way through the band of howling wild men, he cut on every side and forced them back. No one could stand against him. Of all those on the battlefield, he alone was smiling. Of them all he was the single one who could match the iron knights and meet their leader. The Kalevide was inspired and driven by the passion of his dreams, but the Sulevide had purpose. He was confident; he believed in his skill, in his cause, and in the necessity of the war. He knew it was the turning point in the days of Viru. He would fight to see his country the victor, or he would die.

Boldly, powerfully, he paraded on the southern flank to turn the enemy from the forest, to deny them retreat, to drive them back among the rampant horse. He entered battles wherever and whenever his men seemed to falter. He rescued many just as they were about to be overcome, often reversing the tide by his own efforts alone. Others he led back to the battle just as their courage began to fail. By his example he encouraged them to go on. Without his constant attention the flank would have broken, for there were too few there to hold the line, except by heroic effort, but with the Sulevide as their guide, as with the Kalevide elsewhere, the weaker men were given heart. They waged their weary struggles more bravely than they ever could have alone. Slowly, but inexorably, the two main fronts, north and south, right and left, closed together to encompass all the enemy, trapping them, preparing them for defeat.

As the circle closed, the milling mass of men grew tighter. When they were packed together, the men of Viru pushed the Letts still closer. A man could not turn to escape his enemy, and still the Kalevide's troops herded them in. The knights were blocked by the sheer press of bodies against their mounts. Their lances were useless. With the Letts pushing backward on them, they could no longer wield their iron weapons to strike their foe.

For half a day, until the time when twilight neared, the battle raged in the middle of the plain. The Sulevide marshalled his warriors on the southern side and kept them fighting as they were trained, despite the weariness which slowed them. Farmers and craftsmen still held the north. They strove valiantly but were growing ever more fatigued. Many now had scarcely strength enough to raise their weapons or to dodge a killing blow. In complete exhaustion, each one wished that for once he could simply let his arms drop, that he could fall, even die, anything to be spared the effort of more combat. Yet they fought. Behind them was the city, a shadow looming above the plain. Constantly, from the corners of their eyes, they caught glimpses of it, mere glances since there was no time to turn their heads, but they saw enough to remind them that home was there, enough to warn them how desperate the struggle was. Each man clenched his teeth and forced himself to hold his place in the line, telling himself he would not fail. They all fought for the city, for their families and their lovers sheltered behind those walls, and for the lives they hoped to live there once the war was over.

The Kalevide ran among the tightening knots of warring men, pushing through to where the battle seemed thickest, but as the day drew on, although he continued to kill as many of the foe as he could, the madness which had initially carried him from the hilltop alone passed away. It passed, to be replaced by one relentless purpose. Now his eye sought only the captain of the iron knights, the one who rode before the rest, who wore the high-winged helmet to proclaim his mastery of the war. If he could meet him once in close combat, if he could unhorse him, and if his strength would just endure long enough to defeat him despite the iron armor, then the battle would be over; Viru would have won. Once their leader fell, the other knights would flee and not return. The Letts who remained alive would be dispatched with ease, and even pleasure. If he could just capture the great black horse itself, if he could mount it, he would ride gloriously to triumph.

The black mask of the iron knight turned slowly on the Kalevide fighting through the grim confusion of men still caught in combat. Through empty eyeholes stared all the hatred and malevolence that was in the war. The others fell back; men lowered their weapons. A path opened for the Kalevide. Let king fight against king. The tall, proud stallion stood motionless while the field fell silent. Only the groaning of the wounded could be heard. The knight gripped his broadsword in his mailed fists. Its dark, naked, blood-smeared, iron blade radiated ice-cold evil. His shield hung on his saddle; it would not be needed. His reins were looped over the horn; he could control the horse with his will. The master of war waited, poised and still, for the Kalevide to come to him. Not even a breath passed through his iron helm.

The Kalevide began to run. The way was clear for him. A shout of power burst from his lips as he raised his spear to challenge the black figure of death. The knight prompted his horse. The stallion charged, but not toward the Kalevide. He turned and raced away southward, away from the running man. The other knights, as if on a signal, wheeled with their leader and streamed across the field.

Suddenly the Sulevide stepped out of the throng to stand directly in the path of the flying knight. He aimed his sword at the stallion's eye, but the point caught on the protective cup where it flared out from the iron mask. The warhorse shied, but its rider kept it under control, as though the two were in reality a single creature. Majestically, the knight rose in his stirrups and raised his heavy blade high above his head. The Sulevide stared up into the sightless black face; he could not dodge; he could not duck. The sword struck down. It sliced through the air and cried joyfully as it cut, cut deeply into the Sulevide's left arm.

It would have completely severed it if the Kalevide had not at that moment hurled a stone, which struck the knight just as the fatal stroke started to fall. The sword blade faltered; it bit to the bone, but did not kill. The Sulevide collapsed. The iron knight, shaken but not unhorsed, regained his balance and urged his steed through the gap in the line. The Kalevide raced to his fallen comrade.

"Come here!" he shouted desperately to the Alevide, who appeared close by. He had been serving the wounded, fighting to ease their pain.

"Hurry!" cried the Kalevide again. "Help him!"

Blood was pouring out of the Sulevide's wound. While the knights and their Lettish allies fled into the forest, the Alevide bent over his comrade and studied him with concern.

"Do something," cried the Kalevide. "Stop the bleeding; save him."

"What can I do? I am not a healer."

"People say you have power. You must know something of these things. Help him!"

"This needs a wizard. I'm just a man, like you; no wizard."

"They say you are. You know they do, and you let them. You

encourage them to think you have arts. Well, prove it now. He's going to die.''

"It requires knowledge. Do you understand me? Knowledge, not tricks. More knowledge than I have. I need to know the words to stop the bleeding. I need to know the names, the origins, of his wound.''

"He was cut by iron.''

"But what is the origin of iron? That is what I must know. You tell me! You worked with smiths. You must have learned from them. Tell me of iron, then maybe I can heal him.''

"I don't know. I don't. I never learned. Can't you help him without me? Do something. Save him. You must. I have to go after the knights; they're getting away.''

Abruptly the Kalevide turned away and, with a shout, ran after the retreating army. His men followed him, leaving the Alevide and the Sulevide alone on the field, alone but for the fallen.

Weakly, the Sulevide opened his eyes to beseech his friend. "Help me,'' he said faintly.

"I don't know what to do.''

"Stop the bleeding. Fix me up. So I can go and kill those bastards.'' Blood gushed from his arm. The ground around him was soaked with his life.

Anxiously, the Alevide looked around the plain for someone to help him, but all had gone off to keep the war alive, leaving him alone with a dying man. No one could aid him. Furiously, he flung off the Kalevide's golden shield, which he had carried over his back and then forgotten in the mad rush of battle. Now it was only a hindrance, a useless weight which distracted him. The Sulevide groaned, then lapsed into the sleep of pain. The Alevide scooped up two handfuls of dust and opened his arms to the clouds. The dry, gray, powdered earth poured through his fingers while he chanted aloud. He sang the only words that came to him:

> Cease flowing, blood, water,
> honey of life, be still, cease
> streaming. What source opened
> your well; what cause broke
> the bonds that bound you? Blood,
> cease flowing. Like stone be hard;
> be stiff, like oak; cease flowing
> from these stonelike veins; blood,
> be still. Help me, Taara.

[363]

The wound remained open, and the blood continued to flow. The Alevide whispered through clenched teeth, "Help me, Taara!" and pressed his hands over the injured arm to hold the lips of the wound together. Words came into his mouth and he spoke them, although he had no idea where they came from or why he said them. Afterwards he could not remember half of what he had spoken. The words came out of a deep, hidden wellspring, one he had always wanted to possess but never quite believed he owned.

"Hear me, hear me, wound," he cried aloud. His voice became clear and intense. It carried a strength he did not know. As he continued to speak, his words rang louder until they became commands cried forth. "Wound, hear me. Heal. I hold you, I. I am holding you. I, the son of Alev. These are my words. I speak to you now. I, I control you. Wound. Hear me. Cease bleeding. Dry your blood. Bleed no more. No more. No more pain. Be easy. Be kind. I am holding you. Beneath my hands. Feel my hands. I have caught you, wound, and I will cast you forth.

"Flee, wound. Hear me. Now. I banish you from this body. The body of a friend. I command you, wound, pain. I, the son of Alev. You know me. You fear me. Flee, wound. Now. Leave him, leave this man. Go out of him, depart. Go. Far away, wound. Go into the west. Dive, into the western sea, the Amber Sea. Hide, wound, hide yourself beneath a blue stone. Go. Leave him. Now. Wound, now. Now you are going. Now you are fleeing. Now the blood is ceasing to flow. Now the pain is leaving. Wound, go; let this arm heal. Flesh heal. Hear me, wound, hear me. Hear me! Now!"

Like a bubble in him rising, the feeling of power grew. It came from somewhere far inside him and swelled throughout his body and flowed out through his fingertips as he pressed down on the wound and commanded it to heal. His voice was clear. He felt the clarity come over all of him, and then, like a bubble, it rose out of him and blossomed into the gentle breathing air.

The Alevide rocked back on his heels and rested. Suddenly he felt very tired. His body was trembling, and more than anything else he wanted to throw himself onto the earth and sleep. He did not understand what had happened to him, but he longed to savor the new sensations that still sang in his shivering frame. Cautiously, he looked down at his two hands and slowly drew them away from the wound. The cut stayed closed. He smiled. The

Sulevide's eyes flickered twice. "Help me, brother," he said so faintly. Then as the Alevide watched, the wound's white lips slowly parted. Blood welled out of the ugly grin and streamed down the arm to seek the sodden earth.

"Damn! Damn, damn, damn!" he cried. In a desperate last attempt, the Alevide scooped up more dust and, without words, sprinkled it into the bleeding wound itself. Then he took the Sulevide's right hand and dragged it across his body to grip the cut.

"Hold it closed," he commanded, "For your life's sake, hold it, if only for a moment." Then he left him.

Several small clumps of yarrow grew at the edge of the field. Hastily he gathered a handful of their feathered leaves and ran back to the Sulevide, who had fainted again. Crushing the herb in his hands, he plastered it over the dark mud in the wound. Then ripping a long strip from his tunic, he bound it as a bandage around the arm, tying it finally with a length of red woolen yarn from his pouch.

Some time later, when the wound had begun to heal, blood congealing around the earth, flesh knitting with help from the herb, the Sulevide regained consciousness.

"Can you rise?" asked the Alevide.

The Sulevide nodded slightly.

"Can you walk? If I help you?"

Again he nodded.

"Those bastards" hissed the Sulevide when he was finally on his feet. "Those bastards!"

With the Alevide supporting him, he walked into the forest to catch up with the Kalevide and the rest of the men who were pursuing the fleeing Letts and armored knights. Although he leaned on his companion to conserve his strength, the Sulevide was far from done. If he had had to, he could have walked alone. He would have forced himself, if only to obtain revenge. "Those bastards!" he cursed over and over again.

Behind them, as they hobbled away, the dust settled over the battlefield. Calm returned to the plain. Everyone had gone; the war had fled toward the southern marshes. It ran to recover its power and to prepare itself for the second meeting. Only dead men remained where the first battle had raged. Everywhere at intervals six paces apart lay their bodies, Letts and the men who defended Viru. Indiscriminate death had claimed them both for its own. The moans of the wounded grew fainter, then ceased as they, too, died and joined their comrades in the peace of war.

Yet the silence on the battlefield was not complete. Scavengers and carrion-seekers came out from dark hiding places to discover the taste of death. Crows and ravens stalked between corpses and ate the eyes of sightless men. Eagles swooped out of the high clouds to settle on the dead. With their sharp talons they raked the lifeless bellies open and greedily devoured cold entrails. A young wolf cub and a bear scampered from the woods and frolicked amongst the bodies. Playfully, they nosed them over, then flopped down happily to gnaw the bones of broken limbs. Long had they waited for their share of the feast.

As he left the corpse-strewn field and entered the quieter shade of the forest, the Alevide glanced back once briefly to see the desolation and despair that the battle had wrought. Searching among the dead was a small, old woman; her body was shrunken, her belly swollen by hunger. Somewhere she had procured a stick with which to prod the corpses. She turned them over and pawed through their pockets, searching for crumbs. A tall, black-shrouded man stood motionless in the middle of the carnage; a host of flies swarmed around him and settled on the faces of men who had been the Alevide's friends. He could not bear to see it. Turning away, he hurried the Sulevide along the wooded path. In the dust the Kalevide's golden, sun-like shield lay thrown away and forgotten.

38

Fires burned like a ring of red eyes around the shores of a small, shallow lake. Low-burning embers, glowing in circular pits of stone, interrupted the night's somber darkness, but no other lights, no torches, no flares, dispelled the gloom. No stars shined through the thick mantle of clouds draped across the sky. A thin robe of fog floated above the water. The lake slept. The world was quiet. A few men moved around the fires; occasionally a slight rustling of arms or clothing could be heard, or a foot scraping on a stone, or someone weeping, but no other sound great enough to disturb the deep stillness hanging over the night. No one sang; no one laughed. No one spoke anymore of bravery. If anyone whispered, it was low, and it was only to hold off the terrible weight of the silence.

The Kalevide, seated by himself in front of a small fireplace, brooded at the trembling flames. He was as tired as anyone, perhaps more so, for he had fought harder that day than any man alive. His body felt dead; he could not raise his arms. He longed to sleep. As his mind wandered, the image returned and returned again of the black knight, the captain, master of war, mounted on his black stallion, riding away from him across the plain. He could not catch him. In his memory he ran once more, but again he ran too slow. His strength was gone; it seemed sucked out of his body. Once he had overcome the worst forces of the underworld in open combat, and now he let the leader of Viru's foes among men escape. Once he had run the white mare to ground; now the black stallion ran free. Had his victory over the Sarvik cost him so much? Failure weighed so heavily, and he was so weary. Would the dark knight elude him forever? Was final victory lost? So many men had died that day; now the Kalevide mourned their loss. He knew that more battles lay ahead, and more would die.

The Letts, led by their iron masters, had fled desperately through the forest, southward, seeking the bogs and marshes where they might escape the vengeance of Viru after their rout. Only the black knights, riding ahead to choose trails that horses could travel, were undaunted. They rode in retreat, but not flight. Beyond the forest, before the swamplands, they would meet more of their comrades. Reinforced, they would turn. They would strike once more at the heart of Viru. The war was not over; it had just begun.

The Kalevide and his followers had pursued the fleeing Letts until night had compelled them to stop. His troops had caught many stragglers and struck them down easily enough; now their naked bodies littered the roadsides or were piled under the bushes where they were thrown in haste. Although some of Viru's men had also been killed during the chase, they were far fewer than had fallen earlier that day in the battle of the plain. For that the survivors were heartened.

The last two men to come into the camp came quietly. One was wounded and leaned on the other. At the line of fires they were stopped briefly by sentries posted to watch for spies, but the word "Viru," spoken quietly to conceal it from the listening night, sufficed to let them pass. Although several men came forward to relieve the Alevide of the weight of his companion, the wounded man shook them off with a harsh word. Valiantly, the Sulevide stood erect and steeled himself to walk the remaining steps alone. He would not be carried. Though weakened by his wound, he was not crippled. Though his left arm might be useless, the rest of him was sound. His legs would hold him; his right arm was still strong, strong enough to wield a sword. He would show them how strong he was. He needed no man's help to stand. Without a word, the others drifted away to their places to rest. Alone but for the Alevide behind him, the son of Sulev made his way between the fires to find his king.

At their approach the Kalevide raised his eyes from the fire and gazed at them both for a long while silently. He wanted to smile, to put on a brave show of courage in honor of the battle won, but such easy pride had long since slipped away from him.

"I'm glad to see you," he said simply.

"And we you," said the Alevide.

"Are you all right?"

"That bastard. I am going to kill him," the Sulevide growled.

"The Alevide healed your arm? He stopped the bleeding?"

"Well enough. I am well enough to fight. He did what he could. He could not save the arm, but he stopped the blood. The flesh will mend. The arm is dead, but I am not. I can fight. I shall fight. Those bastards."

"The battle was hard today. The men are tired."

"It is war. They will fight again."

"I know."

"Must they?" asked the Alevide softly. "So many die."

"It is war. Fewer died today than might have died. Fewer will die tomorrow. The men fight well; we won the field. But for the knights we would have won more. But for them we might have ended this war. Those bastards."

"We won the field," echoed the Kalevide.

"But we will have to fight again. And perhaps again, before we can claim complete victory."

"Perhaps it will never end," said the Alevide.

"It is war."

"We won the field."

"Can't anything be done about the knights?"

[368]

"They run," mused the Kalevide.

"If not," continued the Alevide, "the battles will come again and again. More and more will die until no one is left in Viru. Isn't there anything we can do to escape this?"

"The knights can be overcome," the Sulevide said. "All men can die. I will kill them."

"How?"

"I have a plan."

"A trick?"

"A plan."

"What is it?"

"When the time comes, you will know."

The Sulevide would say no more; he would not risk another premature springing of his trap.

"They run away," said the Kalevide simply. "They will not fight."

"They will fight me."

"What will you do?"

"When the time comes, you will know. For now, think of this: one word will tell you how to destroy the knights of iron. One word."

The Kalevide turned back to the fire. He did not care for riddles. In his mind once more the black-mounted rider, more menacing than life, wheeled his horse away and galloped for the wood. He could not catch him. He could never catch him.

For three days the men of Viru rested by the lake to recover from the ordeal of their first battle. In those three days they mourned their comrades who were killed. They raised monuments of stone so that those who fell would always be remembered. They sang songs of grieving to guide the spirits of the dead along the paths they were compelled to wander. In those three days the many who were wounded were allowed a brief time to heal. The Alevide went among them and gave what aid he could. Those who were merely weary were granted rest. They regained their strength and the desire to go on. The Olevide and his craftsmen toiled without a break to repair arms and armor. The Sulevide spent his hours methodically honing the edges of his sword and forming plans. Long he sat alone with his weapon's hilt wedged between his knees while he plied the whetstone affectionately to its stout iron blade with his one sound arm. This was a task he would let no other do; it must be done by his own hand. The Kalevide slept. In those three days the enemy, too, was given respite. They moved; they planned. They regrouped their forces for the next attack.

When the men of Viru marched again, they continued southward on the trail of the retreating army. Now and then they met small bands which had left the invader's main force to plunder the outlying districts. There were brief skirmishes, swift, bloody battles which served to remind them all that the war still stalked their land, short bursts of fury in which the outlaws were slain, to whet their taste for the great conflict that loomed ahead of them. The war remained. It was alive, and it lurked somewhere in the southern forest. Nevertheless, for all their searching, they could not find it. It kept always ahead of their march. For seven days the men of Viru pursued the iron knights and their uncouth allies. For seven days they swept the countryside, and still the war eluded them.

The River Vandra flowed deep and wide across Viru, dividing the forest and separating the north's hill country and lakelands from the south's more level ground. Farther south the land would spread in turn into the vast, flat marshland of Kikerpaara, where no men went. Close to the river, on the north side where the grass was fair and the forest rich, the men of Viru found the signs of a great meeting of the enemy. The meadow grass had been trampled by scores of naked feet; the iron shoes of great horses had pressed deep holes in the mud along the waterside. The raw, half-eaten carcasses of small beasts and birds, squirrels and blackbirds, were scattered all around the clearing to show where many men had stopped. The meat was cold, but still fresh. Those who had gathered there and littered the ground could not have gone far away.

"It is the Vends," said the Sulevide reading the signs and noting the direction from which this second force had come. He pointed westward along the river. "Do you see? They have marched from Laane to join the Letts here."

"Then where are they?" asked the Kalevide. "Are they near? Will they fight us now?" He longed for battle, yearned for an end to the war. He was tired.

"Near? Yes, they will be near, and the knights with them. Their army is at full strength once more. They will turn to face us again."

"Could they have crossed the river?" suggested the Alevide. "Perhaps they've had enough by now."

The Sulevide laughed. "Have you?"

"Yes."

"They have not crossed. Nor can they, not here. The armored knights and their horses cannot swim in this current, and the Letts and Vends will not leave them, no matter how much they might like to desert. No, the enemy will be near and waiting. They are ready now for battle. We merely need to lure them to us."

They made camp in the woods away from the river, leaving the bank free and unguarded. Bonfires blazed everywhere between the trees. Flames leaped to the branches as the men heaped fuel on them. It brightened the night. Frightened men lost their fears. Someone began to sing. In the orange light, black silhouettes moved back and forth among the tree trunks.

"Is this wise?" asked the Alevide, tossing another log onto the fire at the Sulevide's request. "Won't the enemy see us and attack?"

"They know well enough where we are already, so there is no harm in telling them. I want them to know. I want them to come. Let them see how they will die. Knight-bastards."

"This is the plan you spoke of? This, this subtle—ambush?"

"You shall see. In the morning. Now I tell you this: this battle is mine. No more mistakes. This time we meet them as I choose, and this time I am going to kill that knight bastard who cut my arm. You may fight the rest. Run the Vends and Letts down for sport. Kill the other knights as I kill their captain, but the captain is mine!"

"But your arm? It's mending well, but it's far from healed. How do you expect to fight anyone, much less that one?"

"You shall see. The arm is useless, if you must know. You did your work well enough. The bleeding has stopped, and the flesh grown together. Most of the pain has gone, but the arm is useless. I cannot lift it, and I never shall, and for that the knight will pay!"

"Are you mad? Do you think you can stand, with one good arm, against an armored man on horseback?"

"I will tie my arm to my side and I will face him bravely. Is this madness? I may be weak, but I am not beaten. I can fight. By Taara, yes, I can fight. I shall kill that bastard, and then the others. All shall die." With a curse he flung another brand onto the fire. Angry sparks exploded in the darkness.

*　　*　　*

When the gray dawn rose over the forest, the company from Viru woke to find their enemy already arrayed in front of them. There were no war horns blowing, no strident chants, no thundering of hooves, only a deathly silence that was more ominous than any clamor, for it left room for fear. The riverbank was lined with men, all standing rigid and waiting, waiting perhaps for a signal, perhaps for a sign of what the Kalevide would do. Perhaps they only waited for the sun to rise. The Vends and the last remaining Letts were mingled together with their backs to the water; their line extended east and west as far as the eye dared to see. With the addition of the new forces, their numbers far surpassed the ones who fought to defend their homes.

The Vends looked much like their more ancient Lettish cousins, but fairer of face and hair. Also, they were clothed and armed with short swords for stabbing. They were clad in simple tunics cut of soft hide; their blades were wrought of bronze. The naked bodies of the Letts glistened with the dew of morning, the golden hair of the Vends streamed brightly in the rising wind, but as they waited in their file, all their faces wore one blank look, and all their eyes were dull, as though none knew anything of his purpose there. They had been assigned their places, and there they abided patiently, pawns in the complex-patterned plan of the war.

In front of the foot soldiers stood the rank of iron-armored knights, mounted, as before, on their black-maned battle steeds. Their numbers, too, had doubled since the battle of the plain. Each knight held his ebon lance at rest in its stirrup cup, each shaft perfectly erect. Each horse was aligned with every other in perfect pose. Each knight bore his white-faced shield balanced on his left arm. Each wore his dark iron helm. None moved. They seemed mute figures cast from a single mold and shaped of one metal of unyielding strength. In front of them all, at the very center of the meadow, was the captain of the knights. His horse was motionless; he was motionless on its back. Beheld close to, to the men of Viru, the two seemed giants of their kind, man and horse, both wrought of iron, both forged of evil. They could not be mortal creatures of the earth. The high-winged helm gleamed coldly in the grim light of early dawn. The black, hidden eyes stared without blinking behind the mask of iron. They held no rage or fury, only the blind hatred of the war.

The Sulevide was the first to rise. Throwing off his cloak, he wrapped a linen band around his body to hold his crippled arm in place. With a curse at each delay, he struggled with the last knots until the Alevide finally came to help him and to help him don his leather tunic, the only garb he would wear for protection, since he was still too weak to bear the weight of mail.

The Alevide looked longingly at the great darkness of the forest behind them. "We can still escape," he said. "Let the oak trees hide us. We do not need to meet these men."

"You would flee? Now? When victory is at hand? What are you thinking of? This is the time for Viru to rise. This is the moment I have been waiting for."

"Are you going out there alone?"

"I am going to kill that bastard. I want him. Then the rest of you may follow. Kill the others as I kill him. Kill them all! —Here, take this," he added, handing his sharp, three-edged sword to the Alevide. Its blade was long and narrow, unlike the broadswords of the knights or the knives carried by the Vends.

"What am I to do with this?"

"Hold it for me. Use it. Do what you want with it."

"You're going out there unarmed?"

"You shall see," the Sulevide said sharply, then turned and left him alone.

When he reached the edge of the forest, the son of Sulev paused for a moment, then bent down and took a brand from the last fire in the camp. Alone he walked forward to face the single knight. Once he swung the glowing branch around his head, to whip it into flame. Fire was the word iron feared. Let fire fight against iron, heat against cold, light against dark. The knight sat motionless in his saddle. His mask could show no feeling or expression. The only sign of his contempt was that the great battle-horse that moment bent its head to crop idly at the dry meadow grass between its feet. This was no way to wage a war.

"Kill him," swore the Sulevide under his breath. He stepped forward. "Kill him now."

At the black knight's silent command, the great horse began to move. It started slowly to overcome its ponderous weight, but gradually gained speed and opened its gait to a gallop. The shock of its hooves thundered in the hard, hollow ground. On the bank the Letts and Vends awoke and let loose a frenzied howl. The men of Viru gazed with horror at their champion. The Sulevide held his torch away from his side, tilted down so it would burn brightly. Black-orange flame licked the length of the stick. The knight lowered his lance. It was aimed at the Sulevide's breast. They seemed so close, horse and rider, yet still they came so slowly. The Sulevide saw every hoof-beat as a separate step. He poised himself, prepared to spring aside at the critical moment of his life. His right arm was drawn back, but already it was growing tired. The torch was heavier than it should have been. He was weaker than he thought. If only he had not been wounded. The noise of the hoofbeats grew louder. He could hear shouting, but the words were lost in the driving pound of those iron hooves. The giant horse seemed almost on top of him. The lance seemed to touch his breast. He could see its iron tip clearly, it came so slowly. The edge where it was honed was white against the iron's black. 'Now,' he thought to himself. 'Now I must step aside.' His legs were wooden; they could not move. Now.

"Viru!" he shouted once aloud as he flung the torch. The lance crashed into his chest.

The burning branch arched high over the horse's head and the shield to strike the knight on the crest of his helm before bouncing harmlessly to the ground. The Sulevide's body was thrown lightly aside as horse and rider wheeled around from the fire. The grass of the meadow, dried by the long drought of summer, seemed to explode. A wall of flame roared between the forest and the river.

Victorious, the black captain galloped along the riverbank, away from the menace of fire which, driven by a northern wind, licked hungrily toward his waiting army. Following their lord and leader, the iron knights rode toward the west, toward the land from which they had come. The Vends and Letts, abandoned by their masters, fled once more in confusion. Flinging themselves into the river, they kicked across the water like frogs. On the far bank they crawled out through the mud to make their sorry escape southwards.

The men of Viru could do nothing, merely stand and stare helplessly while the grass fire raged between them and their retreating foes. Flame and thick black smoke rose up as a curtain to conceal the Vends' hectic flight. No one saw them disappear. The Kalevide ran forward far enough to rescue the Sulevide's body from the worst of the fire. The others, fascinated by the violence of the blaze, were frozen with fear, unable even to move. Finally, when it reached the river, the fire consumed itself and died. All of the enemy had vanished. Only a black field of smoking ash remained to mark the finish of the war.

39   "Don't do it," cried the Kalevide over the body of the Sulevide, cradled in his arms. "Don't leave me. Don't go. Not you. Not now. I need you."

"He is dead now," said the Alevide softly behind him. Tenderly he touched his friend's shoulder. He would have said the Sulevide lived; he would have said he would return, anything, any trick, any lie, to ease the Kalevide's sorrow. But the Sulevide was dead, and no cunning could call him back.

"Dead? Why? Why should he die? Why should he be the one to fall?"

"He died bravely, as he wanted. He believed in battle; it was right that he should die so. He is at peace now."

"Do you think so?"

"He must be."

"He died for us?"

"Yes."

"Then I want you to go after them. I want you to finish his work. You must."

"You want me to attack the iron knights?" The Alevide was amazed, that his words should come to this.

"The knights? No, not them, not the knights. What can you do against knights? No," the Kalevide shook his head heavily. "No, the other ones. Those Vends. Demon Letts. Go after them and drive them away from my land."

"They are already gone; they won't be back."

"I don't want anyone else to die. Too many have died. But I want them out of my country. All of them. You don't have to fight them, just drive them away."

"They're gone."

"Chase them away. Banish them. They killed my friend."

"Are you all right?"

"Yes, I'm all right. The Sulevide is dead. Will you do as I say? For him? Take half the men and go after them. Go, before they come back to kill some more."

"What will you do? Won't you lead the men yourself? They look to you; you are still their king. You should lead them now."

"I can't leave him. Look at him. The Sulevide. I can't leave him like this, all alone, to be eaten by wolves. I will build a mound for him. Yes, a mound, like my father's. He would like that. With the Olevide, together, here, we will build this grave, here, where he fell. We will build it of stone. You go after them. There is no one else to do it. The Sulevide is dead now. He gave you his sword; you must carry on his work."

It was no use for the Alevide to protest that this was not his work. With great regret he bowed to the Kalevide's command. "You will follow later?" he asked.

The Kalevide did not answer. The Alevide turned away to choose the men who would accompany him across the river. So few were left; how many would survive this expedition, he wondered. Once he had left his homeland far away in the east to seek a haven for his people, that he might lead them to a land of peace, and now he was about to lead a band of men into battle. It was the trick of a bitter world.

The Alevide selected those who were trained for the march and the rigors of campaign. They were mostly the Sulevide's men, anxious to avenge their leader. A few had worked for a while with the Olevide in the city; before that they had been hunters and trackers in the wild. None were the farmers and husbandmen with whom he had labored in the fields. He would not risk any of his close companions' lives on such a mission as this. None of the company were men he knew well or was particularly comfortable with, nor they with him. They looked at him with a forced and formal respect and some awe. He was the steward of the land and the companion of the king. Perhaps, too, they feared him a little, for he was reputed to have a wizard's power, although none knew it for a fact of his own account.

While the troop armed itself, the Olevide and his builders threw a hasty framework of floats and timbers across the Vandra to form a bridge. No one of Viru need swim where Vends had fouled the water.

Before the Alevide left camp, the Kalevide called him back for a last word of farewell, only to find that there were no words for such a moment. For a long while he merely gazed at him fondly.

"I want you to wear my armor," he said at last.

"I'm not going to fight."

"Take it."

"Why?"

"In case there's trouble. It will protect you. Please, for my sake."

Reluctantly the Alevide accepted the offer because he knew it was well meant and he would not disappoint the Kalevide further. He donned the golden breastplate and the belt of silver, the gold-plated gauntlets and greaves, and finally the gleaming helm itself, but, to preserve the image of himself, he also drew his own old sheepskin cloak around his shoulders and pulled its hood down over his head as though to hide the armor's splendor from the world. Wearing only his woolen shirt and trousers now, the Kalevide clasped him by the arms.

"The armor suits you," he said. "It makes you handsome. You shouldn't hide it so."

"Are you sure you're all right here?"

"I'm all right. Tired, that's all. I really am tired now. Always tired. Perhaps if I hadn't been so weak I could have saved the Sulevide. I don't know. Perhaps . . ."

"You can't know."

"No."

"Will you follow me?"

"Yes. I will do what I must here, then I'll rest a little. Then I will follow you."

"I don't like to leave you."

"You must. Go. Don't worry. I'll join you soon. We'll go home together. Soon."

The Alevide left him then and followed his company across the bridge to seek the Vends. In the middle of the crossing he turned briefly to look back, flourished the Sulevide's sharp sword once over his head in mock salute, then ran quickly across the rough-hewn timbers to join his men.

The Kalevide watched his best companion cross the bridge. Bridges had always fascinated him. Now, in the confusion of his mind, the rude wooden structure became first an arch of stone and then a high, soaring span suspended gracefully in the sky on filaments of gold. The Alevide was gone.

The enemy's trail was easy enough to find and follow. Like animals, the Letts and Vends had fled in panic, making no attempt to conceal their track. Soon the forest grew thinner and eventually gave way to ranging downlands. The ground became softer and swampier, fields interlaced with small streamlets. The path left by the fleeing army was like a wide beaten road through the grass. Even their footprints remained behind as signals in the spongy earth. Nevertheless, in the two days the Alevide and his band pursued them, they never saw one sight of the retreating outlaws.

The enemy sought refuge in the great swamp of Kikerpaara, which spread beyond the last slow stream of Viru. There, in the loathsome mire from which their race had sprung, they hoped to escape vengeance for their part in the war. Their trail led to the very edge of the marsh, to disappear at last among dead reeds and withered bracken. There the Vends and Letts vanished from the world of living men.

Kikerpaara extended far to the south. No one from Viru knew its breadth, or what lay beyond its foul reach, and none would enter it willingly. The swamp spread as a flat expanse of slime and stagnant water, dotted with low hummocks rising like islands above the mire. Here a man might seek a moment's refuge, a spot of dry ground where he could stand to survey the wilderness around him, but what would that avail? He must always leave that haven eventually, to wade again into the mud of the uncharted fen. The air everywhere was rank, stinking of decay, dismally close, thick with moisture. A few insects swarmed above the water along the marsh's edge, but no life dwelled within the swamp itself. This was no friendly bog where herons wade; whatever entered here fell, a victim of its cloying vapors. Not even toads or vipers crawled within these pools which exuded their own venomous oils. A great silence loomed over the land of waste, unbroken even by the low, unending hum of gnats. No birds flew overhead with songs, no furred animals rustled in the grass. Gray, withered trees stood on the hillocks, but they were dead—twisted shapes from long ago when that country had been alive. Out of shallow, unflowing streams jutted half-rotted snags, as old as the swamp, as old as ages. With the passage of years they slowly crumbled and sank. Perhaps one would fall with a crash and a high shower of foul water, but no man was ever near enough to hear the sound.

Of this company the Alevide alone had seen this wretched land before, and he alone knew its griefs. Since he had briefly penetrated the fringes of its eastern flank on his arrival in Viru, he knew enough not to inflict such trial on these men who had already endured so much. Instead of taking them into the swamp the chase the Vends, he led them eastward around its edge toward the borderlands of Pihkva, so he could honestly say that the enemy had fled and not turned back to threaten further woe on Viru.

Yet even as they marched around the outer margin of Kikerpaara, a miasma of gloom spread over the men to infect them with its hopeless disease. Like poisoned clouds of vapor, the stagnation and stench came over them and smothered their inner sense of strength and pride. They walked slower; they let themselves feel their weariness more. They succumbed to worry, joked less, boasted no longer of their battle prowess. Even the most hardy complained of fatigue and longed to rest, or even turn back. The Letts and Vends were forgotten; the men spoke instead of inhuman demons who were supposed to inhabit such unholy wastes.

To lighten their fears a little, the Alevide told them what he knew of demons. He had met them himself, he said, and found them easily outwitted. Moreover, since the Kalevide, their king, had defeated the Sarvik, demons no longer walked the upper lands, not even such fetid, unkind country as this marsh. There was more to fear there from the quicksands and sinks hidden by the black, stagnant water than from demons, he said, but the men would not believe him.

Worse than demons, indeed, was the madness and despair such desolation breeds, especially in men accustomed to friendly forests and fertile plains. Kikerpaara was like a long-festered sore on the broad, smiling face of the earth.

It was with desperate relief, then, that they turned their backs on the marsh and entered a long, narrow valley where a gentle stream played out of a small, cool lake. Here there was green grass, unaffected by the ancient power of the swamp, untouched even by that summer's drought, soft grass dotted everywhere with sparkling white and yellow wildflowers. Here the men could drink sweet water and bathe away weariness and care. At once their spirits grew lighter; the deep primeval dread spawned by the lifelessness of the marsh was behind them. If the swamp and its gloom had driven off all thoughts of the Vends, their mortal foes, then the valley and its delights now banished those last deep fears. All enemies were forgotten. No traces had been seen anywhere of an army leaving the wastes; the invader was gone, escaped. The iron knights had ridden off, taking strife away to another land. The men were free to look forward to their homes. The war was over. There was no longer any need to fear. They cast their weapons aside and rolled on the grass like children.

The Alevide let them play. He was pleased to see them happy again, even though he knew their exuberance was born more of relief than true gaiety. The toll of the war had been too heavy for anyone to laugh quite freely. All had been touched; all had lost their closest friends; all had felt the hand of death close to their own shoulders, but all that was over now. For these men, the war was finished, and they still lived. As soon as the Kalevide arrived, everyone would go home. They would travel north triumphantly together to seek again the ones they loved.

Wearying at last with their frolic, the men sat on the stones beside the stream, letting their shirts hang open, trailing their feet in the cool water, while they laughed and talked amongst themselves. Again they spoke of their deeds in battle, though now they told them as tales to be shared, tales that would long be told, enhanced and embellished, perhaps, heroic tales rather than the harsh truths so intimately endured. Distant from the others, not really a part of their fellowship, the Alevide stood by himself. Shrouded in his hooded cloak, he gazed eastward across the peaceful valley and remembered times and places far away.

"Don't move," he said quietly, but urgently. At once all fell silent.

Across the stream, three riders emerged over the brow of the hill, then advanced slowly along the bank to water their small, ugly, brown horses at the pool. Casually, they passed the line of men seated by the stream, but stopped directly opposite the Alevide. These were not the iron knights; no one had seen their kind in Viru before. Only the Alevide knew them, for they came out of the east.

In place of heavy armor, these three Riders of the Khan wore thick leather coats with high-flared shoulder pieces and trim of fur. Their shields were small and round, and slung over their backs. At their belts long, curved sabers swung, and each was armed with a long double-arched bow. Their faces were dark and unbearded; their eyes turned at the corners. Their teeth were yellow. Their wide, flat noses seemed almost swallowed by their round, swollen cheekbones. Beneath low, peaked hats of felted wool and fur, their hair was long and black, and fashioned like the tails of their horses.

For a long while they merely sat on their ponies without moving. Although heavily outnumbered, they were relaxed and careless, as if they could not believe the men of Viru were fighters. The leader of the three spoke a few unintelligible words over his shoulder; the other two laughed. When he pointed at the Alevide, they all laughed again. The men on the bank did not stir from their places. The Alevide held himself perfectly still in the face of this new threat. The eastern riders all had heads hanging on their saddles. The two underlings had several, their chief only one.

The Alevide recognized the face of his bailiff, a man he knew well, an elder with whom he had worked for many months and whose friendship he had prized. When the troubles came, this man had, at the Alevide's urging, fled into the forest with his family rather than face the war barred behind the city walls, and now he had come to this, the victim of yet another scourge to cut through Viru. While the Alevide stared at the wretched head, the horseman pulled an arrow out of the quiver at his shoulder. Slowly, deliberately, he drew back his bow, aiming at the Alevide's heart, as though he were no more than a dog to be struck down without a thought. The Alevide watched in disbelief.

Then the rider shot. The arrow flashed across the silver stream, one glint of sunlight, one whisper of motion, before it struck the Alevide's breast. He gasped. Yet the arrow, the messenger of death, the black shaft quivering, projecting from his chest, merely stuck; it did no harm. Beneath his sheepskin cloak, the Kalevide's golden armor, borrowed under protest, had saved his life. The eastern horseman pointed his sharp finger and spoke more gibberish to his companions. They all laughed at the cleverness of the trick: to hide a warrior's armor beneath a peasant's garb. It was the laughter which pierced the Alevide.

Suddenly, without his being conscious of what he was doing, he drew his sword, the Sulevide's sword. Holding it over his head in both hands, pointing it at the horseman, like a single, long, sharp horn from his forehead, he charged across the stream and, before the rider could move, plunged the three-edged blade deep into his belly. The other two easterners immediately turned their horses and galloped away as the men of Viru rose to attack. The Alevide, astonished by his act, wrenched the weapon out and let the dead man fall from his saddle. Then, still clutching the bloody sword, he backed away from the awful corpse. It was the only man he had ever killed. He felt weak; his whole body, his whole being, was shaking and sick from the violent burst which had torn through him. While the others gathered around the body, he staggered to the pool to wash away the blood that covered him. The men hardly noticed him as he slipped away.

The bank of the pool was steep and wet from the others' playful splashing. As the Alevide, still shaking, bent over awkwardly to drink, his foot slipped on a spot of mud, throwing him forward into the water. Weighted down by the unaccustomed armor, he sank swiftly into the depths, to drown before anyone could reach him. The sword fell away from his hand; the helm slipped off his head; when at last the men recovered his body, those two reminders of the war remained at the bottom of the lake. On days when the sun shines brightly, they may still be seen beneath the deep, green water.

When the Kalevide arrived with the rest of Viru's army, he found the Alevide's body laid at peace on the grass beside the lake. Someone had placed a small bouquet of crimson clover on his breast over his heart. Seeing his friend lost without a smile, the last to die in the war, the Kalevide collapsed in his grief. He bent over the Alevide's face and wept without constraint. He had not wept for the Sulevide; then the press of battle had been too fresh and close at hand. Now he wept and groaned and sobbed without shame. Of all the men of Viru, only the Olevide dared approach him.

Without turning around or looking up, the Kalevide spoke to him. His words were quiet and subdued, and surprisingly clear, even cool.

"I want you to build a grave over him," he said. "Here, by the water where he died. Will you do this for me?"

"Yes, of course," replied the Olevide.

"When you have done that, I want you to lead these men. I want you to lead them back to the city. To your city. There you shall rule them; you shall be their king henceforth. Rule the people of Viru; take care of them, as I could not. Go to Lindanisa, the city that you built, if it is not destroyed. If it has been torn down by the war, then gather any who are left and lead them into the forest. Help them to live in any way they can. Will you do this for me? Will you?"

"Yes."

Then a cloud came over the Kalevide and he spoke through its darkness.

"Then you must leave me. You will leave me. Everyone leaves me. Everyone leaves me alone. Alone. The Alevide—he swore to stay with me, and he is gone. The Sulevide—is gone. Everyone. Gone. Where are they? Why do they hide from me? Alone. They hide. The cup-bearer was the first, because I loved him. And then the wizard. No. No, not the first. Not they. First was my mother, Linda, she left me. Because I loved her. Yes? My mother. And Kalev. Left me, before I was born. Kalev was my father; he—No! He left Linda. Mother, and I went after him—her. I took his sword away from him because he abandoned my mother and me. We, and all alone. Now. His sword— where, where is it? Where? It is hiding, hiding. Everything hides. Sword left me, why? A sorcerer stole it, stole my sword, stole my mother, stole my dreams, gave me dreams, and ran away. Ha, ha, catch the robber-thief. Thief. Who's the thief? He runs away, runs away and hides in the ground, hides with the Sarvik and fat demons. Demons all, everyone hiding, hiding in the ground, everybody running, away from me. Hiding from me. I cannot see them. They're afraid. All afraid. The sorcerer. He killed my dog.

"Listen, listen, listen. Listen! What? No, not Musti, not the puppy. What? I cannot hear. Who is it? Horses. Horses, everywhere. Hear them. Here them. Herd them. Heard them. In the ground, pounding. Horses, my father's herd, everywhere galloping across the plains, carrying the riders of Viru, everywhere, across the world. Horses. We shall sweep the lands of men. I ride the black-stallion-charger. With my sword. Sweeping—Wait! There was a white mare. Yes, that was my mare, my horse, my mother, not the black. The white mare. But she left me. I could have ridden her to the end of the world, but I fell asleep. Stupid. She was so beautiful, white, like the girl on the island. Once. No—do not say it—she was my sister. She ran away, ran across the sea. White flyer, died. Why? Where do they go? Where is everyone? Why do they hide?

"Everyone. Sisters and brothers and brothers and sisters. Husbands of wives, three maidens, sisters, wives of husbands, brothers. I had two brothers once and they had me. Once. The son of Alev, the son of Sulev, the son of Kalev, brothers. No, not them. The sons of Kalev, three brothers. Two and me. And they went away and made me be the king and then there was a war and now they are both dead, my brothers, and buried in my arms because I was stronger than they were and I was the king. Kalev's son and the son of Kalev king of Viru Viru's king keeper of the vision of Kalev's dreams. Dreams of visions hopes spun of songs spans hanging in empty air a bridge I saw once and wanted to build. Its keeper was a singer he could hold it in the air a rainbow. I don't know how he did it; I couldn't. Not alone. I never wanted to be king but Kalev made me. They made me. Everybody. Gave me a sword, said, 'Here, king—ha-ha!' Gave me a city. Gave me a war. That's how it is with kings, then they took it all away. The white mare took it, took the sword; took the sword, killed the smith. The smith who took the book. He took the book and gave it to the sorcerer who raped the girl. And the Sarvik laughed. Away we went, the white flyer and I, away to the end of the world to catch the sword and bring it back so we could find my mother,—so she could sing to me. But she wouldn't sing, she went away. She left me again. And again. So she could go away with Kalev, they are hiding in the dark so I will not see them so I must keep searching searching searching forever. Alone. Me. Dark. She—is dead as all are dead as I am dead and my brothers in the war. They made me be the king of Põrgu and I don't want to be anymore.''

The Kalevide rose and shambled away without a look at the others. He wandered around the pool and up the valley until he reached the crest of the hill at its end. On the summit he stopped to gaze northward across the wide, dark forests of Viru where Taara reigned, then he closed his eyes, and spread his arms, and ran headlong forward into the wood.

40   For long months, unreckoned time, while the fields of battle grew clean again and people moved across the land, the Kalevide dwelt far from the eyes of man. No one knew where he was: no one sought him. He found his own hidden haunts and habitats within the wild, where he could live unburdened by the wants of other men. In the wood beside the Koiva River he built himself a tiny hut of pine saplings bent over and piled with brush and branches, which he entered by crawling on his hands and knees. He lived on fish and crayfish taken from the stream, on roots and green herbs, wild apples, acorns, honeycomb, anything that could be foraged from the forest around him. When the weather grew cold, he wrapped himself in hides and slept in the shelter of his hut buried under snow. In the springtime he emerged, ravenous, to scavenge wildly through the woods, seeking food. At times, at night, he moaned with a grief he could not understand; more often he slept in a dreamless sleep, insensible to pain. There were occasions when his wits would clear and he could remember who he was and why he had chosen to retire so far from the world of men, and then he truly wept. More often he was caught in the web of mist and darkness that had fallen over his mind. The past was hidden in the fog; the future was beyond all imagining. He lived from day to day without design, and so became the bear he had always wanted to be.

One morning, when the grass had once again grown green and the sun was shining peacefully, the Kalevide sat splay-legged in front of his hovel, plaiting rushes into a long, flat band. His fingers moved of their own accord, guided only by memories of a distant past. His mind was amused to see the strip taking shape; he no longer remembered the mother who had taught him how. When the band was finished, he would throw it away; it had no more purpose than his life.

While he was concentrating on his creation, three men on horseback emerged from the trees. Laughing and joking, calling to one another over their shoulders, they turned their horses toward the river. It was a fair morning, a time to roam unhurried and unwary. All three were clad in the iron armor of knights, but since this was not a day of war, they rode with their shields at their backs and their swords in their scabbards. They had taken off their heavy helms and thrown back the hoods of their hauberks to let the warm sun smile on their heads. All were handsome, with clean features and light, short-cropped blond hair. Their eyes were blue. They laughed. They looked very young. Barely out of boyhood, yet they had ridden across half the world in the service of the war.

The Kalevide ignored them. He did not even look up. The leader of the knights nearly rode over him before he stopped to gaze down, grinning, from the height of his stallion. He prodded the Kalevide with the butt of his lance.

"What is this?" he called to the others with a laugh. "Is it a man?"

The Kalevide merely stared dully at his plaiting.

"I think it is a man," said the second knight. "Look at his feet."

The Kalevide's feet were bare, his toes exposed. Somewhere he had lost his boots. He had taken them off and left them and now could not remember where or even when, much less why. He had not even missed them until this moment. His toes spread, acting with a will of their own. They wiggled, they danced, they bowed. The knights laughed heartily at such simplicity.

"No, it can be no man," the third rejoined. "Look at its hair. No, it must be a bear."

The Kalevide's golden locks had grown long through the months and now fell about his face. Caked with dirt and pine sap, they were matted with leaves and twigs caught in the tangles. Some feathers and the wing of a bird, which he had found once, were added for ornament.

[385]

"Whatever it is," the first knight joked, "what shall we do with it? Kill it? Or take it with us?"

"Kill him," said the second.

"Take it," said the third.

"And what do you say, creature?" The leader poked him again with his lance. "Do you want to come with us? We are on our way to war. If you are a man and not a bear, you will want to ride with us and help us drive heathen Tatar from your land. We shall push him back across his eastern steppes, if we do not kill him first. Will you join us? There is honor to be won and glory and perhaps rich spoils. The scum have women with them, and we may capture some. Come with us. If you are a man, these are the things you desire: honor, glory, wealth and fame, a woman for your lust. Where else can you win them truly but in war? All men must serve their country; do you hear the call? Of course, if you are a beast and not a man, well, that is quite another matter. Then you are free and may go on your way alone wherever you will."

"Kill it," laughed the other two together.

The Kalevide laid his unfinished braid aside and rose slowly. Still without looking at the intruders, he crossed the grass to the waterside.

The second knight, noticing his shuffle, said, "I think it is a bear."

"If it is a man," said the third, "how can he join us? He has neither horse nor arms, not even a sword."

"You are right," replied the first. "He will never make a knight. Still, he could carry our arms for us. He is large enough, he looks strong."

"A squire!" exclaimed the second.

"An ass!" said the third.

With his back to the knights the Kalevide gazed into the water. He knew what they were saying, but had forgotten how to speak himself. He could neither reply nor tell them to go away. The morning sun poured over the treetops and streamed across the smooth surface of the river. The shadows of rocks undulated underneath the rippling water. He smiled to see the sun; it had come to be his one kind friend. Sometimes crayfish came out of their lairs to walk the streambed in the light. Bending over, he looked deep into the bright-lit water; if he saw one, he would catch it and eat it. While he was staring intently into the depths, having entirely forgotten the knights, a shadow passed over the pool. The sun was eclipsed; the underwater world cast into darkness. In the shadow the Kalevide saw the shape of a long, outstretched arm and in the hand the image of a sword. He screamed.

He whirled to face the iron knight whose sword was raised for a fatal stroke. In an explosion of rage, released from some deeply buried recess that had long lain dormant, the Kalevide ducked under the slashing arm. He caught the wrist, knocked the sword out of the knight's grasp, and seizing his shoulder, pulled him from the saddle. In a single continuous movement he threw the armored man away from him and into the deepest part of the stream. Weighted down by his heavy iron mail, the knight sank swiftly out of sight and drowned.

The other two charged across the bank, one to save his comrade, the other to attack the Kalevide. This one he caught around the middle and dragged off his horse, then flung him with all his might against the trunk of a tall tree at the edge of the wood. The tree shook; its crown swayed as if in a storm. The knight cried once, then crumbled to the ground, his back broken.

The third, who had dismounted to help the one in the water, now turned before he, too, was overthrown by this madman. Even as he drew his sword, however, the Kalevide seized him, with one hand around his neck and the other between his legs. Hoisting him off the ground, armor and all, he whirled him about until the air roared with a rush of wind like the Northern Eagle rising, then still turning, he careened across the clearing to toss the screaming knight into his midden pit, where he sank from view beneath a pile of shells and muck.

Finally, without pausing in his fury, the Kalevide reeled back to the streamside. Gripping his fists together, he raised them over his head, and with all his unspent strength struck the first knight's horse a heavy blow behind the ear. The black war-stallion died on the spot. The other two horses galloped away to safety in the forest. Using the knight's own sword, the Kalevide proceeded to hack off the dead horse's head. The work was difficult, and he performed it crudely, but he did not care. When it was done, he tossed the blood-smeared blade away into the stream.

At last he stood. Calm came over the forest once more. The sun could shine again without fear of shadows. Peace reposed by Koiva, but the quiet that had been was ravaged. The solitude the Kalevide desired had been shattered. The broken body of a knight lay as a reminder in the wood he had roamed. Another loomed overlarge in the pool where he drank and fished. The water itself was fouled by bits of red flesh and blood running from the mangled carcass of the horse. The bank was sodden, and the grass dyed crimson.

With a heavy sigh, the Kalevide hoisted the horse's head onto his back and set off with it, hiking eastward, into the wood.

Carrying his grisly burden, he wandered aimlessly for many days until he came to a small lake with a wide beach of shingle where he might live undisturbed. For shelter he found the hollowed trunk of an ancient beech tree blasted by lightning long ago. The lake and the forest provided his food. He had no other wants. The days grew warmer as spring passed and pretended to be summer. He slept late in the mornings, and never stirred far from his hole.

A young man walked carefully along the edge of the lake, knelt once to wash his face, then climbed the bank to the sheltered shade of a silver tree. His tunic and trousers were well-worn from long travel, even threadbare in places, and many times mended, but they were clean and as neat as could be, as was he. His hair was neatly trimmed, his face glowed from being scrubbed. He had been taught that a man must always look his best if he was to get ahead, that appearances were very important, and what he was taught he believed. Before sitting down, he pulled a small cloth out of his pack and spread it meticulously on the ground to protect his clothes from the dirt and leaves of the earth.

"I'd say you were lost," he said to himself. "You should never have turned off the trail to look at the scenery. No telling where you are now." Nevertheless, despite the danger of being lost in the great forest, he was not discouraged. His voice was confident, even cocky. "Well, I won't think about that now. Never think about the negative, emphasize the positive. That's the way to get ahead. Never look back, always look ahead. I may not know where I am now, but I know where I'm going, and that's more than most young men can say nowadays.

"It can't be more than another day or two to the coast, and then I'm sure I'll find me a place. Didn't that trader from Permu say there were towns and cities being built everywhere to replace the old city that was torn down in the war? Doesn't everyone say this land is becoming a busy center for trade and business now that there is peace and the Old People have gone away? Roads to everywhere, merchants coming and going from the west, the south, the east. Ports opened, traders sailing from Kungla, and where they go you know there's a profit. The country is booming, and I'll be right in the middle of it.

"Yes, sir, I may be lost right now, and I may be poor and without a name, but nothing can stop me when I get started. I'll find a place in a shop or small trading house in one of the new towns where things are growing, start small, learn my trade, work hard, make myself essential to the business. That's the way to make a name. Prove your worth to the company, be noticed, in a few years you'll be bailiff, then steward, one day a partner. Yes, sir, marry the merchant's daughter and take over the entire company. Our son will rule a commercial empire.

"It's rather like the old fairy stories, isn't it? A poor boy comes into the kingdom to seek his fortune; he serves the king and weds the princess, and one day becomes king himself. Only today it's not a children's tale; it's real. And it's commerce, not romance, that opens the way to success."

The sound of his chattering woke the Kalevide, asleep inside the tree. He had been dreaming of squirrels, and thought the noise was them laughing at him. He crawled, half-asleep, out of his hole, with a growl to chase them away so he could sleep some more.

"Oh! I say!" the youth exclaimed with a start. At first he thought the Kalevide was a bear, but noticing his clothes caked with mud, his torn and tangled hair, the stink of his body, his naked feet he decided this must be one of those wild men about whom stories were told. They were believed to be remnants of an elder race, and a few were still said to dwell in the forest, far from the haunts of men, though most thought them merely legend.

The Kalevide towered over the young man without moving, merely staring stupidly down. The youth edged away, decidedly nervous and uncomfortable confronted by someone whose life was so foreign to his own. His first inclination was to flee, but he would not let himself be intimidated by anyone who looked so disreputable.

"Well, I must say, I never expected to find anyone living here," he said. It was almost a challenge, as if the Kalevide by his very presence posed a threat. "All alone, are you? Well, what kind of life is this, I ask you. Look at yourself. Covered with dirt. Why don't you cut your hair? I know, you'll tell me it isn't important and you don't care. You've got fresh air, sunshine, plenty of food, no one to tell you what to do. Sleep as late as you like, don't you? Everything so simple, so natural. But you're wrong. It isn't natural. A man needs more than that if he's to have any self-respect. He needs to work, he needs to make a name for himself. That's what I've been taught, and that's what I believe. What if everyone slept out in the woods and let their hair grow long? What would happen to the world then? No, sir, it's irresponsible, that's what it is, and a man needs responsibility. How can the country grow unless everyone takes part and works hard? How long since you even had a job?''

The Kalevide let the words trip innocently through his ears like the chattering of squirrels. They meant nothing at all to him.

"One thing is certain, you can't stay here. This forest will be cut down so the country can develop. The future lies with the cities. Fortune follows the guilds and trading combines. The roads of commerce will crisscross all the land. The world is changing so fast, and nothing can stop it. And you could be a part of it. Clean yourself up, cut your hair, get some decent clothes, get a job, you could really get somewhere. You're still young, and it's a young man's game now, if you're willing to work hard and learn and look for opportunities instead of frittering away your time. This—This is no life for a man. You must do something, something worthwhile, to fullfill yourself.''

The youth, though addressing the Kalevide, was speaking to himself. He stared earnestly across the lake, but instead of water he saw the vistas of his dreams. The Kalevide was thinking only of the forest, watching the dappled patterns of shadows the sunlight cast passing through leaves, and wondering how high the sun was when it was high. The young man rummaged in his pack for a bit of bread. Suddenly the Kalevide grabbed his shoulder and shook him fiercely. The youth pulled away, but the Kalevide pointed excitedly to a pole braced against a tree stump by the water.

"A fishing pole, how clever,'' the young man said disdainfully.

The Kalevide continued his urgent gesturing, pushing against the air, scooping up with his hands, rubbing his belly, grimacing as though chewing, trying to indicate to the other that if he wanted lunch he should pull up the line, where he would find something better than bread to eat. The youth rose reluctantly, removed his tunic, folding it neatly and setting it aside so it would not be soiled, and walked to the beach to the fishing pole. He wanted nothing more to do with the wild man, but thought if he did what he wished, he could get away that much sooner. To his surprise, he discovered the pole was the entire trunk of a fir tree, root, stump and all. It was far too much for him to handle alone.

Bounding down the bank, the Kalevide pushed him aside, grabbed the rod off its supports, and hauled the line in hand over hand. Waves rolled around his ankles as he disturbed the lake. He ignored them and pulled more furiously. Something very heavy was fastened to the line.

When the thing was nearly to the surface, he gripped the rope firmly in both hands and ran backwards, dragging his catch up the gravel shore. The youth turned away in horror. Attached to the line for bait was the head of the black knight's horse. It had lain in the water a long time, and its flesh was rotting and falling away from the skull. Here and there yellow spots of naked bone showed through the putrid hide. Where it had scraped on the rough stones, a wide strip of skin had been torn off, revealing the decaying meat underneath. The flesh had lost its color; from rich red, it had turned to a livid gray going white, and it was covered with scum. It stank. The stench that rose off the carcass would have smothered a sane man and closed his stomach. Crayfish were crawling over that gruesome feast. Hundreds of them, so many that the scratching of their legs and the clicking of small claws was loud in the quiet noon. They writhed on the horse's rotting head, scrambling in and out of its orifices, into its mouth, where its lips had fallen away, and the soft tongue lay half-devoured, through its nostrils, out its ears. They peered out of the holes where its eyes had been. They worked their way into its brain and crawled out clutching bits of gray flesh in their claws.

The Kalevide, standing proud over his grotesque trophy, held his hands out to the youth. When he opened them, he showed two large, squirming crayfish, a modest lunch. The young man fled. He darted back to the tree, caught up his coat and bag, and, without pausing to take his bearings, plunged into the forest, still to seek the cities of the coast and escape such creatures as dwelt within the wild. The Kalevide did not move. When the other was gone and the sounds of his flight had grown faint, he finally spoke aloud.

"Tell the merchants what you have seen," he said clearly but to no one who could hear.

Then he gorged himself on a feast of raw crayfish and retired to sleep in his nest within the beech tree, to sleep for days undisturbed.

He woke, however, suddenly aware that if the youth really did report his meeting, others would come through the wood to seek him. They would look for him, perhaps pursue him. Sorcerers would find his sleeping place, and they would chase him. No, that was wrong, there were no more sorcerers, but someone would come. Someone always came, and he did not want to be bothered any more. Twice now his peace had been broken; how many more times to come? Who would hound him? Why couldn't he be left alone?

The Kalevide knew he must leave at once before another intrusion caught him by surprise, to seek another, safer, surer refuge, far from the association of men, which brought only pain. He plunged once into the lake to wash away the filth of the last long months. A new freshness came over him. He splashed heartily, even dived below the surface, to come up spouting and sputtering and laughing. His cares, even the regret of leaving his home, fell away into the water. Standing in the shallows, his face half-cleaned of grime, his hair sodden and heavy but free of much of the foreign trash, he shouted bravely at the sky. He had found his tongue again. The sun was shining; clouds were white and friendly, friendlier than people. He rejoiced in their company; he would dwell among the clouds. With his ragged clothes still dripping, he kicked through the water at the lakeside and then ran freely into the deeper forest beyond the shore. On the shingle behind him, forgotten, lay the rotting hulk of the horse's head, given as a gift to the flies.

For three days the Kalevide traveled eastward. At times he followed an old road, once walked by men but since deserted in favor of a newer highway. At other times he scrambled on the tracks taken by the beasts of the wood. Often he left all paths and marked trails to push wantonly through thick tangles of undergrowth, seeking always, so he thought, the origins of the rising sun. Wild roses were in bloom; bright anemones and white violets winked at him all along the wooded ways. When birds sang, he sang with them, raising his voice and shouting at the top of his lungs. It was more a bellow than a song, so loud it drove the flocks away from him and from their homes. The land around him grew still and empty; yet he took no notice as he plowed bravely through the thickets.

Without remembering that he had ever passed that way before, he came into the neighborhood of Lake Peipus and the streams that fed it. Soon the wood gave way to an open glade of water-softened earth covered with a fragrant mat of grass and golden moss. Through the center of the meadow slipped the small brook Kapa. Like a child, the Kalevide jumped into its shallow water with both feet and splashed downstream, merrily frightening small frogs and minnows as he trod the muddy bottom. The brook widened to form a deeper pool, restful and still. Among the water herbs lay a great sword. The Kalevide stretched his right foot out playfully to touch it.

Dreaming undisturbed in its soft green bed in the arms of the water-maid, the sword had lain contemplating the various instructions it had been given, turning them over in its mind, reviewing all the distorted images of its mission in the world. Its body, its long steel blade, untarnished by its sojourn in the water, was still as bright and sharp as ever, but its spirit had become twisted and tormented from being forced to think, remember, understand, decide. The ideas, which had come unbidden into its mind, would not let it rest. It was forced to make a decision, and that was not the way of a sword. A sword is wielded by the hand of another; it has no hands of its own. It should never have to think; it should never have to act on its own.

It had been charged with a great mission, that the sword knew too well, and in its thin mind it had been trying vainly to recall precisely what that mission was. Words came to it out of the past, but it could not keep them clear. Their meanings, blurred by the water, ran together. There were the commands of its maker and the curses of its master; the more the sword considered them, the more confused it became. ''Avenge the murder of my son!'' the smith had said. ''Cut off the legs of the one who brought you here,'' the Kalevide had said. Did he mean the sorcerer? Did he mean another?

Over and over the sword tried to weigh these demands, and the more it thought, the less it understood. What did they mean? It could not read men's minds; that was not the business of a sword. It was not fair to burden it with curses without explaining exactly what they meant. Especially not if they were going to go away and leave it alone to do all the deciding for itself. The sword grew desperate. The curses mingled. The simple sword, its wits addled by a sorcerer's spell, could no longer keep them separate. ''Avenge the one who brought you here!'' ''Cut off the legs of my son!'' It made no sense. What was it? It could not remember. What was it supposed to do? It had no hands of its own. No, not it. It was for others to wield. Why did it have to decide? It was only a sword. The only thing it knew for certain

[393]

was vengeance. Vengeance was demanded; that was the one clear note in both commands, that the iron knew.

As the Kalevide stepped forward, the sword rose from its peaceful bed. Like a giant silver fish, it slid through the water and cut off both his legs above the knee.

"Help me!" cried the Kalevide in agony. No one heard.

He struggled to the bank and pulled himself out of the crimson water. With his hands he dragged himself a short way across the grass before he collapsed. Blood poured out of his legless body.

A white mare walked out of the forest to stand over him. It bent its head and began to drink his blood.

EPILOGUE

The spirit of the Kalevide soared as a bird into the hall of
Ukko behind the clouds. There, surrounded by the gods and the
ancient heroes of Taara, he sat in the firelight with his chin
resting on his wingtip while the elder bards chanted the songs of
his deeds. They sang again all that he had done on Earth, and all
that he had left undone. The lay was long; nothing was forgotten, nothing left unspoken, nothing unnoticed. Vanamuine himself led the singing.

When the words were finished at last, and the last note still,
Ukko, high lord of all, weighed the verses. He measured all the
great deeds done and balanced them against the Kalevide's mis-
deeds. Then, while the son of Kalev waited, seated humbly on a
low stool in a corner of the hall, Ukko called the lords and
powers to meet in secret congregation to decide his fortune.

"This man is too restless to remain here where only songs are
sung," Ukko declared. In that vast hall there were no worlds to
conquer, no beasts or friends to wrestle. There was only wisdom, slowly to be learned.

"Where shall he go?" the other gods inquired.

"Let him return to Earth," said Ukko.

"Is this a punishment for the man?"

"We do not punish; neither do we reward. That is not our
power."

"Why must he go?"

"He is not suited to abide here behind the clouds. Yet neither
can he be sent to the islands of Põrgu. He has grappled with the
Sarvik, death's servant, and bound him in chains."

"At the sacrifice of his country."

"Even so. Let him return to Earth."

"He was not happy there."

"Even so. Let him return."

"Shall he have work to do?"

"Let him be ward and warden at the door between death and life."

So it was decreed.

On wide wings of air the bird that was the Kalevide's spirit glided through the gray roof of cloud and came to earth. He reentered the lifeless body that was his own. Beside him stood the white mare and an old, long-bearded man, clad in a peasant's garb, who had just come out of the wood. This one could heal the pain, but not even the might and wisdom of Taara could restore the Kalevide's legs. Lightly, the old man picked him off the ground and placed him on the white horse's back. With a slow, proud step, she walked across the meadow.

She carried him away from the brook where he had fallen, away from the shores of Lake Peipus, through the valleys of waste and desolation toward the cave that was the gate to Põrgu. The ground was rough and uneven. The Kalevide swayed. He clutched the mare's silver mane for support. Even over the smoothest road it is difficult to ride without legs. In the face of the cliff the dark cave was open. The white mare walked into its mouth.

"Strike the rock with your fist," commanded a voice, the voice of a raven that spoke with a woman's tongue.

The Kalevide smote the cliff and split the stone. His fist caught in the cleft, and he could not draw it out. The white mare stopped and stood patiently waiting for him. This, however, was the post ordained for him, here before the gates of Põrgu. Mounted on the mare, and bound himself, he became the warden set to watch the bonds of others, to ensure that none should ever escape from that grim underworld.

Deep in the cave, demons strive constantly to free the Sarvik from his chains. They pile charcoal and faggots around his bonds to soften them, but each dawn at cock-crow the iron grows hard again. From time to time the Kalevide tries to draw his hand from the cliff, and then the earth trembles, but the hand of Mana that is Death holds him firmly so that he, too, is unable to escape. He can feel cold, stone-like fingers on his wrist and knows he is compelled to keep his station forever.

He sits on the white mare's back in silence, no longer able to speak, no longer able to think what led him there. All words have fled, all memories faded. He tries to recall his life and deeds, but they have left him to pass away with time. The white mare bends her head to crop the meager grass growing in front of the cave. There is little to feed her, however, and soon she will be hungry. Inside the earth the Sarvik moans pitifully, but he, too, is well bound and no longer free. The Kalevide is afraid to move lest, without legs, he fall. He waits.

This too is sung, by the old ones who remember: A day will come when fire will rend the mountain, the rock will break, and the Kalevide's hand will be freed. The chains that bind the Sarvik will melt, and he will come forth from the mouth of the cave. Then the Kalevide will climb down from the white mare's back to face his foe. The two will wrestle. At last the Kalevide will vanquish his enemy, and a new era will begin for Viru.

ABOUT THE AUTHOR

LOU GOBLE was raised in Schenectady, New York (the source of ideas, according to Ursula LeGuin and Harlan Ellison). Schooled at Oberlin College and the University of Pittsburgh, he emerged from the cave a certified philosopher, practiced for a few years under the universities' lamps of learning, then retired to explore long known but long ignored legend and lore. He now lives in the shadows in Eugene, Oregon.

The Kalevide is his first published work.

OUT OF THIS WORLD!

That's the only way to describe Bantam's great series of science fiction classics. These space-age thrillers are filled with terror, fancy and adventure and written by America's most renowned writers of science fiction. Welcome to outer space and have a good trip!

FANTASY AND SCIENCE FICTION FAVORITES

Bantam brings you the recognized classics as well as the current favorites in fantasy and science fiction. Here you will find the beloved Conan books along with recent titles by the most respected authors in the genre.